国际商务英语丛书

国际经济与贸易**专业教材** 涉外商务活动的**英语阶梯**

外经贸英语
阅读教程

A COURSE OF ENGLISH FOR
INTERNATIONAL BUSINESS

蔡惠伟 // 主编

华東理工大学出版社

图书在版编目（CIP）数据

外经贸英语阅读教程／蔡惠伟主编. —上海：华东理工大学出版社，2007.3
ISBN 978－7－5628－1941－7

Ⅰ.外... Ⅱ.蔡... Ⅲ.对外贸易—英语—阅读教学—教材 Ⅳ.H319.4

中国版本图书馆 CIP 数据核字（2007）第 028687 号

外经贸英语阅读教程

主　　编／蔡惠伟
责任编辑／陈　勤
封面设计／戚亮轩
责任校对／张　波
出版发行／华东理工大学出版社
　　　　　地　　址：上海市梅陇路 130 号,200237
　　　　　电　　话：(021)64250306(营销部)
　　　　　　　　　　(021)64252717(编辑室)
　　　　　传　　真：(021)64252707
　　　　　网　　址：www.hdlgpress.com.cn
印　　刷／江苏句容市排印厂
开　　本／787mm×960mm　1/16
印　　张／19
字　　数／391 千字
版　　次／2007 年 3 月第 1 版
印　　次／2007 年 3 月第 1 次
印　　数／1—6050 册
书　　号／ISBN 978－7－5628－1941－7/H·563
定　　价／28.00 元

　　本书内容涉及中国的几个主要贸易伙伴和世界贸易组织等重要国际组织的相关信息。选材广泛,内容实用,可读性强,是配合国际经济与贸易专业基础课程教学而精心设计的一本教材,读者包括全日制本科、继续教育学院和网络教育学院国际经济与贸易专业、与商务相关专业的学生以及广大从事国际商务实际工作、意欲提高专业英语理解与表达水平的第一线专业人员。

内容提要

至 2006 年底,中国加入世界贸易组织整五周年。五年来,中国的对外贸易事业取得了超乎世人想象的成就。出口商品的结构进一步优化,入世时最令人担忧的部分行业和领域,五年后不但没有垮掉,反而取得了历史性、跨越性的进步,有些领域甚至因为入世而使市场份额跃居世界第一。

商务部部长薄熙来在总结入世给中国带来的变化时说:"中国的贸易和产业实现了历史跨越,中国同时成为世界新兴的工厂和市场,中国制造正在成功地转向中国创造。"

薄熙来认为,"入世的最大贡献是促动经济体制改革"。在 WTO 商业规则背景下,中国经济体制改革在更为广泛的领域内提速。在过渡期内,清理并修订的法律法规和部门规章就达 3000 余部。正因为 WTO 带给中国经济社会深层次的推动,薄熙来强调要"勇于开放"。随着时间的推移,中国人民必将更大地受益于入世的抉择。

在欣喜地看到过去成就的同时,我们也应清醒认识到各类资源人均不足、高端人才短缺的国情。人力资源,特别是强英语、厚实务的国际商务人才的培养和开发比以往任何时候都显得更加迫切和重要。预计到 2010 年,中国受高等教育的人数将达 8000 万,到 2020 年,将达到 1.5 亿,这是未来 20 年内我国提升国际竞争力的强大动力。

中国的经济越来越融入世界经济,成为 WTO 成员使我们得以更大程度、更有保障地进入国际市场,经济建设需要我国的高等教育输送更多既懂专业知识,又能用外语同外方有效沟通的国际化人才。然而,现实状况并不容乐观。大量受过高等教育的人,外语口语和书写沟通能力远远满足不了工作的需要。英国《金融时报》曾经公布了咨询公司麦肯锡(McKinsey)的一份报告,该报告称,中国缺乏训练有素的毕业生,这可能会阻碍中国的经济增长以及发展更先进的产业。报告认为,中国大学生缺乏应用技能,英语水平低下,"只有10%的毕业生拥有去外企工作的技能"。有人甚至得出结论,说中国和印度多年来的"龙象之争",有可能最终会输在英语教育上。我们当然不会相信这样一个没有根据的结论,但与邻国印度、巴基斯坦、菲律宾甚至缅甸相比,我们还是感到中国学生的英语熟练程度实在让人汗颜。无论什么学历,考了多少证书,大多数人对自己的外语能力不满意是无可争辩的事实。

另一方面，由于国际贸易研究对象出现新领域、新课题而得到拓展，国际贸易实务出现新方式、新岗位而发生变革，各种新的国际贸易理论应运而生，传统的国际贸易教材已不能很好地适应国际贸易业务快速发展的需要，亟须更新教材，增加新内容、新理论、新实务，以提高跨国经营人才的培养质量。

时代和社会对复合型人才的需求日益迫切，对国际商务英语教学也提出了越来越高的要求。鉴于上述诸方面的原因，我们针对不同层次的读者，为了不同的训练目的而编写了本套国际商务英语丛书，在丛书的总体内容框架中，有注重训练学生口头沟通技巧的，有注重提高学生应用写作能力的，有注重培养学生阅读理解能力的，也有注重强化学生综合应用能力的。本丛书取材真实，编排合理，训练方式灵活，广大读者可根据各自的要求，按需选用。

本套丛书旨在强化学生运用英语从事国际商务活动的能力和技巧，以全球化的眼光关注世界经济贸易活动，特别强调培养学生将英语作为跨国工作语言的能力。本丛书的作者均系高校商学院一线资深教师，他们大都具有多年与外商一起工作、交流的工作经历，实战经验相当丰富，加之长期从事高校相关专业的教学工作，故而既能从企业要求、工作岗位的需要出发来选择内容，又能从教学法的角度来构建组合教材框架。我们深信，本丛书独特的写作视角，娴熟的语言运用，全新的实务知识，一定能使广大读者受益匪浅！

国际商务英语丛书编委会

世界经济一体化是人类文明不可阻挡的大趋势;建设一个和平、繁荣而和谐的世界是每个地球人的崇高义务。我们每个个体以不同的方式,每天以自己脚踏实地的辛勤劳动为之努力。生活在地球各个角落的人们迫切需要跨越语言的障碍,实现彼此的沟通与理解,减少误解与分歧,增加交流与信任,以便使人类的经济活动以最高的效率公平地进行。

经贸英语阅读课程是高等院校国际经济与贸易专业本科生的必修课程。它对经贸知识和英语技能并重,其内容不同于外贸函电。它借助于英语向学生提供了将来从事国际商务活动的工作者需要了解的有关外经贸活动的背景资料、基础知识、国际市场动态等,如中国主要贸易伙伴的相关经贸政策、与我国贸易关系的走向、重要国际经济组织概况及其作用等;在学习经贸知识的同时,通过各种语言现象,进一步巩固和提高学生在基础英语阶段所学到的语言知识和技能,结合具体的经贸内容,有针对性地扩大词汇量(包括认知词汇和运用词汇),培养学生阅读理解有关经贸资料的能力和利用英语表达相关内容的能力。

本书为想要了解国际经济与贸易方方面面基础知识的广大读者提供了理想的平台,它是一本国际经济与贸易专业学生理想的学习界面友好的专业基础教材。本书能帮助读者看懂世界上有关主要经济体和重要国际组织的英文原版资料,培养起相应的阅读能力,积累起一定数量的专业词汇,进而将来结合工作可以去搜索并看懂、使用自己需要的最新的英文资讯。

为便于读者学习,本书对专业资料作了必要而精到的注释,并结合多年教学实践设计了多种题型以构成训练体系,符合教学、培训或自学的需要,相信必将受到广大师生的欢迎。

对读者学习的建议:您可以先看词语注释,然后看英文资料,再对照中文译文。可以一段一段来,每次看半小时至一小时。以理解为重,捎带着积累一些自己原本没有掌握的专业术语。这样的学习顺序是为了减小学习的阻力,养成从外语资讯中吸取有用信息、进而为我所用的习惯。请务必注意本课程的学习重心不是单词,而是检索、理解和翻译需要的专业信息。我们一定要学会摆脱那种以单词为中心、以做语法题目为半径、以考证书为归宿,却永远不会使用的学习模式。这一理念使本书的编排结构、题型构成和训练方式独树一帜,相信一定会使读者诸君受益匪浅。为配合教学需要,本书中的八个单元没有给出中文译文,以便为课堂教学和考试留下必要的空间。

这里要特别感谢英文原文的作者、相关的政府机构以及国际组织,是他们的慷慨和对国际经济与贸易各个方面的专业论述、严谨而优美的语言表达才使编者与读者有了分享知识盛宴和学习的机会。的确,在全球经济一体化的过程中,地球上每个个体都需要学习大量相同的知识,只有让"和平、发展、合作、共赢"成为每个人的共识,世界经济、我们的生活水平才能不断发展和提高。出于对版权的应有尊重,在本书出版后将按原文作者或各类机构的要求,陆续寄出出版物;没有收到的也请与编者及时取得联系。

特别感谢蔡文强翻译了第一和第二单元,姚济雨整理了第十二单元的英文资料。

编者
2007 年 1 月

Contents

目

录

目

录

Unit One

10 Common Misunderstandings about the WTO

Is it a dictatorial tool of the rich and powerful? Does it destroy jobs? Does it ignore the concerns of health, the environment and development?

Emphatically no.

Criticisms of the WTO are often based on fundamental misunderstandings of the way the WTO works.

The debate will probably never end. People have different views of the pros and cons of the WTO's "multilateral" trading system. Indeed, one of the most important reasons for having the system is to serve as a forum for countries to thrash out their differences on trade issues. Individuals can participate, not directly, but through their governments.

However, it is important for the debate to be based on a proper understanding of how the system works. This booklet attempts to clear up 10 common misunderstandings.

The 10 misunderstandings

1. The WTO dictates policy
2. The WTO is for free trade at any cost
3. Commercial interests take priority over development
4. ... over the environment
5. ... over health and safety
6. The WTO destroys jobs, worsens poverty
7. Small countries are powerless in the WTO
8. The WTO is the tool of powerful lobbies
9. Weaker countries are forced to join the WTO
10. The WTO is undemocratic

1. The WTO does NOT tell governments what to do

The WTO does not tell governments how to conduct their trade policies. Rather, it's a "member-driven" organization.

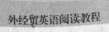

That means:

the rules of the WTO system are agreements resulting from negotiations among member governments,

the rules are ratified by members' parliaments, and

decisions taken in the WTO are virtually all made by consensus among all members.

In other words, decisions taken in the WTO are negotiated, accountable and democratic.

The only occasion when a WTO body can have a direct impact on a government's policies is when a dispute is brought to the WTO and if that leads to a ruling by the Dispute Settlement Body (which consists of all members). Normally the Dispute Settlement Body makes a ruling by adopting the findings of a panel of experts or an appeal report.

Even then, the scope of the ruling is narrow: it is simply a judgement or interpretation of whether a government has broken one of the WTO's agreements—agreements that the infringing government has itself accepted. If a government has broken a commitment, it has to conform.

In all other respects, the WTO does not dictate to governments to adopt or drop certain policies.

As for the WTO Secretariat, it simply provides administrative and technical support for the WTO and its members.

In fact, it's the governments who dictate to the WTO.

2. The WTO is NOT for free trade at any cost

It's really a question of what countries are willing to bargain with each other, of give and take, request and offer.

Yes, one of the principles of the WTO system is for countries to lower their trade barriers and to allow trade to flow more freely. After all, countries benefit from the increased trade that results from lower trade barriers.

But just how low those barriers should go is something member countries bargain with each other. Their negotiating positions, depend on how ready they feel they are to lower the barriers, and on what they want to obtain from other members in return. One country's commitments become another country's rights, and vice versa.

The WTO's role is to provide the forum for negotiating liberalization. It also provides the rules for how liberalization can take place.

The rules written into the agreements allow barriers to be lowered gradually so that domestic producers can adjust.

They have special provisions that take into account the situations that developing countries face. They also spell out when and how governments can protect their domestic producers, for example from imports that are considered to have unfairly low prices because of subsidies or "dumping". Here, the objective is fair trade.

Just as important as freer trade—perhaps more important—are other principles of the WTO system. For example non-discrimination, and making sure the conditions for trade are stable, predictable and transparent.

3. The WTO is NOT only concerned about commercial interests. This does NOT take priority over development

The WTO agreements are full of provisions taking the interests of development into account.

Underlying the WTO's trading system is the fact that freer trade boosts economic growth and supports development. In that sense, commerce and development are good for each other.

At the same time, whether or not developing countries gain enough from the system is a subject of continuing debate in the WTO. But that does not mean to say the system offers nothing for these countries. Far from it. The agreements include many important provisions that specifically take developing countries' interests into account.

Developing countries are allowed more time to apply numerous provisions of the WTO agreements. Least-developed countries receive special treatment, including exemption from many provisions.

The needs of development can also be used to justify actions that might not normally be allowed under the agreements, for example governments giving certain subsidies.

And the negotiations and other work launched at the Doha Ministerial Conference in November 2001 include numerous issues that developing countries want to pursue.

4. In the WTO, commercial interests do NOT take priority over environmental protection

Many provisions take environmental concerns specifically into account.

The preamble of the Marrakesh Agreement Establishing the World Trade Organization includes among its objectives, optimal use of the world's resources, sustainable development and environmental protection.

This is backed up in concrete terms by a range of provisions in the WTO's rules.

Among the most important are umbrella clauses (such as Article 20 of the General Agreement on Tariffs and Trade) which allow countries to take actions to protect human, animal or plant life or health, and to conserve exhaustible natural resources.

Beyond the broad principles, specific agreements on specific subjects also take environmental concerns into account. Subsidies are permitted for environmental protection. Environmental objectives are recognized specifically in the WTO agreements dealing with product standards, food safety, intellectual property protection, etc.

In addition, the system and its rules can help countries allocate scarce resources more efficiently and less wastefully. For example, negotiations have led to reductions in industrial and agricultural subsidies, which in turn reduce wasteful over-production.

A WTO ruling on a dispute about shrimp imports and the protection of sea turtles has reinforced these principles. WTO members can, should and do take measures to protect endangered species and to protect the environment in other ways, the report says. Another ruling upheld a ban on asbestos products on the grounds that WTO agreements give priority to health and safety over trade.

What's important in the WTO's rules is that measures taken to protect the environment must not be unfair. For example, they must not discriminate. You cannot be lenient with your own producers and at the same time be strict with foreign goods and services. Nor can you discriminate between different trading partners. This point was also reinforced in the recent dispute ruling on shrimps and turtles, and an earlier one on gasoline.

Also important is the fact that it's not the WTO's job to set the international rules for environmental protection. That's the task of the environmental agencies and conventions.

An overlap does exist between environmental agreements and the WTO—on trade actions (such as sanctions or other import restrictions) taken to enforce an agreement. So far there has been no conflict between the WTO's agreements and the international environmental agreements.

5. The WTO does NOT dictate to governments on issues such as food safety, and human health and safety. Again commercial interests do NOT override

The agreements were negotiated by WTO member governments, and therefore the agreements reflect their concerns.

Key clauses in the agreements (such as GATT Art. 20) specifically allow governments to take actions to protect human, animal or plant life or health. But these actions are disciplined, for example to prevent them from being used as an excuse for protecting domestic producers— protectionism in disguise.

Some of the agreements deal in greater detail with product standards, and with health and safety for food and other products made from animals and plants. The purpose is to defend governments' rights to ensure the safety of their citizens.

As an exemple, a WTO dispute ruling justified a ban on asbestos products on the grounds that WTO agreements do give priority to health and safety over trade.

At the same time, the agreements are also designed to prevent governments from setting regulations arbitrarily in a way that discriminates against foreign goods and services. Safety regulations must not be protectionism in disguise.

One criterion for meeting these objectives is to base regulations on scientific evidence or on internationally recognized standards.

Again, the WTO does not set the standards itself. In some cases other international agreements are identified in the WTO's agreements. One example is Codex Alimentarius, which sets recommended standards for food safety and comes under the UN Food and Agriculture Organization (FAO) and World Health Organization (WHO).

But there is no compulsion to comply even with internationally negotiated standards such as those of Codex Alimentarius. Governments are free to set their own standards provided they are consistent in the way they try to avoid risks over the full range of products, are not arbitrary, and do not discriminate.

6. The WTO does NOT destroy jobs or widen the gap between rich and poor

The accusation is inaccurate and simplistic. Trade can be a powerful force for creating jobs and reducing poverty. Often it does just that. Sometimes adjustments are necessary to deal with job losses, and here the picture is complicated. In any case, the alternative of protectionism is not the solution. Take a closer look at the details.

The relationship between trade and employment is complex. So is the relationship between trade and equality.

Freer-flowing and more stable trade boosts economic growth. It has the potential to create jobs, it can help to reduce poverty, and frequently it does both.

The biggest beneficiary is the country that lowers its own trade barriers. The countries exporting to it also gain, but less. In many cases, workers in export sectors enjoy higher pay and greater job security.

However, producers and their workers who were previously protected clearly face new competition when trade barriers are lowered. Some survive by becoming more competitive. Others don't. Some adapt quickly (for example by finding new employment), others take longer.

In particular, some countries are better at making the adjustments than others. This is partly because they have more effective adjustment policies. Those without effective policies are missing an opportunity because the boost that trade gives to the economy creates the resources that help adjustments to be made more easily.

The WTO tackles these problems in a number of ways. In the WTO, liberalization is gradual, allowing countries time to make the necessary adjustments. Provisions in the agreements also allow countries to take contingency actions against imports that are particularly damaging, but under strict disciplines.

At the same time, liberalization under the WTO is the result of negotiations. When countries feel the necessary adjustments cannot be made, they can and do resist demands to open the relevant sections of their markets.

There are also many other factors outside the WTO's responsibility that are behind recent changes in wage levels.

Why for example is there a widening gap in developed countries between the pay of skilled and unskilled workers? According to the OECD, imports from low-wage countries account for only 10%–20% of wage changes in developed countries. Much of the rest is attributable to "skill-based technological change". In other words, developed economies are naturally adopting more technologies that require labour with higher levels of skill.

The alternative to trade—protection—is expensive because it raises costs and encourages inefficiency. According to another OECD calculation, imposing a 30% duty on imports from developing countries would actually reduce US unskilled wages by 1% and skilled wages by 5%. Part of the damage that can be caused by protectionism is lower wages in the protectionist country.

At the same time, the focus on goods imports distorts the picture. In developed countries, 70% of economic activity is in services, where the effect of foreign competition on jobs is different—if a foreign telecommunications company sets up business in a country it may employ local people, for example.

Finally, while about 1.15 billion people are still in poverty, research, such as by the World Bank, has shown that trade liberalization since World War II has contributed to lifting billions of people out of poverty. The research has also shown that it is untrue to say that liberalization has increased inequality.

7. Small countries are NOT powerless in the WTO

Small countries would be weaker without the WTO. The WTO increases their bargaining power.

In recent years, developing countries have become considerably more active in WTO negotiations, submitting an unprecedented number of proposals in the agriculture talks, and working actively on the ministerial declarations and decisions issued in Doha, Qatar, in November 2001. They expressed satisfaction with the process leading to the Doha declarations. All of this bears testimony to their confidence in the system.

At the same time, the rules are the result of multilateral negotiations (i. e. negotiations involving all members of GATT, the WTO's predecessor). The most recent negotiation, the Uruguay Round (1986 – 1994), was only possible because developed countries agreed to reform trade in textiles and agriculture—both issues were important for developing countries.

In short, in the WTO trading system, everyone has to follow the same rules.

As a result, in the WTO's dispute settlement procedure, developing countries have successfully challenged some actions taken by developed countries. Without the WTO, these smaller countries would have been powerless to act against their more powerful trading partners.

8. The WTO is NOT the tool of powerful lobbies

The WTO system offers governments a means to reduce the influence of narrow vested interests.

This is a natural result of the "rounds" type of negotiation (i. e. negotiations that encompass, a broad range of sectors). The outcome of a trade round has to be a balance of interests.

Governments can find it easier to reject pressure from particular lobbying groups by arguing that it had to accept the overall package in the interests of the country as a whole.

A related misunderstanding is about the WTO's membership. The WTO is an organization of governments.

The private sector, non-governmental organizations and other lobbying groups do not participate in WTO activities except in special events such as seminars and symposiums.

They can only exert their influence on WTO decisions through their governments.

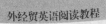

9. Weaker countries do have a choice, they are NOT forced to join the WTO

Most countries do feel that it's better to be in the WTO system than to be outside it. That's why the list of countries negotiating membership includes both large and small trading nations.

The reasons are positive rather than negative. They lie in the WTO's key principles, such as non-discrimination and transparency. By joining the WTO, even a small country automatically enjoys the benefits that all WTO members grant to each other. And small countries have won dispute cases against rich countries—they would not have been able to do so outside the WTO.

The alternative would be to negotiate bilateral trade agreements with each trading partner. That could even include regularly negotiating the regular renewal of commitments to treat trading partners as equals.

For this, governments would need more resources, a serious problem for small countries. And in bilateral negotiations smaller countries are weaker.

By joining the WTO, small countries can also increase their bargaining power by forming alliances with other countries that have common interests.

10. The WTO is NOT undemocratic

Decisions in the WTO are generally by consensus. In principle, that's even more democratic than majority rule because no decision is taken until everyone agrees.

It would be wrong to suggest that every country has the same bargaining power. Nevertheless, the consensus rule means every country has a voice, and every country has to be convinced before it joins a consensus. Quite often reluctant countries are persuaded by being offered something in return.

Consensus also means every country accepts the decisions. There are no dissenters.

What is more, the WTO's trade rules, resulting from the Uruguay Round trade talks, were negotiated by member governments and ratified in members' parliaments.
(*Source：http：// www. wto. org*)

Notes

[1] dictatorial 独裁者的，独裁的，独断的

[2] emphatically 强调地，着重地

[3] pros and cons 正面和反面

[4] dictate 口述，使听写

[5] lobby 游说

[6] conduct 管理，实施

[7] virtually 事实上

[8] findings 调查结果，对事实的认定

[9] panel 专题讨论小组，全体陪审员

[10] appeal 上诉

[11] secretariat 书记处，秘书处

[12] position 立场，位置，职位

[13] liberalization 贸易自由化

[14] preamble 引言，序文，前言

[15] Marrakesh Agreement 马拉喀什协议

[16] optimal 最适当的，最优的

[17] concrete 具体的，实在的

[18] conserve 保存，使(能量等)守恒

[19] exhaustible 可用尽的

[20] scarce 稀罕的，缺乏的

[21] asbestos 石棉

[22] lenient 宽大的，仁慈的

[23] convention 大会，协定

[24] overlap 重叠，重复

[25] sanction 制裁，处罚

[26] override 对……有最后发言权，制服，践踏

[27] disguise 假面目，假装

[28] compulsion 强迫，强制

[29] arbitrary 任意的，恣意的，专制的

[30] accusation 指控，指责

[31] simplistic 过分简单化的

[32] beneficiary 受惠者，受益人

［33］boost 推进，提高，增加

［34］contingency 偶然性，可能性，意外事故

［35］impose 征税

［36］distort 扭曲，歪曲

［37］testimony 证言，证据，声明

［38］vested 既得的，既定的

［39］encompass 包括，包含

［40］seminar 讨论会，专题讨论会

［41］symposium 座谈会，酒会

［42］dissenter 持异议者，不同意者

 Exercises

Ⅰ. Match the following words in Column A and Column B

Column A	Column B
1. findings	a. 专题讨论小组，全体陪审员
2. seminar	b. 调查结果，对事实的认定
3. position	c. 贸易自由化
4. sanction	d. 扭曲，歪曲
5. panel	e. 讨论会，专题讨论会
6. testimony	f. 证言，证据，声明
7. symposium	g. 指控，指责
8. liberalization	h. 偶然性，可能性，意外事故
9. appeal	i. 立场，位置，职位
10. override	j. 上诉
11. distort	k. 座谈会，酒会
12. dissenter	l. 假面目，假装
13. secretariat	m. 对……有最后发言权，制服，践踏
14. disguise	n. 马拉喀什协议
15. accusation	o. 大会，协定
16. preamble	p. 制裁，处罚
17. Marrakesh Agreement	q. 持异议者，不同意者
18. compulsion	r. 强迫，强制
19. convention	s. 书记处，秘书处
20. contingency	t. 引言，序文，前言

Ⅱ. Translate the following sentences into Chinese

1. The only occasion when a WTO body can have a direct impact on a government's policies is when a dispute is brought to the WTO and if that leads to a ruling by the Dispute Settlement Body (which consists of all members).

2. One of the principles of the WTO system is for countries to lower their trade barriers and to allow trade to flow more freely. After all, countries benefit from the increased trade that results from lower trade barriers.

3. At the same time, whether or not developing countries gain enough from the system is a subject of continuing debate in the WTO. But that does not mean to

say the system offers nothing for these countries. Far from it. The agreements include many important provisions that specifically take developing countries' interests into account.

4. The preamble of the Marrakesh Agreement Establishing the World Trade Organization includes among its objectives, optimal use of the world's resources, sustainable development and environmental protection.

5. At the same time, the agreements are also designed to prevent governments from setting regulations arbitrarily in a way that discriminates against foreign goods and services. Safety regulations must not be protectionism in disguise.

6. The WTO tackles these problems in a number of ways. In the WTO, liberalization is gradual, allowing countries time to make the necessary adjustments. Provisions in the agreements also allow countries to take contingency actions against imports that are particularly damaging, but under strict disciplines.

7. As a result, in the WTO's dispute settlement procedure, developing countries have successfully challenged some actions taken by developed countries. Without the WTO, these smaller countries would have been powerless to act against their more powerful trading partners.

8. Governments can find it easier to reject pressure from particular lobbying groups by arguing that it had to accept the overall package in the interests of the country as a whole.

9. The reasons are positive rather than negative. They lie in the WTO's key principles, such as non-discrimination and transparency. By joining the WTO, even a small country automatically enjoys the benefits that all WTO members grant to each other. And small countries have won dispute cases against rich countries—they would not have been able to do so outside the WTO.

10. It would be wrong to suggest that every country has the same bargaining power. Nevertheless, the consensus rule means every country has a voice, and every country has to be convinced before it joins a consensus. Quite often reluctant countries are persuaded by being offered something in return.

III. Cloze

In addition, the system and its rules can help countries allocate scarce resources more efficiently and less wastefully. For example, negotiations have led to reductions _____ industrial and agricultural subsidies, which in turn reduce wasteful over-production.

A WTO ruling _____ a dispute about shrimp imports and the protection of sea turtles has reinforced these principles. WTO members can, should and do take measures to protect endangered species and to protect the environment _____ other ways, the report says. Another ruling upheld a ban on asbestos products on the grounds that WTO agreements give priority _____ health and safety _____ trade.

What's important in the WTO's rules is that measures taken _____ protect the environment must not be unfair. For example, they must not discriminate. You cannot be lenient with your own producers and _____ the same time be strict _____ foreign goods and services. Nor can you discriminate _____ different trading partners. This point was also reinforced in the recent dispute ruling on shrimps and turtles, and an earlier one on gasoline.

Also important is the fact that it's not the WTO's job to set the international rules _____ environmental protection. That's the task of the environmental agencies and conventions.

IV. Underline the important sentences in the text, which give you useful information

V. Retell or write down what you learn from the text in English or in Chinese

参考译文

对世界贸易组织的十大常见误解

它是强权富有的独裁工具吗？它导致失业吗？它忽视了对健康、环境和发展状况的关注吗？

要强调的是，对世贸组织的批评总是建立在对其运作方式的根本误解上。

争论恐怕很难停止。人们对世贸组织的多边贸易体系的利弊有着不同的看法。实际上，保留这种体系的最重要原因是它能给在贸易问题上存在分歧的国家提供一个解决问题的平台。个体也可以参与其中，但不是直接的，必须通过他们的政府。

然而，在正确理解这个体系运行的基础上进行辩论很重要。本文试图理清这十大常见的误解。

十大误区：

1. 世界贸易组织发号施令
2. 世贸组织不惜任何代价推行自由贸易
3. 商业利益优先于发展
4. 商业利益优先于环境
5. 商业利益优先于健康和安全
6. 世贸组织导致失业，加剧贫困
7. 小国在世贸组织中无能为力
8. 世贸组织是强权一方的工具
9. 弱国被迫加入世贸组织
10. 世贸组织是不民主的

1. 世贸组织并没有规定政府该做什么

世贸组织没有规定政府如何制定他们的贸易政策。相反，它是一个"成员驱动"的组织。

这意味着：

- 世贸组织的规则制度是由各成员国共同商议制定的
- 规则由成员国议会批准
- 事实上世贸组织的决定是成员国达成的共识

换言之，世贸组织的决定是经过共同商议的、负责的和民主的。

世贸组织唯一能直接影响一国政府政策的情况是当一个争端提交世贸组织，且争端调解委员会(包括所有成员)作出了裁决的时候。通常争端调解委员会通过专家组的调查结果或一份上诉报告作出裁决。

即使这样,裁决的范围也是狭窄的:仅仅是对一个政府是否违反自己所接受的世贸组织协议的判断或解释。如果一个政府违反了自己的一项承诺,它也得服从规定。

在所有其他方面,世贸组织并没有命令各国政府采取或废除某些政策。

至于世贸组织秘书处,它仅仅向世贸组织及其成员国提供行政和技术性的支持。

事实上,正是政府支配了世贸组织。

2. 世贸组织不会不惜任何代价推行自由贸易

各国政府愿意彼此就什么讨价还价、给予和获得什么、索要和付出什么,的确是一个问题。

不错,世贸组织的原则之一是要求各国降低贸易壁垒,使贸易活动更加自由。毕竟,各国都能从因降低贸易壁垒而引起的贸易增长中获益。

但这个壁垒究竟应该降低到什么程度是各成员国争论的焦点。他们的谈判立场取决于他们对降低壁垒所做的准备以及他们想从其他国家那儿得到什么样的回报。一国的承诺成为另一国的权利,反之亦然。

世贸组织的作用就是为商讨贸易自由化提供平台,同时提供如何实行自由化的规则。

写入协议的规则允许贸易壁垒可以逐步降低,以便让国内生产者能作出调整。

考虑到发展中国家面临的形势,协议有特别的规定。它们还阐明了政府何时及如何能保护其国内生产者,譬如,因补贴或倾销而进行的进口贸易被认为是不公平低价。这里,目标是为了公平贸易。

同自由贸易一样重要,也许比之更重要的是世贸体系的其他原则。譬如,非歧视原则、贸易条件的稳定、可预见性和透明度原则。

3. 世贸组织不是只关心商业利益,它并不优先于发展

世贸组织的协议充满了考虑发展利益的条款。

在世贸组织贸易体系的框架下,更加自由的贸易拉动经济增长,促进发展。从这个角度上说,商业和发展双方是互利的。

与此同时,发展中国家能否在世贸体系中有足够收获是在世贸组织中持续争论的问题,但是这并不等于说这一制度没有带给他们什么东西。事实远非如此,世贸协议,包括许多重要的规定特别考虑了发展中国家的利益。

发展中国家可以有更多的时间用于实行世贸组织协议。最不发达国家得到特别待遇,包括免除实行许多规定。

发展的需要还可以用来证明某些不正常的行为在世贸规则下是不被允许的。例如政府给予某种补贴。

在2001年11月的多哈部长级会议上开启的谈判以及其他工作就包括发展中国家所希望解决的诸多问题。

4. 在世贸组织中,商业利益并不优先于环境保护

许多条款对环境问题作了特别考虑。

《建立世贸组织马拉喀什协定》的前言包括了世贸组织的目标、对全球资源的最佳利用、可持续发展和环境保护。

这是由世贸组织规则的一系列条款的具体规定做后盾的,其中最重要的保护伞条款(如关贸总协定的第20条)允许各国采取行动保护人类、动植物的生命健康以及保存可用尽的自然资源。

大原则之外,具体问题的具体协议同样把环境问题考虑在内。用于环境保护的经济援助是允许的。在世贸组织处理产品标准、食品安全、知识产权等协议中环境目标是被明确认同的。

此外,该制度和规则可以帮助各国更有效率地分配稀有资源减少浪费。例如,谈判导致了削减工业和农业的补贴,从而相应减少产能过剩造成的浪费。

世贸组织一项关于对虾的进口和保护海龟争议的裁决强化了这些原则。世贸组织成员能够、应该且确实采取措施保护濒危物种以及以其他多种形式保护环境。另一个支持禁止在地面使用石棉产品的裁决表明世贸组织协议是把健康和安全优先于贸易考虑的。

世贸规则中重要的是为保护环境而采取的措施必须是公平的。例如,不能有歧视。你不能在严格对待外国商品和服务的同时对本国生产者宽宏大量。也不能区别对待不同的贸易伙伴。这一点也在最近虾和海龟的争端裁决上得到了加强,另一个更早的案例是汽油问题。

同样重要的是,制定环境保护的规则不是世贸组织的工作,那是环保机构和大会的任务。

环境协议与加强世贸组织协议的贸易行动(如制裁或其他进口限制)的确有重叠的地方。迄今为止世贸组织协议与国际环境协议还没有冲突。

5. 世贸组织并没有在食品安全和人类健康和安全等问题上指挥政府,同样商业利益也不会凌驾于一切之上

世贸协议是由各成员国共同商议制订的,因此协议反映了他们共同关心的问题。

该协议主要条款(如关贸总协定第20条)明确允许各国政府采取行动保护人类、动植物的生命健康。但这些行为必须受到规定的制约,以防止他们被用来作为保

护国内生产者的借口,即变相的贸易保护主义。

有些条款非常详细地规定了产品标准、食品健康与安全以及其他动植物产品的标准,目的是维护政府确保公民健康的权利。

世贸组织裁决禁止石棉产品的例子可证明世贸组织协议是把健康和安全优先于贸易来考虑的。

与此同时,协议还制定条款防止各国政府为歧视外国产品和服务而随意设置某些规定。安全法规不得变相地成为贸易保护主义。

实现这些目标的一个依据是以科学证据或者国际公认的标准为基础。

况且,世贸组织本身并不制定标准。在有些情况下,其他国际协议与世贸协议中的条款是一致的。其中一个例子是设立了食品安全推荐标准的食品法典就是按照联合国粮农组织和世界卫生组织的规定制定的。

但组织并无强制要求遵守诸如经国际谈判后而确立的食品法典之类的标准,政府可以自由制定自己的标准,只要他们以一种试图为所有产品避免风险、非专制的、非歧视的方式来做。

6. 世贸组织不会破坏就业环境,也不会拉大贫富差距

这个指责是不准确的,过分简单化的。贸易能有力地创造就业机会、降低贫穷程度,事实往往就是这样的。有时为应对失业状况而进行调整是必要的,而这个情况是非常复杂的。无论如何,保护主义不是解决问题的方法。仔细看一下问题的细节。

贸易与就业之间的关系是复杂的。贸易和平等的关系也是如此。

更自由的流动以及更稳定的贸易促进经济增长。它具有创造就业机会的潜力,有助于减少贫困人口,通常两者同时实现。

降低自己贸易壁垒的国家是最大的受益者。向其做出口贸易的国家也能获利,但相对较少。在许多情况下,出口部门的工人享受高薪以及更好的就业保障。

但是,当贸易壁垒降低时先前受保护的生产者和工人显然要面对新的竞争。有些变得更加具有竞争力而存活下来,另一部分则被淘汰。有些人很快就适应了(例如找到新的就业机会),有些人则要花更长的时间。

特别是有些国家比别人调整得更好。部分原因是因为他们能更有效地调整政策。那些没有有效政策的国家就会失去机会,因为贸易对经济刺激后形成的资源能使调整变得更容易。

世贸组织通过许多方式来处理这些问题。在世贸体系下,自由化是渐进的,给各国留出了时间作必要的调整。协议中的条款允许各国在个别产生破坏性的行业偶尔采取限制进口的措施,但要严格遵守规定。

同时,世贸组织的贸易自由化是谈判的结果。当一国感到无法作出必要的调整时,他们能够且确实可以抵制开放本国相关市场的要求。

在近期工资水平变动的背后还有许多在世贸组织职责之外的因素。

譬如为什么在发达国家熟练工人和非熟练工人的工资差距越来越大？据经合组织统计，与低工资国家的进口贸易导致发达国家的工资变化只有 10% —20%，其余大部分变化源于"技术化的科技变革"。换句话说，发达的经济体自然要采用更高的技术，而这要求拥有高水平技能的劳动力。

贸易的另一种选择——保护——代价是昂贵的，因为贸易保护会提高成本且鼓励无效率。据经合组织的另一项计算，向发展中国家征收 30% 的进口税实际上就减少了美国非熟练工人 1%、熟练工人 5% 的工资。贸易保护的部分危害是在贸易保护的国家导致低工资。

与此同时，对商品进口的高度关注歪曲了事实。在发达国家，70% 的经济活动是在服务业，在这一领域外国竞争对就业的影响是不同的，例如，一家外国电信公司要在国内开展业务可能会聘用当地人。

最后，当 11.5 亿人仍处于贫困水平时，诸如世界银行的研究表明，自从二战以来贸易自由化已经帮助数十亿人摆脱贫困。该研究还表明称贸易自由化扩大差异也是错的。

7. 小国在世贸组织中并非无能为力

没有世贸组织，小国会变得更弱小，世贸组织增强了他们讨价还价的能力。

近几年来发展中国家在世贸谈判中变得相当积极，在农业问题上提交了数量空前的提案，积极执行着在 2001 年 11 月卡塔尔多哈部长级会议上作出的声明和决定。他们对多哈宣言的进程表示满意。这一切证明了他们对世贸体系的信任。

同时，这些规则是多边谈判的结果（即涉及世贸组织前身，关贸总协定的所有成员的谈判）。最近的一次谈判，乌拉圭回合（1986 年至 1994 年）之所以成为可能是因为发达国家同意对纺织品和农产品这两个对发展中国家至关重要的领域进行贸易改革。

简言之，在世贸组织的贸易体系中，所有成员国都要遵循同样的规则。

结果，在世贸组织的争端调解程序中，发展中国家已经成功地挑战了发达国家采取的一些行动。离开了世贸组织，这些小国无力对抗比他们更强大的贸易伙伴。

8. 世贸组织不是强大的利益集团游说的工具

世贸体系为各国政府提供了一种减小目光短浅的既得利益集团影响的途径。

这是"回合"类谈判的一个自然结果（谈判涉及许多部门）。一个贸易谈判回合的结果一定要使各方利益均衡。

政府更容易通过以整个国家利益为重而接受所有贸易谈判条件的方式来抵抗来自特定游说团体的压力。

一个相关的误解是关于世贸组织的成员身份。世贸组织是一个政府组成的机构。

除了诸如研讨会和座谈会之类的特别事件外,私营部门、非政府组织以及其他游说团体不能参加世贸组织的日常工作。

他们只能通过自己的政府对世贸组织的决定施加影响。

9. 弱国是有选择权的,他们不是被迫加入世贸组织的

大多数国家认为加入世贸体系比游离它之外有更多好处。这就是为什么谈判国家的名单中包括大小贸易国。

原因是积极而非消极的。他们依赖于世贸组织的主要原则,如非歧视和透明度原则。加入世贸组织后,即使一个小国也会自动享有所有世贸成员国相互给予的好处。同时小国能够在与大国的贸易争端中获胜,而离开了世贸组织这是不可能的。

不加入的话要与各贸易伙伴进行双边贸易谈判。这需要经常商谈定期更新贸易协议,以使贸易伙伴之间保持平等。

为此,各国政府将需要更多的资源,这对小国而言是个严重的问题。而在双边谈判中,较小的国家显得更加弱小。

通过加入世贸组织,小国家可以同与其利益相关的国家结盟以增加他们讨价还价的能力。

10. 世贸组织不是不民主的

世贸组织中的决策通常都是达到一致同意的。原则上,它比多数原则更民主,因为只有在每个成员同意后才会作出决定。

建议每个国家具有相同的讨价还价的权利是错误的。不过,一致通过的规则意味着每个国家都能发表意见,每个国家都是在确信没有坏处之后才同意多数人的意见。通常,世贸组织会提供一些东西作为回报来换取不赞同国家的认可。

一致通过也表示每个国家都接受决定,没有任何国家持反对意见。

而且,因乌拉圭回合贸易谈判形成的世贸组织贸易协议是所有成员国政府谈判达成的,并经各国议会批准的。

Unit Two

10 Benefits of the WTO Trading System

From the money in our pockets and the goods and services that we use, to a more peaceful world—the WTO and the trading system offer a range of benefits, some well-known, others not so obvious.

The world is complex. This booklet is brief, but it tries to reflect the complex and dynamic nature of trade. It highlights some of the benefits of the WTO's trading system, but it doesn't claim that everything is perfect—otherwise there would be no need for further negotiations and for the system to evolve and reform continually.

Nor does it claim that everyone agrees with everything in the WTO. That's one of the most important reasons for having the system: it's a forum for countries to thrash out their differences on trade issues.

That said, there are many over-riding reasons why we're better off with the system than without it. Here are 10 of them.

The 10 benefits

1. The system helps promote peace

2. Disputes are handled constructively

3. Rules make life easier for all

4. Freer trade cuts the costs of living

5. It provides more choice of products and qualities

6. Trade raises incomes

7. Trade stimulates economic growth

8. The basic principles make life more efficient

9. Governments are shielded from lobbying

10. The system encourages good government

1. The system helps to keep peace

This sounds like an exaggerated claim, and it would be wrong to make too much of it. Nevertheless, the system does contribute to international peace, and if we understand why, we have a clearer picture of what the system actually does.

Peace is partly an outcome of two of the most fundamental principles of the trading system: helping trade to flow smoothly, and providing countries with a constructive and fair outlet for dealing with disputes over trade issues. It is also an outcome of the international confidence and cooperation that the system creates and reinforces.

History is littered with examples of trade disputes turning into war. One of the most vivid is the trade war of the 1930s when countries competed to raise trade barriers in order to protect domestic producers and retaliate against each others' barriers. This worsened the Great Depression and eventually played a part in the outbreak of World War Ⅱ.

Two developments immediately after the Second World War helped to avoid a repeat of the prewar trade tensions. In Europe, international cooperation developed in coal, and in iron and steel. Globally, the General Agreement on Tariffs and Trade (GATT) was created.

Both have proved successful, so much so that they are now considerably expanded—one has become the European Union, the other the World Trade Organization (WTO).

HOW DOES THIS WORK?

Crudely put, sales people are usually reluctant to fight their customers. In other words, if trade flows smoothly and both sides enjoy a healthy commercial relationship, political conflict is less likely.

What's more, smoothly flowing trade also helps people all over the world become better off. People who are more prosperous and contented are also less likely to fight.

But that is not all. The GATT/WTO system is an important confidence-builder. The trade wars in the 1930s are proof of how protectionism can easily plunge countries into a situation where no one wins and everyone loses.

The short-sighted protectionist view is that defending particular sectors against imports is beneficial. But that view ignores how other countries are going to respond. The longer term reality is that one protectionist step by one country can easily lead to retaliation from other countries, a loss of confidence in freer trade, and a slide into serious economic trouble for all—including the sectors that were originally protected. Everyone loses.

Confidence is the key to avoiding that kind of no-win scenario. When governments are confident that others will not raise their trade barriers, they will not be tempted to do the same. They will also be in a much better frame of mind to cooperate with each other.

The WTO trading system plays a vital role in creating and reinforcing that confidence. Particularly important are negotiations that lead to agreement by consensus, and a focus on abiding by the rules.

2. The system allows disputes to be handled constructively

As trade expands in volume, in the numbers of products traded, and in the numbers of countries and companies trading, there is a greater chance that disputes will arise. The WTO system helps resolve these disputes peacefully and constructively.

There could be a down side to trade liberalization and expansion. More trade means more opportunities for disputes to arise. Left to themselves, those disputes could lead to serious conflict. But in reality, a lot of international trade tension is reduced because countries can turn to organizations, in particular the WTO, to settle their trade disputes.

Before World War Ⅱ that option was not available. After the war, the world's community of trading nations negotiated trade rules which are now entrusted to the WTO. Those rules include an obligation for members to bring their disputes to the WTO and not to act unilaterally.

Around 300 disputes have been brought to the WTO since it was set up in 1995. Without a means of tackling these constructively and harmoniously, some could have led to more serious political conflict.

The fact that the disputes are based on WTO agreements means that there is a clear basis for judging who is right or wrong. Once the judgement has been made, the agreements provide the focus for any further actions that need to be taken.

The increasing number of disputes brought to GATT and its successor, the WTO, does not reflect increasing tension in the world. Rather, it reflects the closer economic ties throughout the world, the GATT/WTO's expanding membership and the fact that countries have faith in the system to solve their differences.

Sometimes the exchanges between the countries in conflict can be acrimonious, but they always aim to conform with the agreements and commitments that they themselves negotiated.

When they bring disputes to the WTO, the WTO's procedure focuses their attention on the rules. Once a ruling has been made, countries concentrate on trying to comply with the rules, and perhaps later renegotiating the rules—not on declaring war on each other.

3. A system based on rules rather than power makes life easier for all

The WTO cannot claim to make all countries equal. But it does reduce some inequalities, giving smaller countries more voice, and at the same time freeing the major powers from the complexity of having to negotiate trade agreements with each of their numerous, trading partners.

Decisions in the WTO are made by consensus. The WTO agreements were negotiated by all members, were approved by consensus and were ratified in all members' parliaments. The agreements apply to everyone. Rich and poor countries alike have an equal right to challenge each other in the WTO's dispute settlement procedures.

This makes life easier for all, in several different ways. Smaller countries can enjoy some increased bargaining power. Without a multilateral regime, such as the WTO's system, the more powerful countries would be freer to impose their will unilaterally on their smaller trading partners. Smaller countries would have to deal with each of the major economic powers individually, and would be much less able to resist unwanted pressure.

In addition, smaller countries can perform more effectively if they make use of the opportunities to form alliances and to pool resources. Several are already doing this.

There are matching benefits for larger countries. The major economic powers can use the single forum of the WTO to negotiate with all or most of their trading partners at the same time. This makes life much simpler for the bigger trading countries. The alternative would be continuous and complicated bilateral negotiations with dozens of countries simultaneously. And each country could end up with different conditions for trading with each of its trading partners, making life extremely complicated for its importers and exporters.

The principle of non-discrimination built into the WTO agreements avoids that complexity. The fact that there is a single set of rules applying to all members greatly simplifies the entire trade regime.

And these agreed rules give governments a clearer view of which trade policies are acceptable.

4. Freer trade cuts the cost of living

We are all consumers. The prices we pay for our food and clothing, our necessities and luxuries, and everything else in between, are affected by trade policies.

Protectionism is expensive: it raises prices. The WTO's global system lowers trade barriers through negotiation and applies the principle of non-discrimination. The result is reduced costs of production (because imports used in production are cheaper) and reduced prices of finished goods and services, and ultimately a lower cost of living.

There are plenty of studies showing just what the impacts of protectionism and of freer trade are. These are just a few figures:

FOOD IS CHEAPER

When you protect your agriculture, the cost of your food goes up—by an estimated $1,500 per year for a family of four in the European Union; by the equivalent of a 51% tax on food in Japan (1995); by $3 billion per year added to US consumers' grocery bills just to support sugar in one year (1988).

Negotiating agricultural trade reform is a complex undertaking. Governments are still debating the roles agricultural policies play in a range of issues from food security to environmental protection.

But WTO members are now reducing the subsidies and the trade barriers that are the worst offenders. And in 2000, new talks started on continuing the reform in agriculture. These have now been incorporated into a broader work programme, the Doha Development Agenda, launched at the fourth WTO Ministerial Conference in Doha, Qatar, in November 2001.

CLOTHES ARE CHEAPER

Import restrictions and high customs duties combined to raise US textiles and clothing prices by 58% in the late 1980s.

UK consumers pay an estimated 500 million more per year for their clothing because of these restrictions. For Canadians the bill is around C $780 million. For Australians it would be A $300 annually per average family if Australian customs duties had not been reduced in the late 1980s and early 1990s.

The textiles and clothing trade is going through a major reform—under the WTO—that will be completed in 2005. The programme includes eliminating restrictions on quantities of imports.

If customs duties were also to be eliminated, economists calculate the result could be a gain to the world of around $23 billion, including $12.3 billion for the US, $0.8 billion for Canada, $2.2 billion for the EU and around $8 billion for developing countries.

THE SAME GOES FOR OTHER GOODS...

When the US limited Japanese car imports in the early 1980s, car prices rose by 41% between 1981 and 1984—nearly double the average for all consumer products. The objective was to save American jobs, but the higher prices were an important reason why one million fewer new cars were sold, leading to more job losses.

If Australia had kept its tariffs at 1998 levels, Australian customers would pay on average A $2,900 more per car today. In 1995, aluminium users in the EU paid an extra $472 million due to tariff barriers.

One of the objectives of the Doha Development Agenda (DDA) is another round of cuts in tariffs on industrial products, i. e. manufactured and mining products. Some economists (Robert Stern, Alan Deardorff and Drusilla Brown) predict that cutting these by one third would raise developing countries' income by around $52 billion.

Similar French restrictions added an estimated 33% to French car prices. TVs, radios, videos are, or were, all more expensive under protectionism.

... AND SERVICES

Liberalization in telephone services is making phone calls cheaper—in the 1990s by 4% per year in developing countries and 2% per year in industrial countries, taking inflation into account.

In China, competition from a second mobile phone company was at least part of the reason for a 30% cut in the price of a call. In Ghana the cut was 50%.

The group of economists led by Robert Stern also estimates that lowering services barriers by one third under the Doha Development Agenda would raise developing countries' incomes by around $60 billion.

And so it goes on. The system now entrusted to the WTO has been in place for over 50 years.

In that time there have been eight major rounds of trade negotiations. Trade barriers around the world are lower than they have ever been in modern trading history. They continue to fall, and we are all benefiting.

5. It gives consumers more choice, and a broader range of qualities to choose from

Think of all the things we can now have because we can import them: fruits and vegetables out of season, foods, clothing and other products that used to be considered exotic, cut flowers from any part of the world, all sorts of household goods, books, music, movies, and so on.

Think also of the things people in other countries can have because they buy exports from us and elsewhere. Look around and consider all the things that would disappear if all our imports were taken away from us. Imports allow us more choice—both more goods and services to choose from, and a wider range of qualities. Even the quality of locally-produced goods can improve because of the competition from imports.

The wider choice isn't simply a question of consumers buying foreign finished products. Imports are used as materials, components and equipment for local production.

This expands the range of final products and services that are made by domestic producers, and it increases the range of technologies they can use. When mobile telephone equipment became available, services sprang up even in the countries that did not make the equipment, for example.

Sometimes, the success of an imported product or service on the domestic market can also encourage new local producers to compete, increasing the choice of brands available to consumers as well as increasing the range of goods and services produced locally.

If trade allows us to import more, it also allows others to buy more of our exports. It increases our incomes, providing us with the means of enjoying the increased choice.

6. Trade raises incomes

Lowering trade barriers allows trade to increase, which adds to incomes—national incomes and personal incomes. But some adjustment is necessary.

The WTO's own estimates for the impact of the 1994 Uruguay Round trade deal were between \$109 billion and \$510 billion added to world income (depending on the assumptions of the calculations and allowing for margins of error).

More recent research has produced similar figures. Economists estimate that cutting trade barriers in agriculture, manufacturing and services by one third would boost the world economy by \$613 billion—equivalent to adding an economy the size of Canada to the world economy.

In Europe, the EU Commission calculates that over 1989—1993 EU incomes increased by 1.1% - 1.5% more than they would have done without the Single Market.

So trade clearly boosts incomes. Trade also poses challenges as domestic producers face competition from imports. But the fact that there is additional income means that resources are available for governments to redistribute the benefits from those who gain the most—for example to help companies and workers adapt by becoming more productive and competitive in what they were already doing, or by switching to new activities.

7. Trade stimulates economic growth, and that can be good news for employment

Trade clearly has the potential to create jobs. In practice there is often factual evidence that lower trade barriers have been good for employment. But the picture is complicated by a number of factors. Nevertheless, the alternative—protectionism—is not the way to tackle employment problems.

This is a difficult subject to tackle in simple terms. There is strong evidence that trade boosts economic growth, and that economic growth means more jobs. It is also true that some jobs are lost even when trade is expanding. But a reliable analysis of this poses at least two problems.

First, there are other factors at play. For example, technological advance has also had a strong impact on employment and productivity, benefiting some jobs, hurting others.

Second, while trade clearly boosts national income (and prosperity), this is not always translated into new employment for workers who lost their jobs as a result of competition from imports.

The picture is not the same all over the world. The average length of time a worker takes to find a new job can be much longer in one country than for a similar worker in another country experiencing similar conditions.

In other words, some countries are better at making the adjustment than others. This is partly because some countries have more effective adjustment policies. Those without effective policies are missing an opportunity.

There are many instances where the facts show that the opportunity has been grasped—where freer trade has been healthy for employment. The EU Commission calculates that the creation of its Single Market means that there are somewhere in the range of 300,000—900,000 more jobs than there would be without the Single Market.

Often, job prospects are better in companies involved in trade. In the United States, 12 million people owe their jobs to exports; 1.3 million of those jobs were created between 1994 and 1998. And those jobs tend to be better-paid with better security. In Mexico, the best jobs are those related to export activities: sectors which export 60 per cent or more of their production, pay wages 39% higher than the rest of the economy and maquiladora (in-bond assembly) plants pay 3.5 times the Mexican minimum wage.

The facts also show how protectionism hurts employment. The example of the US car industry has already been mentioned: trade barriers designed to protect US jobs by restricting imports from Japan ended up making cars more expensive in the US, so fewer cars were sold and jobs were lost.

In other words, an attempt to tackle a problem in the short term by restricting trade turned into a bigger problem in the longer term.

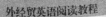

Even when a country has difficulty making adjustments, the alternative of protectionism would simply make matters worse.

8. The basic principles make the system economically more efficient, and they cut costs

Many of the benefits of the trading system are more difficult to summarize in numbers, but they are still important. They are the result of essential principles at the heart of the system, and they make life simpler for the enterprises directly involved in trade and for the producers of goods and services.

Trade allows a division of labour between countries. It allows resources to be used more appropriately and effectively for production. But the WTO's trading system offers more than that. It helps to increase efficiency and to cut costs even more because of important principles enshrined in the system.

Imagine a situation where each country sets different rules and different customs duty rates for imports coming from different trading partners. Imagine that a company in one country wants to import raw materials or components—copper for wiring or printed circuit boards for electrical goods, for example—for its own production.

It would not be enough for this company to look at the prices offered by suppliers around the world. The company would also have to make separate calculations about the different duty rates it would be charged on the imports (which would depend on where the imports came from), and it would have to study each of the regulations that apply to products from each country. Buying some copper or circuit boards would become very complicated.

That, in simple terms, is one of the problems of discrimination. Imagine now that the government announces it will charge the same duty rates on imports from all countries, and it will use the same regulations for all products, no matter where they come from, whether imported or locally produced. Life for the company would be much simpler. Sourcing components would become more efficient and would cost less.

Non-discrimination is just one of the key principles of the WTO's trading system. Others include:

transparency (clear information about policies, rules and regulations);

increased certainty about trading conditions (commitments to lower trade barriers and to increase other countries' access to one's markets are legally binding);

simplification and standardization of customs procedure, removal of red tape, centralized databases of information, and other measures designed to simplify trade that come under the heading "trade facilitation".

Together, they make trading simpler, cutting companies' costs and increasing confidence in the future. That in turn also means more jobs and better goods and services for consumers.

9. The system shields governments from narrow interests

The GATT-WTO system which evolved in the second half of the 20th Century helps governments take a more balanced view of trade policy. Governments are better-placed to defend themselves against lobbying from narrow interest groups by focusing on trade-offs that are made in the interests of everyone in the economy.

One of the lessons of the protectionism that dominated the early decades of the 20th Century was the damage that can be caused if narrow sectoral interests gain an unbalanced share of political influence. The result was increasingly restrictive policy which turned into a trade war that no one won and everyone lost.

Superficially, restricting imports looks like an effective way of supporting an economic sector. But it biases the economy against other sectors which shouldn't be penalized—if you protect your clothing industry, everyone else has to pay for more expensive clothes, which puts pressure on wages in all sectors, for example.

Protectionism can also escalate as other countries retaliate by raising their own trade barriers. That's exactly what happened in the 1920s and 1930s with disastrous effects. Even the sectors demanding protection ended up losing.

Governments need to be armed against pressure from narrow interest groups, and the WTO system can help.

The GATT-WTO system covers a wide range of sectors. So, if during a GATT-WTO trade negotiation one pressure group lobbies its government to be considered as a special case in need of protection, the government can reject the protectionist pressure by arguing that it needs a broad-ranging agreement that will benefit all sectors of the economy. Governments do just that, regularly.

10. The system encourages good government

Under WTO rules, once a commitment has been made to liberalize a sector of trade, it is difficult to reverse. The rules also discourage a range of unwise policies. For businesses, that means greater certainty and clarity about trading conditions. For governments it can often mean good discipline.

The rules include commitments not to backslide into unwise policies. Protectionism in general is unwise because of the damage it causes domestically and internationally, as we have already seen.

Particular types of trade barriers cause additional damage because they provide opportunities for corruption and other forms of bad government.

One kind of trade barrier that the WTO's rules try to tackle is the quota, for example restricting imports or exports to no more than a specific amount each year.

Because quotas limit supply, they artificially raise prices, creating abnormally large profits (economists talk about "quota rent"). That profit can be used to influence policies because more money is available for lobbying.

It can also provide opportunities for corruption, for example in the allocation of quotas among traders. There are plenty of cases where that has happened around the world.

In other words, quotas are a particularly bad way of restricting trade. Governments have agreed through the WTO's rules that their use should be discouraged.

Nevertheless, quotas of various types remain in use in most countries, and governments argue strongly that they are needed. But they are controlled by WTO agreements and there are commitments to reduce or eliminate many of them, particularly in textiles.

Many other areas of the WTO's agreements can also help reduce corruption and bad government.

Transparency (such as making available to the public all information on trade regulations), other aspects of "trade facilitation", clearer criteria for regulations dealing with the safety and standards of products, and non-discrimination also help by reducing the scope for arbitrary decision-making and cheating.

Quite often, governments use the WTO as a welcome external constraint on their policies: "we can't do this because it would violate the WTO agreements." (*Source*: *http://www.wto.org*)

 Notes

[1] brief 简短的

[2] dynamic 动态的，有活力的，不断变化的

[3] highlight 使显著，突出

[4] evolve 进展，进化

[5] thrash out 借讨论而澄清或解决问题

[6] over-riding 不顾及的,不理会的

[7] dispute 纠纷，争端，争议

[8] shield 保护，屏蔽，挡开，避开

[9] undertaking 事业

[10] exaggerated 夸大的，夸张的，言过其实的

[11] claim 断言

[12] outlet 出口，发泄方法

[13] litter 乱丢，铺草，弄乱

[14] retaliate 报复，反击，征收报复性关税

[15] crudely 照自然状态，未成熟地

[16] contented 满足的，心安的

[17] scenario 远景方案,方案，事态

[18] tempt 诱惑

[19] tackle 处理

[20] acrimonious 尖刻的，讥讽的，激烈的

[21] ruling 判决，裁定

[22] numerous 很多的，数目众多的

[23] regime 社会制度，体制

[24] pool 联营，共享

[25] alternative 供替代的选择

[26] offender 罪犯，无礼的人

[27] inflation 通货膨胀

[28] exotic 外国的，外来的,外来物，舶来品

[29] pose 提出，造成

[30] redistribute 重新分配

[31] translate 转化，转变为

[32] Single Market 单一市场

[33] enshrine 嵌入,置于

[34] trade-off 平衡,交换

[35] bias 使有偏见,偏差,偏向

[36] transparency 透明,透明度原则

[37] sector 部门

[38] penalize 惩罚

[39] escalate 逐步扩大,逐步升高,逐步增强

[40] reverse 使逆转,使倒退

[41] backslide 堕落,退步

[42] corruption 腐败,堕落,贪污

[43] quota rent 配额寻租

[44] eliminate 除去,剔除,消除

[45] arbitrary 武断的,独裁的

[46] constraint 强制,约束

 **Exercises**

Ⅰ. Match the following words in Column A and Column B

Column A	Column B
1. over-riding	a. 配额寻租
2. shielded	b. 武断的,独裁的
3. sector	c. 报复,反击,征收报复性关税
4. disputes	d. 远景方案,方案,事态
5. quota rent	e. 逐步扩大,逐步增强
6. reverse	f. 判决,裁定
7. transparency	g. 使逆转,使倒退
8. regime	h. 腐败,堕落,贪污
9. corruption	i. 断言
10. evolve	j. 强制,约束
11. backslide	k. 进展,进化
12. escalate	l. 联营,共享
13. retaliate	m. 透明,透明度原则
14. dynamic	n. 借讨论而澄清或解决问题
15. Single Market	o. 不顾及的,不理会的
16. constraint	p. 社会制度,体制
17. outlet	q. 屏蔽,挡开;避开
18. arbitrary	r. 堕落,退步
19. thrash out	s. 平衡,交换,协定
20. claim	t. 部门
21. alternative	u. 出口,发泄方法
22. scenario	v. 动态的,不断变化的
23. ruling	w. 纠纷,争端,争议
24. pool	x. 供替代的选择
25. trade-off	y. 单一市场

Ⅱ. Translate the following sentences into Chinese

1. Peace is partly an outcome of two of the most fundamental principles of the trading system: helping trade to flow smoothly, and providing countries with a constructive and fair outlet for dealing with disputes over trade issues. It is also

an outcome of the international confidence and cooperation that the system creates and reinforces.

2. The increasing number of disputes brought to GATT and its successor, the WTO, does not reflect increasing tension in the world. Rather, it reflects the closer economic ties throughout the world, the GATT/WTO's expanding membership and the fact that countries have faith in the system to solve their differences.

3. This makes life easier for all, in several different ways. Smaller countries can enjoy some increased bargaining power. Without a multilateral regime, such as the WTO's system, the more powerful countries would be freer to impose their will unilaterally on their smaller trading partners. Smaller countries would have to deal with each of the major economic powers individually, and would be much less able to resist unwanted pressure.

4. Protectionism is expensive: it raises prices. The WTO's global system lowers trade barriers through negotiation and applies the principle of non-discrimination. The result is reduced costs of production (because imports used in production are cheaper) and reduced prices of finished goods and services, and ultimately a lower cost of living.

5. Sometimes, the success of an imported product or service on the domestic market can also encourage new local producers to compete, increasing the choice of brands available to consumers as well as increasing the range of goods and services produced locally.

6. So trade clearly boosts incomes. Trade also poses challenges as domestic producers face competition from imports. But the fact that there is additional income means that resources are available for governments to redistribute the benefits from those who gain the most—for example to help companies and workers adapt by becoming more productive and competitive in what they were already doing, or by switching to new activities.

7. The facts also show how protectionism hurts employment. The example of the US car industry has already been mentioned: trade barriers designed to protect US jobs by restricting imports from Japan ended up making cars more expensive in the US, so fewer cars were sold and jobs were lost.

   In other words, an attempt to tackle a problem in the short term by restricting trade turned into a bigger problem in the longer term.

8. That, in simple terms, is one of the problems of discrimination. Imagine now that the government announces it will charge the same duty rates on imports from

all countries, and it will use the same regulations for all products, no matter where they come from, whether imported or locally produced. Life for the company would be much simpler. Sourcing components would become more efficient and would cost less.

9. The GATT-WTO system covers a wide range of sectors. So, if during a GATT-WTO trade negotiation one pressure group lobbies its government to be considered as a special case in need of protection, the government can reject the protectionist pressure by arguing that it needs a broad-ranging agreement that will benefit all sectors of the economy. Governments do just that, regularly.

10. Because quotas limit supply, they artificially raise prices, creating abnormally large profits (economists talk about "quota rent"). That profit can be used to influence policies because more money is available for lobbying.

III. Cloze

The short-sighted protectionist view is that defending particular sectors _____ imports is beneficial. But that view ignores how other countries are going to respond. The longer term reality is _____ one protectionist step by one country can easily lead to retaliation _____ other countries, a loss _____ confidence _____ freer trade, and a slide into serious economic trouble for all-including the sectors that were originally protected. Everyone loses.

Confidence is the key _____ avoiding that kind of no-win scenario. When governments are confident that others will not raise their trade barriers, they will not be tempted to do the same. They will also be _____ a much better frame _____ mind to cooperate with each other.

The WTO trading system plays a vital role _____ creating and reinforcing that confidence. Particularly important are negotiations that lead to agreement by consensus, and a focus on abiding _____ the rules.

IV. Underline the important sentences in the text, which give you useful information

V. Retell or write down what you learn from the text in English or in Chinese

参考译文

世界贸易组织贸易体系的十大好处

从我们口袋里的钱,我们使用的商品和服务到一个更加和平的世界,世界贸易组织及其贸易体系提供了一系列好处,一些是我们熟知的,而其他的则不那么明显。

世界是纷繁复杂的,这本小册子是简短的,但它试图去反映贸易复杂多变的特性。它突出了世界贸易组织贸易体系的一些好处,但它并不宣称一切都是完美的,否则就没有必要进一步谈判以及继续改革发展这一体系。

在世界贸易组织中对所有事情也不是人人都赞同的。它提供了一个让各国研究解决贸易问题上的分歧的平台,这是这个体系存在的重要原因之一。

有许多更重要的原因可以说明比起没有这一体系为什么现在我们更富裕。这里列举了10条:

十大好处

1. 有利于促进和平;
2. 有建设性地处理分歧;
3. 规则使所有人生活得更舒适;
4. 自由贸易削减生活成本;
5. 提供更多产品和品质的选择;
6. 贸易活动提高了收入;
7. 贸易拉动经济增长;
8. 基本原则使生活更有效率;
9. 政府可以不受游说;
10. 鼓励好的政府。

1. 这个体系有利于维护和平

这听起来有点夸大其词,并且过分坚信这个也是错误的。然而这个体系的确对世界和平作出了贡献,如果我们明白了其中的道理,我们将在心中对这个体系实际所做的事情有个清晰的蓝图。

和平是这个贸易体系的两部分最基本原则的一项成果:方便贸易顺畅流通,在处理贸易纠纷时为成员国提供建设性的并且是公平的解决办法。这也是它所创造并不断加强的国际间的信任与合作的结果。

历史给出了一系列由贸易冲突演变成战争的例子。其中给人印象最深刻的是20

世纪30年代各国竞相提升贸易壁垒以保护本国生产者和报复别国的壁垒措施。这使得大萧条进一步恶化并最终成为第二次世界大战爆发的原因之一。

第二次世界大战后两个国际性组织的发展对避免重蹈战前贸易紧张关系起了很大的作用。在欧洲,国际间合作在煤炭、钢铁领域进行。全球范围内,关税和贸易总协定(简称关贸总协定)创立。

这两者都被证明非常成功,以至于现在已大大地扩张,一个成为了现在的欧洲联盟,另外一个就是世界贸易组织。

这是如何实现的?

简而言之,通常销售人员不愿与他们的顾客对抗。换句话说,如果贸易流通顺畅且双方满意当前健康的商业关系,政治冲突是可能减少的。

何况顺利流畅的贸易有利于世界各国人民富起来。更加繁荣,越发满足的人们也不想打仗。

但这些不是全部。关贸总协定/世贸组织是一个重要的信心建立者。20世纪30年代的贸易战争证明了贸易保护主义能轻易地使各国陷入一个没有赢家只有输家的境地。

目光短浅的保护主义派认为在某些领域对进口实行限制是有利的。但是这种看法忽略了其他国家对此所作出的回应。长期的事实是一国作出的保护措施会轻易地引起他国的报复,失去对自由贸易的信心,并在各方面陷入经济危机,包括原先受保护的领域。双方都遭受损失。

信心是避免这种没有赢家的局面的关键。当政府确信别国不会提高贸易壁垒时,他们也不会尝试去提高。他们还将会在一个更好的框架下进行合作。

世界贸易组织的贸易体系在建立和加强这种信心上发挥着重要作用。更为重要的是能使大家达成共识的谈判,并且大家要共同遵守规则。

2. 这个体系能建设性地处理争端

随着贸易数量、产品种类以及参与的国家和公司的数目的增长,产生贸易冲突的机会也更大。世界贸易组织能有利于和平有效地解决这些冲突。

贸易的自由化和扩张可能会有消极的一面。更多的贸易意味着更多争端出现的机会。如果听之任之,就可能导致严重的冲突。但实际上,许多国际贸易的紧张关系有所缓和,因为相关国家可以诉诸国际组织,尤其是世界贸易组织,以解决其贸易争端。

二次大战前并没有这样的选择。战后世界各贸易国谈判所达成的各种贸易规则现已放进了世贸组织的条款中。其中包括各成员国有义务将争端交由世贸组织处理,而不是单方面采取行动。

自1995年世贸组织成立后,大约有300多起贸易纠纷已被提交。如果没有通过有效和谐的手段解决这些纠纷,有些就可能导致更严重的政治冲突。

事实是根据世贸组织的协议来解决争端为判断孰是孰非提供了一个明确的基础。一旦判决作出,协议就为需要进一步采取的行动提供了方向。

越来越多的争端提请关贸总协定及其后继组织——世贸组织,没有反映出世界各国关系越来越紧张。相反,它反映了世界各国经济联系更加密切、关贸总协定和世贸组织的成员国越来越多,而且事实是各国相信这一体系能解决它们之间的分歧。

有时冲突国家之间的争论是辛辣而激烈的,但他们始终遵从之前谈判达成的协议和承诺。

当成员国向世贸组织提请解决争端时,世贸组织的程序使他们把精力集中在规则上。一旦裁决作出,双方致力于设法遵守规则——可能以后会就规则重新谈判,但不会彼此宣战。

3. 一种基于规则而不是权力的体制使人们的生活更加轻松

世贸组织不能宣称能使所有的国家平等。但它的确消除了一些不平等现象,给小国更多的话语权,同时消除了各大国不得不同众多的贸易伙伴谈判的复杂性。

世贸组织通过成员国一致同意来作出决定。各项贸易协议由全体成员参与商议,需经一致通过,同时由各成员国国会批准。这些协议适用于每个成员国。富国和穷国在世贸组织的争端解决程序中拥有平等的权利,可相互诘问。

这一切使各国在很多方面更轻松了。一些小国可以享有更大的讨价还价的能力。如果没有像世贸组织这样的多边体制,较强的国家将更自由地将自己的意愿单方面地强加给那些较小的贸易伙伴。较小的国家将要各自单独面对主要经济大国,从而更加没有能力抵制不希望有的压力。

另外,如果较小的国家能把握机会组成联盟,共享资源,他们将做得更加有效率。有些国家已经这样做了。

对于较大的国家来说,也有相应的好处。主要的经济大国能利用世贸组织这单一平台与它全部或大部分的贸易伙伴在同一时间进行谈判。这对大的贸易国而言,生活更为简单。否则的话,要同时与几十个国家进行持续而复杂的双边谈判。每个国家将最终与不同贸易伙伴达成各不相同的贸易条件,这对进口商和出口商来说贸易变得极其复杂。

纳入了世贸组织协议的非歧视性原则就避免了那种复杂性。事实上有单一的一套规则适用于所有成员国大大简化了整个贸易体制。

这些既定的规则使各国政府更加清楚地知道什么样的贸易政策可以接受。

4. 更自由的贸易削减生活成本

我们都是消费者。我们为食物、衣服、必需品和奢侈品以及任何一样东西支付的价格都受贸易政策的影响。

保护主义是昂贵的:它提高了价格。世贸组织的全球体系通过谈判降低贸易壁垒、采用非歧视原则。结果是降低生产成本(因为用于生产的进口商品更便宜)和降低制成品和服务的价格,最终形成较低的生活成本。

不少研究表明贸易保护主义和自由贸易到底产生了什么影响。这里有一些数字:

食物更便宜

当你保护你的农业时,食物的费用上涨,估计对于欧盟的一个四口之家来说每年多支出 1500 美元;相当于日本的 51% 的食品税(1995);美国消费者每年增加 30 亿美元的支出来支持糖杂货法案 (1988 年)。

农产品贸易改革谈判是一项复杂的工作。各国政府仍在争论农业政策在从食品安全到环境保护的一系列问题中所起的作用。

但世贸组织成员正在减少农业补贴和性质最严重的贸易壁垒。2000 年,新一轮谈判开始继续讨论农业改革问题。这些问题现已并入一个更广泛的工作方案,即 2001 年 11 月在卡塔尔首都多哈举行的世贸组织第四次部长级会议上发起的多哈发展议程。

衣服更便宜

进口限制和高关税共同作用使 20 世纪 80 年代后期的美国纺织品和服装价格上涨了 58%。

英国消费者由于这类限制估计每年要在服装上多支出 5 亿英镑。加拿大人要多付 7.8 亿加元。如果澳大利亚没有在 20 世纪 80 年代末 90 年代初降低关税的话,每个家庭每年要多支出 300 澳元。

纺织品和服装贸易正在世贸组织的影响下进行重大改革,该改革预计在 2005 年完成。这项计划包括取消进口数量限制。

如果关税也被取消,据经济学家计算,结果将是全世界获利约 230 亿美元,包括美国获得 123 亿美元,加拿大获得 8 亿美元,欧盟获得 22 亿美元,约 80 亿美元归发展中国家。

其他商品也一样……

20 世纪 80 年代初美国限制日本汽车进口,在 1981 到 1984 年间汽车价格上涨 41%,几乎是所有消费品平均涨幅的两倍。这一措施的目的是保证美国的就业,但高昂的代价则是少卖 100 万辆新车的最重要原因,从而导致了更多的失业。

如果澳大利亚保持 1998 年的关税水平,现在澳大利亚人将平均每辆车多花费 2900 多澳元。1995 年,欧盟的铝制品用户由于关税壁垒支付了额外的 4.72 亿美元。

多哈回合(DDA)的目标之一就是新一轮的工业品关税削减,即制造业和采矿业产品。一些经济学家(罗伯特·斯特恩,艾伦·迪奥多夫以及德鲁塞拉·布朗)预言,如果这些关税被削减三分之一将提高发展中国家约 520 亿美元的收入。

法国类似的限制估计使车价提高了 33%。电视机、收音机、录像机在贸易保护主义政策下都更加昂贵。

关于服务

电话服务业的自由化使打电话更便宜,20 世纪 90 年代在发展中国家每年下降 4%,工业化国家每年下降 2%,其中考虑了通货膨胀因素。

在中国,来自第二家手机运营商的竞争至少使电话费用下降 30%。在加纳则要下降 50%。

同时由罗伯特·斯特恩领导的经济学家们估计,多哈回合降低三分之一服务贸易壁垒的措施将使发展中国家收入提高约 600 亿美元。

不仅如此。目前这种体系已经纳入世贸组织 50 多年了。

在当时已经有八个主要的贸易谈判回合。全球贸易壁垒降到了现代贸易史上的最低线,之前从未出现过这种状况。贸易壁垒还在不断降低,同时我们都从中受益了。

5. 提供消费者更多的选择,以及更广泛的品质选择

想想我们现在所拥有的东西是因为我们能够进口:反季节性的蔬菜水果、食物、服装以及其他过去被认为是外国独有的产品,来自世界各地的鲜花、各种家居用品、书本、音乐、电影等等。

想想其他国家的人有的东西,因为他们能购买我们或者其他地方出口的东西。环顾四周,想想那些如果没有进口贸易就将在我们面前消失的东西,进口贸易让我们有更多选择,更多的商品和服务,更广泛的质量选择,甚至当地产品的质量能通过进口产品带来的竞争而被提高。

广泛的选择不是消费者购买外国成品的简单问题。当地生产用的材料、部件和设备都可以进口。

这扩大了国内生产商提供的最终产品和服务的范围,并且增加了他们使用技术的范围。譬如,当有了移动电话设备后,即使在那些没有能力制造设备的国家,移动电话服务也能迅速涌现。

有时候,在国内市场成功引进一种产品或服务也可以鼓励本地生产商加入竞争,增加消费者可以选择的品牌,同时扩大当地产品和服务的范围。

如果贸易让我们进口更多,那么它也允许别人买我们更多的出口商品。它增加了我们的收入,为我们提供了更多享受这些更多选择的方法。

6. 贸易增加收入

降低贸易壁垒使贸易增加,从而使国家收入和个人收入都有所提高。但有必要

作出一些调整。

世界贸易组织自己估计,1994 年的乌拉圭回合产生的全球总收入增加额在 1090 亿美元至 5100 亿美元之间(由假设计算所得并考虑了误差)。

最近更多的研究得出了相同的结论。经济学家估计,削减农业、制造业和服务业贸易壁垒的三分之一将刺激全球经济增长 613 亿美元,相当于增加了一个加拿大经济体。

在欧洲,欧盟委员会计算,与 1989 年至 1993 年间没有实施单一市场相比,欧盟的收入增加了 1.1%—1.5%。

可见贸易显然能增加收入。同时贸易使国内生产者面临进口竞争的挑战。但事实上,政府可以从获益最多的一方那里对额外的收入进行重新分配,例如,帮助企业和员工适应所从事行业生产力和竞争日益增强的现状,或改入新的行业发展。

7. 贸易拉动经济增长,同时对就业是个有利因素

贸易显然有创造就业机会的潜力。在实践中,往往有事实证明降低贸易壁垒能改善就业情况。但有一系列因素使情况显得很复杂。尽管如此,另一种选择——贸易保护主义——并不是解决就业问题的有效途径。

这是个棘手的问题,但能以简单的方式处理。有充分的证据表明贸易能刺激经济增长,而经济增长意味着更多的就业机会。贸易增长导致一些就业机会消失也是事实。但是一项可靠的分析至少提出了两个问题。

首先,有其他因素在起作用。比如,技术的进步对就业和生产也产生了强烈的冲击,对一些工作有益,对另一些则产生不利影响。

其次,当贸易明显刺激国民收入使国家繁荣时,它也不总是为那些由于进口竞争而失业的工人提供新工作。

全世界的情况并不是完全相同的。一个工人在一个国家找一份新工作花费的平均时间可能比另一个有类似经历的同类工人在另一个国家花的时间更长。

换句话说,一些国家比其他国家更好地进行了调整。这是因为有些国家具有更有效的反应调整机制。而那些没有有效政策的国家就会失去机会。

在自由贸易对就业产生正面影响的地方有许多证据表明他们把握住了机会。欧盟估计单一市场的建立意味着相比没有单一市场增加 30 万—90 万的就业机会。

通常从事贸易的公司就业前景较好。在美国,1200 万人的就业机会来自出口行业;在 1994—1998 年间创造了 130 万个岗位。而这些工作趋向于稳定的高收入。在墨西哥,与出口相关的工作是最好的:出口 60% 以上产品的行业比其他行业薪水高39%,而加工出口工厂付的薪水是墨西哥最低薪水的 3.5 倍。

事实也表明保护主义是如何对就业产生不利影响的。美国汽车工业的例子已提到:限制进口日本车的贸易壁垒旨在保护美国的就业,但最终导致美国汽车价格更

高,销量减少,就业机会丢失。

换句话说,试图在短期内限制贸易来解决问题反而在长远变成一个更大的难题。

即使一个国家调整困难,选择保护主义只会使情况变得更糟。

8. 基本原则使经济体制更有效,并降低了成本

贸易体制产生的许多益处无法用数量来形容,但它们仍然很重要。这些好处是这个体制的基本原则的产物,它们使直接参与贸易的公司、生产商和服务提供者更轻松。

贸易允许国际间劳动分工,这使资源得到更恰当有效的利用。但世贸组织的贸易体系带来的不止这些。它有利于提高效率降低成本,因为一些重要原则已融入这个体系中。

想象一下,每个国家对不同的贸易伙伴设定不同的规则和进口关税。设想一下一国的公司想为自己的产品进口原材料或组件,例如电线所需的铜或电器设备的电路板。

光看全球供应商的报价是不够的。公司还得分别计算进口所要支付的不同的关税(取决于从哪里进口),同时得知道适用每个国家产品进口的规定。进口一些铜或电路板会变得非常复杂。

简单地说,这是区别对待造成的。设想现在政府宣布对进口不同国家的商品收取相同的关税,所有的产品无论来自哪里无论进口还是国产都适用相同规则。公司所要做的事会简单得多。组件采购将变得更有效,花费也更少。

非歧视原则是世贸组织贸易制度的一个关键原则。其他原则包括:

· 透明度原则(政策、法规、规则的信息明了);

· 增加贸易条件的确定性(降低贸易壁垒、扩大其他国家的市场准入的义务是有法律约束力的);

· 便利化和海关程序的标准化,去除官僚作风,集中数据库信息,在"贸易便利"的前提下简化其他措施。

总之,这些原则都使贸易更简化,降低公司的花费,增强对未来的信心。相应地,也意味着更多的就业机会以及给消费者更好的商品和服务。

9. 该体制保护政府不受眼前利益损害

20 世纪下半叶从关贸总协定到世贸组织的演变有助于政府以更平衡的视角审视贸易政策,各国政府通过强调为了经济体中每个人的利益而需要平衡,得以更好地捍卫自己免受利益集团的游说。

20 世纪前几十年保护主义大行其道的教训是,如果狭隘的部门利益集团在政治影响中获得了不平衡的影响力,那么危害就会产生。结果是越来越多的限制性政策

最终导致发生没有赢家的贸易大战。

表面上看来,限制进口是支持一个经济部门的有效途径。但它不利于其他不该受影响的部门而使经济发生偏差。比方说,如果你保护服装业,其他所有人必须承受更昂贵的衣服,从而对各部门的工资构成压力。

贸易保护也可以随其他国家通过提高其贸易壁垒的报复而逐步升级。这正是导致20世纪二三十年代的灾难性后果的原因。甚至连要求保护的行业也以损失惨重而告终。

政府需要与狭隘的利益集团抗争,而世贸组织可以提供帮助。

关贸总协定—世贸组织体系涵盖广泛的经济部门。因此,如果在关贸总协定—世贸组织多边贸易谈判中一个利益集团施压游说政府将其视为一个特例来保护,政府可以拒绝保护主义,称这需要有利于经济体所有部门的广泛同意。政府经常都这么做。

10. 这个体制鼓励好的政府

根据世贸组织规则,一旦承诺有了一个行业要实行贸易自由化,反悔是非常困难的。规则还阻止一系列不明智的政策。对企业而言,意味着贸易条件更确定更透明。对政府意味着好的纪律。

规则包括承诺不向不明智的政策倒退。通常贸易保护主义是不明智的,因为我们已经看到它在国内和国际上造成的损害。

某些形式的贸易壁垒会造成更多的损害,因为它们给贪污腐败等恶劣政府行为提供了机会。

配额是世贸组织试图解决的一种贸易壁垒,比如每年进出口限制在一个具体数额内。

因为配额限制供给,他们就人为地提高价格,造成非正常的巨额利润(经济学家称之为"配额寻租")。这些利润可以用来影响政策,因为能有更多的钱被用于游说。

它给腐败提供了机会,例如在贸易商之间的配额分配。世界各地发生过许多这样的案例。

换句话说,配额是一种非常不好的限制贸易的方式。各国政府已同意通过世贸组织的规则,来抵制配额方式。

尽管如此,各种不同形式的配额在大多数国家继续使用,政府据理力争他们需要配额制度。但受制于世贸组织的协议和承诺,他们必须减少或消除一些配额,尤其是在纺织品方面。

许多其他方面的世贸组织的协议也有助于减少腐败和不良政府行为。

透明度原则(向公众提供有关贸易法规的所有信息)、"贸易便利化"的其他方面、有关处理产品安全和标准的更清楚的法规,非歧视原则通过减小随意决策以及作

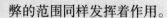
弊的范围同样发挥着作用。

很多时候,政府愿意用世贸组织作为一种外部制约手段:"我们不能这样做,因为这将违反世贸组织的协议。"

Unit Three

European Union

European Union

The European Union (EU) is a union of twenty-five independent states based on the European Communities and founded to enhance political, economic and social co-operation. Formerly known as European Community (EC) or European Economic Community (EEC).

Date of foundation: 1st November, 1993. New members since 1st January, 1995: Austria, Finland, Sweden. For the ten new members as of 1st May, 2004, see below.

Member states (EUR: Euro currency):

Austria (EUR)

Belgium (EUR)

Denmark

Finland (EUR)

France (EUR)

Germany (EUR)

Greece (EUR)

Ireland (EUR)

Italy (EUR)

Luxembourg (EUR)

Netherlands (EUR)

Portugal (EUR)

Spain (EUR)

Sweden

United Kingdom of Great Britain and Northern Ireland

Ten countries have joined the EU on 2004-05-01:

Cyprus (Greek part), the Czech Republic, Estonia, Hungary, Latvia, Lithuania, Malta, Poland, Slovakia and Slovenia.

External Trade

The European Union is the world's biggest trader, accounting for 20% of global imports and exports. Free trade among its members underpinned the successful launch nearly 50 years ago of the EU. The Union is therefore a leading player in efforts to liberalise world trade for the mutual benefit of rich and poor countries alike.

Increased trade boosts world growth to everybody's advantage. It brings consumers a wider range of products to choose from. Competition between imports and local products lowers prices and raises quality. Liberalised trade enables the most efficient producers to compete fairly with rivals in other countries, whose governments have to cut import duties used to protect national firms.

A global player

The EU's basic philosophy is that it will open its market to imports from outside provided its trading partners do likewise. It is also keen to liberalise trade in services. But it is ready to make allowances for developing countries by allowing them to open their markets more slowly than industrialised countries and is helping them integrate into the world trading system.

The removal of barriers to free trade within the EU has made a significant contribution to its prosperity and this has reinforced its commitment to global liberalisation. As the EU member states removed tariffs on trade between them, they also unified their tariffs on goods imported from outside. This meant that products paid the same tariff whether they entered the EU via the ports of Athens or Hamburg. As a result, a car from Japan which pays import duty on arrival in Germany can be shipped to Belgium or Poland and sold there in the same way as a German car. No further duty is charged.

The harmonisation of its common external tariff (CET), as it was known, meant that EU countries had to participate as a single group in international trade negotiations. External trade thus became one of the first instruments of European integration requiring member states to pool their sovereignty.

A firm commitment

As a result, the EU has been a key player along with its trading partners in the successive international rounds of trade liberalisation negotiations. These include the Kennedy Round of the 1960s, the Tokyo Round of the 1980s, the Uruguay Round which was completed in 1994, and the ongoing Doha Development Round which began in 2001. The aim of these rounds, which are now held in the framework of the World Trade Organisation, is to reduce tariffs and remove other barriers to world trade.

Following earlier rounds, the EU's average tariff on industrial imports has now fallen to 4%, one of the lowest in the world.

The collapse of the Cancun conference in September 2003, seen as the midway point in the Doha Round, surprised the EU and other participants. An unexpected gap had opened up between the rich and poor countries on several issues concerning access to each other's markets and the long-running question of agricultural subsidies. The Union is taking an active part in international efforts to get the talks back on track.

The rules-based system

The European Union has invested heavily in trying to make a success of the Doha Round. It is also a firm believer in the rules-based system of the WTO which provides a degree of legal certainty and transparency in the conduct of international trade. The WTO sets conditions under which its members can defend themselves against unfair practices like dumping—selling at below cost—by which exporters compete against local rivals. It provides a dispute settlements procedure when direct disputes arise between two or more trading partners.

A network of agreements

Goods are traded between exporters and importers. Trade rules are multilateral, but trade itself is bilateral—between buyers and sellers, exporters and importers. This is why the EU, in addition to its participation in Doha and previous WTO rounds, has also developed a network of bilateral trade agreements with individual countries and regions across the world.

It has trade agreements with its neighbours in the Mediterranean basin and with Russia and the other republics of the former Soviet Union. When it expanded from 15 to 25 members, the EU declared its intention to develop closer trade and partnership agreements with these neighbours. The creation of such a large EU-centred trade grouping will have an impact on relations with other trading partners.

The wider world

The EU's trade policy is closely linked to its development policy. The Union has granted duty-free or cut-rate preferential access to its market for most of the imports from developing countries and economies in transition under its general system of preferences (GSP). It goes even further for the 49 poorest countries in the world, all of whose exports—with the sole exception of arms—are to enjoy duty-free entry to the EU market under a programme launched in 2001.

The EU has developed a new trade and development strategy with its 78 partners in the Africa—Pacific—Caribbean (ACP) group of countries aimed at integrating them into the world economy. It also has a trade agreement with South Africa that will lead to free trade between the two sides, and it is negotiating a free trade deal with the six members of the Gulf Cooperation Council (GCC)—Bahrain, Kuwait, Oman, Qatar, Saudi Arabia and the United Arab Emirates.

The EU has trade and association agreements with Mexico and Chile in Latin America and has been negotiating a deal to liberalise trade with the Mercosur group—Argentina, Brazil, Paraguay and Uruguay.

It does not, however, have specific trade agreements with its major trading partners among the developed countries like the United States and Japan. Trade is handled through the WTO mechanisms, although the EU has many agreements in individual sectors with both countries.

Given the size of their bilateral trade (the US takes 24% of EU exports and supplies 18% of its imports), it is not surprising that disputes break out between the two from time to time. While a number of these are settled bilaterally, others end up before the WTO dispute-settlement body. Although these disputes make the headlines, they represent less than 2% of total transatlantic trade.

Internal Market

More than ten years on, we take the European single market for granted. With old barriers gone, people, goods, services and money move around Europe as freely as within one country. We travel at will across the EU's internal frontiers for business and pleasure or, if we choose, we can stay at home and enjoy a dazzling array of products from all over the European Union. In 1993, the single market was the EU's greatest achievement; it was also its toughest challenge.

The core of the Union

The single market is the core of today's Union. To make it happen, the EU institutions and the member countries strove doggedly for seven years from 1985 to draft and adopt the hundreds of directives needed to sweep away the technical, regulatory, legal, bureaucratic, cultural and protectionist barriers that stifled free trade and free movement within the Union. They won the race against time, but the victory passed largely unnoticed by the public. The single market never fired the popular imagination in the way the single currency, the other big event of the past decade, did. As the former European Commission president and instigator of the whole project, Jacques Delors, remarked: "you can't fall in love with the single market".

Lovable or not, the single market has, according to the Commission, created 2.5 million new jobs since 1993 and generated more than 800 billion in extra wealth. The opening of national EU markets has brought down the price of national telephone calls to a fraction of what they were ten years ago. Helped by new technology, the Internet is being increasingly used to carry voice telephony. Under pressure of competition, the prices of budget airfares in Europe have fallen significantly. The removal of national restrictions has enabled more than 15 million Europeans to go to another EU country to work or spend their retirement.

When Delors launched his vast single market project in 1985 he knew just how much potential for growth there was and jobs remained locked up behind national frontiers. Tariffs and quotas had been abolished at the end of the 1960s, but many technical and administrative obstacles to free trade still persisted.

How does it work?

When these obstacles are removed and national markets opened, more firms can compete against each other. This means lower prices for the consumer—with the added bonus of a greater choice of goods and services. Firms selling in the single market know they have unrestricted access to more than 450 million consumers in the European Union—enabling them to achieve economies and efficiencies of scale, which translate in turn into lower prices. The single market also provides a useful springboard for European firms to expand into today's globalised markets.

The EU is making it easier to save and invest for retirement. The four freedoms of movement—for goods, services, people and capital—are underpinned by a range of supporting policies. Firms are prevented from fixing prices or carving up markets among them by the EU's robust anti-trust policy. People can move around more freely for work because member states recognise many of each other's academic and professional qualifications. Governments have agreed to take decisions affecting the single market by a system of majority voting rather than by unanimous agreement—which is much harder to achieve.

The creation of the single market gave European Union countries a stronger incentive to liberalise previously protected monopoly markets for utilities such as telecommunications, electricity, gas and water. The independent national regulators who supervise the now-liberalised markets for telecoms and energy coordinate their activity at EU level. Not just big industries, but households and small businesses across Europe are increasingly able to choose who supplies them with electricity and gas.

Some way to go

The undeniable successes of the single market must not blind us to its shortcomings. The services sector, for instance, has opened up more slowly than markets for goods.

This was particularly the case for a wide range of financial services, and for transportation, where separate national markets still exist—especially for rail and air transport.

There is also a need to remove more red tape—those administrative and technical barriers to the free flow of goods and services. These include the reluctance of EU countries to accept each other's standards and norms or sometimes to recognise the equivalence of professional qualifications. The fragmented nature of national tax systems also puts a brake on market integration and efficiency.

The good news is that these dangers have been recognised by member states and the European Commission, and remedial action is under way, although not at a uniform speed and not in all sectors. For financial services, the EU's action plan to develop an integrated market by 2005 has been completed. This will cut the cost of borrowing for firms and consumers, and will offer savers a wider range of investment products—savings plans and pension schemes—which will be available from the European supplier of their choice. Bank charges for cross-border payments have been reduced.

Protecting the single market

The single market relies chiefly on competition and regulatory authorities to maintain a level playing field for the free movement of goods and services. The free movement of people is guaranteed under the Schengen agreement (called after the small Luxembourg town where it was signed). This removes checks at most of the EU's internal frontiers, and strengthens controls at the EU's external borders, including international airports and seaports. The United Kingdom and Ireland have not joined the Schengen system, which does not yet apply to the member states that joined in 2004.

Protection at another level is required to prevent piracy and counterfeiting of genuine EU products. The European Commission estimates that pirates and counterfeiters cost the EU more than 17 000 jobs each year. This is why the Commission and the member states are working on extending copyright and patent protection.

Removing barriers to trade and free movement is a huge plus for those engaged in commerce or travel for legitimate reasons. But criminals of all sorts seek to turn the system to their advantage. The EU response to frontier-free crime has been to create a system of frontier-free police and criminal justice cooperation. Europol, the European police force, is part of that response. So is the Schengen Information System whereby national police exchange information on wanted or suspected wrongdoers. Under the Eurojust project, member states second senior prosecutors, policemen and lawyers to a central team working together to fight organised crime.

Economic and Monetary Affairs

EU member governments run their economies according to similar principles of economic management. They coordinate their policies in order to deliver steady growth, more jobs and a competitive economy across the EU, one which will at the same time preserve the European social model and protect the environment.

All EU member states are part of economic and monetary union (EMU), whose purpose is to integrate the economies of EU countries more effectively. Integration promotes growth and prosperity. It requires closely coordinated economic policy. Member states decide jointly on the basis of proposals from the Commission on the broad approach they will each follow. They are then free to implement these guidelines using the tax and social welfare policy mix which best suits their country.

The single currency

Twelve of the 25 member states have taken integration a major step further by adopting the same currency, the euro. Eleven countries adopted the euro at its launch (as a virtual currency) on 1 January 1999: Austria, Belgium, Germany, Finland, France, Ireland, Italy, Luxembourg, Netherlands, Portugal and Spain. Greece adopted the euro on 1 January 2001. All these countries introduced the euro in cash form on 1 January 2002.

Using the euro lowers the cost of cross-border business. Price comparability across borders increases competition. Individuals also benefit from this process; they make savings by not having to change money when travelling within the euro area, by being able to compare prices more readily, and because the cost of transferring money across borders has come down.

The euro is a recognised international currency used by international travellers and for invoicing commercial transactions with countries outside the euro area, thus reducing risk for euro-area businesses. The euro is also increasingly used by central banks worldwide as a reserve currency.

Adopting the euro

All EMU members are eligible to adopt the euro and all the countries which joined the EU on 1 May 2004 will adopt the euro within the next few years, though there is no fixed timetable. They may choose to wait if they think that their economies are not yet ready. They have to weigh the disadvantages (less control over their inflation, interest and exchange rates) against the likely benefits—which include having the same currency as major trading partners, greater credibility in international financial markets and, consequently, greater flows of investment. Denmark, Sweden and the United Kingdom have chosen to remain outside the euro for the time being.

Citizens of all the new member states will be using the euro within a few years. EMU members wanting to introduce the euro must meet certain economic criteria, including two years of exchange rate stability after joining. Six new member countries—Cyprus, Estonia, Latvia, Lithuania, Malta and Slovenia—have already taken a major step towards meeting this criterion (and adopting the euro) by linking their currencies to the euro through the so-called Exchange Rate Mechanism.

There are four other criteria. These relate to interest rates, the budget deficit, the inflation rate and the debt-to-GDP ratio. Compliance ensures that economies are on broadly similar paths when they join the euro area.

The Stability and Growth Pact

The disciplines of the Stability and Growth Pact (SGP) keep economic developments in the EU, and in the euro-area countries in particular, broadly synchronised. They prevent member states from taking policy measures which would unduly benefit their own economies at the expense of other EU countries.

A key principle of the Pact is the rule that all member states keep their budgets close to balance or in surplus. In a downturn, the deficit must generally not exceed 3% of gross domestic product (GDP). The second anchor of the Pact is the rule that the debt-to-GDP ratio should not be more than 60%.

A revision in March 2005 based on the first five years of experience of the Pact introduced greater flexibility in exceeding the deficit threshold in hard economic times or where the reason for the higher deficit is investment in structural improvements to the economy. Member states are now also allowed longer to reverse their excessive deficits. Ultimately, if they do not bring their economies back into line, corrective measures, or even fines, can be imposed.

This revision did not change the level of the twin anchors and member states re-emphasised as part of the revision the importance of putting more money aside in the good times when budgets are close to or in surplus and reducing government debt to the threshold level.

The European Court of Justice is the ultimate arbiter of how the Pact should be interpreted.

Tools for ensuring economic policy coherence

One of the European Commission's jobs is to assess whether each member state's economic policy is in line with the EU's agreed objectives—economic, social and environmental—and to provide early warnings if it believes a deficit is becoming abnormally high or that some other SGP rule is about to be breached.

The Commission has two tools for doing this:

the Broad Economic Policy Guidelines (BEPG);

the stability and convergence programmes.

The BEPGs are a roadmap for the EU as a whole and for individual member states. They focus on the medium-and long-term changes needed to increase Europe's ability to create jobs and raise productivity growth through more effective competition and better conditions for investment, especially in knowledge and innovation.

Each year, member states provide the Commission with detailed information on their economic policies, and in particular the policies which underpin a disciplined approach to their budgets. Euro-area countries provide this information in so-called stability programmes. For other member states, it takes the form of convergence programmes. The convergence programmes contain one element which is not needed in the stability programmes. This is information on how these economies are performing in relation to the criteria which would apply if they wanted to join the euro.

The role of the ECB

When the euro was launched in 1999, the European Central Bank (ECB) took over full responsibility for monetary policy throughout the euro area. This includes setting benchmark interest rates and managing the euro area's foreign exchange reserves. The ECB also has the job of ensuring that payments move smoothly across all EU borders, not just within the euro area.

Consumers

Every citizen is a consumer and the European Union takes great care to protect their health, safety and economic well-being. It promotes their rights to information and education, takes steps to help them safeguard their interests, and encourages them to set up and run self-help consumer associations.

Empowering Europe's citizens

Consumer policy is part of the Union's strategic objective of improving the quality of life of all its citizens. In addition to direct action to protect their rights, the Union ensures that consumer interests are built into EU legislation in all relevant policy areas. As the single market and the single currency open trading borders, as use of the Internet and electronic commerce grows and as the service sector expands, it is important that all 450 million citizens in the 25-nation Union benefit from the same high level of consumer protection.

Legislation is not the only means. Other methods include co-regulation between consumer and business organisations, and good practice guidelines. Strong consumer organisations, aware of an individual's rights and able to take advantage of them in practice, also have a prominent role to play, especially in the new member states.

Harmonised rules needed

An EU-level consumer policy is a necessary adjunct to the internal market. If the single market functions well, it will stimulate consumer confidence in cross-border transactions and have a positive impact on competition and prices for the benefit of all EU citizens.

But individuals must be confident they have sufficient accurate information before making purchases and enjoy clear legal rights when transactions go wrong. This is why harmonised rules are needed to guarantee citizens an adequate level of protection.

A growing achievement

The policy has ensured consumers a large degree of safety in many areas over the years. In addition to the General Product Safety Directive, adopted in 1992, individual safety measures are now in place for toys, personal protective equipment, electrical appliances, cosmetics, pharmaceuticals, machinery and recreational craft.

A revised Directive came into force in January 2004, introducing new and stricter rules on the recall of defective products. The European Commission receives around 150 notifications of dangerous products each year. The new rules set safety requirements for consumer products like sports and playground equipment, childcare articles, gas appliances and most household products such as textiles and furniture.

EU consumer policy has come a long way since the first programme for consumer information and protection was adopted in 1975. A large number of measures have been taken to safeguard consumers' wider interests in areas such as:

fair business practices;

misleading and comparative advertising;

price indicators;

unfair contract terms;

distance and doorstep selling;

timeshares and package travel.

A comprehensive and integrated approach

The scope of EU consumer protection policy is changing, reflecting a shift in people's needs and expectations. New legislation will set high, harmonised EU safety, security and health standards designed to increase consumer confidence.

The consumer policy strategy for 2002-2006 underlines this shift in emphasis and states that EU consumer policy should:

guarantee essential health and safety standards, so that buyers are sure the products they purchase are safe and that they are protected against illegal and abusive practices by sellers;

enable individuals to understand policies that affect them and to have an input when these policies are made;

establish a coherent and common environment across the Union so that shoppers are confident about making cross-border purchases;

ensure that consumer concerns are integrated into the whole range of relevant EU policy areas from environment and transport to financial services and agriculture.

A high common level of consumer protection

As part of its strategy, the European Commission will propose measures to guarantee the safety of consumer goods and services on items as varied as chemicals, cosmetics and toys. This will be accompanied by legislation to protect people's economic interests when they are involved in transactions like distance selling or timeshare offers.

The European Commission plans guidelines to protect consumers who buy online. With the growth of financial services and electronic commerce, the Commission plans to introduce guidelines for good on-line business practices and provide guarantees for all aspects of consumer credit and non-cash means of payment.

Consumers' interests and benefits are already factored into legislation to inject competition into key public service sectors like transport, electricity and gas, telecommunications and postal services. The new directives and regulations ensure that the public continues to enjoy universal access to high quality services at affordable prices. The European Commission intends to involve consumer organisations more closely in the consultation process when new legislation is being drafted and to fund training courses for their staff. A new European Consumer Consultative Group, bringing together representatives of national consumer organisations and the Commission, began work in December 2003.

Effective enforcement of consumer protection rules

EU rules must be properly implemented and individuals able to obtain redress. This requires better cooperation between member states. Court proceedings, especially in another jurisdiction, can be costly and time-consuming. To encourage out-of-court settlements, the Commission is developing alternative dispute-settlement mechanisms.

In June 2003, the Commission issued a draft directive for adoption by member states which provides for an EU-wide ban on unfair commercial practices. It lists a series of unfair practices and, once adopted, will outlaw them through a single, common and general prohibition. Uncertainty about their rights and fear of exploitation by unscrupulous traders have made consumers wary of cross-border shopping. The new directive aims to give consumers the same protection from sharp business practices and rogue traders whether they buy from the shop around the corner or from a website in another member state. The directive was formally adopted by the EU Council of Ministers and the European Parliament in May 2005. Member states now have 2—1/2 years to bring their national legislation in line with the requirements of the directive.

Consumers already have a limited scope for redress. The EEJ-NET, with contact points in each EU country (www. eejnet. org), acts as a clearinghouse to provide individuals with information and support when making a complaint. A parallel network, FINN-NET, (available on the Commission website at europa. eu. int/comm. /internal_ market) fulfils the same role for cross-border complaints about financial services.

Enterprise

While modern and often successful, European business and industry cannot afford to rest on their laurels. It is a constant challenge to remain competitive, and keep up with technology, and the pace of growth in competing countries. Meeting the challenge successfully is essential for sustainable growth and for our greater prosperity. EU enterprise and industry policy plays its part by fostering innovation, entrepreneurship and competitiveness in manufacturing and services.

Enterprise and industry policy aims to ensure all businesses compete and trade on fair and equal terms and that Europe is an attractive place to invest and work. It nevertheless takes into account the importance of Europe having a sound industrial fabric across the EU. This can mean taking specific needs and characteristics of individual sectors into account, such as the car or textile industries, and ensuring that strategically important industries can flourish. These are industries such as the life sciences, aerospace or biotechnology.

Technology and innovation are key factors in creating an environment for industrial enterprise. The EU funds large amounts of research, finances entrepreneurship, encourages public-private partnerships in order to make the most of what the private and public sectors have to offer and organises technological platforms. It also plans to set up a European Technology Institute.

Managing change

The EU does not take a protectionist or inward-looking approach to meeting these challenges. The basic premise is that sheltering industry from change would only postpone the inevitable and make it costlier and more painful in the long run. What the EU does is to try to anticipate structural change, create a climate which promotes the innovation for meeting the challenge and—where adjustment is needed—then cushions the impact as much as realistically possible for both employer and employee.

This requires a careful balance between meeting society's expectations of high health and environmental standards, for example, while not stifling innovation, greater productivity and job creation with too much red tape. Another element in the equation is adequate and non-discriminatory access at the best price possible to key business support services, such as communications, transport and utilities.

Enterprise policy therefore emphasises the need to integrate policies as diverse as trade, research, the internal market, employment and training, the information society, regional development and taxation—without overlooking the importance of the environment, so that they boost the use of knowledge and innovation across EU industry as a whole. The EU concentrates on removing obstacles to competition across the board, preventing new ones going up, and limiting, improving and simplifying regulation. In addition, individual member states are not allowed to put new obstacles in the way of business from other member states.

Sometimes, barriers to intra-EU trade are dismantled through common product standards, if mandatory product requirements are essential for protecting public health, the consumer or the environment. In other cases, producers are left free to decide what technology to use, providing the end-result is a safe product. The "CE" mark on products provides the authorities and consumers with reassurance that appropriate standards have been met, whether goods are produced in the EU or imported.

Only in exceptional cases, e. g. pharmaceuticals, is upfront approval needed before a product can be put on to the market. The process of obtaining the approvals needed to sell in more than one country is facilitated by the option of applying through the European Medicines Evaluation Agency in London.

Strict rules also apply to some chemicals. These rules are currently being streamlined to achieve a better balance between the need for enterprise to be competitive and for the products not to endanger health or the environment. The plan is to list all chemical substances in a single database and improve risk evaluation though a system called REACH—Registration, Evaluation, and Authorisation of Chemicals. The system will be run by a European Chemicals Agency in Helsinki.

An integrated approach to competitiveness

The Risk Capital Action Plan is one example of the way in which enterprise policy

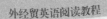

has interacted with other EU policies. It was a single market initiative, but has contributed to entrepreneurship by removing the obstacles small businesses face in obtaining start-up and early-stage finance. Research policy is also vital to entrepreneurship because innovation encompasses not only new technologies but also the development of new business concepts, product design or new ways of distributing or marketing a product.

SMEs are the backbone of EU enterprise

The EU's 25 million small and medium-sized businesses (SMEs) are already the backbone of EU enterprise, but there is unrealised potential to narrow Europe's productivity gap with the United States. Based on its principle of "think small first", the EU has specific programmes which make it easier for SMEs to participate in EU-funded research and innovation projects. In addition, the rules on state aid and other forms of funding are more generous for SMEs than for large firms.

Tourism is the world's largest industry and Europe is the most visited region. The Innovation Relay Centre network in 33 countries, which is part-funded by the Commission, helps SMEs find partners for research and innovation projects, and the Euro Info Centres in 44 countries, including the United States, provide information on policies and opportunities which target SMEs.

Through its Entrepreneurship Action Plan, the Commission is promoting a more entrepreneurial mindset, encouraging more people to set up businesses, helping those businesses grow and become more competitive, improving the flow of finance and creating a more SME-friendly environment. It is spending some 90m annually from 2001 to 2005 for SME-oriented projects in the EU and Bulgaria, Romania and Turkey. It works closely with the European Investment Bank in encouraging small business growth, particularly in the countries which joined the EU in 2004.

Sustainability is crucial

Sustainability is never lost sight of. For example, Europe is the world's most visited tourism region. This calls for a response that does not throttle the development of a major service industry or prevent people taking the holiday of their choice, but protects natural resources and the environment, so that the development of tourist sites does not destroy the very heritage on which the industry is built. Sustainable growth is not just a matter for EU policymakers. Each enterprise is responsible for having socially and environmentally responsible policies, and the European Commission backs initiatives to increase Corporate Social Responsibility (CSR).

Regional Policy

Although the European Union is one of the richest parts of the world, there are striking internal disparities of income and opportunity between its regions. The entry of 10 new member countries in May 2004, whose incomes are well below the EU average, has widened these gaps. Regional policy transfers resources from affluent to poorer regions. It is both an instrument of financial solidarity and a powerful force for economic integration.

Solidarity and cohesion

The two words, solidarity and cohesion, sum up the values behind regional policy in the EU:

solidarity because the policy aims to benefit citizens and regions that are economically and socially deprived compared to EU averages.

cohesion because there are positive benefits for all in narrowing the gaps of income and wealth between the poorer countries and regions and those which are better off.

Big differences in prosperity levels exist both between and within member states. Even before enlargement, the ten most dynamic regions of the EU had a level of prosperity, measured by GDP per capita, which was nearly three times higher than the ten least developed regions. The most prosperous regions are all urban—London, Hamburg and Brussels.

The dynamic effects of EU membership, coupled with a vigorous and targeted regional policy, can bring results. The gap between richest and poorest regions has narrowed over the years. The case of Ireland is particularly heartening. Its GDP, which was 64% of the EU average when it joined in 1973, is now one of the highest in the Union.

One of the current priorities is to bring living standards in the new member states closer to the EU average as quickly as possible.

The causes of inequality

Inequalities have various causes. They may result from longstanding handicaps imposed by geographic remoteness or by more recent social and economic change, or a combination of both. The impact of these disadvantages is frequently evident in social deprivation, poor quality schools, higher unemployment and inadequate infrastructures.

The cost of success

The Regional Fund helps finance the Athens metro. The EU policy to reduce regional disparities is built on four structural funds:

the European Regional Development Fund;

the European Social Fund;

the section of the EU's common agricultural fund devoted to rural development;

financial support for fishing communities as part of the common fisheries policy (CFP).

These funds will pay out about 213 billion, or roughly one third of total EU spending, between 2000 and 2006.

A further 18 billion is allocated to the Cohesion Fund, set up in 1993 to finance transport and environment infrastructure in member states with a GDP less than 90% of the Union average at the time (Greece, Ireland, Spain and Portugal).

Where the money goes

Unlike the cohesion fund, poor or disadvantaged regions in all EU countries can benefit from the four structural funds according to certain criteria or objectives.

A total of 70% of funding goes to so-called Objective 1 regions where GDP is less than 75% of the EU average. About 22% of the Union population live in the 50 regions benefiting from these funds which go to improving basic infrastructure and encouraging business investment.

Another 11.5% of regional spending goes to Objective 2 regions (areas experiencing economic decline because of structural difficulties) to help with economic and social rehabilitation. Some 18% of the EU population live in such areas. An Objective 2 programme in Denmark, receiving 162m from the structural funds, has succeeded in improving transport and telecommunications in small islands and coastal communities with limited access by land and little local fresh water.

Objective 3 focuses on job-creation initiatives and programmes in all regions not covered by Objective 1. 12.3% of funding goes towards the adaptation and modernisation of education and training systems and other initiatives to promote employment.

There are also four special initiatives, accounting between them for 5.35% of the structural funds:

cross-border and inter-regional cooperation (Interreg Ⅲ);

sustainable development of cities and declining urban areas (Urban Ⅱ);

rural development through local initiatives (Leader +);

combating inequalities and discrimination in access to the labour market (Equal).

Looking after new members

With enlargement, the area and population of the Union has expanded by 20% while GDP has increased by less than 5%. The GDP of the newcomers varies from about 72% of Union average in Cyprus to about 35% – 40% in the Baltic States (Estonia,

Latvia and Lithuania). The Union has created tailor-made financial programmes for the period 2000 – 2006 to help the newcomers adjust to membership and to start narrowing the income gap with the rest of the Union.

These programmes are worth about 22 billion in all, with further funding now available for the post-entry period. The components are:

ISPA (the Instrument for Structural Policies for Pre-accession) finances environment and transport projects with a budget of 7. 28 billion;

Sapard (Special Accession Programme for Agriculture and Rural Development) concentrates on agricultural development with a 3. 64 billion budget.

They are additional to the older Phare programme whose budget for 2000 – 2006 is 10. 92 billion and whose priorities are to:

strengthen the administrative and institutional capacity of new members. This accounts for 30% of its budget.

finance investment projects—which absorb the remaining 70%.

To supplement these programmes, the Union has set aside a further 23 billion from the structural and cohesion funds to be spent in the new member states in the period 2004 – 2006.

Beyond the short term

The European Commission has already (in July 2004) published its proposals for a new-look and more integrated regional policy for the period 2007 – 2013 after present programmes run out. Procedures will be simplified and funding concentrated on the most needy regions of the 25 member states. For the new period, the Commission proposes a regional policy budget of 336 billion, still the equivalent of one third of the total EU budget.

The idea is to divide the spending into three categories. Of the total amount, 79% would go on reducing the gap between poor and richer regions while 17% would be spent in increasing the competitiveness of poor regions and creating local jobs there. The remaining 4% would focus on cross-border cooperation between frontier regions.

Taxation

Within the EU, governments retain sole responsibility for direct taxes—the amounts they raise by taxing personal incomes and company profits. EU taxation policy focuses instead on the rates of indirect taxes like value-added tax and excise duties which can directly affect the single market. It also ensures that tax rules do not prevent capital moving freely around the EU and that free movement of capital does not create opportunities for avoiding tax. EU policy also targets tax rules which might limit the rights of EU citizens to work anywhere in the EU.

National governments must have sound public finances and comply with the EU's broad economic policy guidelines. Providing they do this, they are free to decide spending priorities and what taxes to use to raise the necessary money. They are also free to set the rate of tax on company profits and personal incomes, savings and capital gains. Member states' rights are protected by the fact that it requires a unanimous vote to make key changes to EU tax rules. Where there are common rules, including some agreed floors and ceilings for value-added tax (VAT) and excise tax, their purpose is to make sure the single market in goods and financial services works smoothly and that each member state gets a fair share of tax revenues. As some of the EU budget is funded from VAT revenues, a common approach to raising this money means the contributions are fairly distributed across EU governments.

The role of indirect taxes

A degree of uniformity is essential for VAT or excise tax on petrol, drinks or cigarettes, because changes in these taxes can very quickly distort competition. However, there is room for cultural differences, for example in the approach to taxing beer and wine, and for allowing some countries to charge less because they have healthier public finances.

The result can be "bargains" in cross-border shopping. Luxembourg's low excise duties attract motorists and shoppers from its neighbours on all sides. Northern France is a Mecca for British bargain-hunters, especially for beer, wine and tobacco. Differences in rates of taxation on vehicles enable smart buyers to save 20% or more on a new car if they shop around carefully.

Minimum rates

Having minimum tax rates avoids serious distortions. They apply to mineral oils, including petrol, natural gas, electricity and coal. A coherent structure is not only essential for fair competition; it is also a tool the EU can use to encourage energy saving and cleaner fuels, thereby cutting emissions of greenhouse gases. There is nevertheless flexibility in these arrangements to take special national situations into account.

Tax on petrol can serve an environmentally friendly purpose. Minimum rates still leave room for variations to suit national circumstances. There is EU-wide agreement on a minimum rate of 15% for VAT on most goods and services, but exceptions are possible. A higher standard rate is allowed within certain limits. So are lower rates, and exemptions for some items. Generally, these are restricted to goods and services not in competition with goods and services from another member state, like restaurant meals, or to the necessities of daily life, such as food and medicine.

The European Commission tries to limit exceptions as much as possible in the interests of the single market and fair play, so it continues to aim for as much harmonisation as possible. In the meantime, its emphasis is on simplifying the rules and clamping down on fraud, which often takes advantage of the current complexity of a system built up piecemeal. Complexity also adds significantly to the cost of doing business and represents a real barrier to cross-border activities.

At the same time, the Commission is keeping up with developments in technology. The authors of the original VAT rules could not have envisaged that it would one day be possible to download computer software or take pay-per-view television from cyberspace—once a VAT no-man's-land, but now covered by the rules.

Company taxation that is fair for all

In the area of company tax, the EU has two goals: preventing harmful tax competition between member states and supporting the principle of free movement of capital. In the past, member states offered excessive tax incentives to attract foreign investment, sometimes at the expense of another EU country where the investment was economically more justified. Member states are now bound by a Code of Conduct to ensure they do not introduce anti-competitive tax breaks. They are phasing out any that still exist.

There are also EU rules or codes of conduct to ensure, in all member states, comparable tax treatment of cross-border payments of interest, royalties and dividends to sister and parent companies and of cross-border intra-company sales of goods and services (so-called transfer prices). Work is going on to ensure that member states all take the same approach to taxing groups of companies.

An equitable approach to savings and pensions

The EU rarely interferes in personal taxation. Where there are exceptions, they are designed to ensure that there is no discrimination against, or special benefit for anyone taking advantage of the opportunities of working or investing in another country.

For example, EU citizens should be able to accumulate pension rights when moving from one country to another without running into tax barriers and should not pay more tax on dividends on investments in other EU countries than they would pay on domestic investments. The European Commission takes legal action where member states have tax rules which make this difficult.

EU citizens can place their savings where they think they will get the best return. However, tax remains due in their country of residence. EU governments lose legitimate revenue if their residents do not declare interest income on savings held abroad. As a remedy, EU and a number of other European governments have been exchanging information on non-residents' savings since 1 July 2005. Austria, Belgium and Luxembourg will apply withholding tax instead, for the time being, and will transfer a large part of that revenue to the investor's home country, so that the tax ends up where it is actually due. (*Source*：*http*：//*ec. europa. eu*)

Notes

[1] underpinned 加强……的基础，支撑

[2] pool 共享

[3] Cancun conference 坎昆会议

[4] instigator 煽动者

[5] fraction 小部分，分数

[6] abolish 废除，取消

[7] springboard 跳板，出发点

[8] Schengen agreement 申根协议

[9] pirate 盗印者，侵犯专利权者

[10] counterfeiter 伪造者，造假者

[11] wrongdoer 做坏事的人

[12] Eurojust 欧洲司法组织

[13] prosecutor 公诉人，检举人

[14] guideline 指导路线，方针，准则

[15] pact 协定，公约，条约

[16] synchronise （使）同时发生，（使）同步

[17] unduly 不适当地

[18] downturn 衰退，下降趋势

[19] Euro-area countries 欧元区国家

[20] defective 有缺陷的，欠缺的

[21] abusive 被滥用的

[22] redress 赔偿，补救

[23] sharp 骗子

[24] rogue 无赖

[25] laurels 荣誉，胜利，名声

［26］cushion 缓冲，加垫褥

［27］red tape 官样文章

［28］equation 等式，公式

［29］backbone 骨干，支柱

［30］throttle 使窒息，压制

［31］affluent 丰富的，富裕的

［32］heartening 鼓励的，激励的，振奋的

［33］fraud 欺诈，舞弊，骗子

［34］Generalized System of Preference 普遍优惠制度

Exercises

I. Match the following words in Column A and Column B

Column A	Column B
1. Cancun conference	a. 申根协议
2. instigator	b. 无赖
3. springboard	c. 欧元区国家
4. Schengen agreement	d. 欺诈，舞弊，骗子
5. pirate	e. 盗印者，侵犯专利权者
6. counterfeiter	f. 欧洲司法组织
7. wrongdoer	g. 公诉人，检举人
8. Eurojust	h. 坎昆会议
9. prosecutor	i. 煽动者
10. guideline	j. 官样文章
11. pact	k. 衰退，下降趋势
12. downturn	l. 鼓励，激励，振奋
13. Euro-area countries	m. 指导路线，方针，准则
14. redress	n. 骗子
15. sharp	o. 伪造者，造假者
16. rogue	p. 跳板，出发点
17. laurels	q. 荣誉，胜利，名声
18. red tape	r. 协定，公约，条约
19. backbone	s. 做坏事的人
20. heartening	t. 赔偿，补救
21. fraud	u. 骨干，支柱
22. Generalized System of Preference（GSP）	v. 普遍优惠制度

II. Translate the following sentences into Chinese

1. The aim of these rounds, which are now held in the framework of the World Trade Organisation, is to reduce tariffs and remove other barriers to world trade.

2. The WTO sets conditions under which its members can defend themselves against unfair practices like dumping—selling at below cost—by which exporters compete against local rivals. It provides a dispute settlements procedure when

direct disputes arise between two or more trading partners.

3. We travel at will across the EU's internal frontiers for business and pleasure or, if we choose, we can stay at home and enjoy a dazzling array of products from all over the European Union.

4. The single market is the core of today's Union. To make it happen, the EU institutions and the member countries strove doggedly for seven years from 1985 to draft and adopt the hundreds of directives needed to sweep away the technical, regulatory, legal, bureaucratic, cultural and protectionist barriers that stifled free trade and free movement within the Union.

5. The creation of the single market gave European Union countries a stronger incentive to liberalise previously protected monopoly markets for utilities such as telecommunications, electricity, gas and water.

6. The good news is that these dangers have been recognised by member states and the European Commission, and remedial action is under way, although not at a uniform speed and not in all sectors.

7. When the euro was launched in 1999, the European Central Bank (ECB) took over full responsibility for monetary policy throughout the euro area. This includes setting benchmark interest rates and managing the euro area's foreign exchange reserves. The ECB also has the job of ensuring that payments move smoothly across all EU borders, not just within the euro area.

8. Consumer policy is part of the Union's strategic objective of improving the quality of life of all its citizens. In addition to direct action to protect their rights, the Union ensures that consumer interests are built into EU legislation in all relevant policy areas.

9. The EU does not take a protectionist or inward-looking approach to meeting these challenges. The basic premise is that sheltering industry from change would only postpone the inevitable and make it costlier and more painful in the long run.

10. Inequalities have various causes. They may result from longstanding handicaps imposed by geographic remoteness or by more recent social and economic change, or a combination of both.

III. Cloze

The European Commission has already (in July 2004) published its proposals _____ a new-look and more integrated regional policy for the period 2007 – 2013 _____ present programmes run out. Procedures will be simplified and funding concentrated _____ the most needy regions of the 25 member states. _____ the new period, the Commission proposes a regional policy budget _____ 336 billion, still the equivalent of one third _____ the total EU budget.

The idea is _____ divide the spending into three categories. Of the total amount, 79% would go _____ reducing the gap _____ poor and richer regions _____ 17% would be spent on increasing the competitiveness of poor regions and creating local jobs there. The remaining 4% would focus on cross-border cooperation between frontier regions.

IV. Underline the important sentences in the text, which give you useful information

V. Retell or write down what you learn from the text in English or in Chinese

Unit Four

EU-China: Closer Partners, Growing Responsibilities

COMMUNICATION FROM THE COMMISSION TO THE COUNCIL AND THE EUROPEAN PARLIAMENT

EU-China: Closer partners, growing responsibilities

1. What is at stake?

China has re-emerged as a major power in the last decade. It has become the world's 4th economy and 3rd exporter, but also an increasingly important political power. China's economic growth has thrown weight behind a significantly more active and sophisticated Chinese foreign policy. China's desire to grow and seek a place in the world commensurate with its political and economic power is a central tenet of its policy. Given China's size and phenomenal growth, these changes have a profound impact on global politics and trade.

The EU offers the largest market in the world. It is home to a global reserve currency. It enjoys world leadership in key technologies and skills. The EU plays a central role in finding sustainable solutions to today's challenges, on the environment, on energy, on globalisation. It has proved capable of exerting a progressive influence well beyond its borders and is the world's largest provider of development aid.

Europe needs to respond effectively to China's renewed strength. To tackle the key challenges facing Europe today including climate change, employment, migration, security we need to leverage the potential of a dynamic relationship with China based on our values. We also have an interest in supporting China's reform process. This means factoring the China dimension into the full range of EU policies, external and internal. It also means close co-ordination inside the EU to ensure an overall and coherent approach.

To better reflect the importance of their relations, the EU and China agreed on a strategic partnership in 2003. Some differences remain, but are being managed effectively, and relations are increasingly mature and realistic. At the same time China is, with the EU, closely bound to the globalisation process and becoming more integrated into the international system.

The EU's fundamental approach to China must remain one of engagement and partnership. But with a closer strategic partnership, mutual responsibilities increase. The partnership should meet both sides' interests and the EU and China need to work together as they assume more active and responsible international roles, supporting and contributing to a strong and effective multilateral system. The goal should be a situation where China and the EU can bring their respective strengths to bear to offer joint solutions to global problems.

Both the EU and China stand to gain from our trade and economic partnership. If we are to recognise its full potential, closing Europe's doors to Chinese competition is not the answer. But to build and maintain political support for openness towards China, the benefits of engagement must be fully realised in Europe. China should open its own markets and ensure conditions of fair market competition. Adjusting to the competitive challenge and driving a fair bargain with China will be the central challenge of EU trade policy in the decade to come. This key bilateral challenge provides a litmus test for our partnership, and is set out in more detail in a trade policy paper entitled "Competition and Partnership" which accompanies the present Communication.

Europe and China can do more to promote their own interests together than they will ever achieve apart.

2. Context: China's revival

Internal stability remains the key driver for Chinese policy. Over recent decades, stability has been underpinned by delivery of strong economic growth. Since 1980 China has enjoyed 9% annual average growth and has seen its share of world GDP expand tenfold to reach 5% of global GDP. China's growth has resulted in the steepest recorded drop in poverty in world history, and the emergence of a large middle class, better educated and with rising purchasing power and choices.

But the story of this phenomenal growth masks uncertainties and fragility. The Chinese leadership treads a complex daily path, facing a range of important challenges, primarily domestic, but which increasingly resonate beyond national boundaries:

Disparities continue to grow. The wealth gap is significant and growing, as are social, regional and gender imbalances; there is huge stress on healthcare and education systems; and China is already facing significant demographic shifts and the challenges of a rapidly ageing population;

China's demand for energy and raw materials China is already the world's second largest energy consumer is already significant and will continue to grow; and the environmental cost of untrammelled economic and industrial growth is becoming more and more apparent. At the same time growth patterns have not been balanced, with a focus on exports to the detriment of domestic demand.

Growth remains central to China's reform agenda, but increasingly is tempered with measures to address social inequality and ensure more sustainable economic and political development. Paradoxically, in a number of areas, the conditions for stability improve as the Party and State relax control. A more independent judiciary, a stronger civil society, a freer press will ultimately encourage stability, providing necessary checks and balances. Recognition of the need for more balanced development, building a "harmonious society", is encouraging. But further reform will be necessary.

China's regional and international policy also supports domestic imperatives: a secure and peaceful neighbourhood is one conducive to economic growth; and China's wider international engagement remains characterised by pursuit of very specific objectives, including securing the natural resources needed to power growth. At the same time we have seen China's desire to build international respect and recognition. The 2008 Olympic Games in Beijing and the 2010 World Expo in Shanghai will focus the world's attention on China's progress.

China has traditionally described its foreign policy as one of strict non-interference, but as it takes on a more active and assertive international role, this becomes increasingly untenable. The Chinese government is beginning to recognise this, and the international responsibilities commensurate to its economic importance and role as a permanent member of the UN Security Council as illustrated by its increasingly active diplomatic commitments.

The EU and China benefit from globalisation and share common interests in its success. It presents challenges to both and brings further responsibilities. We also share a desire to see an effective multilateral system. But there remain divergences in values, on which dialogue must continue.

As the partnership strengthens, expectations and responsibilities on both sides increase. As China's biggest trading partner, EU trade policy has an important impact on China, as do China's policies on the EU. Increasingly, both sides expect that impact to be taken into account in their partner's policy formulation.

3. The way forward

The EU should continue support for China's internal political and economic reform process, for a strong and stable China which fully respects fundamental rights and freedoms, protects minorities and guarantees the rule of law. The EU will reinforce co-operation to ensure sustainable development, pursue a fair and robust trade policy and work to strengthen and add balance to bilateral relations. The EU and China should work together in support of peace and stability. The EU should increase co-ordination and joint action and improve co-operation with European industry and civil society.

Until now the legal basis for relations has been the 1985 Trade and Co-operation Agreement. This no longer reflects the breadth and scope of the relationship and at the 9th EU-China Summit leaders agreed to launch negotiations on a new, extended Partnership and Co-operation Agreement (PCA) to update the basis for our co-operation. This new agreement presents an important opportunity. It will provide a single framework covering the full range and complexity of our relationship, and at the same time should be forward-looking and reflect the priorities outlined in this Communication.

3.1 Supporting China's transition towards a more open and plural society

The Chinese leadership has repeatedly stated its support for reform, including on basic rights and freedoms. But in this area progress on the ground has been limited. The EU must consider how it can most effectively assist China's reform process, making the case that better protection of human rights, a more open society, and more accountable government would be beneficial to China, and essential for continued economic growth.

Democracy, human rights and the promotion of common values remain fundamental tenets of EU policy and of central importance to bilateral relations. The EU should support and encourage the development of a full, healthy and independent civil society in China. It should support efforts to strengthen the rule of law—an essential basis for all other reform.

At the same time, the EU will continue to encourage full respect of fundamental rights and freedoms in all regions of China; freedom of speech, religion and association, the right to a fair trial and the protection of minorities call for particular attention in all regions of China. The EU will also encourage China to be an active and constructive partner in the Human Rights Council, holding China to the values which the UN embraces, including the International Covenant on Civil and Political Rights.

The twice-yearly human rights dialogue was conceived at an earlier stage in EU-China relations. It remains fit for purpose, but the EU's expectations—which have increased in line with the quality of our partnership are increasingly not being met. The dialogue should be:

More focussed and results-oriented, with higher quality exchanges and concrete results;

More flexible, taking on input from separate seminars and sub-groups;

Better co-ordinated with Member State dialogues.

3.2 Sustainable development

One of today's key global challenges is to ensure our development is sustainable. China will be central to meeting this challenge. China's domestic reform policy is important and the Commission will continue to support this through its co-operation programme, including corporate social responsibility. On issues such as energy, the environment and climate change, respect for international social standards, development assistance, as well as wider macroeconomic issues, the EU and China should ensure close international co-operation. Both sides should:

Ensure secure and sustainable energy supplies. As important players in world energy markets, the EU and China share a common interest and responsibility in ensuring the security and sustainability of energy supplies, improving efficiency and mitigating the environmental impact of energy production and consumption. The EU's priority should be to ensure China's integration into world energy markets and multilateral governance mechanisms and institutions, and to encourage China to become an active and responsible energy partner. On that basis both sides should work together to:

Increase international co-operation, in particular efforts to improve transparency and reliability of energy data and the exchange of information aimed at improving energy security in developing countries, including Africa;

Strengthen China's technical and regulatory expertise, reducing growth in energy demand, increasing energy efficiency and use of clean renewable energy such as wind, biomass and bio fuels, promoting energy standards and savings through the development and deployment of near zero emission coal technology;

Commit to enhance stability through a market-based approach to investment and procurement; dialogue with other major consumers; encouragement of transparent and non-discriminatory regulatory frameworks, including open and effective energy market access; and by promoting the adoption of internationally recognised norms and standards;

Combat climate change and improve the environment. We already have a good basis for co-operation on environment issues and on climate change through the Partnership established at the 2005 EU-China Summit.

The EU should share regulatory expertise, working with China to prevent pollution, safeguard biodiversity, make the use of energy, water and raw materials more efficient, and improve the transparency and the enforcement of environmental legislation. Both

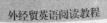

sides should work together to tackle deforestation and illegal logging, sustainable management of fisheries resources and maritime governance;

Both sides should build on the Climate Change Partnership, reinforcing bilateral co-operation, and strengthening international co-operation, meeting shared international responsibilities under the Climate Change Convention and Kyoto Protocol and engage actively in the dialogues on international climate change co-operation post-2012. We should strengthen the use of emissions trading and clean development mechanisms.

Improve exchanges on employment and social issues. China is committed to tackle social disparities and promote more balanced development. The EU and China should:

Intensify co-operation on employment and social issues reinforcing and expanding bilateral dialogue to include issues such as health and safety at work, decent work standards, and meeting the challenges of an ageing population;

Work together to ensure that international commitments on labour and social issues are upheld.

Improve co-ordination on international development. Closer co-operation on international development issues would benefit the EU, China and partners in the developing world. There are significant downsides if we are not able to co-ordinate effectively, particularly in Africa but also in other developing countries. The EU and China should:

Engage in a structured dialogue on Africa's sustainable development. There should be transparency on the activity and priorities of both sides, providing a basis for full discussion;

Support regional efforts to improve governance in Africa;

Explore opportunities for improving China's integration into international efforts to improve aid efficiency, co-ordination and opportunities for practical bilateral co-operation on the ground.

Build sustainable economic growth. China has become a source growth for the EU and the world, but China's current growth model is also the source of important imbalances in EU-China trade. The Chinese government has recognised the importance of meeting macro economic challenges, of forward-looking fiscal, monetary and structural policies, boosting consumption and reducing inequalities. Increasing exchange rate flexibility will be an important factor, helping rebalance growth towards domestic demand and increasing Chinese households' purchasing power. Policies which would lead to a reduction of its current account surplus would increase China's control of its economy and contain risks of overheating, and at the same time meet China's shared responsibility to ensure a stable and balanced world economy.

As key economic powers, the EU and China should further develop their partnership and work together to tackle global economic issues; they should:

Deepen co-operation and share experience in formulating and implementing monetary, fiscal, financial, exchange rate and structural policies;

Co-operate towards the orderly unwinding of global imbalances;

Strengthen and upgrade their macro-economic dialogue.

3.3 Trade and economic relations

China's integration into the global trading system has benefited both Europe and China. The EU is China's largest trading partner, representing more than 19% of China's external trade. European companies trading with and investing in China have contributed to China's growth, bringing capital goods, knowledge and technology that have been instrumental to China's development.

An economically strong China is in Europe's interest. China, especially its rapidly increasing middle class, is a growing market for EU exports. EU exports to China increased by over 100% between 2000 and 2005, much faster than its exports to the rest of the world. EU exports of services to China expanded six-fold in the ten years to 2004. European companies and consumers benefit from competitively priced Chinese inputs and consumer goods. Openness brings benefits to both China and the EU.

Nevertheless, in Europe there is a growing perception that China's as yet incomplete implementation of WTO obligations and new barriers to market access are preventing a genuinely reciprocal trading relationship. Imports from China have added to pressure to adjust to globalisation in Europe. This trend is likely to continue as China moves up the value chain.

For the relationship to be politically and economically sustainable in the long term, Europe should continue to offer open and fair access to China's exports and to adjust to the competitive challenge. The EU needs to develop and consolidate areas of comparative advantage in high-value and high-tech design and production and to help workers retrain. China for its part should reciprocate by strengthening its commitment to open markets and fair competition. Both sides should address concerns over the impact of economic growth on natural resources and the environment. The EU will:

Insist on openness. The EU will continue working with China towards the full implementation of its WTO obligations and will urge China to move beyond its WTO commitments in further opening its market to create opportunities for EU companies. The

EU will accept that it cannot demand openness from China from behind barriers of its own. The EU will urge China to honour its commitment to open accession negotiations on the Government Procurement Agreement in 2008 and work to bring them to a successful conclusion as rapidly as possible.

Level the playing field. Better protection of intellectual property rights in China and ending forced technology transfers are EU priorities, including through implementation by China of WTO obligations and will help create a better investment climate in China. The EU will press China to stop granting prohibited subsidies and reform its banking system, and encourage China to allow market forces to operate in its trade in raw materials.

Support European companies. The Commission will make a major effort to assist companies doing business with China, in particular small and medium sized enterprises while urging them to respect decent work standards. The EU will extend and strengthen the existing information, training and advice on protecting and defending IPR in China. A European Centre in Beijing should be opened. The EU-China Managers Exchange and Training Programme should be extended.

Defend the EU's interests: dialogue first. The EU has a clear preference for resolving trade irritants with China through dialogue and negotiation. The existing EU-China trade related dialogues should be strengthened at all levels, their focus should be sharpened on facilitating trade and improving market access and their scope extended. The EU and China also have an interest in joining their efforts in international rule making and global standard setting bodies. The EU will actively pursue global supervisory and regulatory solutions, promoting open markets and regulatory convergence, and build on co-operation with China through EU-China regulatory dialogues. This will also help to ensure compliance of Chinese imports with EU standards for food and non-food products.

But where other efforts have failed, the Commission will use the WTO dispute settlement system to ensure compliance with multilaterally agreed rules and obligations. Trade defence measures will remain an instrument to ensure fair conditions of trade. The EU is actively working with China with a view to creating the conditions which would permit early granting of MES. Recent progress has been made on some of the conditions. The Commission will continue to work with the Chinese authorities through the mechanisms we have established and will be ready to act quickly once all the conditions are met.

Build a stronger relationship. A key objective of the negotiations for a new

Partnership and Cooperation Agreement, which will also update the 1985 Trade and Co-operation Agreement, will be better access to the Chinese market for European exporters and investors, going beyond WTO commitments, better protection of intellectual property and mutual recognition of geographical indications. China is already a major beneficiary of the international trading system and should assume a responsibility commensurate with those benefits, making a substantial contribution to reviving and completing the WTO Doha round.

Many of these steps are not only in EU's interest. They are strongly in China's interest and an integral part of China's progress towards balanced and sustainable growth and development and global leadership and responsibility. The accompanying trade policy paper sets out a comprehensive approach to EU-China trade and investment relations for the medium term.

3.4 Strengthening bilateral co-operation

Bilateral co-operation spans a wide range of issues, including 7 formal Agreements, 22 sectoral dialogues, covering diverse and important issues from aviation and maritime transport to regional and macro-economic policy. Further development of the structured dialogue to exchange experiences and views on competition matters, as well as technical and capacity-building assistance as regards competition enforcement, remains important. Co-operation has been successful and positive. But more must be done to focus on co-operation and ensure balance and mutual benefit, in all areas, but particularly in flagship areas such as science and technology co-operation. More should be done to strengthen co-operation on migration issues, people-to-people links, and the structures governing our official relations. Both sides should:

Ensure quality and increased co-operation in science and technology. Science and technology co-operation is a priority area for the Chinese government. China spends 1.5% of its GDP on a dynamic and growing research and development programme. Bilateral co-operation is also strong: China is one of the most important third-world countries participating in more EU research projects under the 6th Research Framework Programme, giving it access to 600 million euros of research, and China is an important partner on key projects such as ITER and Galileo. EU participation in Chinese programmes should be increased.

The Joint Declaration from the Science and Technology Forum in May 2005 set the context for taking co-operation forward, based on mutual benefit and reciprocal access and participation. Both sides should:

Consolidate and improve the visibility of co-operation. This will allow both sides to focus and set priorities effectively and to respond to dynamic issues such as emerging pandemics or work on clean energy technologies; make it easier to examine scope for increased reciprocity; and provide a basis for more effective co-ordination with Member States;

Improve joint planning to ensure mutual benefit, and increase flexibility to fund the participation of European researchers in Chinese research programmes. Both sides should facilitate researchers' mobility which in the case of the EU is promoted through specific grants under the Framework Programme.

Build an effective migration relationship. Chinese and other migrants enrich the EU culturally and bring with them important skills and expertise. But there is a significant downside if the process is not managed effectively. There has to be an effective legal framework to facilitate people-to-people exchanges. But we need effective mechanisms to deal with those who abuse the system, with a focus on prevention and return. Both sides should work towards the early conclusion of an effective Readmission Agreement.

The existing consultation mechanism should continue and be extended to cover both legal and illegal migration, and with renewed political commitment to make progress;

Both sides should agree and push forward specific co-operation projects on e. g. the exchange of officials and training; and there should be exchanges on biometric technology;

There should be a dedicated dialogue with the Ministry of Public Security covering migration and the fight against organised crime, terrorism and corruption;

The EU-China Tourism Agreement (ADS) will need continued proactive and practical co-operation to ensure it functions effectively.

Expand people-to-people links. We should strengthen the full range of people-to-people links which underpin our relations through significant and sustained action on both sides, from cultural exchanges and tourism to civil society and academic links.

Civil society and institutional links should provide direct support and impetus for political and trade relations. Both sides should facilitate direct links between civil society groups in the EU and China in all areas, and include them in sectoral dialogues where possible. Official non-governmental links should be strengthened and expanded. The European Parliament plays a central role and should expand co-operation with the Chinese National People's Congress. The EU should also strengthen links between ECOSOC and the Chinese Economic and Social Committee, political parties, and between other semi-official bodies.

Education has been an area of particular success, with 170,000 Chinese students studying in the EU in 2005. We should continue to build on existing co-operation through programmes run by individual Member States and through the China-specific strand of the Erasmus Mundus programme. There have been positive examples of work to set up joint degree courses and joint campuses. We should also implement specific projects such as a European Law School. Both sides will continue to encourage EU students to study in China. To strengthen language capability, the Commission will support a specific programme to train Chinese language teachers to teach in Europe.

Academic expertise in the EU on China needs to be improved and co-ordinated more effectively. Action is needed by both sides to support effective interaction between European and Chinese academia. The Commission should continue to support an academic network on China, drawing together academic expertise to inform EU policy and co-ordinating information-sharing within the academic community; and there should be a small number of prestigious professorships on Chinese studies created and made available to European universities. There should be a permanent regular dialogue between European and Chinese think tanks.

Make bilateral structures more effective. Both sides should reflect on the structures which govern relations and consider whether they should be streamlined, improved or upgraded. The Commission's 2003 Policy Paper sought to expand sectoral dialogue between the EU and China. This has been very successful, and the majority function well and make an important contribution to our partnership. But progress should be reviewed. Both sides should also consider whether there are new bodies or mechanisms which would further contribute to EU-China relations.

Annual Summits provide a good framework for maintaining contacts at head of government level. This should be supported by regular cross-cutting exchange and dialogue at technical, ministerial and more senior level. In addition, both sides should explore further options for flexible and informal opportunities to meet and exchange views;

The recently agreed strategic dialogue at Vice Foreign Minister level should be a key mechanism covering regional and geo-political issues and adding focus, impact and value to the relationship;

Both sides should undertake a thorough examination of the rationale, interrelationship and performance of the sectoral dialogues with the aim of maximising synergies and ensuring mutual benefit, and ensure interested stakeholders are involved where possible. The Commission will produce a series of Working Documents on specific sectoral challenges;

A new independent EU-China Forum should be set up. On the EU side it should be at arms length from the institutions and should draw on civil society, academic, business and cultural expertise, providing policy input to political leaders and impetus to bilateral relations.

The EU should ensure that it speaks with one voice on the panoply of issues related to its relations with China. Given the complexity of the relationship and the importance of continuity, regular, systematic and cross-cutting internal co-ordination will be essential.

The EU's co-operation programme, delivered through the country strategy paper (CSP) and national indicative programmes, should continue to play a role in supporting the partnership between the two sides and China's reform process. But as China moves further away from the status of a typical recipient of overseas development aid, the EU must calibrate its co-operation programme carefully and keep it under review. Co-operation must be in both sides' interests, reflect the EU's own principles and values, and serve to underpin the partnership.

3.5 International and regional co-operation

The EU and China have an interest in promoting peace and security through a reformed and effective multilateral system. They should co-operate closely in the framework of the UN, working to find multilateral solutions to emerging crises, and to combat terrorism and increase regional co-operation, including through involvement by both in emerging regional structures. This common interest, in strong multilateralism, peace and security should also be reflected in closer co-operation and more structured dialogue on the Middle East, Africa and East Asia, and on cross-cutting challenges such as non-proliferation.

East Asia. It is clear the EU has a significant interest in the strategic security situation in East Asia. It should build on the increasing effectiveness of its foreign and security policy and its strategic interest in the region by drawing up public guidelines for its policy.

China has a key role to play in the region and has been working to improve relations with its neighbours, including Russia and India, and with central Asia through the Shanghai Co-operation Organisation. But there remains scope for improvement in Sino-Japanese relations. The EU has an interest in strong relations between the region's major players and in continued regional integration.

Taiwan. The EU has a significant stake in the maintenance of cross-straits peace and stability. On the basis of its One China Policy, and taking account of the strategic balance in the region, the EU should continue to take an active interest, and to make its views known to both sides. Policy should take account of the EU's:

Opposition to any measure which would amount to a unilateral change of the status quo;

Strong opposition to the use of force;

Encouragement for pragmatic solutions and confidence building measures;

Support for dialogue between all parties; and,

Continuing strong economic and trade links with Taiwan.

Non-proliferation. Non-proliferation represents a key area for the strategic partnership. International and bilateral co-operation is based on UNSCR 1540 and the Joint Declaration on Non-Proliferation agreed at the 2004 EU-China Summit. The EU is supportive of China's central role in work on the Korean peninsula and continued Chinese support will be crucial to progress on the Iranian nuclear issue. There has been a good start on dialogue and practical co-operation to strengthen and enforce export controls. The EU should build on this, working with Chinese officials to encourage China to:

Comply with all non-proliferation and disarmament treaties and international instruments, and to promote compliance with them regionally and internationally;

Both sides should work together to share practical experience in implementing and enforcing export controls, including through training for Chinese customs officials. They should consider scope for joint EU/Asia initiatives in the context of the ASEAN Regional Forum.

4. Conclusion

China is one of the EU's most important partners. China's re-emergence is a welcome phenomenon. But to respond positively and effectively, the EU must improve policy co-ordination at all levels, and ensure a focused single European voice on key issues.

We have a strong and growing bilateral relationship. But we must continue build on this. The recommendations in this Communication, which the Council is invited to endorse and complement through Council Conclusions, represent a challenging agenda for the EU to do so, and the Partnership and Co-operation Agreement provides an important practical mechanism to move this agenda forward.

A closer, stronger strategic partnership is in the EU's and China's interests. But with this comes an increase in responsibilities, and a need for openness which will require concerted action by both sides. (*Source: http://ec. europa. eu*)

Notes

[1] at stake 处于胜败关头、处于危险境地

[2] tenet 原则,主义,信条,教义,宗旨

[3] reserve currency 储备货币

[4] sustainable solution 可持续的解决方案

[5] globalisation 全球化

[6] development aid 发展援助

[7] tackle 应付,处理

[8] leverage 发挥杠杆作用

[9] multilateral system

[10] revival 苏醒,复兴

[11] underpinned 巩固,支撑

[12] steep 急剧升降的

[13] resonate 使共鸣、共振

[14] disparity 不同,不一致

[15] untrammelled 不受限制的,自由自在的

[16] detriment 损害,伤害,危害

[17] tempered 缓和

[18] address 对付

[19] paradoxically 自相矛盾地

[20] press 新闻舆论媒体

[21] imperatives 必要的事

[22] conducive 有益于……的

[23] assertive 过分自信的

[24] untenable 不能维持的,支持不住的,(主张等)站不住脚的

[25] commensurate 相称的

[26] divergences 分歧

[27] formulation 明确的表达,确切的陈述

[28] robust 健康的,强健的,坚定的

[29] accountable 负有责任的

[30] embrace 拥抱,包含

[31] covenant 契约,盟约

［32］conceive 构思，认为

［33］corporate 社团的，公司的

［34］mitigate 使缓和，使减轻

［35］governance 统治，统辖，管理

［36］biomass 生物质

［37］deployment 使开始活动或工作

［38］procurement 采购

［39］norms 规范

［40］combat 与……战斗，与……斗争

［41］expertise 专门知识，专家意见

［42］logging（木材）采运作业

［43］emission 排放

［44］decent 得体的，大方的

［45］uphold 支持，确定

［46］downsides 下降趋势，底侧

［47］boost 推进

［48］current account surplus 经常项目顺差

［49］unwinding 循环

［50］instrumental 可作为手段的

［51］perception 感觉，领悟力

［52］genuinely 真诚地，诚实地

［53］reciprocal 相互的，互惠的，有往来的

［54］consolidate 巩固

［55］reciprocate 回报，互换，酬答

［56］honour its commitment 履行其义务

［57］level 使……平等

［58］defend 防护，辩护

［59］preference 偏爱，优先，喜爱物，优先权

［60］irritants 刺激物

［61］convergence 集中

［62］market economy status（MES）市场经济地位

［63］assume 承担

［64］integral 固有的

［65］readmission 重新接纳

［66］consultation mechanism 磋商机制

［67］biometric technology 生物特征识别技术

［68］proactive 前置的

［69］impetus 推动力

［70］sectoral 部门的

［71］official 正式的

［72］ECOSOC（联合国）经济及社会理事会

［73］strand 线,绳

［74］academia 学术界

［75］prestigious 享有声望的

［76］concerted 商定的,一致的

 **Exercises**

I. Match the following terms in Column A and Column B

Column A	Column B
1. tenet	a. 复兴
2. reserve currency	b. 自相矛盾地
3. globalisation	c. 经常项目顺差
4. development aid	d. 相互的，互惠的，有往来的
5. multilateral system	e. 新闻舆论媒体
6. revival	f. 必要的事
7. disparities	g. 不同,不一致
8. detriment	h. 相称的
9. paradoxically	i. 损害，伤害，危害
10. press	j. 分歧
11. imperatives	k. 原则,宗旨
12. commensurate	l. 发展援助
13. divergence	m. 市场经济地位
14. formulation	n. 多边体系
15. covenant	o. 契约，盟约
16. conceive	p. 储备货币
17. procurement	q. 确切的陈述
18. norms	r. 全球化
19. expertise	s. 构思，认为
20. logging	t. 规范
21. current account surplus	u. 生物特征识别技术
22. reciprocal	v. 享有声望的
23. consolidate	w. 专门知识，专家意见
24. reciprocate	x. (联合国)经济及社会理事会
25. MES: market economy status	y. 学术界
26. consultation mechanism	z. (木材)采运作业
27. biometric technology	A. 巩固
28. ECOSOC	B. 采购
29. academia	C. 回报，互换，酬答
30. prestigious	D. 磋商机制

II. Translate the following sentences into Chinese

1. It will provide a single framework covering the full range and complexity of our relationship, and at the same time should be forward-looking and reflect the priorities outlined in this Communication.

2. Nevertheless, in Europe there is a growing perception that China's as yet incomplete implementation of WTO obligations and new barriers to market access are preventing a genuinely reciprocal trading relationship. Imports from China have added to pressure to adjust to globalisation in Europe. This trend is likely to continue as China moves up the value chain.

3. The EU will continue working with China towards the full implementation of its WTO obligations and will urge China to move beyond its WTO commitments in further opening its market to create opportunities for EU companies. The EU will accept that it cannot demand openness from China from behind barriers of its own.

4. The EU will press China to stop granting prohibited subsidies and reform its banking system, and encourage China to allow market forces to operate in its trade in raw materials.

5. The EU and China also have an interest in joining their efforts in international rule making and global standard setting bodies. The EU will actively pursue global supervisory and regulatory solutions, promoting open markets and regulatory convergence and build on co-operation with China through EU-China regulatory dialogues.

6. But where other efforts have failed, the Commission will use the WTO dispute settlement system to ensure compliance with multilaterally agreed rules and obligations. Trade defence measures will remain an instrument to ensure fair conditions of trade.

7. We should strengthen the full range of people-to-people links which underpin our relations through significant and sustained action on both sides, from cultural exchanges and tourism to civil society and academic links.

8. Both sides will continue to encourage EU students to study in China. To strengthen language capability, the Commission will support a specific programme to train Chinese language teachers to teach in Europe.

9. China is one of the EU's most important partners. China's re-emergence is a welcome phenomenon. But to respond positively and effectively, the EU must improve policy co-ordination at all levels, and ensure a focused single European

voice on key issues.

10. A closer, stronger strategic partnership is in the EU's and China's interests. But
   with this comes an increase in responsibilities, and a need for openness which
   will require concerted action by both sides.

III. Cloze

Build a stronger relationship. A key objective of the negotiations for a new
Partnership and Cooperation Agreement, which will also update the 1985 Trade and
Co-operation Agreement, will be better access to the Chinese market for European
exporters and investors, going _____ WTO commitments, better protection _____
intellectual property and mutual recognition _____ geographical indications. China is
already a major beneficiary _____ the international trading system and should assume
a responsibility commensurate _____ those benefits, making a substantial contribution
_____ reviving and completing the WTO Doha round.

Many of these steps are not only _____ EU's interest. They are strongly in
China's interest and an integral part of China's progress _____ balanced and
sustainable growth and development and global leadership and responsibility. The
accompanying trade policy paper sets out a comprehensive approach _____ EU-China
trade and investment relations _____ the medium term.

IV. Underline the important sentences in the text, which give you useful information

V. Retell or write down what you learn from the text in English or in Chinese

参考译文

委员会致理事会和欧洲议会的沟通文件

欧盟一中国:伙伴关系,责任共进

1.双方面临的挑战

在过去十年中,中国重新成为了世界主要国家。它已经成为世界第四经济体和第三大出口国,而且政治实力不断增强。中国的经济增长巩固了中国更主动更老到的外交政策。中国希望发展并寻求符合其政治与经济力量的世界地位是中国政策的中心原则。鉴于中国的规模与显著的发展,中国的变化对全球的政治和贸易产生了深远的影响。

欧盟向世界提供了最大的市场。它是全球储备货币的基地。在主要技术和技能方面占有世界领先地位。欧盟在寻找可持续地解决环境、能源、全球化等世界当今面临的问题上一直起着主要作用。事实证明欧盟有能力在其边境之外产生积极影响,并提供了世界上最大的发展援助。

欧洲需要对中国复兴的力量作出有效的反应。为应对欧洲当今所面临的主要挑战——包括气候变化、就业、移民以及安全——我们需要根据我们的价值观很好地利用与中国活跃关系的潜力。支持中国的改革进程也符合我们的利益。这意味着欧盟所有政策范围之内,包括内外政策,都需要考虑到中国的因素,也意味着欧盟内部需要紧密协调,以确保整体一致的方法。

为了更好地反映双方对此关系的重视,欧盟和中国在2003年同意结成战略伙伴关系。虽然双方仍然存在分歧,但是都在进行有效的解决,并且双方的关系越来越成熟和切合实际。同时,中国和欧盟离不开全球化进程,而且越来越深地融入到国际体制当中。

欧盟对中国的根本方针必须体现合作和伙伴精神的统一。但是伴随着更紧密的战略伙伴关系意味着双方责任的增强。伙伴关系应该符合双方的利益,而欧盟和中国需要共同努力,因为它们想要承担更主动和有责任的国际角色,为建立一个强有力的、有效的多边体系提供支持和作出贡献。目标是中国和欧盟能够通过发挥各自的长处从而对全球问题提出联合解决方案。

欧盟和中国都会持久地从我们的贸易和经济伙伴关系中获利。如果我们意识到中国的充分潜力,对中国的竞争关上欧洲的大门就不是答案了。但是要建立并保持对中国开放的政治支持,对这种契约的利益必须在欧洲实现。中国应该开放它的市场并确保公平的市场竞争。适应竞争挑战和与中国实现公平竞争是欧盟贸易政策在未来十年将面临的中心挑战。这一关键的双边挑战给我们的伙伴关系带来了很好的考验,这在与本文件一起提交的"竞争与伙伴关系"贸易政策文件中得到了更详细的描述。

欧盟和中国通过共同努力可以更好地促进双方的利益,比各自推动将取得更好的成绩。

2. 背景:中国的复兴

内部稳定仍是中国政策的主要动力。近几十年,强有力的经济增长巩固了稳定性。自从1980年以来中国享有了年均9%的增长率,而中国占全球国内生产总值的比例增长了10倍,达到了全球GDP的5%。中国的增长在世界历史上最大幅度地削减了贫困,并产生了一个庞大的中产阶级,他们接受更好的教育并具有更强的购买力和选择能力。

但是中国庞大的增长隐藏着一些不确定和脆弱的因素。中国领导每天面临着重要挑战,主要属于国内挑战,但是这些挑战的影响力逐渐超越了国家界限:

差距仍然在扩大。贫富差距显著而且在继续扩大,社会、地区和性别不平衡也是如此,医疗和教育体制的压力很大。而中国也面临着重大的人口变化和人口快速老龄化的挑战。

中国已经是世界能源消费第二大国,中国对能源和原材料的需求已经很大而且将继续增长,未加约束的经济和工业增长所付出的环境代价越来越明显。与此同时,增长模式还没有得到平衡,重点仍然放在出口,却以损害国内需求为代价。

增长仍然是中国改革议程的中心部分,但是越来越随着社会不平等的解决措施和对更可持续的经济和政治发展的保障措施得到减缓。矛盾的是,在不少领域,随着党和国家控制的放松,情况反而变得更稳定。更独立的司法机制、更强的民间社会及更自由的媒体最终将鼓励稳定,提供必要的制衡。认识到更平衡发展的需求、建立"和谐社会"令人鼓舞,但进一步的改革还是必要的。

中国的地区和国际政策也支持着国内必要的事情:稳定而和平的邻国关系有利于经济增长;并且中国广泛的国际活动的特点仍然是对具体目标的追求,包括确保增长所需要的自然资源。同时我们看到了中国希望获得国际尊重和认可的愿望。2008年在北京举行的奥运会和2010年在上海举行的世博会将使世界关注中国的进步。

中国外交政策一直宣称是互不干涉的政策,但是随着中国承担起更自信和主动的国际角色,这种政策变得越来越不可维系。中国政府开始认识到这一点,与其经济地位和联合国安理会常任理事国角色相匹配的国际责任在其日益主动的外交工作中得以体现。

欧盟和中国都从全球化获益,并在全球化成功中享有共同利益。全球化给双方带来了挑战和进一步的责任。我们也都希望能看到一个有效多边体系的建立。但是价值观方面仍然存在分歧,因此双方应该继续这方面的对话。

随着伙伴关系的加强,双方的期待和责任也相应扩大。作为中国最大贸易伙伴,欧盟贸易政策对中国的影响重大,同时,中国的政策对欧盟的影响也是如此。双方逐渐地希望对方能够在制定各自政策过程当中考虑到这个影响力。

3. 未来的道路

欧盟应该继续通过鼓励并支持中国的内部政治及经济改革进程,以便实现一个强有力的、稳定的、并全面遵守基本权利和自由、保护少数民族以及保证法治的中国。欧盟将加强合作以便确保可持续发展,寻求公平和坚定的贸易政策,并且努力加强和进一步平衡双边关系。欧盟和中国应该共同努力支持和平与稳定。欧盟应当增加协调和共同行动,并完善与欧洲企业和民间社会的合作。

截至目前,双方关系的法律基础是1985年签署的贸易与合作协定。这个协定不再能够反映关系的广度和范围了,因此在第9次中欧领导人会晤时,双方领导同意就一个新的、进一步扩大的伙伴与合作协议启动谈判,以更新我们合作的基础。这个新协议带来了一个重要的机遇。它将提供一个单独的框架来管理我们关系的整体范围和丰富内容,同时,这个协议应该具有前瞻性并应当反映出本文件所强调的重点。

3.1 支持中国转型为更加开放的多元社会

中国领导人多次阐明支持包括基本权利和自由在内的改革。但是在这一点上,实际取得的进步很有限。欧盟必须考虑如何更有效地帮助中国的改革,使其认识到更好的保护人权,更加开放的社会、更负责任的政府对中国有利,对持续经济增长至关重要。

民主、人权和促进共同价值始终是欧盟政策的基本原则,对双边关系极为重要。欧盟将支持并鼓励在中国发展一个全面、健康、独立的文明社会。欧盟将支持强化法治的各项努力,法治是一切其他改革的核心基础。

与此同时,欧盟将继续鼓励在中国所有地区完全尊重基本权利和自由;言论、宗教、结社自由、公平审判的权利以及少数民族的保护都应当受到特别的关注。欧盟还将鼓励中国在人权理事会成为一名积极富有建设性的成员,希望中国接受联合国认可的价值观,其中包括公民权利和政治权利国际公约。

此前中欧已经决定一年举行两次人权对话。目前的对话虽然符合双方初衷,但是欧盟的期望随着双方伙伴关系的增进已经不断提高,不能得到满足。人权对话应该:

更加突出重点,注重成果,提高交流的质量,取得实在的成果;

更加灵活,吸取其他研讨会和小组的意见;

与欧盟其他成员国的对话更好地协调。

3.2 可持续发展

当今一个重要的世界性挑战就是确保我们的发展是可持续的。中国将成为面对这一挑战的中坚力量。中国国内的改革政策非常重要,委员会将继续通过合作项目支持它。在诸如能源、环境和气候变化、发展援助以及更为广泛的宏观经济问题上,欧盟和中国应当确保紧密合作。双方应当:

确保安全可持续的能源供应　欧盟和中国作为世界能源市场的重要参与者,在保证能源供应的安全和可持续性,提高效率,减少能源生产和消耗对环境的影响上具有共同的利益和责任。欧盟的重点应该是确保中国融入世界能源市场和多边管理体制与机构,鼓励中国成为积极且负责任的能源伙伴。在此基础上双方应当共同努力:

扩大国际合作,特别是提高能源数据的透明度和可靠性,加强与包括非洲在内的发展中国家而进行的信息交流以便提高能源安全;

强化中国的技术和管理经验,减少能源需求的增长,提高能源使用效率,使用诸如风能、生物质能、生物燃料等清洁可再生能源,提高能源标准,并通过发展和使用近零排放煤炭技术节约能源;

致力于通过以市场为基础的投资采购来稳定市场;与其他消费大国对话;鼓励透明且无歧视的立法监督体系,包括开放有效的能源市场准入;推动采纳国际认可的规范和标准。

应对气候变化和改善环境　我们已经就环境和气候变化问题通过在 2005 中欧领导人会晤时建立的伙伴关系确立了良好的合作基础。

欧盟应该分享立法监督方面的经验,与中国一起努力防止污染,保护生物多样性,更加有效地使用能源、水和原材料,提高环境立法的透明度和执行力度。双方应当共同解决森林过度采伐非法采伐的问题和渔业资源以及海洋治理可持续管理的问题;

双方应在已建立的气候变化伙伴关系基础上,加强双边合作,巩固国际合作,承担气候变化公约与京都议定书之下共同的国际责任,并在 2012 年之后积极参与关于气候变化的国际对话。我们应当加强利用排放贸易和清洁发展机制。

提高有关就业和社会问题的交流　中国坚持应对社会不平等问题并推动更加平衡的发展。欧盟和中国应该:

加强关于就业和社会问题的合作,以加强和扩大将包括工作卫生和安全、良好的工作标准和应对老龄化人口等话题的双边对话;

共同努力确保有关劳动和社会问题的国际承诺得到履行。

加强在国际发展问题上的协调　在国际发展问题上更紧密的合作对欧盟、中国和发展中国家都有利。如果我们不能有效地协调,特别是对非洲但也包括其他的发展中国家,会有明显的负面影响。欧盟和中国应该:

参与有组织的关于非洲可持续发展。双方的活动和重点应当公开,提供全面讨

论的基础;

支持提高非洲治理的地区工作;探讨如何使中国融入国际救助力量,提高救助的效率和协调,并寻求在实地救助时双方合作。

可持续经济增长　中国已经成为欧盟和世界增长源头,但是中国目前的增长模式也导致了中欧贸易的严重不平衡。中国政府已经认识到应对宏观经济挑战、具有前瞻性的财政政策、货币政策和产业结构政策、刺激消费和消除不平等一系列问题的重要性。提高汇率灵活性将是一个重要因素,有助于重新平衡国内需求增长并增加中国家庭的购买力。削减中国经常项目顺差的系列政策将提高中国对自身经济的控制并防止过热风险,同时,也使中国承担起保证世界经济稳定平衡的责任。

作为重要的经济大国,欧盟和中国应该继续发展伙伴关系,共同努力解决全球性经济问题,双方应该:

深化合作,在制定和实施货币政策、财政政策、汇率政策、产业结构政策方面分享经验;

互相合作有序调整全球不平衡;

加强并提升双方的宏观经济对话。

3.3 贸易及经济关系

中国融入全球贸易体系给欧盟和中国都带来了利益。欧盟是中国最大贸易伙伴,占了中国对外贸易总额的19%。在中国进行贸易和投资的欧盟企业对中国的增长作出了贡献,引入了对中国发展起过重要作用的资本货物、知识和技术。

一个经济富强的中国符合欧盟的利益。中国,特别是中国快速发展的中产阶级,是欧盟出口产品不断扩大的市场。2000年和2005年期间,欧盟到中国的出口以100%的速度增长,远远快于到其他地区的出口增长。直到2004年的10年间,欧盟往中国出口的服务产品增长了6倍。欧盟企业和消费者从中国具有价格竞争力的产品和消费品中获利。开放对中国和欧盟都是有利的。

然而,欧洲逐渐有人认为中国没有全面地履行对世贸组织的承诺和新的市场准入壁垒阻碍了实现真正互惠的贸易关系。从中国的进口增加了欧洲适应全球化的压力。随着中国在价值链中位置的提升,这个趋势有可能会持续。

为了保证关系长期的政治及经济可持续性,欧盟应该继续向中国出口提供开放和公平的准入,并且应该继续适应竞争的挑战。欧盟应该巩固并进一步地发展在高价值和高技术设计与生产领域的比较优势,并且应该帮助工人重新培训。中国应该加强其对开放市场和公平竞争的承诺。双方应该应对经济增长对自然资源和环境所带来的影响。欧盟将:

坚持开放和市场准入　欧盟将继续与中国合作全面履行中国入世承诺。欧盟将敦促中国在2008年按其承诺如期启动加入政府采购协议的谈判并尽早成功结束,以便能显著地进一步开放其政府采购市场。欧盟将敦促中国在其世贸承诺之外进一步开放市场为欧盟企业创造机会。欧盟承认欧盟不会自己设置壁垒却强迫中国开放。

提供平等竞争平台　欧盟的首要任务是确保在华知识产权的更好保护并结束被迫的技术转让,包括通过中国入世承诺的履行和创造更好的在华投资环境。欧盟将促使中国停止发放被禁止的补贴,改革其银行体系,而且将鼓励中国允许各种市场力量在原材料贸易中发挥作用。

支持欧洲企业　委员会做出巨大的努力帮助在华企业,特别是中小企业,敦促他们遵守良好的工作标准。欧盟将扩大并加强已有的保护知识产权方面的信息、培训和咨询。在北京将应该设立一个欧洲中心。欧盟－中国经理交换培训项目将应该得到扩大。

保护欧盟的利益:对话为先　欧盟清楚地表明优先选择对话和谈判解决对华贸易摩擦。已有的中欧贸易对话应当在各个层次全面得到加强,突出对话的重点为方便贸易与提高市场准入,并扩大对话的范围。欧盟和中国对在制定国际规则和全球标准的国际组织中的合作具有共同的利益。欧盟将积极寻求建立全球监督管理模式,促进市场开放和集中管理,通过中欧监管对话与中国合作。这将有助于确保中国进口的食品和非食品产品符合欧盟的标准。

但是当其他方式失败的时候,委员会将利用世界贸易组织争端解决机制来保证多边规则和义务得以执行和履行。贸易保护措施将仍是保证公平贸易的手段。欧盟正在同中国一起努力创造条件尽早给予中国市场经济地位。在某些方面,近期已经取得了进展。委员会将继续与中国政府通过已经建立的机制共同努力,并做好准备在条件成熟的时候快速反应。

加强双边关系　中欧新伙伴合作协议将更新1985年的贸易合作协议。新协议谈判的一个重要目标就是使中国市场对欧洲出口商和投资者比中国的世贸承诺更为开放,更好地保护知识产权,互相承认地理标识。中国已经成为国际贸易体系的重要受益人,也应当承担与其受益程度相当的责任,为恢复并完成世界贸易组织多哈回合作出重要贡献。

这些行动很多都不仅仅对欧盟有利,对中国也非常有利,并且是中国走向平衡可持续发展、成为负责任的全球领导者过程中不可或缺的部分。同时提交的贸易政策文件为中欧贸易投资关系确立了全面的中期发展方针。

3.4 加强双边合作

双边合作涵盖了广泛的内容,包括7个正式协议和22个涵盖如航空和海洋运输、地区和宏观经济政策等重要问题在内的行业对话。进一步发展有组织的对话,交流在竞争问题上的经验和看法,并对执行竞争的技术和能力建设提供支持,这些仍然非常重要。双方合作取得了积极良好的成果。但是还必须不断努力来调整合作,保证双方在各个领域平衡对等地受益,尤其是科技合作等旗舰领域。在移民问题上,在人与人之间的联系上,以及在管理双边正式关系的组织机构问题上,都需要做更多的工作。双方应该：

确保高质量不断增加的科技合作 科技合作是中国政府优先关注的领域。中国将其国内生产总值的 1.5% 用于充满活力并不断成长的研发项目。双边合作同样强劲：中国是参与第六研究框架计划下的欧盟研究项目最重要的第三世界国家之一，能够参与总投资 6 亿欧元的研究项目，而且，中国还是国际热核试验反应堆和伽利略等重大国际项目的重要参与方。欧盟在中国项目中的参与应该增加。

2005 年 5 月在科学技术论坛上发表的联合声明确定了推动合作的框架并设定了以共同受益和平等参与为基础。双方应当：

巩固并提高合作的知名度。这样能使双方集中精力，有效确定优先发展目标，应对如流行传染疾病等突发问题或努力发展清洁能源技术；便于探索扩大平等合作范围的潜力；为成员国之间有效协调提供基础。

促进双方共同规划以保证互利互惠，在资助欧盟研究人员参与中国研究项目的问题上增加灵活性。双方应该为研究人员的流动提供便利。在欧盟，这项工作是通过框架计划下的特定赠款而推进的。

建立一个有效的移民关系 来自中国和其他地区的移民丰富了欧盟的文化，带来了重要的技能和专业知识。但若不有效地加以管理，会有很大的负面效果。必须建立一个有效的法律体系，以促进人与人之间的往来，但在以预防和遣返为主的同时，我们需要有效的机制来应对滥用这套体系的人。双方应共同努力，早日签署一部有效的重新接纳协议。

应继续执行现有的磋商机制，将其涵盖范围扩大至合法移民与非法移民，并从政治上致力于取得新的进展；

双方应同意并推进诸如官员交流与培训等具体合作项目；应当建立生物特征识别技术领域的交流；

应当建立与公安部之间的对话，以应对移民以及打击组织犯罪、恐怖主义及腐败问题；

应当继续积极而务实地推动中欧旅游协议（ADS）的合作，以保障协议有效地执行。

扩大人与人之间的联系 双方应采取有力而持续的行动，全面加强巩固我们关系的人与人之间从文化交流与旅游到民间社会及学术之间的联系。

民间社会和机构之间的联系应当为政治与贸易关系带来直接的支持与推动力。双方应促进欧盟与中国的民间组织在所有领域的直接联系，并尽可能让他们参与行业对话。应当加强并扩大正式的非政府联系。欧洲议会发挥着中心作用，应扩大与中国人民代表大会的合作。欧盟应加强其经济和社会理事会与中国经济和社会委员会、政党、及其他半官方机构之间的联系。

教育领域取得了显著的成绩，2005 年，有 170,000 名中国学生在欧盟留学。我们应继续通过各成员国的项目及伊拉斯谟·曼德斯对中国的项目加强现有的合作。在建立联合学位课程及联合学院方面已经产生了成功的案例。我们还应执行例如一个欧洲法学院等的具体项目。双方将继续鼓励欧盟的学生到中国学习。为了增强语言能力，委员会将支持旨在培训汉语教师到欧洲教学的具体计划。

欧盟研究中国的学术能力需要得到改善及更加有效的协调。双方都需采取行动支持中欧学术界之间的有效交流。委员会应继续支持研究中国的学术网络，收集学术意见供欧盟政策参考，协调学术界内部的信息沟通；应在欧洲高校建立并提供少数中国研究方面的、高声望的教授职位。中欧智囊机构之间应建立永久性的定期对话。

让双边体系更有效 双方应研究指导双边关系的体系，并考虑是否需调整、改进或升级。委员会2003年政策报告寻求扩大欧盟与中国间的行业对话，这一政策非常成功，大部分对话运行良好并为我们的伙伴关系作出了重要贡献。但应回顾这一进程，双方也应考虑是否有新的机构或机制能够进一步促进中欧关系。

年度高层会晤为保持政府首脑间的接触提供了良好的框架，这一框架应得到技术层面、部长级或更高级别等多层次和跨部门定期交流和对话的支持。另外，双方应寻求其他灵活而非正式的途径，进行会晤并交流看法；

最近达成的副外长级战略性对话应成为涵盖区域性和地缘政治事务的关键性机制并使双边关系更明确，增加其影响力和价值；

双方应本着使合力最大化和保障共同利益的目的，对行业对话的原则、相互关系及效果进行全面的检查，应保证尽可能涉及相关各方。委员会将制定一系列关于各行业挑战的工作文件；

应建立新的独立的欧盟-中国论坛。在欧盟方面，论坛应独立于欧盟机构并应吸收民间团体、学术界、商界和文化界的专业知识，为政治领袖提供政策建议并为双边关系提供推动力。

欧盟应保证在有关中国关系的所有问题上保持一致观点。鉴于这一关系的复杂性和保持连贯的重要性，定期的、系统的和跨部门间的内部协调将至关重要。

欧盟通过国家战略文件和国家指导性项目实施的合作计划应继续在支持双边伙伴关系和中国的改革进程中发挥作用。但是随着中国进一步偏离典型的海外发展援助接受国这一地位，欧盟必须认真调整并随时审议其合作计划。合作必须有利于双方的利益，反映欧盟自身的原则和价值，并利于巩固这一伙伴关系。

3.5 国际与地区合作

通过改革的和有效的多边体系来促进和平与安全是符合欧盟与中国的利益的。他们应当在联合国的框架下密切合作，共同努力为凸现的危机寻求多边解决方案，打击恐怖主义，提升区域性合作，包括通过双方参与新出现的区域性组织。在强有力的多边主义、和平与安全方面共同的利益也应当在中东、非洲和东亚地区密切合作和更加有组织的对话中以及在防止核扩散等多边挑战中得到体现。

　　东亚　显而易见,欧盟十分关注东亚地区的战略性安全局势,应当通过制定政策指导方针,逐步提高欧盟在本地区的外交与安全政策的有效性及战略利益。

　　中国在本地区发挥着主要作用,不断改善着与其邻国包括俄罗斯与印度的关系,并通过上海合作组织改善着与中亚的关系。但中日关系仍存在需要改善的方面。这一地区主要国家的牢固关系以及该地区持续的团结符合欧盟的利益。

　　中国台湾　欧盟十分关注海峡两岸的和平与稳定。在一个中国的政策基础上,并考虑到该地区的战略性平衡,欧盟应继续予以积极的关注,并让海峡两岸都了解欧盟的观点。政策的制定应当考虑欧盟的如下立场:

　　反对任何能够导致现状单方面变化的措施;

　　强烈反对使用武力;

　　鼓励使用务实的解决方案和利于互信的措施;

　　支持所有各方进行对话;

　　继续保持与台湾牢固的经济与贸易联系。

　　防止核扩散　防止核扩散是战略性伙伴关系的关键领域。国际与双边合作的基础是联合国安理会第 1540 号决议以及 2004 年中欧高层会晤达成的关于防止核扩散的联合声明。欧盟支持中国在朝鲜半岛问题上的中心作用,中国持续的支持对伊朗核问题的进展至关重要。旨在巩固和加强出口控制的对话取得了良好的开端,开展了务实的合作。欧盟应以此为基础,与中国政府共同努力,鼓励中国:

　　履行所有防止核扩散和裁军条约以及国际协议,并推动协议在地区和国际间的履行;

　　双方应共同努力,交流在执行和加强出口控制方面的实际经验,包括通过对中国海关官员的培训。应当考虑在东盟区域性论坛背景下欧亚联合行动的领域。

4. 结论

　　中国是欧盟最重要的伙伴之一。中国的再度崛起是一个受欢迎的现象。但是为了积极而有效地回应,欧盟必须改善各个层次的政策协调,并保证在关键问题上拥有集中而统一的欧洲声音。

　　我们拥有牢固而成长的双边关系,但是我们必须在此基础上继续发展。本文件提出的建议尚需欧洲理事会签署并通过"理事会结论"加以补充,这些建议对欧盟而言,是一项富有挑战性的议程,伙伴关系以及合作协议为推动这一议程的进展提供了重要而务实的机制。

　　更加密切而牢固的战略性伙伴关系符合欧盟与中国的利益,但随之而来的,是更多的责任和对开放的需要,这将要求双方共同行动。

Unit Five

International Chamber
of Commerce

ICC (International Chamber of Commerce) is the voice of world business championing the global economy as a force for economic growth, job creation and prosperity.

Because national economies are now so closely interwoven, government decisions have far stronger international repercussions than in the past.

ICC— the world's only truly global business organization responds by being more assertive in expressing business views.

ICC activities cover a broad spectrum, from arbitration and dispute resolution to making the case for open trade and the market economy system, business self-regulation, fighting corruption or combating commercial crime.

ICC has direct access to national governments all over the world through its national committees. The organization's Paris-based international secretariat feeds business views into intergovernmental organizations on issues that directly affect business operations.

Setting rules and standards

Arbitration under the rules of the ICC International Court of Arbitration is on the increase. Since 1999, the Court has received new cases at a rate of more than 500 a year.

ICC's Uniform Customs and Practice for Documentary Credits (UCP 500) are the rules that banks apply to finance billions of dollars worth of world trade every year.

ICC Incoterms are standard international trade definitions used every day in countless thousands of contracts. ICC model contracts make life easier for small companies that cannot afford big legal departments.

ICC is a pioneer in business self-regulation of e-commerce. ICC codes on advertising and marketing are frequently reflected in national legislation and the codes of professional associations.

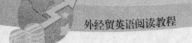

Promoting growth and prosperity

ICC supports government efforts to make a success of the Doha trade round. ICC provides world business recommendations to the World Trade Organization.

ICC speaks for world business when governments take up such issues as intellectual property rights, transport policy, trade law or the environment.

Signed articles by ICC leaders in major newspapers and radio and TV interviews reinforce the ICC stance on trade, investment and other business topics.

Every year, the ICC Presidency meets with the leader of the G8 host country to provide business input to the summit.

ICC is the main business partner of the United Nations and its agencies.

Spreading business expertise

At UN summits on sustainable development, financing for development and the information society, ICC spearheads the business contribution.

Together with the United Nations Conference on Trade and Development (UNCTAD), ICC helps some of the world's poorest countries to attract foreign direct investment.

In partnership with UNCTAD, ICC has set up an Investment Advisory Council for the least-developed countries.

ICC mobilizes business support for the New Partnership for Africa's Development. At ICC World Congresses every two years, business executives tackle the most urgent international economic issues.

The World Chambers Congress, also biennial, provides a global forum for chambers of commerce.

Regular ICC regional conferences focus on the concerns of business in Africa, Asia, the Arab World and Latin America.

Advocate for international business

ICC speaks for world business whenever governments make decisions that crucially affect corporate strategies and the bottom line.

ICC's advocacy has never been more relevant to the interests of thousands of member companies and business associations in every part of the world.

Equally vital is ICC's role in forging internationally agreed rules and standards that companies adopt voluntarily and can be incorporated in binding contracts.

ICC provides business input to the United Nations, the World Trade Organization, and many other intergovernmental bodies, both international and regional.

For information on how to join ICC and ensure your company exerts influence where it counts, contact ICC Membership Department in Paris by Email or telephone +33 (0)1 49 53 28 49.

History of the International Chamber of Commerce

The ICC's origins

The International Chamber of Commerce was founded in 1919 with an overriding aim that remains unchanged: to serve world business by promoting trade and investment, open markets for goods and services, and the free flow of capital.

Much of ICC's initial impetus came from its first president, Etienne Clémentel, a former French minister of commerce. Under his influence, the organization's international secretariat was established in Paris and he was instrumental in creating the ICC International Court of Arbitration in 1923.

ICC has evolved beyond recognition since those early post-war days when business leaders from the allied nations met for the first time in Atlantic City. The original nucleus representing the private sectors of Belgium, Britain, France, Italy and the United States, has expanded to become a world business organization with thousands of member companies and associations in around 130 countries. Members include many of the world's most influential companies and represent every major industrial and service sector.

The voice of international business

Traditionally, ICC has acted on behalf of business in making representations to governments and intergovernmental organizations. Three prominent ICC members served on the Dawes Commission which forged the international treaty on war reparations in 1924, seen as a breakthrough in international relations at the time.

A year after the creation of the United Nations in San Francisco in 1945, ICC was granted the highest level consultative status with the UN and its specialized agencies. Ever since, it has ensured that the international business view receives due weight within the UN system and before intergovernmental bodies and meetings such as the G8 where decisions affecting the conduct of business are made.

Defender of the multilateral trading system

ICC's reach and the complexity of its work have kept pace with the globalization of

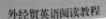

business and technology. In the 1920s ICC focused on reparations and war debts. A decade later, it struggled vainly through the years of depression to hold back the tide of protectionism and economic nationalism. After war came in 1939, ICC assured continuity by transferring its operations to neutral Sweden.

In the post-war years, ICC remained a diligent defender of the open multilateral trading system. As membership grew to include more and more countries of the developing world, the organization stepped up demands for the opening of world markets to the products of developing countries. ICC continues to argue that trade is better than aid.

In the 1980s and the early 1990s, ICC resisted the resurgence of protectionism in new guises such as reciprocal trading arrangements, voluntary export restraints and curbs introduced under the euphemism of "managed trade".

Challenges of the 21st Century

As the world enters the 21st century, ICC is building a stronger presence in Asia, Africa, Latin America, the Middle East, and the emerging economies of eastern and central Europe.

Today, 16 ICC commissions of experts from the private sector cover every specialized field of concern to international business. Subjects range from banking techniques to financial services and taxation, from competition law to intellectual property rights, telecommunications and information technology, from air and maritime transport to international investment regimes and trade policy.

Self-regulation is a common thread running through the work of the commissions. The conviction that business operates most effectively with a minimum of government intervention inspired ICC's voluntary codes. Marketing codes cover sponsoring, advertising practice, sales promotion, marketing and social research, direct sales practice, and marketing on the Internet. Launched in 1991, ICC's Business Charter for Sustainable Development provides 16 principles for good environmental conduct that have been endorsed by more than 2300 companies and business associations.

Practical services to business

ICC keeps in touch with members all over the world through its conferences and biennial congresses—in 2004 the world congress was held in Marrakesh. As a member-driven organization, with national committees in 84 countries, it has adapted its structures to meet the changing needs of business. Many of them are practical services, like the ICC International Court of Arbitration, which is the longest established ICC institution. The Court is the world's leading body for resolving international commercial disputes by arbitration. In 2004, 561 Requests for Arbitration were filed with the ICC Court, concerning 1 682 parties from 116 different countries and independent territories.

The first Uniform Customs and Practice for Documentary Credits came out in 1933 and the latest version, UCP 500, came into effect in January 1994. These rules are used by banks throughout the world. A supplement to UCP 500, called the eUCP, was added in 2002 to deal with the presentation of all electronic or part electronic documents. In 1936, the first nine Incoterms were published, providing standard definitions of universally employed terms like Ex quay CIF and FOB, and whenever necessary they are revised. Incoterms 2000 came into force on 1 January 2000.

In 1951 the International Bureau of Chambers of Commerce (IBCC) was created. It quickly became a focal point for cooperation between chambers of commerce in developing and industrial countries, and took on added importance as chambers of commerce of transition economies responded to the stimulus of the market economy. In 2001, on the occasion of the 2nd World Chambers Congress in Korea, IBCC was renamed the World Chambers Federation (WCF), clarifying WCF as the world business organization's department for chamber of commerce affairs. WCF also administers the ATA Carnet system for temporary duty-free imports, a service delivered by chambers of commerce, which started in 1958 and is now operating in over 57 countries.

Another ICC service, the Institute for World Business Law was created in 1979 to study legal issues relating to international business. At the Cannes film festival every year, the Institute holds a conference on audiovisual law.

The fight against commercial crime

In the early 1980s, ICC set up three London-based services to combat commercial crime: the International Maritime Bureau, dealing with all types of maritime crime; the Counterfeiting Intelligence Bureau; and the Financial Investigation Bureau. A cybercrime unit was added in 1998. An umbrella organization, ICC Commercial Crime Services, coordinates the activities of the specialized anti-crime services.

All these activities fulfil the pledge made in a key article of the ICC's constitution: "to assure effective and consistent action in the economic and legal fields in order to contribute to the harmonious growth and the freedom of international commerce."

How ICC works

Council

The ICC World Council is the equivalent of the general assembly of a major intergovernmental organization. The big difference is that the delegates are business executives and not government officials. There is a federal structure, based on the Council as ICC's supreme governing body. National committees name delegates to the Council, which normally meets twice a year. Ten direct members—from countries where there is no national committee—may also be invited to participate in the Council's work.

National committees and groups

They represent the ICC in their respective countries. The national committees and groups make sure that ICC takes account of their national business concerns in its policy recommendations to governments and international organizations.

The Chairmanship and Executive Board

The Council elects the Chairman and Vice-Chairman for two-year terms. The Chairman, his immediate predecessor and the Vice-Chairman form the Chairmanship. The Council also elects the Executive Board, responsible for implementing ICC policy, on the Chairman's recommendation. The Executive Board has between 15 and 30 members, who serve for three years, with one third retiring at the end of each year.

Secretary General

The Secretary General heads the International Secretariat and works closely with the national committees to carry out ICC's work programme. The Secretary General is appointed by the Council at the initiative of the Presidency and on the recommendation of the Executive Board.

Commissions

Member companies and business associations can shape the ICC stance on any given business issue by participating in the work of ICC commissions. Commissions are the bedrock of ICC, composed of a total of more than 500 business experts who give freely their time to formulate ICC policy and elaborate its rules. Commissions scrutinize proposed international and national government initiatives affecting their subject areas and prepare business positions for submission to international organizations and governments.

Working with the United Nations

Since 1946, ICC has engaged in a broad range of activities with the United Nations and its specialized agencies. In addition, ICC has actively participated in global UN conferences such as the Conference on Financing for Development, the World Summit on Sustainable Development and the World Summit on the Information Society. Throughout the years ICC has been actively involved in the work of The Economic and Social Council, the Commission on Sustainable Development, the Commission for Social Development, the UN Information and Communication Task Force, the UN Economic Commission for Europe, the UN Commission on International Trade Law, the UN Conference on Trade and Development (UNCTAD), the UN Development Program (UNDP), the UN Environment Program (UNEP) and the UN World Aids Campaign among others.

Working with IGOs

ICC relations and projects with Inter-Governmental Organizations (IGOs)

The International Chamber of Commerce enjoys a close working relationship with the United Nations and other intergovernmental organizations. With IGOs increasingly involved in matters of concern to the business community, it is important that its representatives be "at the table" when such matters are discussed. The emphasis on the crucial role of the private sector in the achievement of the international community's development goals makes its participation in IGO discussions even more necessary.

This is a partial list of IGOs and other intergovernmental entities with which ICC collaborates:

UN Economic and Social Council (ECOSOC)

UN Commission on Sustainable Development

UN Commission for Social Development

UN Commission on International Trade Law (UNCITRAL)

UN Industrial Development Organization

UN Information and Communication Task Force

UN Environmental Programme (UNEP)

UN Office on Drugs and Crime

World Trade Organization (WTO)

Organization for Economic Cooperation and Development (OECD)

Office of the UN High Commissioner for Human Rights and Commission on Human

Rights

UN Conference on Trade and Development (UNCTAD)

Food and Agriculture Organization (FAO)

International Civil Aviation Organization (ICAO)

International Maritime Organization (IMO)

International Telecommunications Union (ITU)

World Health Organization (WHO)

World Intellectual Property Organization (WIPO)

World Bank Group

The International Chamber of Commerce has been in partnerships with various intergovernmental organizations for specific projects. It also has Memoranda of Understanding with the following: World Customs Organization, Interpol, World Trade Organization (WTO), United Nations Development Programme (UNDP), United Nations Economic Commission for Europe (UNECE) and the World Bank.

Since 1946, ICC has engaged in a broad range of activities with the United Nations and its specialized agencies.

Examples of important projects:

The Global Compact

Financing for Development process

ICC/UNCTAD Investment Guides for Least Developed Countries

ICC/UNCTAD Investment Advisory Council (IAC)

New Partnership for Africa's Development (NEPAD)

UN World Aids Campaign

UN Conferences in which ICC has participated:

The International Conference on Financing for Development in Monterrey, Mexico (FfD)

The World Summit on Sustainable Development in Johannesburg, South Africa (WSSD)

The World Summit on the Information Society in Geneva, Switzerland and Tunis, Tunisia (WSIS)

The International Ministerial Conference of Landlocked and Transit Developing Countries on Transit Transport Cooperation in Almaty, Kazakhstan

The International Chamber of Commerce chairs the following groups:

Coordinating Committee of Business Interlocutors (CCBI) for WSIS

Business Committee on Financing for Development (BCFD)

Who can become a member of ICC?

— Corporations and companies in all sectors;

— National professional and sectoral associations;

— Business and employers federations;

— Law firms and consultancies;

— Chambers of commerce;

— Individuals involved in international business.

How does ICC membership work for you?

ICC members belong to an organization representing businesses from all sectors all over the world. ICC is the only world business organization. It promotes business enterprise and investment as the most effective way of raising living standards and creating wealth. ICC works for the liberalization of trade and investment within the multilateral trading system.

Being a member of ICC enables you to take part in the work of ICC's commissions and special working groups, composed of a total of more than 500 business experts who regularly meet to scrutinize proposed international and government initiatives affecting their subject areas. Members of ICC learn what really matters for their companies at an early stage and win time to make the right decisions.

Through ICC's many working bodies, members shape ICC's policy and elaborate its rules. ICC gives priority to the issues that most urgently concern its members. It is the members who set ICC's agenda.

ICC members are at the forefront of business self-regulation. ICC is world leader in setting voluntary rules, standards and codes for the conduct of international trade that are accepted by all business sectors and observed in thousands of transactions every day.

Member companies and business associations are instrumental in the development of such key international trading instruments as Incoterms, the Uniform Customs and Practice for Documentary Credit (UCP 500) and GUIDEC (a set of guidelines for ensuring trustworthy digital transactions over the Internet).

ICC's privileged links with major international organizations, including the UN and its specialized agencies and the World Trade Organization, allow the organization to effectively represent the interests of its members in international fora. ICC members prepare business positions for submission to international organizations and also, through ICC's global network of national committees, to governments.

By being part of ICC, members gain influence both at national and international level.

ICC offers members many of the advantages of belonging to a prestigious club and the chance to forge business relationships at the highest level at exclusive ICC events.

How to join ICC

There are two ways to become a member of ICC:

1. Through affiliation with an ICC national committee or group (please click on the relevant part of the map to find national committees in your area);

2. By direct membership with the ICC International Secretariat when a national committee/group has not yet been established in your country/territory.

What is the cost of ICC membership?

National committees pay an annual subscription to ICC's International Secretariat in Paris to meet the organization's administrative expenses. The rate is proportionate to the economic importance of the country they represent. National committees are financially independent of the central body and are free to establish the level of their own membership subscriptions.

Direct members fall into two categories with their annual dues as follows:

— 1500 EUR (approximately US $1500) per year for local members, i. e. local chambers of commerce, local companies, professional individuals;

— 3000 EUR (approximately US $3000) per year for national members, i. e. national chambers of commerce, national trade associations, national business organizations, as well as companies with a predominant international activity, and occupying a leading position in the country.

Who can establish a national committee?

Business and trade associations as well as individual companies and firms can apply for approval from ICC's World Council to establish an ICC national committee.

The ICC World Council considers the following criteria before giving its approval:

— Members of the proposed national committee must represent the main economic forces in the country concerned, which in turn should adhere to market economy principles;

— The national committee must be able to participate regularly and effectively in ICC's work. (*Source: http://www. iccwbo. org*)

 Notes

[1] business 企业，商业

[2] champion 支持,拥护,冠军

[3] interweave 使交织,使混杂

[4] repercussion 反响,反射

[5] respond 承担责任

[6] assertive 断定的,过分自信的

[7] spectrum 光谱

[8] International Court of Arbitration 国际仲裁庭

[9] finance 供给……经费，负担经费,筹措资金

[10] code 代码，法规

[11] legislation 立法，法律

[12] recommendation 劝告,建议书

[13] stance 地位，形势

[14] spearhead 做先锋，带头

[15] biennial 两年一次的

[16] advocate 主张，提倡

[17] advocacy 主张，鼓吹，辩护

[18] forging 打造,锻造

[19] incorporate 合并

[20] impetus 动力，推动力，动量

[21] nucleus 核心，原子核，起点

[22] treaty 条约，谈判,协议

[23] reparation 赔款

[24] breakthrough 突破，新发现，新进展

[25] vainly 枉然地，无益地，徒然

[26] hold back 阻止

[27] step up 促进,增加

[28] aid 援助

[29] resurgence 复活，再现

[30] guise 相似，伪装

[31] curb 限制

[32] euphemism 委婉说法，委婉语

［33］disintegration 瓦解

［34］maritime 海的，海上的

［35］conviction 信服，坚信

［36］endorse 支持，赞同

［37］file 归档，申请

［38］presentation 提示，交单

［39］federation 联合，联盟

［40］clarify 阐明

［41］ATA Carnet system 暂准进口单证册制度

［42］combat 对抗

［43］cybercrime 计算机犯罪

［44］constitution 章程

［45］assembly 大会

［46］supreme 最高的

［47］direct members 直接会员

［48］chairmanship 主席的身份或资格

［49］predecessor 前任

［50］bedrock 基础

［51］elaborate 详细地说明

［52］scrutinize 仔细检查，审查

［53］initiative 初步行动，主动行动

［54］Inter-Governmental Organizations（IGOs）政府间组织

［55］commissioner 特派员

［56］chair 使入座，使就任要职

［57］interlocutor 对话者，谈话者

［58］fora(forum 的复数形式)论坛，讨论会，座谈会

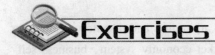Exercises

Ⅰ. **Match the following words in Column A and Column B**

Column A   Column B

1. repercussion   a. 主张，鼓吹，辩护

2. International Court of Arbitration   b. 前任

3. legislation   c. 动力，推动力，动量

4. advocacy   d. 委婉说法，委婉语

5. impetus   e. 政府间组织

6. treaty   f. 基础

7. reparation   g. 条约，谈判，协议

8. breakthrough   h. 特派员

9. resurgence   i. 国际仲裁庭

10. euphemism   j. 提示，交单

11. disintegration   k. 计算机犯罪

12. conviction   l. 对话者，谈话者

13. presentation   m. 章程

14. federation   n. 联合，联盟

15. ATA Carnet system   o. 主席的身份或资格

16. cybercrime   p. 复活，再现

17. constitution   q. 瓦解

18. assembly   r. 反响，反射

19. direct members   s. 立法，法律

20. chairmanship   t. 突破，新发现，新进展

21. predecessor   u. 信服，坚信

22. bedrock   v. ATA 单证册制度

23. initiative   w. 直接会员

24. Inter-Governmental Organization   x. 赔款

25. commissioner   y. 大会

26. interlocutor   z. 初步行动，主动行动

Ⅱ. **Translate the following sentences into Chinese**

1. ICC（International Chamber of Commerce）is the voice of world business championing the global economy as a force for economic growth, job creation

and prosperity.

2. ICC activities cover a broad spectrum, from arbitration and dispute resolution to making the case for open trade and the market economy system, business self-regulation, fighting corruption or combating commercial crime.

3. ICC has direct access to national governments all over the world through its national committees. The organization's Paris-based international secretariat feeds business views into intergovernmental organizations on issues that directly affect business operations.

4. ICC supports government efforts to make a success of the Doha trade round. ICC provides world business recommendations to the World Trade Organization.

5. Together with the United Nations Conference on Trade and Development (UNCTAD), ICC helps some of the world's poorest countries to attract foreign direct investment.

6. The International Chamber of Commerce was founded in 1919 with an overriding aim that remains unchanged: to serve world business by promoting trade and investment, open markets for goods and services, and the free flow of capital.

7. As a member-driven organization, with national committees in 84 countries, it has adapted its structures to meet the changing needs of business.

8. Since 1946, ICC has engaged in a broad range of activities with the United Nations and its specialized agencies.

9. ICC's privileged links with major international organizations, including the UN and its specialized agencies and the World Trade Organization, allow the organization to effectively represent the interests of its members in international fora.

10. National committees pay an annual subscription to ICC's International Secretariat in Paris to meet the organization's administrative expenses. The rate is proportionate to the economic importance of the country they represent.

III. Cloze

ICC members belong to an organization representing businesses _____ all sectors all over the world. ICC is the only world business organization. It promotes business enterprise and investment _____ the most effective way of raising living standards and creating wealth. ICC works _____ the liberalization of trade and investment _____ the multilateral trading system.

Being a member of ICC enables you to take part in the work of ICC's commissions and special working groups, composed _____ a total of more than 500 business experts who regularly meet to scrutinize proposed international and government initiatives affecting their subject areas. Members of ICC learn what really matters _____ their companies _____ an early stage and win time to make the right decisions.

Through ICC's many working bodies, members shape ICC's policy and elaborate its rules. ICC gives priority _____ the issues that most urgently concern its members. It is the members who set ICC's agenda.

ICC members are _____ the forefront of business self-regulation. ICC is world leader in setting voluntary rules, standards and codes for the conduct of international trade that are accepted by all business sectors and observed _____ thousands of transactions every day.

Ⅳ. Underline the important sentences in the text, which give you useful information

Ⅴ. Retell or write down what you learn from the text in English or in Chinese

Unit Six

Trade and Development Report

UNCTAD/TDR/2005（Overview）

UNITED NATIONS CONFERENCE ON TRADE AND DEVELOPMENT

GENEVA

TRADE AND DEVELOPMENT REPORT, 2005

UNITED NATIONS

New York and Geneva, 2005

Overview

Note

Symbols of United Nations documents are composed of capital letters combined with figures. Mention of such a symbol indicates a reference to a United Nations document.

The designations employed and the presentation of the material in this publication do not imply the expression of any opinion whatsoever on the part of the Secretariat of the United Nations concerning the legal status of any country, territory, city or area, or of its authorities, or concerning the delimitation of its frontiers or boundaries.

Material in this publication may be freely quoted or reprinted, but acknowledgement is requested, together with a reference to the document number. A copy of the publication containing the quotation or reprint should be sent to the UNCTAD secretariat.

The Overview contained herein is also issued as part of the Trade and Development Report, 2005 (UNCTAD/TDR/2005, sales number E. 05. Ⅱ. D. 13).

UNCTAD/TDR/2005（Overview）

Overview

Looking at recent trends in the world economy from the perspective of the Millennium Development Goals (MDGs), the good news is that in 2004 growth in the developing countries was rapid and more broad-based than it had been for many years. Strong per capita income growth continued in China and India, the two countries with the largest number of people living in absolute poverty. Latin America has seen a rebound from its deep economic crisis, and a return to faster growth, fuelled by export expansion. Africa again reached a growth rate of more than 4. 5 per cent in 2004. Moreover, relatively strong growth in many African countries is envisaged in the short-term, owing to continuing strong demand for a number of their primary commodities. The bad news is that even growth rates of close to 5 per cent in sub-Saharan Africa are insufficient to attain the MDGs, and that the outlook for 2005, overshadowed by increasing global imbalances, is for slower growth in the developed countries with attendant effects on the developing countries.

Since the beginning of the new millennium, the performance of the world economy has been shaped by the increasingly important role of China and India. Rapid growth in these two large economies has spilled over to many other developing countries and has established East and South Asia as a new growth pole in the world economy. Their ascent has been accompanied by new features of global interdependence, such as a brighter outlook for exporters of primary commodities, rising trade among developing countries, increasing exports of capital from the developing to the developed countries, but also intensified competition on the global markets for certain types of manufactures.

Global prospects and imbalances

The slowdown in global output growth in 2005 is mainly due to a deceleration in the major developed economies and some emerging economies in Latin America and East Asia. The temporary weakness in the United States economy has not been compensated by stronger growth performance in the euro area and in Japan. Both continue to lack the dynamism needed to redress domestic imbalances and to contribute to an adjustment of the global trade imbalance. Indeed, beginning in the second half of 2004, output growth in the euro area and Japan has slowed down markedly, causing forecasts for 2005 to be revised downwards. While greatly benefiting from the global expansion over the past three years, and especially the Asian boom, neither the euro area nor Japan has managed to revive domestic demand.

Another reason for concern about global economic prospects is the increase in oil prices, which have doubled since mid-2002, to reach $58 per barrel in July 2005, despite flexible supply adjustments on the part of oil producers. However, the much feared shock of surging oil prices on economic activity and inflation in developed countries, an impact of the kind witnessed in the 1970s, has so far not occurred, for two reasons. First, developed countries have become less oil dependent, as energy is being used more efficiently. At the same time, the share of services in their GDP has gained in importance at the expense of industry, where more energy is used per unit of output. Second, the recent oil price increase was not the result of a big supply shock, but of a gradual increase in demand. Under these conditions, the wage and monetary policy responses in the developed countries have been measured, and have not jeopardized price stability or output growth.

The recent surge in oil prices has a stronger impact on oil-importing developing economies, especially in countries where industrialization has led to greater dependence on oil imports. In Brazil, for example, the oil intensity of domestic production is 40 per cent higher than the OECD average; in China and Thailand it is more than twice as high, and in India almost three times as high as in the OECD countries. Therefore, it is primarily in developing countries where inflationary pressures resulting from further rising oil prices imply risks for the sustainability of the growth process. Even though inflation has so far been modest, monetary policy has already been tightened in some countries.

On the other side, not only oil exporters but also many developing countries exporting non-oil primary commodities benefited from increased demand and rising prices for their exports. Since 2002, strong demand from East and South Asia, in particular China and India, has been the main factor behind the hike in commodity prices. In the markets for some primary commodities, emerging supply constraints have also contributed to the strong price reaction. Asian demand for primary commodities, particularly for oil and minerals such as copper, iron ore and nickel, as well as for natural rubber and soybeans, is likely to remain strong, boosting the earnings of the exporters of these products. But further developments on the markets for primary commodities will also critically depend on how much additional supply capacity will be created by recent new investments, how fast this capacity will go on-stream, and how commodity demand from developed countries will be affected by the need to correct the existing trade imbalances.

Despite the increasing importance of the fast growing developing countries for international commodity markets, developed countries, which still account for two thirds of global non-fuel commodity imports, will continue to play an important role. It is unlikely that the growing imports of primary commodities by China and India alone will bring about a permanent reversal of the declining trend in real commodity prices. Indeed, in real terms, commodity prices are still more than one third below their 1960—1985 average. Moreover, the sharp fluctuations in commodity prices constrain the ability of many developing countries to attain a path of stable and sustained growth and employment creation that could benefit all segments of their population and allow them to reach the MDGs.

The large global current-account imbalances represent the greatest short-term risk for stable growth in the world economy. The United States trade deficit has continued to grow despite the depreciation of the dollar; it has lost 18 per cent of its value on a trade-weighted basis since February 2002. And the United States current-account deficit accounts for two thirds of the combined global surpluses. The deficit has increased in recent years vis-a-vis virtually all its trading partners; the increase has been the most pronounced in trade with Western Europe and China. On the other hand, China's trade is in surplus not only with the United States but also with many other developed countries. However, despite these surpluses, China's imports from these countries have also increased rapidly, as have its imports from neighbouring countries and other developing countries.

A well coordinated international macroeconomic approach would considerably enhance the chances of the poorer countries to consolidate the recent improvements in their growth performance. Such an approach would also have to involve the major developing countries and aim at avoiding deflationary adjustments to the global imbalances.

East and South Asia as a new growth pole

Asia has been a region of economic dynamism over the past four decades, with different economies in the region successively experiencing rapid growth. The large size of the countries that entered this process most recently, China and India, has established the East and South Asian region as a new growth pole in the world economy. Due to the high dependence of these large Asian economies on imports of primary commodities for industrial output growth, in particular fuels and industrial raw materials, and the resulting linkages with other developing countries, variations in their growth performance will have strong repercussions on the terms of trade and export earnings of other developing countries. This inevitably raises the question of the sustainability of the pace of growth of these two economic powers in the medium and long term.

In terms of per capita GDP, both China and India still have a long way to go to approach the levels of the leading economies. Their potential for catching up is enormous. To realize this potential, it will be crucial for both countries to achieve further productivity gains in manufacturing activities and ensure that all segments of their population participate in income growth. Broad-based income growth is essential for accelerating the eradication of poverty and gaining widespread social acceptance of the required structural changes; but wage increases throughout the economy in line with rising productivity are also a central pillar for the expansion of domestic consumption and, thus, the sustainability and stability of output growth. Fixed capital formation depends on favourable demand expectations in general, and not just on exports, which are subject to the vagaries of the world market and to changes in international competitiveness.

Shifting trade patterns in China and India

Sustained rapid growth and rising living standards in China and India have been accompanied by a dramatic increase in Asia's shares of world exports and raw material consumption. Given the large size of the Chinese and Indian economies and their specific patterns of demand, changes in their structure of supply and demand have a much larger impact on the composition of world trade than did those of other late industrializers in Asia during their economic ascent. The impact of China's growth on international product markets and global trade flows is already apparent. India's merchandise trade structure may follow a sequence of changes similar to that of China, with a lag of one or two decades, if industrialization in India gains the same importance in its further economic ascent as it did in the other fast growing Asian economies.

Metal use in China—and to a lesser extent in India—has strongly increased over the past few decades, particularly since the mid-1990s. In China, growth in the use of aluminium, copper, nickel and steel now exceeds that of GDP. Part of this recent increase coincides with very high rates of investment, especially in infrastructure. However, this recent rapid rise in China's intensity of metal use, and the concomitant increase in its imports of minerals and mining products, may well slow down once investment growth, especially in construction and infrastructure, decelerates. By contrast, India's intensity of metal use has remained fairly stable over the past four decades, reflecting the country's slower pace of industrialization and the relatively small share of investment in infrastructure in its GDP.

China's energy use has steadily increased since the 1960s, but at a slower rate than its GDP. Its future energy use will depend on how opposing trends play out: on the one hand, continued rapid industrialization, higher living standards and improved transport infrastructure will tend to further increase energy use; on the other hand, there remains considerable potential for the adoption of energy-saving technologies. In either case, China's energy demand is likely to continue to outpace the future growth of domestic supply.

Agricultural imports will be determined by a number of factors. To the extent that imports of raw materials for industrial use are needed as production inputs for the expanding domestic market, import demand will grow further. This is likely to be the case for rubber and wood. On the other hand, imports of cotton, which to a large extent have depended on the production of textiles and clothing for export, can be expected to slow down as the composition of exports shifts to more technology-intensive products.

A continuous increase in average living standards and further progress in poverty reduction in China will also lead to higher demand for food and to a change in its dietary composition. So far, China has remained largely self-sufficient in all major food items. But with increasing consumption it is likely to become more dependent on food imports in the future, notwithstanding possible productivity and output growth in its domestic agricultural sector as a result of recent agricultural policy reforms. Given the size of its economy, even small changes in self-sufficiency ratios can have a considerable impact on China's agricultural imports.

Since the mid-1980s China has substantially upgraded its export basket, in which labour- and resource-intensive manufactures and, increasingly, electronics, have become dominant. China's exports still have a relatively high import content, but there are indications of a rise in the share of domestic value added in China's processing trade, particularly in the electronics sector. India has not experienced the kind of manufacturing export boom that has characterized the other rapidly growing economies in Asia. It has become a leading exporter of software and IT-enabled services, particularly to the United States, but it is highly uncertain whether their share in India's export earnings can rise much further. Over the next few years, the absolute value of these services' exports may continue to grow, but export dynamism in manufacturing is likely to become stronger.

The growth dynamics in China and other Asian economies have positive effects for many developed and developing countries. This is true for those countries that benefit directly from the surge in import demand from the fast growing Asian economies. It is also true for those that benefit indirectly through the positive growth effects in the economies of their main trading partners. Still others have achieved higher export and income growth as a result of the rise in commodity prices, even though their exports to the fast growing Asian economies are relatively small. But it also has to be recognized that China's increasing participation in international trade poses new challenges for many countries. Its weight in international markets due to the very large size of its economy may contribute to a fall in the export prices of manufactures that it produces and exports along with other developing countries, such as clothing, footwear and certain types of information and communication technology products. The rise of China's clothing exports, in particular, occurred at a time when several developing countries had adopted more outward-oriented development strategies, and many had developed production and export activities in the clothing sector partly in response to the quota regulations under the Multi-Fibre Arrangement.

There is little doubt that the pace of development in the populous Asian economies, and especially in China, requires accelerated structural change in many other countries—developing and developed alike. In some sectors, such as the clothing industry and, more generally, in activities at the low-skill end of the economy, the adjustment pressure is stronger than in others where there is less competition from low-wage producers with relatively high productivity. There are widespread fears in many countries that the pace of structural change could result in higher unemployment and lower output. Paradoxically, among the developed countries, those with large deficits in their trade balance, such as Australia, Spain, the United Kingdom and the United States, have performed much better in terms of domestic growth and employment than countries that have been recording large trade surpluses and greater competitiveness, such as Germany and Japan. Challenging the commitment of all countries to develop a global partnership for development and responding to the integration of large and poor countries by giving in to protectionist pressures would be counterproductive: most of the earnings of developing countries from their exports to the developed countries are translated into higher import demand for advanced industrial products, and thus flow back, directly or indirectly, to the latter.

The growing importance of South-South trade

Trade among developing countries has sometimes been promoted as an alternative to the traditional trade pattern where developing-country trade relies mainly on primary commodity exports to developed countries in exchange for imports of manufactures. The rapid rise in the importance of South-South trade, particularly over the past two decades, reflects a number of factors. First, there has been an upswing following the downturn of such trade during the 1980s. Second, the move towards the adoption of more outward-oriented development strategies, along with trade reform and regional trade agreements, in a wide range of developing countries has significantly improved access to their markets, including for imports from other developing countries. But the most important reason for the rapid growth of South-South trade is that output growth in some large developing economies, particularly China, has been much faster than in the developed countries. Moreover, these countries' buoyant growth performance has been closely linked with increasing intraregional specialization and production-sharing.

While increased South-South trade is a fact, recent developments in the developing countries as a whole require a careful assessment of the statistical data. Indeed, such an assessment calls for a number of qualifications to the prima facie impression that trade among developing countries has grown massively over the past decade or so, and that exports of manufactures account for much of that rise.

The growing role of developing countries in world trade flows appears to be the result, above all, of the above-average growth performance of a few Asian economies, and the associated shifts in the level and composition of their external trade. A substantial part of the statistical increase in South-South trade in manufactures is due to double-counting associated with intraregional production-sharing in East Asia for products eventually destined for export to developed countries. It is also due to double-counting associated with the function of Hong Kong (China) and Singapore as transhipment ports or regional hub ports. The important role of triangular trade in the measured rise of South-South trade in manufactures implies that the bulk of such trade has not reduced the dependence of developing countries' manufactured exports on aggregate demand in developed-country markets. As long as final demand from developed countries—notably the United States, which is East Asia's most important export market—remains high for products for which production-sharing within East Asia plays an important role, triangular trade and, thus, South-South trade, will remain strong. On the other hand, the economic rebound in Latin America has improved the prospects for South-South trade in manufactures that is not related to triangular trade.

The rise of South-South trade in primary commodities appears more modest in trade statistics. However, it has involved a larger number of countries than the strong rise of South-South trade in manufactures. It has allowed Africa, as well as Latin America and the Caribbean to recoup some of the market shares in total South-South trade that they had lost in the 1980s. Indeed, the rise in South-South exports of primary commodities to the rapidly growing Asian developing countries is likely to evolve into the most resilient feature of what has come to be called the "new geography of trade".

The promotion of South-South trade remains a desirable objective for a variety of reasons. First, sluggish growth in developed countries and their continued trade barriers against products of export interest to developing countries implies that developing countries need to give greater attention to each other's markets to promote export growth in order to achieve their economic growth targets. Second, the vast size of the rapidly growing Asian economies reduces the need for developing countries to seek developed-country markets in order to benefit from economies of scale. Third, continued dependence on developed-country markets exposes developing countries to possible pressure that links better access to those markets with binding commitments to rapid trade and financial liberalization, protection of intellectual property and an open-door policy for FDI. More generally, it also entails the risk of increasingly narrowing the policy space for developing countries.

Terms of trade revisited

The recent and ongoing changes in international trade, with respect to both product composition and direction of trade, is affecting developing countries in different ways, depending on the product composition of their exports and imports. On the export side, the impact differs according to the shares of manufactures and primary commodities, and on the import side, it is especially the dependence on fuels and industrial raw materials that determines the outcome for individual countries.

The same factors that improved the terms of trade of some groups of countries, especially the higher prices of oil and minerals and mining products, led to a worsening of the terms of trade in others. In some countries, particularly in Latin America, but also in Africa, the positive effect of price movements on the purchasing power of exports was reinforced by an increase in export volumes; whereas in others, gains from higher export unit values were compensated, or even over-compensated, by higher import prices. Since 2002, economies with a high share of oil and minerals and mining products in their total merchandise exports have gained the most from recent developments in international product markets. The terms of trade of countries with a dominant share of oil exports increased by almost 30 per cent between 2002 and 2004, and those of countries with a dominant share of minerals and mining products in their exports increased by about 15 per cent. Terms-of-trade developments have varied the most among economies where agricultural commodities have dominated total merchandise exports. This reflects large differences in the movement of prices for specific products within this category, differences in the shares of other primary commodities in their exports and the share of oil in their merchandise imports.

Developing countries for which manufactures are the dominant category of exports, and which are at the same time net importers of oil and minerals and metals have seen a deterioration in their terms of trade in the past two or three years. The deterioration, due to the combined effects of rising prices of imported primary commodities and stagnating or falling prices of their manufactured exports, could well become a longer term feature in their external trade. There are two reasons for this: first, there are indications that the prices for their manufactured exports are falling relative to the prices of the manufactures they are importing from the developed countries; second, prices for primary commodities are likely to remain strong as long as industrial growth remains vigorous in the large Asian economies and the imbalances in the developed world can be settled without entering into a recession.

Indeed, the terms-of-trade losses of exporters of manufactures among the developing countries are partly explained by the pace of the catch-up process in some of these countries, particularly in China and India. This process has been driven by higher productivity in the export sectors, which has given them a competitive edge and led to higher import demand. The variations in the global pattern of demand and their impact on individual countries have resulted in a redistribution of income, not only between developed and developing countries, but also, and to an increasing extent, between different groups of developing countries. However, it is important to recognize that a change in the distribution of real income does not necessarily imply absolute losses. As long as output growth is strong enough, all countries can gain in terms of real income, with some gaining more than others, depending on the structure of their exports and the international competitiveness of their producers: a terms-of-trade deterioration can be compensated by rising export volume. The probability for this to happen is much greater if exports consist of manufactures, for which the price elasticity of demand is high, than if they consist of primary commodities.

The productivity gains in Asia have led not only to higher company profits, but also to higher wages; they have also benefited consumers at home and abroad through lower prices. Higher export earnings, despite lower export prices, have enabled Asian countries to pay higher prices for imported inputs, which, in turn, has represented terms-of-trade gains for many primary commodity exporters. Moreover, exports from Asia also benefit from rising demand in those developing countries that have seen their export earnings rise thanks to growing Asian demand for their commodities.

Policies for managing the new forms of global interdependence

Although continuing growth in East and South Asia and recovery in other regions of the developing world are likely to sustain the demand for primary commodities, the basic problem of instability in these prices and their long-term tendency to deteriorate in real terms vis-a-vis the prices of manufactures, especially those exported by developed countries, remains unresolved. Therefore, it is imperative for developing countries not to become complacent about industrialization and diversification. There is a risk that the recent recovery of primary commodity markets could lead to a shift away from investment—both domestic and foreign—in the nascent manufacturing sectors of commodity-exporting countries in favour of extractive industries. While higher investment in that area may be beneficial in terms of creating additional supply capacity and raising productivity, this should not be at the expense of investment in manufacturing. Exporters of primary commodities that have recently benefited from higher prices and, in some cases, from higher export volumes, have to continue their efforts towards greater diversification within the primary commodity sector, as well as upgrading their manufacturing and services sectors. The recent windfall gains from higher primary commodity earnings provide an opportunity to step up investment in infrastructure and productive capacity—both essential for boosting development.

At the national level, this raises the question of the sharing of export revenues from extractive industries, which has always been a central concern in development strategy. Higher global demand and international prices for fuels and mining products have been attracting additional FDI to these sectors in a number of developing countries, and this may increase the scope in these countries for mobilizing additional resources for development. However, government revenues from taxes on profits in these sectors have typically been very low, partly due to a policy since the beginning of the 1990s of attracting FDI through the offer of fiscal incentives. Such a policy risks engaging potential host countries in "a race to the bottom" which, clearly, should be avoided.

Additional sources of fiscal revenue from primary export-oriented activities may be royalties, the conclusion of joint ventures or full public ownership of the operating firms. However, efforts to obtain adequate fiscal revenue should not deprive the operators, private or public, of the financial resources they need to increase their productivity and supply capacity, or their international competitiveness. Recent upward trends in world market prices of fuels and minerals and mining products as a result of growing demand from East and South Asia provide an opportunity to review the existing fiscal and ownership regimes. Such a review—which is already under way in several countries— and possible strategic policy adjustments could be more effective if oil and mineral exporting countries would cooperate in the formulation of some generally agreed principles relating to the fiscal treatment of foreign investors. Moreover, a higher share of the public sector or consumers in the rent generated by extractive industries does not automatically enhance development and progress towards the MDGs; it has to be accompanied by strategic use of the proceeds for investment that would enhance productive capacity in other sectors, as well as in education, health and infrastructure.

At the international level, recent increases in the prices of some primary commodities and improvements in the terms of trade of a number of developing countries may not have changed the long-term trend in real commodity prices or altered the problem of their volatility. Wide fluctuations in primary commodity prices are not in the interest of either producers or consumers. This has also been recognized by the IMF's International Monetary and Financial Committee, which, at its April 2005 meeting, inter alia, underscored "the importance of stability in oil markets for global prosperity" and encouraged "closer dialogue between oil exporters and importers". Although primary commodities other than oil may be less important for the developed countries, they are nevertheless equally, if not more important for those developing countries that depend on exports of such commodities. And since in many of the latter countries extreme poverty is a pressing problem, the issue of commodity price stability is of crucial importance not only for the achievement of the MDGs but also for global prosperity in general. Consequently, in the spirit of a global partnership for development, the international community might consider reviewing mechanisms at the global or regional level that could serve to reduce the instability of prices of a wider range of commodities, not just oil, to mitigate its impact on the national incomes of exporting countries.

In the short term, however, the central policy issue concerns the correction of existing global trade imbalances. It is often argued that the decision of central banks in the developing world, and in particular in Asia, to intervene in the currency market is the main reason for these imbalances. Indeed, most of the intervening countries explicitly try to avoid currency appreciation that could result from speculative capital inflows, in order to ensure that the international competitiveness of the majority of their producers is not put at risk. Most of the East Asian countries adopted a system of unilateral fixing of their exchange rates following the Asian financial crisis, while most Latin American turned to managed floating. In both cases, the aim has been to maintain the real exchange rate at a competitive level while gaining a certain degree of independence from international capital markets.

In the absence of a multilateral exchange rate system that takes account of the concerns of small and open developing economies, such unilateral stabilization of the exchange rate at a competitive level appears to be an effective means of crisis prevention. Individual central banks do have the capacity for successful and credible counter-attacks when their own currency is under "threat" or pressure to appreciate. By contrast, they are practically powerless to stabilize an exchange rate that has come under threat or pressure to depreciate, even if central banks have accumulated huge reserves of international currency. It would require multilateral cooperation and policy coherence to address this type of asymmetry. The premature liberalization of capital markets has seriously heightened the vulnerability of developing countries to external financial shocks. Moreover, it has become clear that strengthening domestic financial systems is not enough to significantly reduce that vulnerability.

For a smooth redressing of the global imbalances, it is essential to avoid a recession in developed countries—where growth has been depending excessively on the United States economy—and a marked slowdown in developing countries. A scenario which seeks to correct the global imbalances, and most importantly the external deficit of the United States, through massive exchange rate appreciation and lower domestic absorption in China and other developing countries in Asia, will almost inevitably have a deflationary impact on the world economy. It will not only jeopardize China's attempts to integrate a vast pool of rural workers and, more generally, reduce poverty, but will also adversely affect the efforts of other developing countries towards achieving the MDGs.

By contrast, adjusting the global imbalances will be less deflationary if demand from the euro area and Japan grows faster. It should not be forgotten that much of the counterpart to the United States' external deficit is to be found in the surpluses of other developed countries. The current-account surpluses of the euro area and Japan with the rest of the world are mushrooming—despite rising import bills for oil and other primary commodities. Indeed, Japan and Germany together accounted for $268 billion or about 30 per cent of the combined global current-account surplus in 2004. This compares with an overall current-account surplus of $193 billion in East and South Asia. China, the country on which revaluation pressure has been most intense, accounts for just over one third of this amount, or less than 8 per cent of the combined global surplus.

Supachai Panitchpakdi Secretary-General of UNCTAD

International initiatives to alleviate poverty and to reach the MDGs should not ignore the importance of a smooth correction of the global imbalances so as to ensure the sustainability of the "Asian miracle". Indeed, further economic catch-up by China and India will have expansionary effects for most developing countries. Any slowing down or disruption of this process would carry the risk of intensifying global price competition on the markets for manufactures exported by developing countries, while weakening the expansionary effects resulting from the growing demand from Asia.

Supachai Panitchpakdi
Secretary-General of UNCTAD

[1] perspective（观察问题的）视角

[2] rebound 回弹

[3] fuel 加燃料

[4] envisage 面对，正视，想象

[5] attain 达到，获得

[6] attendant 伴随的

[7] spill 使溢出

[8] ascent 上升，提高

[9] intensify 加强

[10] manufacture 制成品

[11] successively 接连,继续地

[12] dependence 依赖，依存

[13] variation 变更，变化,差异

[14] repercussion 弹回，反响，反射

[15] segment 部分，分部，部门

[16] eradication 根除,消灭

[17] central pillar 核心支柱

[18] vagary 反复无常的行为

[19] lag 落后延迟，间隔期间（时日）

[20] intensity 强烈，紧张，强度

[21] concomitant 相伴的，伴随的

[22] mining 采矿

[23] decelerate （使）减速

[24] outpace 超过……速度

[25] notwithstanding 尽管,虽然

[26] ɔoom 繁荣

[27] dynamism 活力

[28] dynamics 动力学,活力

[29] surge 大涨

[30] widespread 普及的,流传广的

[31] deficit 赤字,不足

[32] counterproductive 使达不到预期目标的

[33] upswing 上升,向上摆动

[34] buoyant 降而复升的,保持高价的

[35] destined 预定的,注定的

[36] hub 中继站

[37] modest 适当的

[38] recoup 补偿

[39] resilient 有弹力的

[40] sluggish 萧条的,呆滞的

[41] entail 使承担

Exercises

I. Match the following terms in Column A and Column B

Column A	Column B
1. dependence	a. 根除，消灭
2. repercussion	b. 制成品
3. eradication	c. 赤字，不足
4. rebound	d. 回弹
5. envisage	e. 上升，提高
6. attendant	f. 中继站
7. ascent	g. 弹回，反响，反射
8. manufacture	h. 核心支柱
9. segment	i. 依赖，依存
10. boom	j. 面对，正视，想象
11. surge	k. 大涨
12. widespread	l. 使达不到预期目标的
13. deficit	m. 相伴的，伴随的
14. central pillar	n. 部分，分部，部门
15. intensity	o. 繁荣
16. concomitant	p. 普及的，流传广的
17. lag	q. 伴随的
18. counterproductive	r. 强烈，紧张，强度
19. hub	s. 落后延迟，间隔期间（时日）
20. recoup	t. 补偿

II. Translate the following sentences into Chinese

1. Since the beginning of the new millennium, the performance of the world economy has been shaped by the increasingly important role of China and India. Rapid growth in these two large economies has spilled over to many other developing countries and has established East and South Asia as a new growth pole in the world economy.

2. Asia has been a region of economic dynamism over the past four decades, with different economies in the region successively experiencing rapid growth. The large size of the countries that entered this process most recently, China and

India, has established the East and South Asian region as a new growth pole in the world economy.

3. Sustained rapid growth and rising living standards in China and India have been accompanied by a dramatic increase in Asia's shares of world exports and raw material consumption. Given the large size of the Chinese and Indian economies and their specific patterns of demand, changes in their structure of supply and demand have a much larger impact on the composition of world trade than did those of other late industrializers in Asia during their economic ascent.

4. China's energy use has steadily increased since the 1960s, but at a slower rate than its GDP. Its future energy use will depend on how opposing trends play out: on the one hand, continued rapid industrialization, higher living standards and improved transport infrastructure will tend to further increase energy use; on the other hand, there remains considerable potential for the adoption of energy-saving technologies. In either case, China's energy demand is likely to continue to outpace the future growth of domestic supply.

5. A continuous increase in average living standards and further progress in poverty reduction in China will also lead to higher demand for food and to a change in its dietary composition. So far, China has remained largely self-sufficient in all major food items. But with increasing consumption it is likely to become more dependent on food imports in the future, notwithstanding possible productivity and output growth in its domestic agricultural sector as a result of recent agricultural policy reforms.

6. Since the mid-1980s China has substantially upgraded its export basket, in which labour-and resource-intensive manufactures and, increasingly, electronics, have become dominant. China's exports still have a relatively high import content, but there are indications of a rise in the share of domestic value added in China's processing trade, particularly in the electronics sector.

7. But it also has to be recognized that China's increasing participation in international trade poses new challenges for many countries. Its weight in international markets due to the very large size of its economy may contribute to a fall in the export prices of manufactures that it produces and exports along with other developing countries, such as clothing, footwear and certain types of information and communication technology products.

8. Trade among developing countries has sometimes been promoted as an alternative to the traditional trade pattern where developing-country trade relies mainly on

primary commodity exports to developed countries in exchange for imports of manufactures. The rapid rise in the importance of South-South trade, particularly over the past two decades, reflects a number of factors.

9. The recent and ongoing changes in international trade, with respect to both product composition and direction of trade, is affecting developing countries in different ways, depending on the product composition of their exports and imports. On the export side, the impact differs according to the shares of manufactures and primary commodities, and on the import side, it is especially the dependence on fuels and industrial raw materials that determines the outcome for individual countries.

10. At the national level, this raises the question of the sharing of export revenues from extractive industries, which has always been a central concern in development strategy. Higher global demand and international prices for fuels and mining products have been attracting additional FDI to these sectors in a number of developing countries, and this may increase the scope in these countries for mobilizing additional resources for development.

III. Cloze

At the international level, recent increases _____ the prices of some primary commodities and improvements in the terms of trade of a number of developing countries may not have changed the long-term trend in real commodity prices or altered the problem _____ their volatility. Wide fluctuations in primary commodity prices are not _____ the interest of either producers _____ consumers. This has also been recognized _____ the IMF's International Monetary and Financial Committee, which, _____ its April 2005 meeting, inter alia, underscored "the importance of stability in oil markets _____ global prosperity" and encouraged "closer dialogue _____ oil exporters and importers". Although primary commodities other than oil may be less important _____ the developed countries, they are nevertheless equally, if not more important for those developing countries that depend _____ exports _____ such commodities. And since in many of the latter countries extreme poverty is a pressing problem, the issue of commodity price stability is _____ crucial importance not only for the achievement of the MDGs but also for global prosperity in general. Consequently, _____ the spirit of a global partnership for development, the international community might consider reviewing mechanisms _____ the global or regional level that could serve to reduce the instability of prices _____ a wider range of commodities, not just oil, to mitigate its impact on the national incomes of exporting countries.

IV. Underline the important sentences in the text, which give you useful information

V. Retell or write down what you learn from the text in English or in Chinese

参考译文

联合国贸易与发展会议

日内瓦
2005 年贸易与发展报告
概述
联合国
纽约和日内瓦,2005 年

说明

· 联合国文件都用英文大写字母附加数字编号。凡是提到这种编号,就是指联合国的某一个文件。

· 本出版物所采用的名称及其材料的编写方式,并不意味着联合国秘书处对于任何国家、领土、城市、地区或其当局的法律地位,或对于其边界或界线的划分,表示任何意见。

· 本出版物的材料可自由援引或翻印,但需说明出处及文件号码。应向贸易与发展会议秘书处提交一份载有文件引文或翻印部分的出版物。

本文所载的概述也作为 2005 年贸易与发展报告(UNCTAD/TDR/2005,出售品编号 E. 05. Ⅱ. D. 13)的一部分印发。

UNCTAD/TDR/2005(概述)

概述

从《千年发展目标》的视角看,世界经济的近期走向喜忧参半。好消息是,2004 年发展中国家发展迅速,增长范围之广是前所未有的。中国和印度这两个绝对贫困人口最多的国家持续实现了较大的人均收入增长趋势。拉丁美洲在出口扩张的带动下摆脱了深度的经济危机,恢复了较快的发展。非洲在 2004 年再度达到了 4. 5% 以上的增长率。另外,许多非洲国家由于对一些初级商品的需求持续强劲,预计这些国家的增长在短期内会保持相对有力。坏消息是,尽管非洲撒哈拉以南的增长率接近 5% ,但仍不足以达到《千年发展目标》。而且,2005 年的前景处在全球失衡加剧的阴影笼罩之下,发达国家的发展会更慢,并对发展中国家造成种种附带影响。

自新千年开始以来,中国和印度起着日趋重要的作用,左右了世界经济的发展状况。这两个大型经济体的高速增长向许多其他发展中国家外溢,使东亚和南亚成为了世界经济中的一个新的增长点。在中国和印度经济地位提升的同时,全球相互依存关系出现了一些新的特点,例如,初级商品出口国有了较为光明的前景,发展中国家之间的贸易不断扩大,发展中国家向发达国家的资本出口正在上升,但某些制成品在全球市场上的竞争也有所加剧。

全球前景与失衡

全球产出增长率在 2005 年放慢的主要原因是,各主要发达经济体和拉丁美洲及东亚的某些新兴经济体减慢了速度。欧元区和日本并没有能够用较强的增长业绩填补美国经济的暂时疲软,两者都仍然缺乏纠正国内失衡和推动调整全球贸易不平衡所需要的活力。事实上,从 2004 年下半年开始,欧元区和日本的产出增长率一直明显下降,造成了 2005 年预测的下调。虽然欧元区和日本在过去三年中极大地获益于全球扩张,尤其是亚洲的繁荣,但都未能设法重振内需。

全球经济前景令人担忧的另一个原因是石油价格的上涨。虽然某些石油生产国作了灵活的供货调整,但是油价自 2002 年中期以来翻了一番,在 2005 年 7 月达到了每桶 58 美元。这令人焦虑重重,生怕像 20 世纪 70 年代那样出现油价飙升致使发达国家的经济活动受到冲击和通货膨胀的现象,然而,到目前为止,由于两方面的原因,这种情况并没有发生。首先,由于提高了能源的使用率,发达国家减少了对石油的依赖。同时,服务业在这些国家国内生产总值中所占份额的扩大,压缩了单位产出能耗较大的工业所占的比重。第二,油价近期上涨不是由于供货受到猛烈冲击造成的,而是需求逐步扩大的结果。在这种情况下,发达国家出台的工资和货币对策把握了分寸,并没有破坏价格稳定或产出增长。

油价近期大涨对发展中石油进口经济体,尤其是那些因为开展工业化而更多地依赖进口石油的国家,冲击较为剧烈。例如,巴西国内生产活动中的石油消耗密度比经合组织平均值高 40%,中国和泰国高出一倍以上,而印度几乎比经合组织成员国高两倍。因此,石油价格进一步上涨造成的通胀压力,主要是在发展中国家具有破坏增长进程可持续性的危险。虽然迄今为止通货膨胀幅度有限,但一些国家已经收紧了货币政策。

另一方面,获益于需求扩大和出口价格上涨的,不仅是石油出口国,而且还有许多出口非石油初级商品的发展中国家。自 2002 年以来,东亚和南亚特别是中国和印度的高需求,是初级商品价格大幅提升的主要原因。在某些初级商品的市场上,正在出现的供方制约也促成了价格上涨的强力反应。亚洲对于各种初级商品,尤其是对石油和铜、铁矿石、镍等矿产品以及天然胶和大豆的需求可能会保持强劲,增加这些产品出口国的收入。但是,初级商品市场的进一步发展动态还将取决于其他一些关键因素:近期的新投资将能增创多大的供应能力;这种能力的投产速度有多快;纠正现有贸易不平衡的必要性会对发达国家的初级商品需求产生何种影响。

虽然高速增长的发展中国家对国际初级商品市场的重要性与日俱增,但发达国家仍占全球非燃料初级商品进口的三分之二,还将继续发挥重要作用。单靠中国和印度增加初级商品进口,不可能永久扭转初级商品实际价格不断下滑的趋势。实际上,以实际值衡量,初级商品价格现在仍然不到1960—1985年平均水平的三分之二。除此之外,初级商品价格的急剧波动限制了许多发展中国家走上稳定和持续增长和创造就业的道路,造福于人口的所有层次并实现千年发展目标的能力。

全球经常项目的巨额失衡,是世界经济稳定增长面临的最大短期风险。虽然美元贬值,但美国的贸易逆差继续扩大:2002年2月以来美元的贸易额加权币值损失了18%。而美国的经常项目逆差占了全球顺差总量的三分之二。近些年来,美国对几乎所有贸易伙伴的逆差都在扩大,增加幅度最明显的是对西欧和对中国的贸易。另一方面,中国不仅对美贸易存在顺差,而且,对许多其他发达国家的贸易也是顺差。可是,尽管存在这些顺差,中国从这些国家的进口与从周边国家和其他发展中国家的进口相似,也是高速增长。

如果能够实行一种周密协调的国际宏观经济方略,就能大大提高较贫穷国家巩固提高近期发展业绩的机会。这种方法必须得到主要发展中国家的参与,并且着眼于避免使用通货紧缩手段调整全球失衡。

东亚和南亚——新的增长极

在过去的四十年当中,亚洲是富有经济活力的区域,区域内的不同经济体先后实现了高速增长。中国和印度是最近跨入这个进程的国家。由于两国幅员辽阔,东亚和南亚区域已经被建成了世界经济增长的新的一极。这两个大型亚洲经济体的工业产出增长,高度依赖于初级商品尤其是燃料和工业原材料的进口以及由此而来与其他发展中国家的联系,因此,中国和印度增长业绩的变化会对其他发展中国家的贸易条件和出口收入产生强烈的影响。这不可避免地引出了这两个经济大国中、长期增长速度可持续性的问题。

从人均国内生产总值看,中国和印度要达到先进经济体的水平还有很长一段路要走。两国都有巨大的追赶潜力。发挥这一潜力的关键,是两国实现制造业活动的更高生产率收益,确保人口所有层次都能增加。对于加快脱贫,争取社会广泛接受必要的结构变革而言,收入的大面积增长至为关键。但是,随着生产率的上升,在整个经济中不断提高工资,也是扩大国内需求的一个核心支柱,这样才能实现产出增长的持续和稳定。固定资本形成取决于总体上的良性需求期望,并不仅仅取决于出口,出口受制于世界市场的无常和国际竞争力的变化。

中国和印度贸易格局的转变

在中国和印度实现持续高速增长和不断提高生活水平的同时,亚洲在世界出口和原材料消费中的份额激增。中国和印度的经济规模巨大,有着独特的需求格局,因此,这两个国家供求结构中的变化对于世界贸易构成具有的影响,远大于亚洲其他后起工业化国家在经济崛起过程中的供求变化所产生的影响。中国的增长对国际产品市场和全球贸易流动的影响已经清晰可见。如果印度的工业化能够如同亚洲其他高速增长的经济体那样,在进一步的经济提升过程中占据同样的重要地位,印度的商品贸易结构就有可能沿袭与中国相似的一系列变革,虽然印度在时间上将晚于中国十年或二十年。

在过去数十年中,尤其是自20世纪90年代中期以来,中国的金属用量大幅度上升,印度与之相似,程度略低。中国的铝、铜、镍和钢铁的用量增长率现在已经超过国内生产总值的增长率。这一近期增长的一部分与尤其是基础设施的极高投资率相重合。但是,一旦投资增长速度放慢,尤其是建筑业和基础设施的投资减缓,中国金属使用密度的这种近期高速增长以及矿物和矿产品进口的同期增加就很可能减速。相比之下,印度的金属使用密度在过去四十年中一直相当稳定,反映出该国的工业化速度较慢,国内生产总值中基础设施投资的份额相对较小。

中国的能源用量自20世纪60年代起一直稳步增加,但速度低于国内生产总值的提高。未来的能源用量将取决于两种互逆趋势的此消彼长:一方面,持续的高速工业化、更高的生活水平和有所改善的交通运输基础设施将使能源用量进一步加大;另一方面,仍然存在着采用节能技术的巨大潜力。无论是哪种情况,中国的能源需求增长速度可能会继续大于今后的国内供应增长速度。

农产品进口将由若干因素决定。只要还需要进口工业用原材料作为不断扩大的国内市场的生产投入,进口需求将会进一步增长。橡胶和木材可能就属于这种情况。另一方面,纺织品和服装的出口量在很大程度上决定着棉花的进口,随着出口构成向技术密度高的产品转化,可以预期棉花进口将会放慢增速。

中国持续提高平均生活水平和不断取得减贫进展,也将带来食品需求的增加和饮食结构的变化。到目前为止,中国的所有主要食品基本上保持着自给自足。尽管近期的农业政策改革可能会使国内农业提高生产力和产出增长率,但随着消费的增加,今后有可能加大对进口食品的依赖。由于经济规模巨大,即使是自给自足比率发生细微的变化,也会对中国的农产品进口产生巨大影响。

自20世纪80年代中期以来,中国的出口产品极大地提高了档次,其中,劳动密集型和资源密集型制成品以及越来越多的电子产品已经占有了主导地位。中国的出口仍有相对较高的进口成分,但有迹象表明,在中国的加工贸易尤其是电子产业中,国内增加值所占份额正在加大。印度并没有经历亚洲其他高速增长经济体曾经有过的那种制造业出口繁荣。印度已经成为出口以软件和信息技术为支撑的服务的大国,尤其是向美国出口,但是,这种服务在印度出口收入中的份额能否进一步大增,存在着极大的不确定性。在今后数年,这些服务出口的绝对值有可能继续增长,但制造业的出口可能会变得更为强劲。

中国和其他亚洲经济体的增长活力对于许多发达国家和发展中国家具有积极效应,对于直接获益于亚洲高速增长经济体进口需求激增的国家是这样,对于间接获益于主要贸易伙伴的经济积极增长效应的国家也是如此。还有其他一些经济体由于初级商品价格的提高而实现了更高的出口和收入增长率,尽管这些国家对亚洲高速增长经济体的出口相对较少。但还应该认识到,中国扩大了对国际贸易的参与,这给许多国家带来了新的挑战。中国的经济规模巨大,在与其他发展中国家一道生产和出口制成品的领域当中,中国在国际市场上的份量有可能造成出口价格下跌,如服装、鞋类和某些类型的信息和通信技术产品。具体而言,中国服装出口的兴起,恰恰就是在一些发展中国家实行了较为外向的发展战略,很多发展中国家部分上为了应对《多种纤维安排》的配额规定而发展起服装生产和出口的时候实现的。

人口众多的亚洲经济体特别是中国的发展速度,无疑需要许多其他国家加快结构变革,无论是发展中国家还是发达国家。在有些产业,来自低工资、高生产率国家的竞争较少,与之相比,服装业和较一般而言在经济的低技能端开展的活动实行调整的压力较大。许多国家存在着普遍的担心,以为结构变革的步伐会造成失业率上升和产出下降。恰恰相反,在发达国家当中,贸易平衡存在巨额逆差的国家,如澳大利亚、西班牙、大不列颠及北爱尔兰联合王国和美国,国内增长率和就业方面的业绩远远胜过保持了大量贸易顺差和具有较强竞争力的国家,如德国和日本。如果对保护主义妥协让步,违背与所有国家结成全球发展伙伴关系和积极回应贫穷大国融入的承诺,就会适得其反,道理在于,发展中国家从对发达国家的出口中获得收入,大部分转化成了对先进工业产品的更高进口需求,因而也就直接或间接地回流到了发达国家。

南南贸易日趋壮大

在传统的贸易格局中,发展中国家主要依赖对发达国家出口初级商品换取制成品进口。促进南南贸易有时被用作替代这种贸易格局的手段。南南贸易重要性的迅速上升,尤其是在过去二十年中的发展,是若干因素的表现。首先,这一贸易在20世纪80年代滑坡之后重新恢复了元气。第二,大量发展中国家在实行贸易改革和缔结区域贸易协定的同时采取了更为外向型的发展战略,这一走势极大地改善了进入其市场的机会,包括从其他发展中国家进口产品的准入。但是,南南贸易迅速发展的最重要原因是,一些大型发展中经济体,特别是中国的产出增长速度远远高于发达国家。另外,这些国家生机勃勃的增长业绩与区域之内的专门化和生产分工密切相关。

南南贸易的壮大是个事实,但是,要明了发展中国家作为一个整体的近期动态,就应当对统计数据认真加以评估。实际上,发展中国家间贸易在过去十年左右增长斐然,而且制成品出口在这一崛起中占有重要地位是一种表面印象,在开展此种评估时应当对这一表面印象加以某些限定。

发展中国家在世界贸易流动中不断增强的作用似乎首先来自于少数亚洲经济体高于平均水平的增长业绩，以及这些经济体对外贸易水平和构成随之而来发生的转变。南南贸易制成品统计量上升的很大一部分，是由于东亚区域内分工生产最终向发达国家出口的产品而发生双重统计所造成的。另一个原因是，由于中国香港和新加坡具有转运港口或区域集散港的作用，也存在着重复统计的情况。在南南贸易制成品稳缓增长的过程中，三角贸易占有重要地位，这意味着，南南贸易制成品的主要部分并没有降低发展中国家制成品出口对于发达国家市场总需求的依赖程度。只要发达国家，特别是作为东亚最重要出口市场的美国，对于在东亚之内生产分工过程中发挥重要作用的产品保持高位的最终需求，三角贸易和由此而来的南南贸易就能维持强劲。另一方面，拉丁美洲的经济回弹为与三角贸易无关的南南贸易中的制成品交易改善了前景。

从贸易统计数据看，南南贸易中的初级商品增幅较为一般。但是，这种贸易涉及的国家数目，多于南南贸易制成品有力增长涉及的国家。非洲以及拉丁美洲和加勒比地区借助初级商品南南贸易，赢回了在20世纪80年代失去的、在南南总贸易中原有的部分市场份额。对亚洲高速增长发展中国家的初级商品南南出口不断扩大，这在被称为"新贸易地理"的布局中，确实有可能演变为最具活力的特征。

出于多种原因，应当始终把促进南南贸易定为一个目标。第一，发达国家增长乏力，对涉及发展中国家出口利益的产品仍然设置着贸易壁垒，这意味着发展中国家为了促进出口增长就需要更多地注意相互间的市场。第二，亚洲高速增长经济体的规模巨大，减少了发展中国家为了获益于规模经济而争取发达国家市场的必要性。第三，继续依赖于发达国家市场可能会使发展中国家面临压力：要想使进入这些国家的市场准入得到改善，就必须迅速实行贸易和金融自由化、保护知识产权、对外国直接投资实行开放政策。较一般而言，这种挂钩压力会使发展中国家的政策空间面临受到更大挤压的风险。

再论贸易条件

国际贸易在产品构成和贸易流向上的近期和当前变化，因发展中国家的进出口产品构成而定，以不同的方式影响着这些国家。从出口看，这种影响按照制成品和初级商品的比例而变化，从进口看，决定各个国家面临何种影响的，主要是对燃料和工业原材料的依赖程度。

使得某些国家的贸易条件得到改善的因素，尤其是石油和矿物以及矿产品价格的上涨，恰恰就是使其他一些国家的贸易条件发生恶化的因素。在有些国家，尤其是在拉丁美洲，还有非洲，价格走向对于出口品购买力的积极效应由于出口量的增加而强化；而在其他一些国家，通过出口单位价值提高的产品而得到的收益因进口价格的上涨被抵消，甚至入不敷出。2002年以来，商品总出口中石油和矿物及矿产品份额较高的经济体在国际产品市场近期动态中获益最大。出口以石油为主的国家,2002 至 2004 年期间的贸易条件提高了近 30%;出口以矿物和矿产品为主的国家,贸易条件提高了约 15%。商品总出口主要由初级农产品构成的经济体,贸易条件的上下波动最大。这反映出此类经济体内具体产品价格走向的巨大差异、其他初级商品所占出口份额的差异以及石油在商品进口中所占份额的差异。

对于以制成品为主要出口产品、同时又是石油和矿物及金属净进口国的发展中国家,贸易条件在过去两三年中发生恶化。这种恶化是进口初级商品价格上涨和制成品出口价格停滞或下跌的双重效应造成的,很可能会成为这些国家对外贸易的一种长期特征。这有两个原因:首先,有迹象表明,这些国家的制成品出口价格相对于从发达国家进口的制成品价格而言正在下跌;其次,只要大型亚洲经济体的工业增长保持强劲,发达世界在避免进入衰退的同时能够纠正失衡,初级商品价格就有可能维持坚挺。

事实上,发展中国家行列中制成品出口国的贸易条件损失,部分是由于其中一些国家特别是中国和印度的赶超速度造成的。推动这一赶超进程的,是出口产业生产率的提高,使这些国家掌握了竞争优势,也增加了进口需求。全球需求格局的变化及其对各个国家的影响引起了收入的再分配,这不仅是在发达国家与发展中国家之间的再分配,而且越来越多地是在不同类别发展中国家之间的再分配。然而,必须认识到,实际收入的分配变化并不必然意味着绝对损失。只要产出增长足够有力,所有国家的实际收入都可能获益,有些国家可能获益较大,这取决于出口结构和厂商的国际竞争力:贸易条件的恶化有可能通过加大出口量来弥补。制成品的需求价格弹性高,通过制成品出口使得贸易条件恶化得到弥补的概率,远大于初级商品出口。

亚洲在生产率上取得的收益不仅带来了更高的公司利润,而且也增加了工资,另外,由于降低了价格,也使国内外消费者得到了好处。虽然出口价格下跌,但仍然增加了出口收入,使亚洲国家能够为进口投入支付更高的价格,而这对许多初级商品出口国而言也就意味着贸易条件的好转。除此之外,一些发展中国家的出口收入由于亚洲对其初级商品的需求不断扩大而增加,由此而带动了这些国家需求的扩大,这也有利于亚洲的出口。

驾驭新型全球相互依存关系的政策

东亚和南亚的持续增长以及发展中世界其他区域的复苏有可能维持住初级商品的需求,尽管如此,初级商品价格不稳及其相对于制成品价格尤其是发达国家出口的制成品价格而发生实质恶化的长期趋势这个基本问题,并没有得到解决。因此,发展中国家对于工业化和多样化决不能沾沾自喜。现存的一种危险是,初级商品市场的近期复苏有可能使国内外投资移出初级商品出口国的新生制造业部门,转向采掘产业。在采掘产业领域内增加投资可能会有利于创建更多的供应能力,提高生产率,但是,这不应当以挤占对制造业的投资为代价。由于初级商品价格提高和出口量加大而在近期获益的初级商品出口国,必须继续努力扩大初级商品产业内的多样化,提升自己的制造业和服务业。由于初级商品收入提高而在最近得到的这种巨大意外收益,带来了加大基础设施和生产能力投资的机会,对推动发展而言,这两者都是不可或缺的。

如何分享采掘业出口收入的问题,始终是国家发展战略的一个核心关注。燃料和矿产品全球需求和国际价格的上涨,吸引了更多的外国直接投资流入一些发展中国家的这些产业,这有可能扩大这些国家为发展筹集更多资金的余地。但是,政府通过对这些部门的利润抽税得到的收入一向很低,其部分原因是20世纪90年代开始以来实行了通过多种财政优惠办法鼓励吸引外资的政策。这一政策有可能会使潜在的投资接受国进入一场"冲底让利的竞赛",显然应当避免这样的竞赛。

通过初级商品出口活动增加财政收入的来源可能是特许权使用费、合资经营或运营中企业的完全国有权。但是,取得足够财政收入的努力不应当剥夺公共或民办运营商提高生产率和扩大供应能力所需要的资金或削弱其国际竞争力。燃料和矿物及矿产品世界市场价格由于东亚和南亚需求的增加而在近期上扬的趋势,带来了审查现行财政和所有权制度的一次机会。有些国家已经开始了这种审查。如果石油和矿物出口国能够开展合作,就外国投资人的财政待遇制定某些普遍同意的原则,这种审查以及可能的战略政策调整就能更为有效。另外,公共部门或消费者加大在采掘业获取的利润中占有的份额,并不会自动地增强发展和加大争取千年发展目标的进展,必须与此同时将收益用于投资,提高其他产业的生产能力以及增加教育、卫生部门和基础设施的投资。

在国际层次,某些初级商品价格的近期上涨和一些发展中国家贸易条件的改善,或许并没有改变初级商品实际价格的长期趋势或此类价格的波动性问题。初级商品价格的大幅波动既不符合生产者的利益,也不符合消费者的利益。国际货币基金组织的国际货币和金融委员会也承认这一点,在2005年4月的会议上除其他问题外,强调了"石油市场稳定对全球繁荣的重要性"并鼓励"石油出口国与进口国加强对话"。虽然除石油以外的初级商品对发达国家的重要性可能较低,但对依赖出口此类初级商品的发展中国家来说,这些初级商品即使不比石油更为要紧,至少也是同样重要。在这类国家,极端贫困是一个紧迫问题,因此,初级商品价格的稳定不仅对于实现千年发展目标,而且对于总体上的全球繁荣至关重要。所以,国际社会可本着全球发展伙伴关系的精神考虑在全球或区域层次审查多种机制,借以在较大范围上减少初级商品而不仅仅是石油的价格不稳定性,从而减轻出口国国民收入受到的影响。

然而,短期内的核心政策问题是纠正现有的全球贸易不平衡。经常有人说,发展中世界尤其是亚洲一些中央银行干预货币市场的决定是造成这些失衡的主要原因。其实,大多数实行干预的国家显然是要力图避免投机性资本流动可能带来的货币升值,以便确保大部分本国生产厂商的国际竞争力不会面临风险。多数东亚国家在亚洲金融危机之后都实行了单方面固定汇率制度,而多数拉丁美洲国家转而采用了有调控的浮动汇率。这两者的目标都是保持实际汇率的竞争力水平,同时在一定程度上取得相对国际资本市场的独立地位。

目前并不存在一个能够对小型和开放发展中经济体的关注加以考虑的多边汇率体系,在这种条件下,将汇率稳定在有竞争力水平上的单方面措施看来是预防危机的有效手段之一。各国央行确实具有在本国货币受到升值"威胁"或压力时进行成功和可靠反击的能力。相比之下,即便这些央行积累了大量的国际货币储备,在汇率面临贬值的威胁和压力而需要稳定汇率的时候,它们实际上是无能为力的。如果要解决这种类型的不对称,就需要开展多边合作和实现政策上的协调一致。条件不成熟就开放资本市场,已经严重加剧了发展中国家在外部金融冲击面前的脆弱性。而且,现在可以清楚地看到,仅凭加强国内金融体制并不足以真正减少这种脆弱性。

为了平稳地纠正全球失衡现象,必须避免发达国家发生衰退——这些国家的增长过分依赖于美国经济,也必须避免发展中国家的增长明显减速。依靠中国和亚洲其他发展中国家的汇率大幅升值和降低国内吸收能力来纠正全球失衡以及首先是美国的对外逆差,几乎不可避免地会对世界经济产生通货紧缩影响。这不仅会破坏中国吸纳庞大的农村民工队伍和更普遍减贫的尝试,而且还会对其他发展中国家争取实现千年发展目标的努力产生有害影响。

相比之下,如果欧元区和日本加速扩大需求,则调整全球失衡而引起的通货紧缩影响就会较小。不应忘记,美国对外逆差的很大一部分实际上是其他发达国家的相应顺差。欧元区和日本虽然为进口石油和其他初级商品增加了付出的代价,但对世界其他地区的经常项目顺差正在急剧膨胀。实际上,日本和德国两家在 2004 年就占了全球经常项目顺差总额的大约 30% ,为 2,680 亿美元。这远远超过了东亚和南亚 1,930 亿美元的经常项目顺差总额。中国是受调整币值压力最大的国家,可在这一顺差中所占的比例仅略大于三分之一,还不到全球顺差总额的 8% 。

减轻贫困和争取千年发展目标的国际举措不应忽视平稳纠正全球失衡的重要意义,这样才能确保"亚洲奇迹"的持续。中国和印度的进一步经济赶超确实会对大多数发展中国家产生扩张效应。这一进程如果发生任何减速或中断,就会带来在发展中国家制成品出口市场上加剧全球价格竞争的危险,并且削弱亚洲需求不断扩大所产生的经济扩张效应。

贸易与发展会议秘书长

素帕猜·帕尼奇帕克迪

Unit Seven

US-China Joint Commission on Commerce and Trade

US-China Joint Commission on Commerce and Trade (JCCT)

JCCT. The US-China Joint Commission on Commerce and Trade (JCCT) was established in 1983 as a forum for high-level dialogue on bilateral trade issues and a vehicle for promoting commercial relations. The JCCT works to resolve problems affecting US companies and serves as an umbrella for trade events and World Trade Organization (WTO) technical assistance programs. The JCCT is co-chaired by US Secretary of Commerce and China's Minister of Commerce and enjoys strong interagency support on both sides. The Commission consists of three working groups covering trade and investment issues, business development and industrial cooperation, and commercial law, as well as a side dialogue on export controls. Cabinet-level plenary sessions, typically are held annually, while sub-cabinet sessions and subgroup meetings are more frequent and ongoing. The Department of Commerce (DOC) consults closely with US industry prior to each session to ensure that companies' most pressing concerns are addressed. Companies are encouraged to express their concerns to relevant DOC JCCT contacts.

2004 session of Joint Commission on Commerce and Trade (JCCT) will take place on April 21, 2004. The elevated JCCT will be co-chaired by Secretary of Commerce Donald Evans and US Trade Representative Robert Zoellick on the US side and by Vice Premier Wu Yi on the Chinese side. The JCCT will cover a wide range of US-China economic issues, including Intellectual Property Rights, Trade Expansion Initiatives, and Export Controls.

The Trade and Investment Working Group (T & IWG). The T & IWG, co-chaired by the DOC Assistant Secretary for Market Access and Compliance and China's Ministry of Commerce (MOFCOM) Director General for the Americas, covers issues related to market access, trade finance, and investment and business facilitation. T & IWG also provides an important venue where outstanding commercial dispute cases are reviewed and addressed.

The last T & IWG meeting convened at the directorial level in Washington, DC on August 11, 2003. The US side raised a number of issues including establishing further cooperation on standards development and stronger intellectual property rights protection. The US side also proposed strengthening and reinvigorating the T & IWG mechanism by designating a coordinator on each side, regularizing meetings, and maintaining a direct line of communication between working group meetings.

The Business Development and Industrial Cooperation Working Group (BDICWG). The BDICWG, co-chaired by DOC Assistant Secretary for Trade Development and MOFCOM Director General of the Department of Science and Technology, promotes greater commercial cooperation on an industry sector basis. Industry sub-groups in environmental technologies, medical and pharmaceuticals, information industries, aviation and airport infrastructure, electric power technologies, and motor vehicle and allied products provide an ongoing policy forum for sector-focused discussion of market access and regulatory issues, and commercial cooperation. US Government agencies such as the EPA, FDA, and the FAA are important partners in supporting sub-group activities.

The BDICWG last convened in Washington in April 2003 to discuss industry sector' specific issues, review industry subgroup progress, and agree upon new priorities and principles for bilateral cooperation. The co-chairs agreed that all subgroups should undertake stronger cooperation on standards as a part of their overall efforts.

Commercial Law Working Group (CLWG). The CLWG, co-chaired by the Department of Commerce General Counsel and MOFCOM Director General for Treaty and Law, works to improve commercial relations between the United States and China through discussion of legal issues of mutual interest. The CLWG has proven a useful forum for seeking reform of China's commercial law system in areas of concern to US companies. Through the CLWG there have been successful discussions on measures to enhance the recognition and enforcement of arbitral awards in China and the inequitable application of China's border trade policy to goods that compete with US products.

The CLWG last convened in April 2002 in Beijing, where the US raised several concerns including lack of transparency in Chinese regulatory practices, problems with the method of promulgation and content of measures regulating foreign law firms issued by China's Ministry of Justice, and the process of granting marketing approval for generic drugs.

The CLWG also sponsors the US-China Legal Exchange, a series of joint legal seminars that foster mutual understanding of the legal regimes governing trade and investment in both countries. The seminars offer US audiences the opportunity to learn about the legal reforms taking place in China and provide Chinese participants the chance to learn about US practices. Under this program, the United States and China send delegations of legal experts to speak on topics of current interest. Both private sector and government attorneys have been featured at the seminars, which are open to government officials and academicians as well as the local business and legal communities. In December 2002, Vice Minister of Foreign Trade Long Yongtu led a delegation of Chinese legal experts to the United States to talk about the legal changes necessary for China to implement its WTO accession commitments. General Counsel Kassinger reciprocated, leading the most recent Legal Exchange delegation to China in November 2003 to discuss both recent developments in corporate governance practices in the United States as well as to discuss a variety of trade remedy measures used to safeguard fair trade between the United States and its trading partners, including China.

Export Controls Dialogue. The Bureau of Industry and Security (BIS) meets with officials from MOFCOM's Department of Science and Technology under the Export Controls Side Dialogue of the JCCT. BIS has generally used the regularized exchange of the JCCT forum to encourage more cooperation from MOFCOM on end-use checks for US strategic goods licensed to China.

The Bureau of Industry and Security co-hosted the Sino-US Export Control Outreach Seminar in Shanghai, China with China's Ministry of Commerce on September 17—18, 2003. The conference highlighted basic elements of US and Chinese export controls, regulations, and enforcement and was attended by 275 business and Chinese Government participants. Presenters at the conference consisted of both US and Chinese export control government representatives. Speakers from both governments were able to share their experience and knowledge of export controls with industry attendees. (*Source:http://www. ustr. gov*)

 Notes

[1] vehicle 传播媒介

[2] Cabinet-level 内阁

[3] plenary 正式的，充分的，全体出席的

[4] session 会议，对话

［5］address 发表,对付

［6］compliance 遵从,顺从

［7］venue 发生地点

［8］outstanding 未解决的

［9］convene 集合,召集

［10］directorial 主管的

［11］reinvigorate 使再振作,使复兴

［12］designate 指定,指派

［13］regularize 调整,使系统化

［14］EPA（Environment Protection Agency）美国环境保护署

［15］FDA（Food and Drug Administration）美国食品与药物管理局

［16］FAA（Federal Aviation Administration）美国联邦航空管理局

［17］enforcement 执行,强制

［18］arbitral award 仲裁裁决

［19］promulgation 颁布,公布

［20］generic 基因的

［21］sponsor 发起,赞助

［22］feature 特写

［23］outreach 超出……的范围

［24］attendee 出席人,参加者

Exercises

I. Match the following words in Column A and Column B

Column A	Column B
1. vehicle	a. 遵从，顺从
2. plenary	b. 集合，召集
3. session	c. 美国联邦航空管理局
4. compliance	d. 颁布，公布
5. venue	e. 发起，赞助
6. outstanding	f. 正式的,全体出席的
7. convene	g. 执行，强制
8. directorial	h. 传播媒介
9. Environment Protection Agency（EPA）	i. 会议，对话
10. Food and Drug Administration（FDA）	j. 美国食品与药物管理局
11. Federal Aviation Administration（FAA）	k. 发生地点
12. enforcement	l. 美国环境保护署
13. arbitral award	m. 仲裁裁决
14. promulgation	n. 出席人，参加者
15. sponsor	o. 未解决的
16. attendee	p. 主管的

II. Translate the following sentences into Chinese

1. The US-China Joint Commission on Commerce and Trade（JCCT）was established in 1983 as a forum for high-level dialogue on bilateral trade issues and a vehicle for promoting commercial relations.

2. The JCCT works to resolve problems affecting US companies and serves as an umbrella for trade events and World Trade Organization（WTO）technical assistance programs.

3. The Commission consists of three working groups covering trade and investment issues, business development and industrial cooperation, and commercial law, as well as a side dialogue on export controls.

4. The Trade and Investment Working Group（T & IWG）covers issues related to market access, trade finance, and investment and business facilitation.

5. The US side also proposed strengthening and reinvigorating the T & I WG

mechanism by designating a coordinator on each side, regularizing meetings, and maintaining a direct line of communication between working group meetings.

6. The Business Development and Industrial Cooperation Working Group (BDICWG) promotes greater commercial cooperation on an industry sector basis.

7. Commercial Law Working Group (CLWG) works to improve commercial relations between the United States and China through discussion of legal issues of mutual interest.

8. The US raised several concerns including lack of transparency in Chinese regulatory practices, problems with the method of promulgation and content of measures regulating foreign law firms issued by China's Ministry of Justice, and the process of granting marketing approval for generic drugs.

9. The Bureau of Industry and Security (BIS) has generally used the regularized exchange of the JCCT forum to encourage more cooperation from MOFCOM on end-use checks for US strategic goods licensed to China.

10. The conference highlighted basic elements of US and Chinese export controls, regulations, and enforcement and was attended by 275 business and Chinese Government participants.

III. Cloze

The CLWG also sponsors the US-China Legal Exchange, a series of joint legal seminars that foster mutual understanding _____ the legal regimes governing trade and investment _____ both countries. The seminars offer US audiences the opportunity to learn _____ the legal reforms taking place in China and provide Chinese participants the chance to learn about US practices. _____ this program, the United States and China send delegations of legal experts to speak _____ topics of current interest. Both private sector and government attorneys have been featured _____ the seminars, which are open _____ government officials and academicians as well as the local business and legal communities. In December 2002, Vice Minister of Foreign Trade Long Yongtu led a delegation of Chinese legal experts to the United States _____ talk about the legal changes necessary for China to implement its WTO accession commitments. General Counsel Kassinger reciprocated, leading the most recent Legal Exchange delegation to China in November 2003 to discuss both recent developments _____ corporate governance practices in the United States as well as to discuss a variety _____ trade remedy measures used _____ safeguard fair trade between the United States _____ its trading partners, including China.

IV. Underline the important sentences in the text, which give you useful information

V. Retell or write down what you learn from the text in English or in Chinese

Unit Eight

Association of
Southeast Asian Nations

Overview

ASSOCIATION OF SOUTHEAST ASIAN NATIONS

ESTABLISHMENT

The Association of Southeast Asian Nations or ASEAN was established on 8 August 1967 in Bangkok by the five original Member Countries, namely, Indonesia, Malaysia, Philippines, Singapore, and Thailand. Brunei Darussalam joined on 8 January 1984, Vietnam on 28 July 1995, Lao PDR and Myanmar on 23 July 1997, and Cambodia on 30 April 1999.

The ASEAN region has a population of about 500 million, a total area of 4. 5 million square kilometers, a combined gross domestic product of almost US $ 700 billion, and a total trade of about US $ 850 billion.

OBJECTIVES

The ASEAN Declaration states that the aims and purposes of the Association are: (1) to accelerate economic growth, social progress and cultural development in the region and (2) to promote regional peace and stability through abiding respect for justice and the rule of law in the relationship among countries in the region and adherence to the principles of the United Nations Charter.

The ASEAN Vision 2020, adopted by the ASEAN Leaders on the 30th Anniversary of ASEAN, agreed on a shared vision of ASEAN as a concert of Southeast Asian nations, outward looking, living in peace, stability and prosperity, bonded together in partnership in dynamic development and in a community of caring societies.

In 2003, the ASEAN Leaders resolved that an ASEAN Community shall be established comprising three pillars, namely, ASEAN Security Community, ASEAN Economic Community and ASEAN Socio-Cultural Community.

FUNDAMENTAL PRINCIPLES

ASEAN Member Countries have adopted the following fundamental principles in their relations with one another, as contained in the Treaty of Amity and Cooperation in Southeast Asia (TAC):

 * mutual respect for the independence, sovereignty, equality, territorial integrity, and national identity of all nations;

 * the right of every State to lead its national existence free from external interference, subversion or coercion;

 * non-interference in the internal affairs of one another;

 * settlement of differences or disputes by peaceful manner;

 * renunciation of the threat or use of force; and

 * effective cooperation among themselves.

ASEAN SECURITY COMMUNITY

Through political dialogue and confidence building, no tension has escalated into armed confrontation among ASEAN Member Countries since its establishment more than three decades ago.

To build on what has been constructed over the years in the field of political and security cooperation, the ASEAN Leaders have agreed to establish the ASEAN Security Community (ASC). The ASC shall aim to ensure that countries in the region live at peace with one another and with the world in a just, democratic and harmonious environment.

The members of the Community pledge to rely exclusively on peaceful processes in the settlement of intra-regional differences and regard their security as fundamentally linked to one another and bound by geographic location, common vision and objectives. It has the following components: political development; shaping and sharing of norms; conflict prevention; conflict resolution; post-conflict peace building; and implementing mechanisms. It will be built on the strong foundation of ASEAN processes, principles, agreements, and structures, which evolved over the years and are contained in the following major political agreements:

 * ASEAN Declaration, Bangkok, 8 August 1967;

 * Zone of Peace, Freedom and Neutrality Declaration, Kuala Lumpur, 27 November 1971;

 * Declaration of ASEAN Concord, Bali, 24 February 1976;

* Treaty of Amity and Cooperation in Southeast Asia, Bali, 24 February 1976;

* ASEAN Declaration on the South China Sea, Manila, 22 July 1992;

* Treaty on the Southeast Asia Nuclear Weapon—Free Zone, Bangkok, 15 December 1997;

* ASEAN Vision 2020, Kuala Lumpur, 15 December 1997; and

* Declaration of ASEAN Concord Ⅱ, Bali, 7 October 2003.

In recognition of security interdependence in the Asia-Pacific region, ASEAN established the ASEAN Regional Forum (ARF) in 1994. The ARF's agenda aims to evolve in three broad stages, namely the promotion of confidence building, development of preventive diplomacy and elaboration of approaches to conflicts.

The present participants in the ARF include: Australia, Brunei Darussalam, Cambodia, Canada, China, European Union, India, Indonesia, Japan, Democratic Republic of Korea, Republic of Korea (ROK), Lao PDR, Malaysia, Mongolia, Myanmar, New Zealand, Pakistan, Papua New Guinea, the Philippines, the Russian Federation, Singapore, Thailand, the United States, and Viet Nam.

The ARF discusses major regional security issues in the region, including the relationship amongst the major powers, non-proliferation, counter-terrorism, transnational crime, South China Sea and the Korean Peninsula, among others.

ASEAN ECONOMIC COMMUNITY

The ASEAN Economic Community shall be the end-goal of economic integration measures as outlined in the ASEAN Vision 2020. Its goal is to create a stable, prosperous and highly competitive ASEAN economic region in which there is a free flow of goods, services, investment and a freer flow of capital, equitable economic development and reduced poverty and socio-economic disparities in year 2020.

The ASEAN Economic Community shall establish ASEAN as a single market and production base, turning the diversity that characterises the region into opportunities for business complementation and making the ASEAN a more dynamic and stronger segment of the global supply chain. ASEAN's strategy shall consist of the integration of ASEAN and enhancing ASEAN's economic competitiveness.

In moving towards the ASEAN Economic Community, ASEAN has agreed on the following:

* institute new mechanisms and measures to strengthen the implementation of its existing economic initiatives including the ASEAN Free Trade Area (AFTA), ASEAN Framework Agreement on Services (AFAS) and ASEAN Investment Area (AIA);

* accelerate regional integration in the following priority sectors by 2010: air travel, agro-based products, automotives, e-commerce, electronics, fisheries, healthcare, rubber-based products, textiles and apparels, tourism, and wood-based products.

* facilitate movement of business persons, skilled labour and talents; and

* strengthen the institutional mechanisms of ASEAN, including the improvement of the existing ASEAN Dispute Settlement Mechanism to ensure expeditious and legally-binding resolution of any economic disputes.

Launched in 1992, the ASEAN Free Trade Area (AFTA) is now in place. It aims to promote the region's competitive advantage as a single production unit. The elimination of tariff and non-tariff barriers among Member Countries is expected to promote greater economic efficiency, productivity, and competitiveness.

As of 1 January 2005, tariffs on almost 99 percent of the products in the Inclusion List of the ASEAN-6 (Brunei Darussalam, Indonesia, Malaysia, the Philippines, Singapore, and Thailand) have been reduced to no more than 5 percent. More than 60 percent of these products have zero tariffs. The average tariff for ASEAN-6 has been brought down from more than 12 percent when AFTA started to 2 percent today. For the newer Member Countries, namely, Cambodia, Lao PDR, Myanmar, and Viet Nam (CLMV), tariffs on about 81 percent of their Inclusion List have been brought down to within the 0-5 percent range.

Other major integration-related economic activities of ASEAN include the following:

* Roadmap for Financial and Monetary Integration of ASEAN in four areas, namely, capital market development, capital account liberalisation, liberalisation of financial services and currency cooperation;

* trans-ASEAN transportation network consisting of major inter-state highway and railway networks, including the Singapore to Kunming Rail-Link, principal ports, and sea lanes for maritime traffic, inland waterway transport, and major civil aviation links;

* Roadmap for Integration of Air Travel Sector;

* interoperability and interconnectivity of national telecommunications equipment and services, including the ASEAN Telecommunications Regulators Council Sectoral Mutual Recognition Arrangement (ATRC-MRA) on Conformity Assessment for Telecommunications Equipment;

* trans-ASEAN energy networks, which consist of the ASEAN Power Grid and the Trans-ASEAN Gas Pipeline Projects;

∗ Initiative for ASEAN Integration (IAI) focusing on infrastructure, human resource development, information and communications technology, and regional economic integration primarily in the CLMV countries;

∗ Visit ASEAN Campaign and the private sector-led ASEAN Hip-Hop Pass to promote intra-ASEAN tourism; and

∗ Agreement on the ASEAN Food Security Reserve.

ASEAN SOCIO-CULTURAL COMMUNITY

The ASEAN Socio-Cultural Community, in consonance with the goal set by ASEAN Vision 2020, envisages a Southeast Asia bonded together in partnership as a community of caring societies and founded on a common regional identity.

The Community shall foster cooperation in social development aimed at raising the standard of living of disadvantaged groups and the rural population, and shall seek the active involvement of all sectors of society, in particular women, youth, and local communities.

ASEAN shall ensure that its work force shall be prepared for, and benefit from, economic integration by investing more resources for basic and higher education, training, science and technology development, job creation, and social protection.

ASEAN shall further intensify cooperation in the area of public health, including in the prevention and control of infectious and communicable diseases.

The development and enhancement of human resources is a key strategy for employment generation, alleviating poverty and socio-economic disparities, and ensuring economic growth with equity.

Among the on-going activities of ASEAN in this area include the following:

∗ ASEAN Work Programme for Social Welfare, Family, and Population;

∗ ASEAN Work Programme on HIV/AIDS;

∗ ASEAN Work Programme on Community-Based Care for the Elderly;

∗ ASEAN Occupational Safety and Health Network;

∗ ASEAN Work Programme on Preparing ASEAN Youth for Sustainable Employment and Other Challenges of Globalisation;

∗ ASEAN University Network (AUN) promoting collaboration among seventeen member universities ASEAN;

∗ ASEAN Students Exchange Programme, Youth Cultural Forum, and the ASEAN Young Speakers Forum;

∗ The Annual ASEAN Culture Week, ASEAN Youth Camp and ASEAN Quiz;

* ASEAN Media Exchange Programme; and

* Framework for Environmentally Sustainable Cities (ESC) and ASEAN Agreement on Transboundary Haze Pollution.

EXTERNAL RELATIONS

The ASEAN Vision 2020 affirmed an outward-looking ASEAN playing a pivotal role in the international community and advancing ASEAN's common interests.

Building on the Joint Statement on East Asia Cooperation of 1999, cooperation between the Southeast and Northeast Asian countries has accelerated with the holding of an annual summit among the leaders of ASEAN, China, Japan, and the Republic of Korea (ROK) within the ASEAN Plus Three process.

ASEAN Plus Three relations continue to expand and deepen in the areas of security dialogue and cooperation, transnational crime, trade and investment, environment, finance and monetary, agriculture and forestry, energy, tourism, health, labour, culture and the arts, science and technology, information and communication technology, social welfare and development, youth, and rural development and poverty eradication. There are now thirteen ministerial-level meetings under the ASEAN Plus Three process.

Bilateral trading arrangements have been or are being forged between ASEAN Member Countries and China, Japan, and the ROK. These arrangements will serve as the building blocks of an East Asian Free Trade Area as a long term goal.

ASEAN continues to develop cooperative relations with its Dialogue Partners, namely, Australia, Canada, China, the European Union, India, Japan, the ROK, New Zealand, the Russian Federation, the United States of America, and the United Nations Development Programme. ASEAN also promotes cooperation with Pakistan in some areas of mutual interest.

Consistent with its resolve to enhance cooperation with other developing regions, ASEAN maintains contact with other inter-governmental organisations, namely, the Economic Cooperation Organisation, the Gulf Cooperation Council, the Rio Group, the South Asian Association for Regional Cooperation, the South Pacific Forum, and through the recently established Asian-African Sub-Regional Organisation Conference.

Most ASEAN Member Countries also participate actively in the activities of the Asia-Pacific Economic Cooperation (APEC), the Asia-Europe Meeting (ASEM), and the East Asia-Latin America Forum (EALAF).

STRUCTURES AND MECHANISMS

The highest decision-making organ of ASEAN is the Meeting of the ASEAN Heads of State and Government. The ASEAN Summit is convened every year. The ASEAN Ministerial Meeting (Foreign Ministers) is held annually.

Ministerial meetings on the following sectors are also held regularly: agriculture and forestry, economics (trade), energy, environment, finance, health, information, investment, labour, law, regional haze, rural development and poverty alleviation, science and technology, social welfare, telecommunications, transnational crime, transportation, tourism, youth. Supporting these ministerial bodies are committees of senior officials, technical working groups and task forces.

To support the conduct of ASEAN's external relations, ASEAN has established committees composed of heads of diplomatic missions in the following capitals: Beijing, Berlin, Brussels, Canberra, Geneva, Islamabad, London, Moscow, New Delhi, New York, Ottawa, Paris, Riyadh, Seoul, Tokyo, Washington D. C. and Wellington.

The Secretary-General of ASEAN is appointed on merit and accorded ministerial status. The Secretary-General of ASEAN, who has a five-year term, is mandated to initiate, advise, coordinate, and implement ASEAN activities. The members of the professional staff of the ASEAN Secretariat are appointed on the principle of open recruitment and region-wide competition.

ASEAN has several specialized bodies and arrangements promoting inter-governmental cooperation in various fields including the following: ASEAN Agricultural Development Planning Centre, ASEAN-EC Management Centre, ASEAN Centre for Energy, ASEAN Earthquake Information Centre, ASEAN Foundation, ASEAN Poultry Research and Training Centre, ASEAN Regional Centre for Biodiversity Conservation, ASEAN Rural Youth Development Centre, ASEAN Specialized Meteorological Centre, ASEAN Timber Technology Centre, ASEAN Tourism Information Centre, and the ASEAN University Network.

In addition, ASEAN promotes dialogue and consultations with professional and business organisations with related aims and purposes, such as the ASEAN-Chambers of Commerce and Industry, ASEAN Business Forum, ASEAN Tourism Association, ASEAN Council on Petroleum, ASEAN Ports Association, Federation of ASEAN Shipowners, ASEAN Confederation of Employers, ASEAN Fisheries Federation, ASEAN Vegetable Oils Club, ASEAN Intellectual Property Association, and the ASEAN-Institutes for Strategic and International Studies. Furthermore, there are 58 Non-

Governmental Organizations（NGOs）, which have formal affiliations with ASEAN.
(*Source*：http：//www. aseansec. org)

Notes

[1] Brunei Darussalam 文莱达鲁萨兰

[2] Lao PDR 老挝人民民主共和国

[3] Myanmar 缅甸

[4] accelerate 加速，促进

[5] concert 一致，协调

[6] pillar 支柱

[7] amity 友好，亲善关系

[8] national identity of all nations 各国的民族特性

[9] national existence 保持其民族生存的权利

[10] subversion 颠覆

[11] coercion 强迫,高压政治

[12] renunciation 放弃

[13] equitable 公平的

[14] disparity 不同，差距

[15] complementation 互补

[16] institute 建立

[17] implementation 实施

[18] apparels 衣服

[19] institutional 公共机构的

[20] expeditious 迅速的

[21] elimination 消除

[22] inclusion 包含

[23] sea lane 航线

[24] interoperability 互用性,协同工作的能力

[25] interconnectivity 互接

[26] grid 网，格子

[27] pivotal 关键的，起中心作用的

[28] eradication 根除

[29] the ROK（the Republic of Korea）大韩民国

［30］ the Rio Group 里约集团

［31］ ASEAN Free Trade Area（AFTA）东盟自由贸易区

［32］ CLMV countries（Cambodia, Lao PDR, Myanmar, and Viet Nam）柬埔寨、老挝、
缅甸、越南

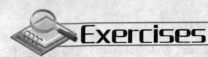 Exercises

Ⅰ. **Match the following words in Column A and Column B**

Column A	Column B
1. concert	a. 民族特性
2. pillar	b. 颠覆
3. amity	c. 包含
4. national identity	d. 起中心作用的
5. national existence	e. 友好，亲善关系
6. subversion	f. 互补
7. coercion	g. 一致，协调
8. renunciation	h. 民族生存的权利
9. disparity	i. 实施
10. complementation	j. 不同，差距
11. implementation	k. 消除
12. expeditious	l. 强迫
13. elimination	m. 互接
14. inclusion	n. 根除
15. interoperability	o. 放弃
16. interconnectivity	p. 迅速的
17. pivotal	q. 支柱
18. eradication	r. 互用性

Ⅱ. **Translate the following sentences into Chinese**

1. The ASEAN region has a population of about 500 million, a total area of 4. 5 million square kilometers, a combined gross domestic product of almost US $ 700 billion, and a total trade of about US $ 850 billion.

2. The ASEAN Declaration states that the aims and purposes of the Association are: (1) to accelerate economic growth, social progress and cultural development in the region and (2) to promote regional peace and stability through abiding respect for justice and the rule of law in the relationship among countries in the region and adherence to the principles of the United Nations Charter.

3. The ASEAN Economic Community shall be the end-goal of economic integration measures as outlined in the ASEAN Vision 2020. Its goal is to create a stable,

prosperous and highly competitive ASEAN economic region in which there is a free flow of goods, services, investment and a freer flow of capital, equitable economic development and reduced poverty and socio-economic disparities in year 2020.

4. The ASEAN Economic Community shall establish ASEAN as a single market and production base, turning the diversity that characterises the region into opportunities for business complementation and making the ASEAN a more dynamic and stronger segment of the global supply chain.

5. The Community shall foster cooperation in social development aimed at raising the standard of living of disadvantaged groups and the rural population, and shall seek the active involvement of all sectors of society, in particular women, youth, and local communities.

6. ASEAN shall ensure that its work force shall be prepared for, and benefit from, economic integration by investing more resources for basic and higher education, training, science and technology development, job creation, and social protection.

7. The development and enhancement of human resources is a key strategy for employment generation, alleviating poverty and socio-economic disparities, and ensuring economic growth with equity.

8. Building on the Joint Statement on East Asia Cooperation of 1999, cooperation between the Southeast and Northeast Asian countries has accelerated with the holding of an annual summit among the leaders of ASEAN, China, Japan, and the Republic of Korea (ROK) within the ASEAN Plus Three process.

9. ASEAN Plus Three relations continue to expand and deepen in the areas of security dialogue and cooperation, transnational crime, trade and investment, environment, finance and monetary, agriculture and forestry, energy, tourism, health, labour, culture and the arts, science and technology, information and communication technology, social welfare and development, youth, and rural development and poverty eradication.

10. Bilateral trading arrangements have been or are being forged between ASEAN Member Countries and China, Japan, and the ROK. These arrangements will serve as the building blocks of an East Asian Free Trade Area as a long term goal.

III. Cloze

ASEAN's strategy shall consist of the integration _____ ASEAN and enhancing ASEAN's economic competitiveness.

In moving towards the ASEAN Economic Community, ASEAN has agreed _____ the following:

* institute new mechanisms and measures _____ strengthen the implementation _____ its existing economic initiatives including the ASEAN Free Trade Area (AFTA), ASEAN Framework Agreement on Services (AFAS) and ASEAN Investment Area (AIA);

* accelerate regional integration _____ the following priority sectors _____ 2010: air travel, agro-based products, automotives, e-commerce, electronics, fisheries, healthcare, rubber-based products, textiles and apparels, tourism, and wood-based products.

* facilitate movement _____ business persons, skilled labour and talents; and

* strengthen the institutional mechanisms _____ ASEAN, including the improvement of the existing ASEAN Dispute Settlement Mechanism _____ ensure expeditious and legally-binding resolution _____ any economic disputes.

IV. Underline the important sentences in the text, which give you useful information

V. Retell or write down what you learn from the text in English or in Chinese

Unit Nine

Declaration of the Beijing Summit of the Forum on China-Africa Co-operation

Declaration of the Beijing Summit of the Forum on China-Africa Co-operation

We, the heads of state and (or) government of the People's Republic of China and 48 African countries, met in Beijing from 4th to 5th November 2006 for the Summit of the Forum on China-Africa Co-operation.

We applaud the summit held on the occasion of the 50th anniversary of the inauguration of diplomatic relations between the People's Republic of China and African countries.

For the purpose of promoting "friendship, peace, co-operation and development," we have reviewed the sincere friendship, solidarity and co-operation between China and Africa over the past half century, discussed the common goals and direction for growing China-Africa co-operation in the new era, and decided to enhance the role of the Forum.

We hold that the world today is undergoing complex and profound changes, and that the pursuit of peace, development and co-operation has become the trend of the times.

We call for the development of friendly relations and co-operation among countries in accordance with the UN Charter, the Five Principles of Peaceful Co-existence and other generally recognized norms governing international relations.

We propose to enhance South-South co-operation and North-South dialogue to promote balanced, co-ordinated and sustainable development of the global economy to enable all countries to share its benefits and realize common development and prosperity.

We hold that the United Nations should strengthen its role through reforms, pay greater attention to the issue of development and give priority to increasing the representation and say of African countries in UN agencies.

China reaffirms its support for African countries in their efforts to strengthen themselves through unity and independently resolve African problems, its support for African regional and sub-regional organizations in their efforts to promote economic integration and its support for African countries in implementing the "New Partnership for African Development" programmes.

We call on the international community to encourage and support Africa's efforts to pursue peace and development. In particular, we urge developed countries to increase official development assistance and honour their commitment to opening markets and debt relief to enhance Africa's capacity in poverty and disaster reduction and prevention and control of desertification, and help Africa realize the UN Millennium Development Goals.

We hold that the adherence of China, the world's largest developing country, to peaceful development and the commitment of Africa, a continent with the largest number of developing countries, to stability, development and renaissance, are in themselves significant contributions to world peace and development.

African countries are greatly inspired by China's rapid economic development and extend congratulations to China. They reiterated that they adhere to the one-China policy and support China's peaceful reunification.

China and Africa enjoy traditional solidarity and co-operation and China-Africa friendship enjoys immense popularity.

We hereby solemnly proclaim the establishment of a new type of strategic partnership between China and Africa featuring political equality and mutual trust, economic win-win co-operation and cultural exchanges. For this purpose, we will:

- Increase high-level visits, conduct strategic dialogue and enhance mutual political trust.
- Deepen and broaden mutually beneficial co-operation and give top priority to co-operation in agriculture, infrastructure, industry, fishing, IT, public health and personnel training to draw on each other's strengths.
- Increase exchange of views on governance and development to learn from each other.
- Increase dialogue between different cultures and promote people-to-people exchanges, particularly those between the young people.
- Enhance international co-operation.
- Enhance the Forum on China-Africa Co-operation.
- Properly handle issues and challenges that may arise in the course of co-operation in keeping with China-Africa friendship and the long-term interests of the two sides.

We hold that the establishment of a new type of strategic partnership is the shared desire of China and Africa, serves our common interests, and will help enhance solidarity and mutual assistance among developing countries and contribute to lasting peace and harmonious development in the world. (*Source*: *China Daily*, *Nov.* 6. 2006 *p.* 3)

Notes

[1] inauguration 开启

[2] solidarity 团结

[3] undergo 遭受,经历

[4] the UN Charter《联合国宪章》

[5] the Five Principles of Peaceful Co-existence 和平共处五项原则

[6] norm 准则,基准,标准

[7] priority 优先,优先权

[8] say 意见,发言权

[9] integration 综合,集成,整合,一体化

[10] New Partnership for African Development 非洲发展新伙伴计划

[11] official development assistance 官方发展援助

[12] honour their commitment 履行其义务

[13] the UN Millennium Development Goals 联合国千年发展目标

[14] renaissance 振兴,复兴,文艺复兴

[15] draw on 吸收,利用

 **Exercises**

I. Match the following words in Column A and Column B

Column A	Column B
a. strategic dialogue	1. 义务
b. political trust	2. 宪章
c. norm	3. 准则
d. solidarity	4. 复兴
e. charter	5. 团结
f. say	6. 意见,发言权
g. integration	7. 政治互信
h. development assistance	8. 发展援助
i. commitment	9. 一体化,整合
j. renaissance	10. 战略对话

II. Translate the following sentences into Chinese

1. We have reviewed the sincere friendship, solidarity and co-operation between China and Africa over the past half century, discussed the common goals and direction for growing China-Africa co-operation in the new era, and decided to enhance the role of the Forum.

2. We call for the development of friendly relations and co-operation among countries in accordance with the UN Charter, the Five Principles of Peaceful Co-existence and other generally recognized norms governing international relations.

3. We propose to enhance South-South co-operation and North-South dialogue to promote balanced, co-ordinated and sustainable development of the global economy to enable all countries to share its benefits and realize common development and prosperity.

4. We hold that the United Nations should strengthen its role through reforms, pay greater attention to the issue of development and give priority to increasing the representation and say of African countries in UN agencies.

5. China reaffirms its support for African countries in their efforts to strengthen themselves through unity and independently resolve African problems, its support for African regional and sub-regional organizations in their efforts to promote economic integration and its support for African countries in implementing the "New Partnership for African Development" programmes.

6. In particular, we urge developed countries to increase official development assistance and honour their commitment to opening markets and debt relief to enhance Africa's capacity in poverty and disaster reduction and prevention and control of desertification, and help Africa realize the UN Millennium Development Goals.

7. We hold that the adherence of China, the world's largest developing country, to peaceful development and the commitment of Africa, a continent with the largest number of developing countries, to stability, development and renaissance, are in themselves significant contributions to world peace and development.

8. African countries are greatly inspired by China's rapid economic development and extend congratulations to China. They reiterated that they adhere to the one-China policy and support China's peaceful reunification.

9. We hereby solemnly proclaim the establishment of a new type of strategic partnership between China and Africa featuring political equality and mutual trust, economic win-win co-operation and cultural exchanges.

10. We hold that the establishment of a new type of strategic partnership is the shared desire of China and Africa, serves our common interests, and will help enhance solidarity and mutual assistance among developing countries and contribute to lasting peace and harmonious development in the world.

III. Cloze

We hereby solemnly proclaim the establishment _____ a new type of strategic partnership _____ China and Africa featuring political equality and mutual trust, economic win-win co-operation and cultural exchanges. _____ this purpose, we will:

- ■ Deepen and broaden mutually beneficial co-operation and give top priority _____ co-operation _____ agriculture, infrastructure, industry, fishing, IT, public health and personnel training _____ draw _____ each other's strengths.

- ■ Increase exchange of views _____ governance and development to learn _____ each other.

- ■ Enhance the Forum _____ China-Africa Co-operation.

IV. Underline the important sentences in the text, which give you useful information

V. Retell or write down what you learn from the text in English or in Chinese

参考译文

《中非合作论坛北京峰会宣言》

中华人民共和国和 48 个非洲国家的国家元首、政府首脑和代表团团长于 2006 年 11 月 4 日至 5 日在北京举行中非合作论坛峰会。

我们高度评价在中华人民共和国同非洲国家建交 50 周年之际举行的此次峰会。

我们本着"友谊、和平、合作、发展"的宗旨,回顾了半个世纪以来中非之间的真挚友谊和团结合作,探讨了新世纪中非合作的共同目标和发展方向,决心进一步发挥中非合作论坛的作用。

我们认为,当前国际形势正经历着复杂、深刻的变化,求和平、促发展、谋合作已经成为时代的潮流。

我们主张根据联合国宪章与和平共处五项原则以及其他被普遍认同的支配国际关系的准则发展友好合作关系。

我们主张加强南南合作和南北对话,推动全球经济均衡、协调和可持续发展,实现各国共享成果、普遍发展、共同繁荣。

我们主张通过改革加强联合国作用,更加重视发展问题,优先增加非洲国家在联合国各机构的代表性和充分参与。

中国重申支持非洲国家联合自强,自主解决非洲问题,支持非洲地区组织和次地区组织推动经济一体化的努力,支持非洲国家实施"非洲发展新伙伴计划"。

我们呼吁国际社会鼓励并支持非洲谋求和平与发展的努力,特别呼吁发达国家增加官方发展援助,切实兑现开放市场和减免债务等承诺,增强非洲脱贫、减灾、防治荒漠化的能力,帮助非洲实现联合国千年发展目标。

我们认为,中国作为世界上最大的发展中国家坚持走和平发展道路,非洲作为发展中国家最集中的大陆致力于稳定、发展和振兴,是对世界和平与发展事业的重大贡献。

非洲国家对中国经济快速发展深感鼓舞并表示祝贺;重申坚持一个中国立场,支持中国和平统一大业。

我们认为,中非之间有着良好的团结与合作传统,中非友谊深入人心。

在此,我们郑重宣示,中非建立政治上平等互信、经济上合作共赢、文化上交流互鉴的新型战略伙伴关系;并为此:

加强高层交往,开展战略对话,增进政治互信;

加强互利合作,拓展合作领域,重点加强在农业、基础设施建设、工业、渔业、信息

技术、医疗卫生和人力资源培训等领域合作,实现优势互补;

加强治国理政和发展经验的交流和借鉴;

加强人文对话,促进人民之间特别是青年一代的联系;

加强国际合作;

促进中非合作论坛建设;

从中非友好大局和双方长远利益出发,妥善处理合作中出现的新课题、新挑战。

我们认为,建立新型战略伙伴关系是中非双方的共同愿望,符合双方利益,有利于增进发展中国家的团结互助,也有利于促进世界的持久和平与和谐发展。(根据2006年11月6日《中国日报》第三版翻译)

Unit Ten

Declaration on Fifth Anniversary of Shanghai Cooperation Organisation

Declaration on Fifth Anniversary of Shanghai Cooperation Organisation
(Shanghai, 15 June 2006)

On the occasion of the fifth anniversary of the establishment of the Shanghai Cooperation Organisation (hereinafter referred to as the SCO), the heads of SCO member states—President Nursultan Nazarbaev of the Republic of Kazakhstan, President Hu Jintao of the People's Republic of China, President Kurmanbek Bakiev of the Kyrgyz Republic, President Vladimir Putin of the Russian Federation, President Emomali Rakhmonov of the Republic of Tajikistan and President Islam Karimov of the Republic of Uzbekistan—met in Shanghai, the SCO's birthplace, and stated as follows:

I

The SCO was founded in Shanghai five years ago pursuant to a strategic decision made by its member states to meet challenges and threats of the twenty-first century and bring about durable peace and sustainable development of the region. This decision, which ushered in a new historical phase of regional cooperation, is of great importance to the establishment and maintenance of peace and stability and the creation of an inclusive environment for cooperation in the SCO region.

With volatile changes taking place in the international and regional environment, the SCO has become an important mechanism for deepening good-neighborly cooperation, friendship and partnership among its members. It is a good example of dialogue among civilizations and an active force for promoting democracy in international relations.

II

Through its endeavour over the past few years, the SCO has laid a solid foundation for its steady and sustained growth and gained extensive international recognition.

1. The SCO has completed building of institution and legal framework, which

ensures its effective functioning.

2. It has carried out close security cooperation focusing on addressing non-traditional security threats and challenges such as fighting terrorism, separatism, extremism and drug trafficking.

3. It has adopted a long-term plan, set direction for regional economic cooperation and identified the goal, priority areas and major tasks of economic cooperation among member states. It has set up the SCO Business Council and the Interbank Association.

4. Following the principles of openness, non-alliance and not targeting at any third party, it has actively engaged in dialogue, exchange and cooperation of various forms with countries and international organisations that, like the SCO, are ready to carry out cooperation on an equal and constructive basis with mutual respect to safeguard regional peace, security and stability.

The SCO owes its smooth growth to its consistent adherence to the "Spirit of Shanghai" based on "mutual trust, mutual benefit, equality, consultations, respect for the diversity of cultures and aspiration towards common development". This spirit is the underlying philosophy and the most important code of conduct of the SCO. It enriches the theory and practice of contemporary international relations and embodies the shared aspiration of the international community for realising democracy in international relations. The "Spirit of Shanghai" is therefore of critical importance to the international community's pursuit of a new and non-confrontational model of international relations, a model that calls for discarding the Cold War mentality and transcending ideological differences.

The SCO will remain dedicated to the purposes and principles established at its founding and strengthened in the documents, declarations and statements adopted thereafter.

III

The world and international relations today are going through unprecedented and profound changes. There is increasing trend toward multipolarisation and economic globalisation amid twists and turns. The establishment of a new international order in the twenty-first century is a slow and uneven process. Interdependence among countries is growing. The international community faces favourable opportunities for ensuring stability, peace and common development, but is also confronted with complicated traditional and non-traditional security challenges and threats.

The SCO is committed to enhancing strategic stability, strengthening the international regime of non-proliferation of weapons of mass destruction and upholding order in international law, and will contribute its share to accomplishing these important missions.

The SCO holds that the United Nations, being the universal and the most representative and authoritative international organisation, is entrusted with primary responsibility in international affairs and is at the core of formulating and implementing the basic norms of international law. The United Nations should improve efficiency and strengthen its capacity for responding to new threats and challenges by carrying out proper and necessary reforms in light of the changing international environment. In carrying out Security Council reform, the principles of equitable geographical distribution and seeking the broadest consensus should be observed. No time limit should be set for the reform, nor should a vote be forced on any proposal over which there are major differences. The SCO holds that the next Secretary-General of the United Nations should come from Asia.

Threats and challenges can be effectively met only when there is broad cooperation among all countries and international organisations concerned. What specific means and mechanism should be adopted to safeguard security of the region is the right and responsibility of countries in the region.

The SCO will make a constructive contribution to the establishment of a new global security architecture of mutual trust, mutual benefit, equality and mutual respect. Such architecture is based on the widely recognised principles of international law. It discards "double standards" and seeks to settle disputes through negotiation on the basis of mutual understanding. It respects the right of all countries to safeguard national unity and their national interests, pursue particular models of development and formulate domestic and foreign policies independently and participate in international affairs on an equal basis.

Diversity of cultures and model of development must be respected and upheld. Differences in cultural traditions, political and social systems, values and model of development formed in the course of history should not be taken as pretexts to interfere in other countries' internal affairs. Model of social development should not be "exported". Differences in civilisations should be respected, and exchanges among civilisations should be conducted on an equal basis to draw on each other's strengths and enhance harmonious development.

IV

There is general stability in the Central Asia. Countries in this region have achieved historic success in political and economic reforms and social development. The unique historical and cultural traditions of Central Asian nations deserve respect and understanding of the international community. The governments of Central Asian countries should be supported in their efforts to safeguard security and stability, maintain social and economic development and improve people's livelihood.

SCO member states will continue to tap the potential of the Organisation, enhance its role and work to turn this region into one that is peaceful, coordinated in development, open, prosperous and harmonious.

SCO member states will remain friends from generation to generation and will never be enemies against one another. They are committed to the all-round growth of good-neighborly relations of mutual respect and mutually beneficial cooperation. They support each other in their principled positions on and efforts in safeguarding sovereignty, security and territorial integrity. They will not join any alliance or international organisation that undermines the sovereignty, security and territorial integrity of SCO member states. They do not allow their territories to be used to undermine the sovereignty, security or territorial integrity of other member states, and they prohibit activities by organisations or gangs in their territories that are detrimental to the interests of other member states. To this end, SCO member states will conduct, within the SCO framework, consultation on the conclusion of a multilateral legal document of long-term good-neighborly relations, friendship and cooperation.

SCO member states will continue to strengthen coordination and cooperation in international and regional affairs and take a common position on matters involving the SCO's interests.

The SCO has the potential to play an independent role in safeguarding stability and security in this region. In case of emergencies that threaten regional peace, stability and security, SCO member states will have immediate consultation on effectively responding to the emergency to fully protect the interests of both the SCO and its member states. Study will be made on the possibility of establishing a regional conflict prevention mechanism within the SCO framework.

To comprehensively deepen cooperation in combating terrorism, separatism, extremism and drug trafficking is a priority area for the SCO. The SCO will take steps to strengthen the regional anti-terrorism agency and carry out cooperation with relevant international organisations.

To expand economic cooperation among them, SCO member states need to coordinate their efforts in implementing the Programme of Multilateral Trade and Economic Cooperation among SCO Member States by carrying out major priority projects of regional economic cooperation. They need to work together to promote trade and investment facilitation and gradually realise the free flow of commodities, capital, services and technologies.

The SCO welcomes participation by relevant partners in specific projects in priority areas like energy, transportation, information and communications and agriculture. The SCO will endeavour to actively participate in international campaigns against communicable diseases and contribute to environmental protection and rational use of natural resources.

To strengthen and expand the social foundation for friendship and mutual understanding among SCO member states is an important way to ensure the SCO's resilience and vitality. To this end, SCO member states need to institutionalise bilateral and multilateral cooperation in culture, arts, education, sports, tourism and media. With the unique and rich cultural heritage of its member states, the SCO can surely serve as a model in promoting dialogue among civilisations and building a harmonious world.

This Declaration is issued on the occasion of the 5th anniversary of the SCO. We, heads of SCO member states, are firm in the belief that the SCO will fully realise the noble objective and mission declared at its establishment and contribute to the cause of peace, cooperation and development. (*Source*: *http*://*www. sectsco. org*)

Notes

[1] occasion 场合，时机，机会
[2] anniversary 周年纪念
[3] usher 引导，招待
[4] inclusive 包含的，包括的
[5] volatile 可变的，不稳定的
[6] civilization 文明，文化，文明国家的总称
[7] function 发挥职能
[8] trafficking 交易，做买卖，运输
[9] non-alliance 不结盟
[10] adherence 依附，坚持
[11] consultation 协商
[12] diversity 差异，多样性
[13] aspiration 热望，志向，渴望
[14] underlying 在下面的

[15] philosophy 哲理，基本原理，哲学，人生观

[16] embody 具体表达，使具体化

[17] non-confrontational 非对抗

[18] discard 抛弃，放弃

[19] mentality 心态

[20] transcending 超越

[21] ideological 意识形态的

[22] dedicated 专注的，献身的

[23] unprecedented 空前的，无前例的

[24] multipolarisation 多极化

[25] twist 曲折，螺旋状

[26] uneven 不平坦的，不均等的

[27] confronted 使面对，对抗，遭遇

[28] non-proliferation 不扩散，不激增

[29] mission 使命，任务

[30] distribution 地域分配

[31] consensus 合意，一致，同感

[32] Secretary-General 秘书长

[33] dispute 纠纷，争端，争议

[34] pretext 借口，托词

[35] deserve 应得，值得

[36] livelihood 生计，营生，生活

[37] sovereignty 主权，独立国

[38] territorial integrity 领土完整

[39] alliance 同盟，联盟

[40] undermines 渐渐破坏，暗地里破坏

[41] detrimental 有害的

[42] facilitation 便利化

[43] communicable 有传染性的

[44] rational 理性的，合理的

[45] resilience 有弹力，恢复力

[46] vitality 活力，生命力

[47] heritage 遗产，祖先遗留物，继承物

[48] cause 原因，目标

Exercises

I . Match the following words in Column A and Column B

Column A	Column B
1. diversity	a. 便利化
2. aspiration	b. 地域分配
3. facilitation	c. 心态
4. unprecedented	d. 文明，文化，文明国家的总称
5. anniversary	e. 发挥职能
6. civilization	f. 哲理，基本原理，哲学，人生观
7. function	g. 合意，一致，同感
8. trafficking	h. 不扩散，不激增
9. non-alliance	i. 协商
10. consultations	j. 周年纪念
11. philosophy	k. 交易，做买卖，运输
12. non-confrontational	l. 差异，多样性
13. mentality	m. 热望，志向，渴望
14. distribution	n. 领土完整
15. consensus	o. 生计，营生，生活
16. Secretary-General	p. 空前的，无前例的
17. territorial integrity	q. 原因，目标
18. pretext	r. 使命，任务
19. livelihood	s. 不结盟
20. vitality	t. 活力，生命力
21. heritage	u. 借口，托词
22. cause	v. 遗产，祖先遗留物，继承物
23. multipolarisation	w. 多极化
24. sovereignty	x. 非对抗
25. non-proliferation	y. 秘书长
26. mission	z. 主权，独立国

II . Translate the following sentences into Chinese

1. This decision, which ushered in a new historical phase of regional cooperation, is of great importance to the establishment and maintenance of peace and stability

and the creation of an inclusive environment for cooperation in the SCO region.

2. It is a good example of dialogue among civilizations and an active force for promoting democracy in international relations.

3. Following the principles of openness, non-alliance and not targeting at any third party, it has actively engaged in dialogue, exchange and cooperation of various forms with countries and international organisations that, like the SCO, are ready to carry out cooperation on an equal and constructive basis with mutual respect to safeguard regional peace, security and stability.

4. The SCO owes its smooth growth to its consistent adherence to the "Spirit of Shanghai" based on "mutual trust, mutual benefit, equality, consultations, respect for the diversity of cultures and aspiration towards common development".

5. It enriches the theory and practice of contemporary international relations and embodies the shared aspiration of the international community for realising democracy in international relations.

6. The "Spirit of Shanghai" is therefore of critical importance to the international community's pursuit of a new and non-confrontational model of international relations, a model that calls for discarding the Cold War mentality and transcending ideological differences.

7. The world and international relations today are going through unprecedented and profound changes. There is increasing trend toward multipolarisation and economic globalisation amid twists and turns.

8. The SCO holds that the United Nations, being the universal and the most representative and authoritative international organisation, is entrusted with primary responsibility in international affairs and is at the core of formulating and implementing the basic norms of international law.

9. Diversity of cultures and model of development must be respected and upheld. Differences in cultural traditions, political and social systems, values and model of development formed in the course of history should not be taken as pretexts to interfere in other countries' internal affairs.

10. Differences in civilisations should be respected, and exchanges among civilisations should be conducted on an equal basis to draw on each other's strengths and enhance harmonious development.

III. Cloze

To expand economic cooperation _____ them, SCO member states need to coordinate their efforts _____ implementing the Programme of Multilateral Trade and Economic Cooperation among SCO Member States _____ carrying out major priority projects of regional economic cooperation. They need to work together _____ promote trade and investment facilitation and gradually realise the free flow _____ commodities, capital, services and technologies.

The SCO welcomes participation _____ relevant partners in specific projects _____ priority areas like energy, transportation, information and communications and agriculture. The SCO will endeavour to actively participate in international campaigns _____ communicable diseases and contribute to environmental protection and rational use _____ natural resources.

To strengthen and expand the social foundation for friendship and mutual understanding among SCO member states is an important way to ensure the SCO's resilience and vitality. To this end, SCO member states need to institutionalise bilateral and multilateral cooperation _____ culture, arts, education, sports, tourism and media. _____ the unique and rich cultural heritage of its member states, the SCO can surely serve _____ a model in promoting dialogue among civilisations and building a harmonious world.

IV. Underline the important sentences in the text, which give you useful information

V. Retell or write down what you learn from the text in English or in Chinese

参考译文

上海合作组织五周年宣言

值此上海合作组织（以下简称"本组织"）成立五周年之际，本组织成员国元首——哈萨克斯坦共和国总统纳扎尔巴耶夫、中华人民共和国主席胡锦涛、吉尔吉斯斯坦共和国总统巴基耶夫、俄罗斯联邦总统普京、塔吉克斯坦共和国总统拉赫莫诺夫、乌兹别克斯坦共和国总统卡里莫夫在本组织诞生地——上海举行会议，声明如下：

一、本组织五年前在上海宣告成立，是所有成员国基于 21 世纪的挑战和威胁，为实现本地区的持久和平与可持续发展而作出的战略抉择。这一决定推动地区合作迈入新的历史阶段，对于本组织所在地区建立和保持和平与稳定，建设合作和开放的环境具有重要意义。

在国际和地区局势风云变幻的情况下，本组织已成为成员国深化睦邻友好合作和伙伴关系的重要机制，开展文明对话的典范，是推动国际关系民主化的积极力量。

二、过去几年的工作为本组织稳定和持续发展奠定了坚实基础，已得到国际社会的广泛认同。

第一，顺利完成了机制和法律建设任务，确保本组织有效发挥职能。

第二，展开安全领域的密切合作，中心任务是打击恐怖主义、分裂主义、极端主义和非法贩运毒品，应对非传统威胁与挑战。

第三，制定了区域经济合作长期计划和方向，明确了成员国经济合作的目标、优先方向和首要任务，建立了实业家委员会和银行联合体。

第四，奉行对外开放、不针对第三方和不结盟原则，积极与像本组织一样愿在平等、相互尊重和建设性基础上进行合作的国家和国际组织开展多种形式的对话、交流与合作，以维护地区和平、安全与稳定。

本组织顺利发展，在于它一直遵循"互信、互利、平等、协商，尊重多样文明，谋求共同发展"的"上海精神"。作为本组织一个完整的基本理念和最重要的行为准则，它丰富了当代国际关系的理论和实践，体现了国际社会对实现国际关系民主化的普遍要求。"上海精神"对国际社会寻求新型的、非对抗性的国际关系模式具有非常重要的意义，这种模式要求摒弃冷战思维，超越意识形态差异。

本组织将毫不动摇地坚持成立之初确立的、并在通过的文件、宣言和声明中得到巩固的宗旨及原则。

三、当今世界形势和国际关系经历着前所未有的深刻变化。世界多极化和经济全球化的趋势在曲折中向前发展,建立 21 世纪国际新秩序是一个缓慢而曲折的进程,各国相互联系与依存日益加深。国际社会拥有实现稳定、和平和普遍发展的良好机遇,也面临着一系列复杂的传统和非传统安全挑战和威胁。

本组织一贯主张加强战略稳定和不扩散大规模杀伤性武器的国际体系,支持维护国际法秩序,将为实现上述重大任务作出自己的贡献。

本组织认为,联合国是世界上最具普遍性、代表性和权威性的国际组织,被赋予在国际事务中发挥主导作用的责任,成为制定和执行国际法基本准则的核心。联合国应根据世界形势变化进行合理、必要的改革,以提高效率,增强应对新威胁和新挑战的能力。安理会的改革,应遵循公平地域分配原则和最广泛协商一致的原则,不应为改革设立时限或强行推动表决尚有重大分歧的方案。本组织主张,下届联合国秘书长应来自亚洲。

只有所有相关国家和国际组织开展广泛合作,才能有效应对挑战和威胁,而确定维护地区安全的具体方式和机制,是该地区国家的权利和责任。

本组织将为建立互信、互利、平等、相互尊重的新型全球安全架构作出建设性贡献。此架构基于公认的国际法准则,摒弃"双重标准",在互谅基础上通过谈判解决争端,尊重各国维护国家统一和保障民族利益的权利,尊重各国独立自主选择发展道路和制定内外政策的权利,尊重各国平等参与国际事务的权利。

必须尊重和保持世界文明及发展道路的多样性。历史形成的文化传统、政治社会体制、价值观和发展道路的差异不应被用于干涉他国内政的借口。社会发展的具体模式不能成为"输出品"。应互相尊重文明差异,各种文明应平等交流,取长补短,和谐发展。

四、中亚地区形势总体保持稳定。各国在政治经济改革和社会发展领域取得了历史性成就。中亚国家拥有独特的历史文化传统,应得到国际社会的尊重和理解。应支持中亚国家政府为维护安全与稳定、保持社会经济发展及不断改善人民生活所作的努力。

将继续挖掘本组织潜力,加强本组织作用,为促进成员国合作,建立和平、协作、开放、繁荣与和谐的地区作出积极贡献。

成员国将世代友好,永不为敌,将全面发展睦邻友好、互相尊重和互利合作的关系,相互支持维护国家主权、安全和领土完整的原则立场和努力,不参加损害成员国主权、安全和领土完整的联盟或国际组织,不允许利用其领土损害其他成员国主权、安全和领土完整,禁止损害其他成员国利益的组织或团伙在本国领土活动。为此,成员国将协商缔结本组织框架内长期睦邻友好合作多边法律文件的问题。

成员国将一如既往地就国际和地区事务加强协调与合作,就涉及本组织利益的问题形成共同立场。

本组织拥有在本地区维护稳定与安全方面发挥独立作用的潜力。当出现威胁地区和平、稳定与安全的紧急事件时,成员国将立即联系并就共同有效应对进行磋商,以最大限度地维护本组织和成员国的利益。将研究在本组织框架内建立预防地区冲突机制的可能性。

全面加强联合打击恐怖主义、分裂主义和极端主义及非法贩运毒品行为的力度是本组织的优先方向。本组织将采取措施,以加强地区反恐机构的管理并与相关国际机构开展合作。

为进一步扩大经济合作,需协调成员国通过实施区域经济合作重大优先项目而落实《上海合作组织成员国多边经贸合作纲要》所作的努力,协调各方推进贸易和投资便利化,逐步实现商品、资本、服务和技术的自由流动。

本组织欢迎有关伙伴参与能源、交通运输、信息通信、农业等优先领域的具体项目。本组织将尽己所能,积极参与防治传染病的国际行动,为环境保护和合理利用自然资源作出贡献。

巩固和扩大成员国友好和相互理解的社会基础,是确保本组织持久生命力的重要手段。为此,需要将文化艺术、教育、体育、旅游、传媒等领域双边和多边合作机制化。鉴于成员国拥有独特、丰富的文化遗产,本组织在促进文明对话、建立和谐世界方面,完全可以发挥促进和示范作用。

值此本组织成立五周年之际发表此宣言,我们,成员国元首深信,本组织将更加有效地致力于实现其创建时宣告的崇高目标和任务,为和平、合作和发展事业作出贡献。

Unit Eleven

Deepening Economic Interdependency
between China and Japan
and Challenges for the Future

Deepening Economic Interdependency between China and Japan and Challenges for the Future

Keynote Address by Osamu Watanabe, Chairman and CEO of JETRO

at the Symposium on Japan-China Business Alliance in Beijing

on June 8th, 2006

1. Introduction

Let me first express my gratitude from the bottom of my heart to Mr. Lu Kejian, Honorable Director-General of the Department of Asian Affairs in the Ministry of Commerce. Thank you very much for taking time out of your busy schedule to join us today and for giving us your heartfelt greeting.

I would also like to thank Mr. Yu Ping, Honorable Vice-Chairman of the China Council for the Promotion of International Trade (CCPIT), for your all-out support in helping us organize today's symposium.

Finally, I'd like to thank everyone in the audience for coming and extend special thanks to the people, on both the Japan and China sides, who worked so hard to make this event a reality: without your help we would not have been able to hold this follow-up seminar to last year's "Japan-China Business Alliance Symposium", also held here in Beijing.

Today's symposium, held under the theme of "Japan-China Business Alliances in the Era of Economic Interdependency in East Asia", will feature a keynote speech by Dr. Li Xiaoxi, Director of the Institute of Economic and Resource Management, Beijing Normal University. There will also be a panel discussion involving representatives from companies and research institutes from both Japan and China, who will share their views on ways the two countries can build closer economic ties and cooperation.

I will begin by sharing my personal views on East Asia's economic integration and the roles Japan and China are expected to play in the region.

2. The Japanese economy

After more than a decade of sluggish growth, the Japanese economy is firmly on the road to recovery. Companies are again focusing on profitability, after completing years of restructuring efforts to eliminate past excesses of capacity, employment and debt.

Japan is back. Corporate profits increased for the fourth straight year in 2005; and I expect the economy will remain strong, even surpassing, this November, Japan's longest postwar economic expansion of 57 months (from 1965 to 1970).

This strong economic turnaround owes much to restructuring efforts made in both the public and private sectors over the past decade. But there is another important factor: the steady growth of economic relations between Japan and China.

Between 2001 and 2005, Japan's exports to China grew by 2.5 times. During this time, firms in iron & steel, non-ferrous metal and construction machinery saw their businesses turn around. This is one way in which increased exports to China have helped Japan's economic recovery.

3. Deepening Economic Interdependency between Japan and China

Japan-China trade has been growing in tandem with growth in Japanese investment in China, suggesting that the complementary economic relationship between the two countries has also been deepening. In one example, Japan's IT and audio-visual machinery firms have been increasingly shifting their production bases into China; with this has come increased local procurement of parts and materials by these firms.

In turn, however, Japan's exports to China have slowed somewhat. But a growing number of finished products made in China by Japanese firms, such as personal computers, are sold on the Japan market. This is further proof that the economic relationship between the two countries is becoming increasingly complimentary.

Japan's trade with China reached a record of US $ 190 billion in 2005, when Japan's exports to and imports from China had marked growth for the seventh straight year. China is now Japan's largest import source and second largest export destination.

Japanese investment in China also grew last year, led mainly by auto industries. And while investment in China by manufacturers from other countries has been declining, Japanese investment in the country has marked record growth for the last three years in a row.

Japan's big three automakers (namely, Toyota, Nissan and Honda) all have production bases in Guangzhou; this is something that no single area in Japan can boast!

Last April's anti-Japan demonstrations in China came as a shock to the Japanese people—and also firms, who grew cautious about investing in China afterwards. But a year on, firms were gradually regaining their confidence in doing business in the country.

Japanese investment in China in 2005 was 2.2 times what it was in 1999, totaling some US $53 billion. The number of Japanese firms registered in China in 2005 stood at around 20,000.

A Chinese government survey revealed that Japanese firms in the country employed some 9.2 million workers (both directly and indirectly) in 2004, and that firms paid 49 billion *yuan* in taxes to the government—or 12% of China's total corporate taxes collected.

Leaders of Chinese provinces and cities are eager to visit Japan to attract more Japanese firms to their regions, knowing well how such investment can benefit their economies.

Here it is important not to overlook that Japan's growing investment in China has also boosted transfer of advanced Japanese technologies to China. For instance, Japan was the second largest provider of such technology in 2005. And on a contract basis, Japan accounts for 20% of China's technology transfers from abroad.

But when I visit China, I sometimes hear people say that Japanese firms are indeed investing in the country—but they are not transferring their technology in the process. But such transfer of technology is happening, and it is bringing the two countries closer.

A JETRO survey conducted last year revealed that more than 70% of Japanese firms operating in China made a profit and have plans to expand their business operations in the country.

One of the biggest concerns facing Japan today is a declining birthrate combined with an ageing population. To counter this, Japan has to grow together with China and the rest of East Asia.

Last year, an American economist friend of mine said to me that, since Japan has entered the era of an aged society and its population is declining, its capital accumulation will slow down and that the country's GDP will start to shrink. He said that with the declining population, Japan would barely be able to maintain its per capita GDP.

In response, I admitted that, yes, Japan's population and capital accumulation were shrinking, but I explained how the country can overcome these challenges by leading with innovation and improving productivity.

Given its size, Japan cannot receive immigrants like the US, I said. Instead, Japan has to go out and make use of the young, capable and abundant human resources available elsewhere in East Asia, namely ASEAN and China.

The distance between Japan and Bangkok is almost the same as that between New York and Los Angeles, I said. If you think of the whole of East Asia as one single economic sphere, the production factors of East Asia stand at almost the same level as those of the United States. I finished by saying that Japan, utilizing the pool of talented young workers in East Asia, can indeed grow as the region as a whole grows.

He was impressed with this explanation, saying that this is what lies in the creation of an East Asia community.

I may have exaggerated a little, but I see bright prospects for the Japanese economy. Japan in the 21st century will grow stronger together with East Asia, and economic interdependency between Japan and China will be further deepened.

4. Challenges for China and Japan's Cooperation

China's economy is growing at a tremendous pace, while transforming itself into a market economy. But the country faces a number of key challenges.

Firstly, China must deal with the growing disparity (between the rich and the poor and between coastal and inland provinces).

China is facing a huge income gap between its urban and rural/agricultural areas, which was pointed out in the government's "11th Five Year Plan for National Economic and Social Development". In the plan, the central government placed the highest priority on building a "new socialist countryside", with the aim of curbing growing disparities and addressing China's three farm-related problems.

Regarding the farm-related problems, China must continue shifting population from rural areas to cities. Urban development and job creation are imperative to facilitate this population flow. And to create new employment, labor-intensive industries must be promoted.

My suggestion here is to encourage Japanese small and medium-sized enterprises (SMEs) seeking low cost/high quality labor to invest in China, provided China's investment climate is favorable for them. The SMEs will bring with them their advanced technologies—the same technologies that make Japanese industry competitive. And this technology will invariably contribute to strengthening China's industrial base.

Secondly, China must deal with issues associated with natural resources, energy and the environment. Over a period of more than 20 years since 1978—the year China adopted a policy of reform and opening-up to the outside world—the country's economy has grown steadily and its GDP quadrupled.

Through the tireless efforts of the Chinese people, the country has successfully built a "wen bao" society, where everyone is adequately fed and clothed. The country is now working towards the next step—to build a "xiaokang", or "well-off" society. For this to happen, the Chinese government estimates that the country's GDP must again quadruple in size (from its level in 2000).

But the Chinese economy is structurally very energy-consuming: its energy consumption per unit GDP is about nine times that of Japan and 3.3 times that of the US. With continued global energy shortages and rising world energy prices—as well as continued environmental destruction in China (including air, river and soil pollution), China will have a difficult time expanding its GDP by this amount, while at the same time overcoming these energy and environmental problems.

The effects of China's rapid rise—namely insatiable energy consumption and environmental destruction—have serious consequences not just for China but for the whole planet. Taking this into consideration, the Chinese government included in its "11th Five Year Plan" the goal of reducing its energy consumption per unit of GDP by around 20%. I think this is move in the right direction, but I think there is still considerable room for China to do more towards becoming an energy efficient and environmentally-friendly country.

Japan can share with China its wisdom of tackling environmental issues. In the 1960s and 70s, during Japan's rapid growth, the country experienced very serious environmental problems and energy crises of its own. To overcome these issues, Japan's public and private sectors joined hands to implement strict energy-saving and environment-friendly measures, and worked to shift Japan's industrial structure towards a more energy-efficient one. The country also worked to raise awareness among Japanese people of the need for and benefits of an energy-saving/energy-friendly lifestyle.

During this period, I was working at the Ministry of International Trade and Industry (now METI) to help address these issues. I can say that through Japan's efforts during this difficult time, Japan today boasts some of the world's most advanced, energy-efficient and environment-friendly technologies.

I strongly hope that this experience and knowledge can be shared with China, and that Japan's advanced environment-related technologies can be transferred to China to help the country develop. I also hope that, in the future, the two countries play an important role in helping the world to address global environmental issues.

5. Challenges in Building Stronger Japan-China Business Alliances

I think Japan-China business alliances can hold a key in helping to address the two issues facing China that I just mentioned. But for the two countries to work in true harmony, several challenges must be worked out *together*.

The first challenge relates to concluding a bilateral investment agreement.

A JETRO survey revealed that a majority of Japanese firms operating in China cited a lack of transparency in China's investment environment, including unclear administrative procedures, arbitrary application of legal and economic systems as well as a lack of harmony in these systems between central and regional governments.

For Japanese FDI in China to continue to grow, a bilateral investment agreement needs to be put in place to ensure transparency in the country's investment environment. We know there is some cautious concern on the Chinese side about concluding such an agreement, but thinking of future technological cooperation between both countries, I suggest that both parties take a forward-looking approach.

The second issue regards intellectual property (IP) protection. Since its accession to WTO, China has been working hard to improve its legal systems concerning this important area. I am here again as a co-leader of Japan's government—private sector joint mission on IP protection and have been deeply impressed by the sincere attitudes of Chinese officials in addressing IP issues.

I am fully aware of the difficulty they face in enforcing laws in such a vast and populous country. But China must ensure effective enforcement without delay, or risk losing out on gaining international credibility and acquiring technologies from foreign companies. Relevant parties from China and Japan have been discussing and implementing measures to improve IP enforcement, such as holding joint seminars; this sort of cooperation, the mission pledged, would continue in the years to come. Through their efforts to date, Chinese authorities have improved greatly; it seems to me the rest is just a matter of speed.

6. Towards Creating an East Asia Free Business Zone

As I mentioned, amid increasing economic interdependency between Japan and China, there are challenges the two countries should jointly work out. Through bilateral cooperation, the two countries are expected to contribute not only to their further development of two countries, but also to the development of East Asia as a whole.

East Asia has been drawing the world's attention as an economic growth center.

East Asia is quickening its pace of de facto integration, and the move in the region is now toward concluding free trade agreements (FTAs) and economic partnership agreements (EPAs). This is giving government-level form to this integration and keeping country borders from hindering regional integration.

ASEAN is leading this move. Currently, ASEAN is negotiating five FTAs with its partners in the region, namely: China, Japan, Korea, India and Australia/New Zealand—all of which are expected to be in place by the end of 2007. In December of last year, the first East Asia Summit was held in Kuala Lumpur to discuss the creation of an East Asian community, which gave a further boost to the region's integration. I am confident that by 2015 there will be an East Asia free business zone covering the five "ASEAN Plus One" FTAs.

While Japan represents 60% of East Asia's total GDP, China accounts for 20%. The two countries—which together account for such a large portion of the region's economy—must join hands to facilitate the creation of an East Asia free business zone and work towards sustained growth and stability for the whole region.

7. JETRO's Roles

Now I would like to talk about four of JETRO's efforts—amid this increasing economic interdependency between the two countries—aimed at accelerating China-Japan business alliances and promoting bilateral cooperation towards the creation of the free business zone I just mentioned.

Firstly, JETRO continues to support the efforts of Japanese firms, mainly SMEs, seeking to expand their business into China. JETRO's offices in China also give wide support to firms already in China, advising them on issues concerning local regulations, labor and legal matters, taxation and IP protection.

Information gathered through such activities is communicated to relevant Chinese organizations and government bureaus, which then use the information to improve local administrative procedures.

Secondly, JETRO operates Invest Japan Business Support Centers (IBSCs) in Japan, which help foreign firms, including those from China, enter Japan's markets.

Located in major metropolitan areas, including Tokyo, Osaka, Yokohama, Nagoya, Kobe and Fukuoka, IBSCs serve as one-stop resources for firms interested in setting up business in Japan. Companies can take advantage of the IBSC's vast resources and use private office space free for up to two months. The Tokyo IBSC alone has some 36 offices.

The Chinese government is encouraging Chinese companies to invest overseas. I hope many Chinese companies will advance into the Japanese market and actively utilize the IBSCs, building win-win business partnerships along the way.

The third area in which JETRO can play a role is by helping foster Japan-China business alliances and collaborations.

This past March, JETRO, together with CCPIT and the Korea Trade Investment Promotion Agency (KOTRA), and in cooperation with China's Ministry of Commerce, held the China—Japan—Korea Industrial Fair 2006 in Qingdao.

The fair was comprised of three parts: an exhibition, a symposium and industrial tour for missions visiting the country. The exhibition was a success, with nearly 600 exhibitors from China, Japan and Korea; the total number of attendees and visitors to the fair (Industrial Fair) exceeded 15,000. CCPIT, KOTRA and JETRO have agreed to hold a similar event in Korea next June and one in Japan in 2008.

JETRO, together with relevant organizations and associations, also holds the Japan-China Economic Conference every autumn in Osaka, bringing together key Chinese entrepreneurs and Japanese firms interested in doing business in China's fast-growing economy. Some 330 representatives from over 200 Japanese firms and 170 representatives from 120 Chinese firms took part in last year's conference.

A business-matching event is held concurrently with the event, which, in the past years, has led to quite a number of successful business deals. I cordially invite Chinese firms and interested parties to take part in this year's conference, which will take place on November 16th and 17th.

Fourthly, the JETRO Institute of Developing Economies (IDE) and Chinese research institutes continue to work together to conduct joint studies.

IDE conducts comprehensive research on issues concerning developing countries and regions; the institute's findings and reports are highly valued.

IDE is currently conducting a joint study with the Chinese Academy of Social Sciences (CASS) to examine ways to promote trade and investment that will benefit the whole of East Asia.

There are many other areas in which IDE and Chinese research institutes can conduct joint studies; for example, on topics such as energy conservation and natural resources. By sharing study findings with business communities and the governments of both countries, JETRO hopes to contribute to helping Japan and China build a win-win relationship.

8. Closing

In closing, I would like to talk about the future of the Japan-China relationship.

Despite the many important roles expected of both countries, present relations between the two countries are less than good. But it is not uncommon for two neighboring countries, especially major ones, to have differing views and outstanding issues. I believe that Japan and China should make every effort to improve and develop bilateral relations through active exchange on public and private levels, and seek to resolve differences in opinions through finding common ground.

Last week, Mr. Bo Xilai, China's commerce minister, visited Japan to join a Japan-China joint symposium on energy conservation and environmental protection, which was co-hosted by Japan's Economy, Trade and Industry Minister Mr. Toshihiro Nikai and was attended by a number of Chinese delegates and representatives from leading Japanese firms. The event—which featured a symposium and tours of hybrid car factories, wind-power plants and other energy-efficient facilities and technologies—was considered a success.

Japan and China share the same boat, so to speak, and the two countries need to row together towards a better future.

I see bright prospects for the future of the Japan-China relationship. I have this optimism because I strongly believe that frank and candid dialogue will pave the way for true mutual understanding.

Thank you very much.

Supplementary:

JETRO, or the Japan External Trade Organization, is a government-related organization that works to promote mutual trade and investment between Japan and the rest of the world. Originally established in 1958 to promote Japanese exports abroad, JETRO's core focus in the 21st century has shifted toward promoting foreign direct investment into Japan and helping small to medium sized Japanese firms maximize their global export potential. (*Source*: *http://www. jetro. go. jp*)

Notes

[1] interdependency 互相依赖

[2] Japan External Trade Organization(JETRO)日本贸易振兴机构

[3] symposium 讨论会

[4] alliance 联合,联盟

[5] honorable 可敬的

[6] keynote speech 主旨演讲

[7] economic integration 经济一体化

[8] excess of capacity 产能过剩

[9] turnaround 突然好转,转向

[10] in tandem with 同……合作, 与……串联

[11] complementary economic relationship 互补的经济关系

[12] local procurement 就地采购

[13] automaker 汽车制造商

[14] demonstration 游行

[15] capital accumulation 资本积累

[16] shrink 收缩

[17] exaggerate 夸大

[18] tremendous 巨大的

[19] new socialist countryside 社会主义新农村

[20] China's three farm-related problems 中国的三农问题

[21] small and medium-sized enterprises (SMEs) 中小企业

[22] quadruple 使成四倍

[23] insatiable 不知足的

[24] 11th Five Year Plan "十一五"计划

[25] de facto 事实上的, 实际的

[26] free trade agreements (FTAs) 自由贸易安排

[27] economic partnership agreements (EPAs) 经济伙伴协议

[28] common ground 共同点

Exercises

I. Match the following words in Column A and Column B

Column A	Column B
1. interdependency	a. 经济伙伴协议
2. JETRO	b. 突然好转
3. SMEs	c. 互相依赖
4. EPAs	d. 产能过剩
5. symposium	e. 中小企业
6. alliance	f. 日本贸易振兴机构
7. keynote speech	g. 共同点
8. economic integration	h. 互补的经济关系
9. excess of capacity	i. 汽车制造商
10. turnaround	j. 联合,联盟
11. complementary economic relationship	k. 就地采购
12. local procurement	l. 讨论会
13. automaker	m. 主旨演讲
14. capital accumulation	n. 资本积累
15. China's three farm-related problems	o. 经济一体化
16. common ground	p. 中国的三农问题

II. Translate the following sentences into Chinese

1. Japan's trade with China reached a record of US $190 billion in 2005, when Japan's exports to and imports from China had marked growth for the seventh straight year. China is now Japan's largest import source and second largest export destination.

2. A Chinese government survey revealed that Japanese firms in the country employed some 9.2 million workers (both directly and indirectly) in 2004, and that firms paid 49 billion yuan in taxes to the government—or 12% of China's total corporate taxes collected.

3. The distance between Japan and Bangkok is almost the same as that between New York and Los Angeles, I said. If you think of the whole of East Asia as one single economic sphere, the production factors of East Asia stand at almost the same level as those of the United States. I finished by saying that Japan, utilizing

the pool of talented young workers in East Asia, can indeed grow as the region as a whole grows.

4. The Chinese economy is structurally very energy consuming: its energy consumption per unit GDP is about nine times that of Japan and 3.3 times that of the US. With continued global energy shortages and rising world energy prices— as well as continued environmental destruction in China (including air, river and soil pollution), China will have a difficult time expanding its GDP by this amount, while at the same time overcoming these energy and environmental problems.

5. Japan can share with China its wisdom of tackling environmental issues. In the 1960s and 70s, during Japan's rapid growth, the country experienced very serious environmental problems and energy crises of its own. To overcome these issues, Japan's public and private sectors joined hands to implement strict energy-saving and environment-friendly measures, and worked to shift Japan's industrial structure towards a more energy-efficient one.

6. A JETRO survey revealed that a majority of Japanese firms operating in China cited a lack of transparency in China's investment environment, including unclear administrative procedures, arbitrary application of legal and economic systems as well as a lack of harmony in these systems between central and regional governments.

7. I am fully aware of the difficulty they face in enforcing laws in such a vast and populous country. But China must ensure effective enforcement without delay, or risk losing out on gaining international credibility and acquiring technologies from foreign companies.

8. While Japan represents 60% of East Asia's total GDP, China accounts for 20%. The two countries—which together account for such a large portion of the region's economy—must join hands to facilitate the creation of an East Asia free business zone and work towards sustained growth and stability for the whole region.

9. JETRO continues to support the efforts of Japanese firms, mainly SMEs, seeking to expand their business into China. JETRO's offices in China also give wide support to firms already in China, advising them on issues concerning local regulations, labor and legal matters, taxation and IP protection.

10. JETRO operates Invest Japan Business Support Centers (IBSCs) in Japan, which help foreign firms, including those from China, enter Japan's markets.

Located in major metropolitan areas, including Tokyo, Osaka, Yokohama, Nagoya, Kobe and Fukuoka, IBSCs serve as one-stop resources for firms interested in setting up business in Japan.

III. Cloze

The fair was comprised _____ three parts: an exhibition, a symposium and industrial tour for missions visiting the country. The exhibition was a success, _____ nearly 600 exhibitors from China, Japan and Korea; the total number of attendees and visitors _____ the fair (Industrial Fair) exceeded 15,000. CCPIT, KOTRA and JETRO have agreed to hold a similar event in Korea next June and one in Japan in 2008.

JETRO, together with relevant organizations and associations, also holds the Japan-China Economic Conference every autumn in Osaka, bringing _____ key Chinese entrepreneurs and Japanese firms interested _____ doing business in China's fast-growing economy. Some 330 representatives from _____ 200 Japanese firms and 170 representatives _____ 120 Chinese firms took part in last year's conference.

A business-matching event is held concurrently _____ the event, which, in the past years, has led to quite a number _____ successful business deals. I cordially invite Chinese firms and interested parties _____ take part in this year's conference, which will take place on November 16th and 17th.

IV. Underline the important sentences in the text, which give you useful information

V. Retell or write down what you learn from the text in English or in Chinese

Unit Twelve

Investor's Guidebook to Russia

Economy on the Rebound

Over the time that elaspsed since 1991, Russia's economy has drastically changed. Obvious positive results, connected with the changeover to market principles for the economy's organization, were accompanied by some considerable drawbacks. At the early stage of the reforms, as a result of the decline in industrial production, the national economy had significantly "lost in weight". Adding to that was also curtailment of the production of armaments that constituted the backbone of the Soviet planned economy, along with the influx to the domestic consumer market of cheaper and higher quality imported goods that posed serious competition to the local manufacturing industry.

Nonetheless, today the Russian economy demonstrates enviable growth rates. Suffice it to mention the constant growth of GDP. In 2005 the GDP growth rate was 6.4%. Hence, the welfare of the population is growing and the living standards are rising. There is yet another feature of Russia's economic development worth mentioning. The years of socio-economic changes have formed a new stratum of modern managers that have embraced European business practices, a factor not to be overlooked by the private investors interested in efficient management of their capitals.

Gross Domestic Product

Starting in 2000 the country has witnessed the highest growth rates of its economy over the last 35 years. According to government projections, in 2006 GDP will increase by 6.6%, in 2007 by 6.0%, and in 2008 by 5.8%. However, even these relatively high by-world-standards growth rates are still lower than they were in the not-so-distant past (in 2003 and 2004, the GDP grew at 7% each year). Many economists believe this process is quite natural insomuch as the far-reaching structural changes presently underway in the Russian economy have led not only to the rapid growth in certain sectors and in manufacturing, but simultaneously to curtailment of unprofitable production assets

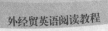

in a number of industries inherited from the inefficient Soviet economy.

Growth of Industrial Production

The pace of the industrial production growth over recent years has slowed down as well, which is a fact the analysts also attribute to the ongoing structural reforms. For example, in 1999 and 2000 Russian manufacturing grew by more than 11% per year, in 2001 it increased by 4.9%, and in 2002 by 3.1%. In 2003, however, the growth recovered to 7.3% and 6.1% in 2004. In 2005 industrial growth again plummeted to 4%, but in the first half of 2006, it grew to 4.4%.

Budget

The favorable situation in the world energy market has enabled Russia to not only ensure a significant growth of the country's revenue into the budget, but to make the budget with a surplus. In 2004 revenues exceeded expenditures by RUB 3.4 trillion and in 2005 the surplus was already RUB 5.0 trillion; the figures for 2006 are expected to be approximately RUB 6.2 trillion. With the budget revenues going up, so are the budget expenses, albeit not that fast: 2004—RUB 2.7 trillion; 2005—approximately RUB 3.5 trillion; 2006—RUB 4.3 trillion. The surplus enabled the Ministry of Finance to create, out of primarily excess profits from high oil prices, a Stabilization Fund. It is these funds that Russia uses for the early repayment of its foreign debts. For instance, in January 2005 the debt to IMF was fully discharged, and in August 2006, repayment was completed of almost the entire sum of foreign debt to the Paris Club in the amount of US $23.8 billion.

The 2007 budget has been drafted. Here are some of its figures: budget revenues are planned at RUB 6.97 trillion and expenditures at RUB 5.46 trillion, respectively, i.e. a budget surplus of RUB 1.5 trillion (or 4.8% of GDP) is planned provided Urals prices are US $61.0 per barrel of oil on average. The government assumes that in 2007 inflation will be in the area of 6.5% to 8.0%, while an average annual ruble rate will be RUB 26.5 for one US dollar. The Stabilization Fund will also grow to reach presumably RUB 2.5 trillion by the end of 2006. In 2006, for the first time ever, special funds have been earmarked for the implementation (with the participation of private capital) of projects of paramount importance. In 2007, the amount of this investment fund is planned to be RUB 110.6 billion.

The 2007 budget stands out by its scale of social expenditures growth. Allocations for education are planned at RUB 277.7 billion, for culture at RUB 64.1 billion, for healthcare and sports at RUB 205.4 billion, and for social policy at RUB 212.0 billion. The so-called interbudgetary transfers (i. e. revenues allocated from the federal budget to the regional budgets for the implementation of social projects) will amount to RUB 0.8 trillion.

National Projects: Investments in Human Capital

In September 2005, the President of Russia Vladimir Putin promulgated four national priority programs combined under the common principle—investments in human capital—that deal with education, healthcare, housing, and agriculture. A considerable increase of salaries in education and healthcare along with affordable terms of home loans (although they may hardly be called the chief priorities and the most capital-intensive objectives under the new nationwide projects) will cost the state RUB 180 billion in 2006. But these are the so-called "short-term" objectives which will be followed by qualitative changes in the above mentioned areas.

Plans are to improve the existing system of education and ensure the training of skilled specialists meeting the present day requirements for the national economy. In the next two years, additional funds will be allocated for the acquisition of laboratory equipment and software by universities and schools that actively implement innovative educational programs. These funds are also earmarked for the upgrade of classrooms and teachers' training. It is planned that in the period from 2006 through 2008 compensation of qualified scientific personnel will be RUB 30,000 per month on average. At least 5,000 individual grants for schoolchildren, students, and young specialists will be issued to support young talents. Incomes of teachers will also increase accordingly. It is planned that all these initiatives will be conducive to the improvement of the general level of education, giving young talented people an opportunity to meet their aspirations at home in Russia—effectively stemming the drain of intelligence and talent sought after worldwide.

Equally massive investments are planned for the upgrade and modernization of medical institutions: in the next two years over 10,000 municipal outpatient clinics (of which over two-thirds are in rural areas), a significant number of regional in-patient clinics, and paramedical posts will receive diagnostic equipment; the fleet of ambulance cars will be significantly replaced. Starting in 2006 salaries of district physicians, pediatricians, and general practice doctors and nurses will be raised.

Significant funds from the budgets of all levels will be allocated for the solution to housing problems. Fulfillment of this program is associated primarily with the growth of housing construction, the modernization of utilities infrastructure, and the development of mortgaging. The state does not limit its participation in this area by the development of a regulatory base for the issue of mortgage securities or the mechanisms to finance home loans. Budget funds and serious government guarantees have been used to significantly increase the charter capital of the Mortgage and Housing Lending Agency enabling provision of home loans to the population at lower interest rates.

Finally, priority will be given to the program of rural areas' support. It is planned that agricultural enterprises are given real access to debt financing while additional funds will be allocated from the federal budget to subsidize bank interest rates. Special benefits will be due for those entities that will engage in the construction of and investment in the upgrade of stock breeding farms. It is proposed that import duties for stock breeding technological equipment be abolished, provided these have no internally produced equivalents. For the purposes of developing the human capital potential in agriculture, money has been earmarked to build houses for young professionals coming to work in the rural areas.

All of the above four national projects have been adopted and their financing at least for 2006 is ensured by budget revenues, while the government and Central Bank of the Russian Federation have prepared a package of measures to hold down inflation in connection with these huge investments.

Inflation

The extremely thrifty spending of the Stabilization Fund has not only been prompted by the desire to improve Russia's image in the eyes of foreign partners (a fact that has undoubtedly been considered in granting Russia an investment-grade sovereign rating by leading rating agencies), but to deter the growth of monetary supply not supported by the corresponding production growth. Yet, the level of inflation has not so far met the expectations. The government planned to hold down inflation in 2005 at 10%, but it was 10.9% as of the year-end. Even though this figure is lower than for similar periods in the past years (2000—20%; 2001—18.6%; 2002—15.1%, 2003—12%; 2004—11.7%), it is still too high. The discrepancy between the actual and the planned figures is accounted for among other things by the ongoing economic reforms in Russia, for instance, in the utilities sector whereby tariffs there increased some 25%—30%. Nonetheless, the Government is confident that it in the coming years inflation growth rates will decrease, and in 2006 it will be about 9%, in 2007—6.5% to 8% and in 2008—4.5% to 6%. According to Alexei Kudrin, Minister of Finance, decreasing inflation will be high on the government's agenda in the next three years.

The Ruble Rate

The Central Bank of Russia pursues a well-balanced policy in establishing the exchange rate of the national currency. If the Russian ruble is significantly undervalued, inflation will increase; if it is overvalued, Russian goods will lose their competitiveness at the world market. Russia managed to restrain the sharp ruble fluctuations. For instance, the average annual dollar rate in 2000 was RUB 28.1; in 2001—RUB 29.2; in 2002—RUB 31.3; in 2003—RUB 30.7; in 2004—RUB 28.8 and in 2005—RUB 28.3. Analysts note the strengthening of the ruble's real effective exchange rate (REER). It is projected that in 2007 it will increase by 4.8%, in 2008—1.4%, and in 2009—1%.

Russia's Participation in World Trade

According to WTO data, Russia's share in world exports does not exceed 1.5%, and in imports, it does not exceed 0.7%, whereas Russia's participation in the global services trade is purely symbolic. Nonetheless, over the years of economic reforms, exports have become the largest sector of the economy, accounting for over one-fourth of GDP (in the former Soviet Union this figure did not exceed 10%). Twenty to 80% of the national production of basic commodities and semi-finished goods are bound for the world markets. It should be noted that qualitative indicators of exports do not resolve the task of raising competitiveness of the Russian-made products at the world markets so long as the structure of the Russian exports has an obvious energy and commodities leaning. The structure of exports is evident of the lopsided development of the Russian economy with high-tech industries still lagging behind.

The share of machinery and equipment in Russian exports was a mere 5.6% in 2005. The imports are dominated by consumer goods (primarily foodstuffs and raw materials for their production and household appliances), accounting for about one half of the total Russian imports.

Given the economic globalization, development of interstate trade and economic relations, and the international division of labor, Russia rivets an increasingly greater attention of foreign partners. The negotiations on Russia's accession to the WTO that have entered their final stage, along with the continued negotiations on the OECD membership, are indicative of such interest and the recognition of Russia as a market economy. Until recently, Russia has been regarded as a transitional economy for which it has not always been treated equally by the world business community.

Economic Reforms

A task of paramount importance for which the economic changes are being primarily introduced is the improvement of the economic structure and Russia's entry into the postindustrial era. First, the country is striving to end its "oil addiction", or more precisely the overdependence of the national economy and the budget on oil and gas exports that today account for nearly 60% of the country's earnings. Economists are concerned with the Dutch disease suffered by the Russian economy whereby excessive profits in the energy sector hamper development in other areas. And it is not that anyone is going to cut exports of oil and gas. Objectively, Russia will remain an energy donor in the years to come. It ranks first in the world by proven reserves of natural gas (48 trillioncum at the end of 2004, or 26.7% of the world's proven reserves of natural gas) and ranks seventh by its proven oil reserves (9.9 billion tons or 6.1% of the world's oil reserves). Currently, in Russia's bid to get the most mileage out of the favorable market situation, it exports even more oil that Saudi Arabia, but analysts believe that in the near future its share will fall to the current level of 9% to 4%—5%. It is true, though, that no cuts in the production and exports of natural gas are planned. According to the forecast of the World Energy Council, in 2020 Russia's share in the world production of natural gas will be 20%, and in world trade, 30%—35%. Russia will have to invest funds in the development of innovative technologies by drawing on its export capabilities in order to keep up with world economic trends.

The current reforms to overhaul the national economy in Russia pervade practically all sectors and industries. For instance, new antimonopoly legislation provides for the liberalization of market of shares of the Russian gas monopoly Gazprom, which its contributors think will encourage investments in its expansion and modernization while discouraging the monopoly from systematic price hikes. Transformation of another energy monopolist—RAO UES—will create competition at the electricity market which will be conducive to the industry's development and improve the consumer qualities of its products.

These reforms have been dragging for years, and they have made the government believe that it is impossible to reform only the largest corporations while leaving other sectors of the economy (and as it later transpired, government institutions and social relations) intact.

The tax reform resulted in the formalization of relations between the state and taxpayers and significant reduction of the tax burden.

As a result, there is not a single industry currently in Russia that does not undergo, to a greater or a lesser extent, reforms aiming at the creation of a qualitatively new economy. As not only been limited to the economy, as equally important changes are simultaneously made in the regulatory and judicial systems and location administration. These reforms will ultimately enable the creation of an administrative and legal basis for an investor-friendly environment for Russian and foreign businesses alike.

How to Invest

Forms and Types of Investment Activities

Russia mobilizes capital in the form of direct and portfolio investments, capital investment loans, and through the placement of bonds at international capital markets.

There are no restrictions for foreign investors in Russia from the viewpoint of legal form: their companies may be registered under any legal form stipulated in the legislation.

Those who may be foreign investors are the following: foreign legal entities including any company, firm, enterprise, organization, and association established and entitled to invest in accordance with the laws of the country of their residence; foreign citizens or individuals without citizenship; Russian citizens residing permanently abroad if they are duly registered in the country of citizenship or permanent residence; as well as foreign governments and international organizations.

Foreign investments in the Russian Federation may be made into any assets which are not proscribed in the legislation. These may include new and modernized capital and current assets in all sectors of the economy, securities, target deposits, high-tech goods, and other property rights.

Foreign investors are entitled to make investment in the Russian Federation in the form of:

Shares in ventures established jointly with Russian legal entities and citizens;

Establishment of ventures owned fully by foreign investors, as well as the establishment of branches of foreign legal entities;

Purchase of ventures, estates, buildings, constructions, shares in ventures, units of investment trusts, stocks, bonds, and other securities, as well as other assets which may be owned by foreign investors in accordance with the effective legislation (usually through auction, tender, competition, or purchase at the secondary market);

Purchase of the rights on the use of land plots and other natural resources (usually in the form of lease or the purchase of constructions on a land plot allocated thereto or the acquisition of a Russian venture holding the title to a land plot, or the establishment of joint-stock companies with entities which contribute land plots to the Charter Fund).

Purchase of other ownership rights

Issuance of loans, contribution of assets and ownership rights.

Ventures with foreign investment may operate under different legal forms to include joint-stock companies and other companies and partnerships stipulated in the legislation of the Russian Federation. These may include:

a) Ventures with foreign shares (joint ventures), as well as their subsidiaries and branches;

b) Ventures owned fully by foreign investors, as well as their subsidiaries and branches;

c) Branches of foreign legal entities.

Evidently, in such cases investments are made through the establishment of entities with 100% capital owned by foreign investors or with foreign investors' shares, acquisition of operating entities or their shares, establishment of branches and representative offices, and conclusion of investment agreements. The investment agreement is defined to include accords between investment entities on the fulfillment of certain actions to implement an investment project.

The system of investment agreements may include bargain and sale agreements (namely, the sale of real estate, ventures, and securities), financial lease, building contract, provision of chargeable services, commercial concession, trust, special partnership, and founding agreements.

The law "On Production Sharing Agreements" (PSA) was adopted in Russia ten years ago—the first investment law which paved the way for market-oriented civil contractual relations pertaining to the use of natural resources, a sphere formerly closed to foreign investors. PSAs have been used so far only for development of the oil and gas fields in Sakhalin and the shelf thereof.

New Investment Mechanisms in Russia

Concession agreements. The law "On Concession Agreements" was adopted in Russia in 2005. Pursuant to the top officials of the Ministry of Economic Development, the law will serve as a basis for the development of public-private partnership (PPP).

In accordance with a concession agreement, the state or a municipal entity (the conceder) provides for the other party (the concessionary) state or municipal property for the use on a time and chargeable basis, at such concessionary's risk and under the condition that the concessionary has made the investments as stipulated in the concession agreement; and grants the right to set up (build) a concessionary entity and the use (business use) thereof after it has been set up (built) during an established period and at the conditions as stipulated in the concession agreement with its subsequent return to the public or municipal ownership, as well as the right to perform work or provide services. The law states precisely that access to the infrastructure installations which are the subject matter of a concession agreement may be granted to foreign citizens.

In general the concession agreement is nothing but a public-private partnership in which the private sector and the government accept all the risks associated with a project. The share of expenses under a project incurred by the government may be stated as the terms and conditions of a tender for the right to conclude a concession agreement. Thus, the budget for 2006 includes the allocation for the Investment Fund (nearly RUB 70 billion). Pursuant to the government concept, the Investment Fund will be used, as the first priority, to develop the infrastructure, national innovations, and carry out large-scale restructuring. That is to say, some of its funds may be used for the co-financing of concession agreements. Besides the Investment Fund, the federal target programs (totaling, approximately, RUB 340 billion) will be an additional incentive for the investors seeking to conclude concession agreements with the government. A certain share of the foregoing funds should be used for the construction and modernization of major transport facilities, as well as the implementation of technological programs.

The new law regulates the relations arising from the preparation, conclusion, performance, and termination of concession agreements, and it establishes the rights and legitimate interests of the parties thereto. Its scope includes the assets which may not be privatized. Concession presumes that the government retains the ownership rights on an asset and grants its use to a private entity for a certain period. Parties to a concession agreement, i. e. federal, regional, and municipal government entities, as well as concessionaries, are entitled to set the foregoing period.

The law stipulates the list of concessionary entities to include highways and engineering facilities of the transport infrastructure; railway and pipeline transport installations; sea and river ports; seaships and river-ships, sea-and river-going ships (combined), icebreakers, surveying ships, research ships, ferries, docks; airports; water-development works; facilities for generation, transmission and distribution of electric and heat energy; utilities systems and installations; underground railway and other public transport; facilities used for medical treatment and recreation, provision of medical services, tourism; public health facilities, educational, cultural, and sporting facilities, as well as other social entities and entities providing services to households. Subsoil assets may not be the subject matter of a concession agreement.

The concessionary and the state may conclude a concession agreement only with respect to public assets. If an asset is held in joint ownership, the government must register its exceptional ownership right on such assets before it may grant concession on its use.

As the adopted law has an evident slant towards the infrastructure, one can assume that it will have an impact on the mobilization of private investment, particularly, for the construction of real estate or the restructuring of publicly owned real estate entities.

The progressive nature of the law on concession is manifested also by the fact that it sets up conditions for the participation of small-and medium-sized companies, as well as small investors in large-scale projects.

In fact, there are many minor projects in the utilities sector which are a constant headache to municipal and village authorities. If the matter at stake is a local boiler or water intake, one may seek to become a concessionary even with the capital of US $ 10,000. Hence the obstacles preventing private companies and private investors to access this sphere have been removed.

It was assumed that the law "On Concession Agreements" would be directly applicable. However, it has become evident even now that the preservation of other effective legislative provisions regulating the investment process, in individual branches included, is a significant obstacle for its implementation. It has turned out that a whole range of laws and legal acts on railways, power generation, and, particularly, the laws on federal and municipal property will contradict the law on concession agreements. Problems may arise with the placement of public assets in concession, as well as the conflict resolution practice of arbitration courts with respect to concession agreements. Moreover, as mentioned above, the law formed a basis for development of the legislation on public-private partnership. For such reasons one should expect amendments of the effective legislation and the adoption of federal laws "On Seaports, On Toll Highways," etc.

One should also take into account that regional laws may be adopted in certain regions seeking to conclude concession agreements. Thus, a regional law stipulating ten types of concession contracts was drafted in Saint Petersburg. Under one of them, the concessionary is to build a real estate entity at its expense in order to receive its tenure for up to 50 years. Another scenario presumes that a public asset can be placed in trust for the same period. One of the contracts establishes the right to a long-term lease of a real estate entity which has been set up with its subsequent buy-out. Still another scenario provides for the reimbursement of construction costs to a company from the budget after an entity has been put into use.

Special Economic Zones. Leaders of the Russian government realize that the reliance on the country's natural resources without taking into account its intellectual resources would be erroneous. Russian scientists and engineers have made so many designs and inventions in all branches of science and technology that their implementation would require more than one Silicon Valley. However, up to now the effective legislation had no provisions granting any significant preferences to the projects capable of bringing the Russian engineering and technology to a new qualitative level. Only now the consideration of such projects as technoparks and business incubators, where the foregoing objectives can be achieved with financial support of the federal government and regional authorities, has begun.

The President of the Russian Federation signed the federal law "On Special Economic Zones in the Russian Federation" on July 22, 2005. A Special Economic Zone (SEZ) is a territory established by the government within the Russian Federation with a special regime for conducting business. Special tax, customs, licensing, and visa regimes are effective in a Special Economic Zone. Strictly speaking, the law on SEZ deals only with the establishment of the customs regime of a free economic zone. It means that foreign goods may be stored and used within a Special Economic Zone without contribution of the customs duties and the value-added tax, as well as that the interdictions and restrictions of an economic nature established in the Russian legislation on state regulation of foreign trade are not applicable to such goods. In this context Russian goods are stored and used under the conditions set for the customs export regime with contribution of the excises, but exempt from the export tariffs. As far as the taxation is concerned, pursuant to Article 36 of the law on Special Economic Zones, the residents thereof are taxed in accordance with the Russian legislation on taxes and levies. The only exemption is provided in Article 38 which stipulates guarantees versus the adoption of unfavorable amendments to the Russian legislation and sets the conditions under which legal acts regulating taxes and levies are suppressed if they deteriorate the position of taxpayers—SEZ residents.

The directive of the Government of August 19, 2005 No. 530 charges the newly established federal executive agency Federal Agency for SEZ Governance under the

Ministry of Economic Development and Trade of Russian Federation.

New Special Economic Zones are set up for the term of 20 years which is non-renewable. The law presumes the establishment of technological and industrial production zones for the implementation of R & D projects and, consequently, the development of industrial production. Manufacturing zones are set up on land plots not to exceed 20 sq. km, and for technological zones, on not more than two land plots with the total area not to exceed 2 sq. km.

The main condition established for residents of industrial production zones is to invest no less than EUR 10 million in manufacturing, of which no less than EUR 1 million must be invested during the first year. The law does not stipulate any investment threshold for the residents of technological Special Economic Zones.

The law stipulates an interdiction of certain types of activities within the SEZ: metallurgy, extraction, and beneficiation of mineral resources, production, and assembly of excisable goods with the exception of motorbikes and cars.

Foreign investors are particularly interested in Special Economic Zones established in Russia. Furthermore, they propose to minimize restrictions.

The tender commission selected successful participants after the consideration and assessment of each project on the basis of supplied documentation. Seventy-two applications were sent to the tender, of which 29 were for the establishment of technological-innovative SEZs and 43 were for industrial production SEZs. They will operate in Zelenograd (microelectronics), Dubna, Moskovskaya Oblast (nuclear technologies and technologies related to modern physics), Saint Petersburg (development of information technologies), and Tomsk (new materials). Two projects were selected out of 43 applications for the establishment of industrial production zones: the production of household electric appliances and, possibly, furniture in Lipetskaya Oblast and the production of spare parts for the automotive industry, and high-tech petrochemical products in the city of Yelabuga in Tatarstan.

SEZ specialization was expanded recently. Amendments to the law concerning Special Economic Zones that were adopted on June 3, 2006 provide for the establishment of a new SEZ type—tourist and recreational. A resident of a tourist and recreational SEZ may engage only in tourist and recreational activities subject to terms and conditions stipulated in the relevant agreement. These activities involve construction, refurbishment, and operations in the tourism industry, sanatorium and spa treatment, medical rehabilitation, recreation facilities, as well as tourist activity and activity that involves the development of mineral water deposits, therapeutic mud fields, and other natural therapeutic resources.

The tender for the establishment of tourist and recreational SEZs was announced on September 15, 2006. Preliminary results will be available soon.

Investment Fund. The 2006 budget will have one more recipient of budget funds— the Investment Fund. Pursuant to the draft budget prepared by the Government of the Russian Federation, the Investment Fund was set at RUB 69. 7 billion (RUB 110. 6 billion in 2007 and RUB 104. 3 billion in 2008). The amount may not seem particularly high in comparison with other government investments allocated for the federal target programs (approximately, RUB 400 billion). However, Minister of Economic Development and Trade German Gref, who proposed to establish the Fund, believes that implementation of the national-scale projects financed by the Fund will provide for the annual GDP growth of 0. 4% – 0. 5%. Pursuant to the Minister's concept, the government investment should help the private capital which does not want to invest in long-term projects to overcome the fear of economic disruptions and political unpredictability. The focus is made on public-private partnerships; the Investment Fund will be used to finance projects where the share of mobilized private capital will be no less than 25% of the total project cost.

Naturally, there may be projects where private companies will seek to invest half of the project cost or even more. However, the matter at hand is the branches in which the private sector has been reluctant to invest in so far. The Investment Fund will be used for development of the following infrastructures: construction of utilities, roads, airports, sea and river ports, etc. Realization of such projects jointly with the private sector is such a high priority for the government that it will be prepared to allocate the required funds. If private investors mobilize loans for implementation of such projects, the government will guarantee their obligations to credit organizations. The Regulations on the Investment Fund read: "Government guarantees are extended, amongst others, to borrowers in favor of credit organizations, credit organizations with foreign investment included. "

The government mobilizes funds to pay for its shares in the projects from two sources: the budget windfall from high oil prices and the interest savings resulting from the ahead-of-schedule foreign debt repayment.

Regional entities of the Russian Federation and municipalities or private companies operating in Russia may initiate projects to be realized jointly with the government. Naturally, not all proposals will be good enough to receive budget financing. Firstly, there are restrictions with respect to the amount of funds that can be allocated and the deadline of project realization. These should be large-scale national projects worth no less than RUB 5 billion. The period for the provision of public support is not to exceed five years.

Additional criteria for the selection of investment projects have been set: the availability of a prospective private investor that has confirmed its preparedness to take part in the project, the compliance of a project with the priorities of Russia's socioeconomic development and the industrial development strategy, as well as project's financial, budget, and economic efficiency.

In addition, initiators of such a project will have to substantiate the impossibility of its implementation without the government's support and provide favorable opinion of the branch ministry and the investment advisor. Advisors will have to be chosen from among the reputed firms working over large-scale projects. The Commission headed by Minister German Gref will select projects which will be financed by the Investment Fund. The Commission will include all cabinet ministers, as well as representatives of the State Duma, the Federation Council, and Government staff.

Guarantee of Foreign Investment in Russia

Despite the aforementioned difficulties of the transition period, the generally favorable development of the Russian economy and the establishment of a rule-of-law state provided for the assignment of a high investment rating to Russia. Based on the specific indicators of legal security of all business entities, Moody's and S & P rating agencies concluded the evolvement of a favorable investment climate in Russia. It has been achieved primarily due to a high level of political stability. However, the general state of economy and the government policy of economic development also play a pivotal role in this context.

Improvement of the legal system is an essential condition for raising the investment attractiveness of a country. The investment procedure in Russia is regulated both by the national as well as international legal standards ensuring the safety and operations of investment and the establishment of appropriate safeguards at all levels.

The government promotes investors' participation in privatization of public property in Russia. Mandatory licensing is required only for privatization of hi-tech manufacturing facilities and defense plants undergoing conversion and enterprises of the fuel and energy complex. The set of national security measures provides for such restrictions as the interdiction to foreign investors to privatize certain entities, the establishment of a ceiling for their shares in the authorized capital of a joint-stock company for up to three years, and preservation in the public ownership of the block of shares entitling to veto or give the decisive vote.

The federal law "On Foreign Investment in the Russian Federation" adopted in 1999 regulates the terms and conditions of investment and the guarantees thereof. Article 3 of the law stipulates that foreign investments in Russia are regulated by Russian laws and legal acts, as well as by international agreements.

The effective legislation provides full-fledged and unconditional legal safeguards to foreign investors. It also provides guarantees against forced property confiscation or the illegal actions of government agencies and officials, and it assumes that compensation should be paid in the amount of inflicted damage, missed interest included.

Thus, Article 8 of the law reads "foreign investments in the Russian Federation are not subject to the confiscation, nationalization, and requisition included" except as stipulated in the law of the Russian Federation or its international agreements. At the same time, the legislation has a provision that in the event of nationalization or requisition, which should be of nondiscriminatory nature, the foreign investor is entitled to receive compensation in the same currency as the investment was made and in accordance with its current value.

Conclusion of the bilateral intergovernmental agreements on promoting capital investments and the mutual protection thereof is one of the effective forms of providing guarantees to foreign investors. The legal relevance of such agreements is based on the superiority of international law over national law which is amended following international standards during the economic restructuring. The Constitution of the Russian Federation stipulates that "if an international agreement of the Russian Federation establishes rules other than established in its law, the rules of such international agreement shall apply."

From the viewpoint of international investment law, the procedure regulating access of foreign investment has primary significance for the legal regulation of foreign capital investment. Notably, it is inseparable from the issue of safeguarding investment because the access procedure, particularly, establishes a legal basis for the successful completion of a foreign investment project in a given country. It is common knowledge that the essence of legal relations in the foreign investment sphere includes the establishment of essential conditions and guarantees to investors through the development of appropriate legal provisions regulating investment.

The bilateral agreements concluded by the Russian Federation with other countries on the promotion and mutual safeguards of capital investment establish transparent and enforceable rules ensuring and promoting access of foreign investment to a recipient country. The definition of a general legal regime has a prominent position within such rules, for a clear-cut description of the general legal regime is essential for the establishment of a favorable investment climate in any given country.

It should be mentioned that in addition to the most favored nation clause, the Russian Federation undertook to provide the national regime for foreign investors, also viewed in industrialized countries as a basic requirement for investment activities. Where such a regime is granted with respect to foreign capital investment, domestic and foreign entrepreneurs enjoy equal rights at the domestic market with some exceptions. In most cases the domestic laws, and not the laws of the country of origin, regulate an investors' right in a host county. In this context the regime granted to foreign investment may not be less favorable than the regime granted to Russian investors.

Russia has reserved the right to make exemptions from the national regime in such industries and activities as power generation, production of uranium, other fissionable materials, and the products thereof, ownership rights on land, use of subsoil assets and natural resources, ownership rights on real estate entities, and performance of the transactions therewith, etc. The international investment law allows also for the restrictions which are enforced pursuant to public health and environmental requirements. The law on foreign investment in the Russian Federation includes a similar provision.

Guarantee of the repatriation of foreign investor's receipts is an essential element of legal safeguards for foreign investments. The law on foreign investment (Article 8) stipulates that "property of a foreign investor or business entity with foreign investment shall not be subject to confiscation including nationalization and requisition, with the exception of events and reasons as established by federal law or international agreement of the Russian Federation." It also reads, "In the event of nationalization, the cost of the nationalized property and other losses shall be compensated to a foreign investor or a business entity."

The ownership right is one of the basic economic rights granted to individuals in the context of civil relations and, concurrently, it is a legal form for the fixation of property to individuals. Due to such reasons, legislative guarantees of the ownership right, foreign investors' rights included, is a prerequisite not only for the stable development of market-driven relations, but for democratic transformations in general.

Legal protection of the foregoing right in Russia is guaranteed pursuant to the principles and standards of international law and the Constitution of the Russian Federation. The aforementioned constitutional and international provisions have been developed further in the Russian civil legislation and judicial practice.

The Russian judicial practice relies on standards established in resolutions of the European Court of Human Rights. The protection of ownership rights and the provision of guarantees to owners is an essential function of the judiciary in the Russian Federation. The principles of universality and absence of discrimination prevail amongst the general principles of international law. They presume the inadmissibility of discrimination of the persons that own, use, and dispose of property based on race, nationality, ethnic origin, color of skin, gender, political, social and religious adherence.

Laws adopted in regional entities of the Russian Federation stipulate foreign investors' rights and the guarantees extended to them. With a view to mobilizing higher amounts of foreign capital, regional entities establish preferences pertaining, among others, to taxation.

Risk Insurance

Insurance of political risks is a prerequisite of foreign direct investment. If one takes into account the specifics of such insurance it will become evident that only the insurance companies independent of the country where the investments have been made are capable of providing such a type of insurance. Furthermore, such a company should not specialize exceptionally in the risks associated with the Russian market; its operations must include several countries.

The insurance system for such types of risks evolved long before. Both specialized public agencies, as well as private insurance companies provide the investment insurance. The OPIC (Overseas Private Investment Corporation) is a US insurer of investments to developing countries. A similar agency, the ECGD (Export Credits Guarantee Department), operates in the UK. Among European insurers operating at the investment insurance market, there is Coface of France (together with Unistrat which is part and parcel of the same group), Euler Hermes of Germany, as well as Gerling NCM. The said companies have begun to provide insurance of the Russian risks.

Notably, the OPIC will sign an insurance agreement and provide guarantees only with respect to projects in the countries which have signed agreements on OPIC programs with the US government. The Agreement of 1992 between the United States of America and the Russian Federation is one of such agreements. The Ministry of Foreign Economic Relations and the Overseas Private Investment Corporation signed the agreement on principles of their cooperation on September 27, 1994. In particular, the agreement reads: "The Ministry and the OPIC will cooperate to develop programs establishing incentives for the investment and the related activities in Russia; to identify enterprises and projects in Russia that would benefit from the financing programs and political risk insurance provided by the Overseas Private Investment Corporation. "

In 2003 the ECGD provided a guarantee to Aeroflot for export credit in the amount of US \$ 24 million under the contract between the Russian aviation company and Airbus for acquisition of 21 A—320 airplanes. In 2005 the ECGD was the underwriter in the transaction between Motorola of Sweden and MTS of Russia for provision of mobile communication equipment in the amount of US \$ 28 million to Russia. Experts noted that it was for the first time that the ECGD insured the Russian company's risk all by itself and did not require any third party's guarantee, e. g. of a Russian bank.

As far as the Euler Hermes group is concerned, it provided insurance for export credits in 2002 under the agreement signed by MENATEP SPb bank and Bankgesellschaft Berlin AG credit organization. The agreement dealt with cooperation in the sphere of long-term credits for development of trade between Russia and Germany. Euler Hermes was the guarantor of the credit agreement for the term of seven years in the amount of EUR 5.5 million between MDM—Bank and Bayerische Landesbank Girozentrale bank. The credit was used to finance the contract between Deutsche Voest—Alpine Industrieanlagenbau and Nizhnetagilskiy Integrated Iron-and-steel Works (NTMK) for construction of an installation reducing the sulphur content in cast iron. The said contract is the first stage of the project for construction of a continuous casting plant and 160—ton ladle furnace at NTMK.

On July 8,2004 the Euler Hermes group signed an agreement with ROSNO Russian insurance company on cooperation in the sphere of credit risk insurance in Russia. Pursuant to the agreement, ROSNO, among other activities, will reinsure at Euler Hermes the credit risks arising from the purchase of goods and services with delayed payment by Russian enterprises. Obligatory insurance is provided versus the default risk.

Another Russian company Ingosstrakh and Gerling group signed an agreement on cooperation for development of the credit-insurance market in Russia. An insurance policy for the export credits received by Russian companies was developed at the initial stage which was completed successfully. In this case, the medium-and long-term objectives of Russian-German cooperation is to develop an effective know-how with respect to credit underwriting, debt collection, and loss prevention in Russia. Thus, Ingosstrakh and Gerling will seek to meet the constantly growing needs in the insurance of Russian credit risks and to insure export shipments to this country.

Western companies operating in Russia often insure political risks related to the possibility of nationalization or expropriation of their property. The foregoing practice was introduced by major international corporations which accessed the Russian market in the beginning of the 1990s. They made a rule of insuring risks related to government policy changes then and have done so ever since.

Russian-Chinese Business Center

The Russian-Chinese Business Center establishes a forum for exchange of opinion and business cooperation between experts and managers of service and manufacturing companies of the Russian Federation and the People's Republic of China. The Center holds seminars on topical issues with the participation of Chinese and Russian experts, consultations, conferences, and exhibits.

The Center safeguards interests of the business community in general and, particularly, those of its member-companies. The Center lobbies for its members' interests in the government agencies which impact their operations, sets up favorable conditions for business development, promotes continuous information exchange between the Business Center members, unites business-people to raise efficiency and reduce costs in such spheres as market communication, advertising, advisory, and legal services. Association with the Business Center is open for all Chinese and Russian companies, Sino-Russian joint ventures, and companies with different ownership structures.

The Business Center provides support in

Promotion of Chinese goods and services in the Russian market;

Promotion of Russian goods and services in the Chinese market;

Placement of advertising in Russian and Chinese mass media;

Search for and selection of potential Russian business partners at the request of Chinese companies;

Establishment of contacts with government agencies of the Russian Federation;

Registration of companies, representative offices, opening of shops and maintenance of their financial and business activities.

Purchase of real estate

Organization of workshops, presentations, anniversaries, and conferences.

Evidently, we have listed far from all the organizations providing advisory services to foreign investors. There are different business associations in Russia. The Russian Union of Industrialists and Entrepreneurs includes mostly large companies. Medium-sized companies have set up the Delovaia Rossia business association. Small-sized companies are associated with OPORa—an all-Russian nongovernmental association of small-and medium-sized companies. Bankers have their own professional associations, e. g. the Association of Russian Banks（ARB）and the Association of Russian Regional Banks（Rossia）, while managers have the Russian Managers' Association, similar to other professions, such as chemists, oil engineers and oilmen, metallurgists, etc. The forementioned organizations support foreign investors. Please see their e-mail addresses at the end of this publication.（*Source*：*Extracts from Investor's Guidebook to Russia*）

Notes

[1] changeover 完全转变，转型

[2] drawback 缺点，障碍

[3] curtailment 缩减，缩短

[4] armament 军备，武器

[5] planned economy 计划经济

[6] influx 流入

[7] stratum 社会阶层

[8] RUB, ruble 卢布（俄罗斯货币）

[9] revenue 国家收入，税收

[10] trillion 万亿

[11] surplus 盈余

[12] stabilization fund 平准基金

[13] barrel 桶

[14] earmark 指定（款项等的）用途

[15] mortgage 抵押

[16] deter 阻止

[17] inflation 通货膨胀

[18] undervalue 低估

[19] overvalue 高估

[20] lopsided 不平衡的

[21] division of labor 劳动分工

[22] rivet 固定

[23] market economy 市场经济

［24］transitional economy 转型经济

［25］overhaul 检查

［26］pervade 遍及

［27］direct investment 直接投资

［28］portfolio investment 间接投资

［29］secondary market 二级市场

［30］joint-stock company 股份公司

［31］concession agreement 特许协议

［32］infrastructure 基础设施

［33］privatize 私有化

［34］toll highway 收费公路

［35］tenure 使用期限,任期

［36］reimbursement 偿付,退还

［37］erroneous 错误的

［38］incubator 孵化器

［39］Special Economic Zone（SEZ）经济特区

［40］deteriorate（使）恶化

［41］threshold 开始,开端

［42］metallurgy 冶金,冶金术

［43］beneficiation 选矿

［44］sanatorium 疗养院,休养地

［45］windfall 横财

［46］municipality 市政当局

［47］cabinet minister 内阁大臣

［48］pivotal 关键的

［49］confiscation 没收,征用

［50］nondiscriminatory 一视同仁的

［51］repatriation 汇回国内,遣送回国

［52］prerequisite 先决条件

［53］underwriter 保险商

［54］insurance policy 保单

［55］export credit 出口信贷

［56］political risk 政治风险

 **Exercises**

I. Match the following words in Column A and Column B

Column A	Column B
1. changeover	a. 社会阶层
2. curtailment	b. 孵化器
3. planned economy	c. 疗养院,休养地
4. stratum	d. 平准基金
5. surplus	e. 劳动分工
6. stabilization fund	f. 没收,征用
7. barrel	g. 选矿
8. mortgage	h. 市场经济
9. inflation	i. 完全转变,转型
10. division of labor	j. 经济特区
11. market economy	k. 计划经济
12. transitional economy	l. 转型经济
13. portfolio investment	m. 缩减,缩短
14. secondary market	n. 先决条件
15. joint-stock company	o. 二级市场
16. concession agreement	p. 通货膨胀
17. toll highway	q. 特许协议
18. tenure	r. 桶
19. incubator	s. 内阁大臣
20. Special Economic Zone（SEZ）	t. 间接投资
21. beneficiation	u. 抵押
22. sanatorium	v. 股份公司
23. windfall	w. 收费公路
24. cabinet minister	x. 盈余
25. confiscation	y. 使用期限,任期
26. prerequisite	z. 横财

II. Translate the following sentences into Chinese

1. The years of socio-economic changes have formed a new stratum of modern managers that have embraced European business practices, a factor not to be

overlooked by the private investors interested in efficient management of their capitals.

2. Given the economic globalization, development of interstate trade and economic relations, and the international division of labor, Russia rivets an increasingly greater attention of foreign partners.

3. The country is striving to end its "oil addiction", or more precisely the overdependence of the national economy and the budget on oil and gas exports that today account for nearly 60% of the country's earnings.

4. A Special Economic Zone (SEZ) is a territory established by the government within the Russian Federation with a special regime for conducting business. Special tax, customs, licensing, and visa regimes are effective in a Special Economic Zone.

5. The effective legislation provides full-fledged and unconditional legal safeguards to foreign investors. It also provides guarantees against forced property confiscation or the illegal actions of government agencies and officials, and it assumes that compensation should be paid in the amount of inflicted damage, missed interest included.

6. Conclusion of the bilateral intergovernmental agreements on promoting capital investments and the mutual protection thereof is one of the effective forms of providing guarantees to foreign investors.

7. The bilateral agreements concluded by the Russian Federation with other countries on the promotion and mutual safeguards of capital investment establish transparent and enforceable rules ensuring and promoting access of foreign investment to a recipient country.

8. The law on foreign investment (Article 8) stipulates that "property of a foreign investor or business entity with foreign investment shall not be subject to confiscation including nationalization and requisition, with the exception of events and reasons as established by federal law or international agreement of the Russian Federation." It also reads, "In the event of nationalization, the cost of the nationalized property and other losses shall be compensated to a foreign investor or a business entity."

9. The Russian-Chinese Business Center establishes a forum for exchange of opinion and business cooperation between experts and managers of service and manufacturing companies of the Russian Federation and the People's Republic of China.

10. The Center lobbies for its members' interests in the government agencies which impact their operations, sets up favorable conditions for business development, promotes continuous information exchange between the Business Center members, unites business and people to raise efficiency and reduce costs in such spheres as market communication, advertising, advisory, and legal services.

III. Cloze

According to WTO data, Russia's share _____ world exports does not exceed 1.5%, and in imports, it does not exceed 0.7%, whereas Russia's participation _____ the global services trade is purely symbolic. Nonetheless, _____ the years of economic reforms, exports have become the largest sector of the economy, accounting _____ over one-fourth of GDP (in the former Sovet Union this figure did not exceed 10%). Twenty to 80% of the national production of basic commodities and semi-finished goods are bound _____ the world markets. It should be noted that qualitative indicators of exports do not resolve the task of raising competitiveness of the Russian-made products at the world markets so long as the structure of the Russian exports has _____ obvious energy and commodities leaning. The structure of exports is evident _____ the lopsided development of the Russian economy _____ high-tech industries still lagging behind.

The share of machinery and equipment in Russian exports was a mere 5.6% in 2005. The imports are dominated _____ consumer goods (primarily foodstuffs and raw materials for their production and household appliances), accounting for about one half _____ the total Russian imports.

IV. Underline the important sentences in the text, which give you useful information

V. Retell or write down what you learn from the text in English or in Chinese

Unit Thirteen

The Doha Agenda

At the Fourth Ministerial Conference in Doha, Qatar, in November 2001 WTO member governments agreed to launch new negotiations. They also agreed to work on other issues, in particular the implementation of the present agreements. The entire package is called the Doha Development Agenda (DDA).

The negotiations take place in the Trade Negotiations Committee and its subsidiaries, which are usually, either regular councils and committees meeting in "special sessions", or specially-created negotiating groups. Other work under the work programme takes place in other WTO councils and committees.

The Fifth Ministerial Conference in Cancún, Mexico, in September 2003, was intended as a stock-taking meeting where members would agree on how to complete the rest of the negotiations. But the meeting was soured by discord on agricultural issues, including cotton, and ended in deadlock on the "Singapore issues" (see below). Real progress on the Singapore issues and agriculture was not evident until the early hours of 1 August 2004 with a set of decisions in the General Council (sometimes called the July 2004 package). The original 1 January 2005 deadline was missed. After that, members unofficially aimed to finish the negotiations by the end of 2006.

There are 19—21 subjects listed in the Doha Declaration, depending on whether to count the "rules" subjects as one or three. Most of them involve negotiations; other work includes actions under "implementation", analysis and monitoring. This is an unofficial explanation of what the declaration mandates (listed with the declaration's paragraphs that refer to them):

Implementation-related issues and concerns

"Implementation" is short-hand for developing countries' problems in implementing the current WTO Agreements, i. e. the agreements arising from the Uruguay Round negotiations.

No area of WTO work received more attention or generated more controversy during nearly three years of hard bargaining before the Doha Ministerial Conference. Around

100 issues were raised during that period. The result was a two-pronged approach：

- More than 40 items under 12 headings were settled at or before the Doha conference, for immediate delivery.

- The vast majority of the remaining items immediately became the subject of negotiations.

This was spelt out in a separate ministerial decision on implementation, combined with paragraph 12 of the main Doha Declaration.

The implementation decision includes the following (detailed explanations can be seen on the WTO website)：

General Agreement on Tariffs and Trade(GATT)

- Balance-of-payments exception：clarifying less stringent conditions in GATT for developing countries if they restrict imports in order to protect their balance-of-payments.

- Market-access commitments：clarifying eligibility to negotiate or be consulted on quota allocation.

Agriculture

- Rural development and food security for developing countries
- Least-developed and net food-importing developing countries
- Export credits, export credit guarantees or insurance programmes
- Tariff rate quotas

Sanitary and phytosanitary (SPS) measure

- More time for developing countries to comply with other countries' new SPS (Sanitary and phytosanitary) measures

- "Reasonable interval" between publication of a country's new SPS measure and its entry into force

- Equivalence：putting into practice the principle that governments should accept that different measures used by other governments can be equivalent to their own measures for providing the same level of health protection for food, animals and plants.

- Review of the SPS Agreement
- Developing countries' participation in setting international SPS standards
- Financial and technical assistance

Textiles and clothing

- "Effective" use of the agreement's provisions on early integration of products into normal GATT rules, and elimination of quotas.

- Restraint in anti-dumping actions.

- The possibility of examining governments' new rules of origin.

- Members to consider favourable quota treatment for small suppliers and least-developed countries, and larger quotas in general.

Technical barriers to trade

- Technical assistance for least-developed countries, and reviews of technical assistance in general.

- When possible, a six-month "reasonable interval" for developing countries to adapt to new measures.

- The WTO director-general encouraged to continue efforts to help developing countries participate in setting international standards.

Trade-related investment measures(TRIMS)

- The Goods Council is "to consider positively" requests from least-developed countries to extend the seven-year transition period for eliminating measures that are inconsistent with the agreement.

Anit-dumping

- No second anti-dumping investigation within a year unless circumstances have changed.

- How to put into operation a special provision for developing countries (Article 15 of the Anti-Dumping Agreement), which recognizes that developed countries must give "special regard" to the situation of developing countries when considering applying anti-dumping measures.

- Clarification sought on the time period for determining whether the volume of dumped imported products is negligible, and therefore no anti-dumping action should be taken.

- Annual reviews of the agreement's implementation to be improved.

Customs valuation

- Extending the deadline for developing countries to implement the agreement

- Dealing with fraud: how to cooperate in exchanging information, including on export values

Rules of origin

- Completing the harmonization of rules of origin among member governments

- Dealing with interim arrangements in the transition to the new, harmonized rules of origin.

Subsidies and countervailing measures

- Sorting out how to determine whether some developing countries meet the test of being below US $ 1,000 per capita GNP allowing them to pay subsidies that require the recipient to export.

- Noting proposed new rules allowing developing countries to subsidize under programmes that have "legitimate development goals" without having to face countervailing or other action.
- Review of provisions on countervailing duty investigations.
- Reaffirming that least-developed countries are exempt from the ban on export subsidies.
- Directing the Subsidies Committee to extend the transition period for certain developing countries.

Trade-related aspects of intellectual property rights(TRIPS)

- "Non-violation" complaints: the unresolved question of how to deal with possible TRIPS disputes involving loss of an expected benefit even if the TRIPS Agreement has not actually been violated.
- Technology transfer to least-developed countries

Cross-cutting issues

- Which special and differential treatment provisions are mandatory? What are the implications of making mandatory those that are currently non-binding?
- How can special and differential treatment provisions be made more effective?
- How can special and differential treatment be incorporated in the new negotiations?
- Developed countries are urged to grant preferences in a generalized and non-discriminatory manner, i. e. to all developing countries rather than to a selected group.

Outstanding implementation issues

- To be handled under paragraph 12 of the main Doha Declaration.

Final provisions

- The WTO Director-General is to ensure that WTO technical assistance gives priority to helping developing countries implement existing WTO obligations, and to increase their capacity to participate more effectively in future negotiations.
- The WTO Secretariat is to cooperate more closely with other international organizations so that technical assistance is more efficient and effective.

The implementation decision is tied into the main Doha Declaration, where ministers agreed on a future work programme to deal with unsettled implementation questions. "Negotiations on outstanding implementation issues shall be an integral part of the Work Programme" in the coming years, they declared.

In the declaration, the ministers established a two-track approach. Those issues for which there was an agreed negotiating mandate in the declaration would be dealt with under the terms of that mandate.

Those implementation issues, where there is no mandate to negotiate, would be taken up as "a matter of priority" by relevant WTO councils and committees. These bodies were to report on their progress to the Trade Negotiations Committee by the end of 2002 for "appropriate action".

Agriculture

Negotiations on agriculture began in early 2000, under Article 20 of the WTO Agriculture Agreement. By November 2001 and the Doha Ministerial Conference, 121 governments had submitted a large number of negotiating proposals.

These negotiations have continued, but now with the mandate given by the Doha Declaration, which also includes a series of deadlines. The declaration builds on the work already undertaken, confirms and elaborates the objectives, and sets a timetable. Agriculture is now part of the single undertaking in which virtually all the linked negotiations were to end by 1 January 2005, now with the unofficial target of the end of 2006.

The declaration reconfirms the long-term objective already agreed in the present WTO Agreement: to establish a fair and market-oriented trading system through a programme of fundamental reform. The programme encompasses strengthened rules, and specific commitments on government support and protection for agriculture. The purpose is to correct and prevent restrictions and distortions in world agricultural markets.

Without prejudging the outcome, member governments commit themselves to comprehensive negotiations aimed at:

- market access: substantial reductions
- exports subsidies: reductions of, with a view to phasing out, all forms of these (in the 1 August 2004 "framework" members agreed to eliminate export subsidies by a date to be negotiated)
- domestic support: substantial reductions for supports that distort trade (in the 1 August 2004 "framework", developed countries pledged to slash trade-distorting domestic subsidies by 20% from the first day any Doha Agenda agreement is implemented.

The declaration makes special and differential treatment for developing countries integral throughout the negotiations, both in countries' new commitments and in any relevant new or revised rules and disciplines. It says the outcome should be effective in practice and should enable developing countries to meet their needs, in particular in food security and rural development.

The ministers also take note of the non-trade concerns (such as environmental protection, food security, rural development, etc.) reflected in the negotiating proposals already submitted. They confirm that the negotiations will take these into account, as provided for in the Agriculture Agreement.

A first step along the road to final agreement was reached on 1 August 2004 when members agreed on a "framework" (Annex A of the General Council decision).

The negotiations take place in "special sessions" of the Agriculture Committee.

Key dates: agriculture

Start: early 2000

"Framework" agreed: 1 August 2004

Formulas and other "modalities" for countries' commitments: originally 31 March 2003, now by 6th Ministerial Conference, 2005 (in Hong Kong, China)

Countries' comprehensive draft commitments and stock taking : originally by 5th Ministerial Conference, 2003 (in Mexico)

Deadline: originally by 1 January 2005, now unofficially by end of 2006, part of single undertaking

Services

Negotiations on services were already almost two years old when they were incorporated into the new Doha agenda.

The WTO General Agreement on Trade in Services (GATS) commits member governments to undertake negotiations on specific issues and to enter into successive rounds of negotiations to progressively liberalize trade in services. The first round had to start no later than five years from 1995.

Accordingly, the services negotiations started officially in early 2000 under the Council for Trade in Services. In March 2001, the Services Council fulfilled a key element in the negotiating mandate by establishing the negotiating guidelines and procedures.

The Doha Declaration endorses the work already done, reaffirms the negotiating guidelines and procedures; and establishes some key elements of the timetable including, most importantly, the deadline for concluding the negotiations as part of a single undertaking.

The negotiations take place in "special sessions" of the Services Council and regular meetings of its relevant subsidiary committees or working parties.

Key dates: services

Start: early 2000

Negotiating guidelines and procedures: March 2001

Initial requests for market access: by 30 June 2002

Initial offers of market access: by 31 March 2003

Stock taking: originally 5th Ministerial Conference, 2003 (in Mexico)

Revised market-access offers: by 31 May 2005

Deadline: originally by 1 January 2005, now unofficially end of 2006, part of single undertaking

Market access for non-agricultural products

The ministers agreed to launch tariff-cutting negotiations on all non-agricultural products. The aim is "to reduce, or as appropriate eliminate tariffs, including the reduction or elimination of tariff peaks, high tariffs, and tariff escalation, as well as non-tariff barriers, in particular on products of export interest to developing countries". These negotiations shall take fully into account the special needs and interests of developing and least-developed countries, and recognize that these countries do not need to match or reciprocate in full tariff-reduction commitments by other participants.

At the start, participants have to reach agreement on how ("modalities") to conduct the tariff-cutting exercise (in the Tokyo Round, the participants used an agreed mathematical formula to cut tariffs across the board; in the Uruguay Round, participants negotiated cuts product by product). The agreed procedures would include studies and capacity-building measures that would help least-developed countries participate effectively in the negotiations. Back in Geneva, negotiators decided that the "modalities" should be agreed by 31 May 2003. When that date was missed, members agreed on 1 August 2004 on a new target: the Hong Kong Ministerial Conference in December 2005.

While average customs duties are now at their lowest levels after eight GATT Rounds, certain tariffs continue to restrict trade, especially on exports of developing countries—for instance "tariff peaks", which are relatively high tariffs, usually on "sensitive" products, amidst generally low tariff levels. For industrialized countries, tariffs of 15% and above are generally recognized as "tariff peaks".

Another example is "tariff escalation", in which higher import duties are applied to semi-processed products than to raw materials, and higher still to finished products. This practice protects domestic processing industries and discourages the development of processing activity in the countries where raw materials originate.

The negotiations take place in a Market Access Negotiating Group.

Key dates: market access

Start：January 2002

Stock taking：5th Ministerial Conference，2003（in Mexico）

Deadline：originally by 1 January 2005，now unofficially by end 2006，part of single undertaking

Trade-related aspects of intellectual property rights（TRIPS）

TRIPS and public health. In the declaration，ministers stress that it is important to implement and interpret the TRIPS Agreement in a way that supports public health—by promoting both access to existing medicines and the creation of new medicines. They refer to their separate declaration on this subject.

This separate declaration on TRIPS and public health is designed to respond to concerns about the possible implications of the TRIPS Agreement for access to medicines.

It emphasizes that the TRIPS Agreement does not and should not prevent member governments from acting to protect public health. It affirms governments' right to use the agreement's flexibilities in order to avoid any reticence the governments may feel.

The separate declaration clarifies some of the forms of flexibility available，in particular compulsory licensing and parallel importing. （For an explanation of these issues，go to the main TRIPS pages on the WTO website）

For the Doha agenda，this separate declaration sets two specific task. The TRIPS Council has to find a solution to the problems countries may face in making use of compulsory licensing if they have too little or no pharmaceutical manufacturing capacity，reporting to the General Council on this by the end of 2002. （This was achieved in August，2003，see intellectual property section of the "Agreements" chapter. ）The declaration also extends the deadline for least-developed countries to apply provisions on pharmaceutical patents until 1 January 2016.

Geographical indications—the registration system. Geographical indications are place names（in some countries also words associated with a place）used to identify products with particular characteristics because they come from specific places. The WTO TRIPS Council has already started work on a multilateral registration system for geographical indications for wines and spirits. The Doha Declaration sets a deadline for completing the negotiations：the Fifth Ministerial Conference in 2003.

These negotiations take place in "special sessions" of the TRIPS Council.

Geographical indications—extending the "higher level of protection" to other products. The TRIPS Agreement provides a higher level of protection to geographical indications for wines and spirits. This means they should be protected even if there is no risk of misleading consumers or unfair competition. A number of countries want to negotiate extending this higher level to other products. Others oppose the move, and the debate in the TRIPS Council has included the question of whether the relevant provisions of the TRIPS Agreement provide a mandate for extending coverage beyond wines and spirits.

The Doha Declaration notes that the TRIPS Council will handle this under the declaration's paragraph 12 (which deals with implementation issues). Paragraph 12 offers two tracks: "(a) where we provide a specific negotiating mandate in this Declaration, the relevant implementation issues shall be addressed under that mandate; (b) the other outstanding implementation issues shall be addressed as a matter of priority by the relevant WTO bodies, which shall report to the Trade Negotiations Committee [TNC], established under paragraph 46 below, by the end of 2002 for appropriate action. "

In papers circulated at the Ministerial Conference, member governments expressed different interpretations of this mandate.

Argentina said it understands " there is no agreement to negotiate the other outstanding implementation issues' referred to under (b) and that, by the end of 2002, consensus will be required in order to launch any negotiations on these issues".

Bulgaria, the Czech Republic, EU, Hungary, India, Liechtenstein, Kenya, Mauritius, Nigeria, Pakistan, the Slovak Republic, Slovenia, Sri Lanka, Switzerland, Thailand and Turkey argued that there is a clear mandate to negotiate immediately.

Reviews of TRIPS provisions. Two reviews have been taking place in the TRIPS Council, as required by the TRIPS Agreement: a review of Article 27. 3(b) which deals with patentability or non-patentability of plant and animal inventions, and the protection of plant varieties; and a review of the entire TRIPS Agreement (required by Article 71. 1).

The Doha Declaration says that work in the TRIPS Council on these reviews or any other implementation issue should also look at: the relationship between the TRIPS Agreement and the UN Convention on Biodiversity; the protection of traditional knowledge and folklore; and other relevant new developments that member governments raise in the review of the TRIPS Agreement. It adds that the TRIPS Council's work on these topics is to be guided by the TRIPS Agreement's objectives (Article 7) and principles (Article 8), and must take development fully into account.

Key dates: intellectual property

Report to the General Council-solution on compulsory licensing and lack of pharmaceutical production capacity: originally by end of 2002, decision agreed 30 April 2003.

Report to TNC—action on outstanding implementation issues under par 12: by end of 2002 (missed)

Deadline—negotiations on geographical indications registration system (wines and spirits): by 5th Ministerial Conference, 2003 (in Mexico) (missed)

Deadline—negotiations specifically mandated in Doha Declaration: originally by 1 January 2005, now unofficially by the end of 2006

Least-developed countries to apply pharmaceutical patent provisions: 2016

The four Singapore' issues: no negotiations until...

For trade and investment, trade and competition policy, transparency in government procurement and trade facilitation, the 2001 Doha declaration does not launch negotiations immediately. It says "negotiations will take place after the Fifth Session of the Ministerial Conference on the basis of a decision to be taken, by explicit consensus, at that session on modalities of negotiations [i. e. how the negotiations are to be conducted]." But consensus eluded members on negotiating the four subjects. Finally agreement was reached on 1 August 2004 to negotiate trade facilitation alone. The three other subjects were dropped from the Doha agenda.

Relationship between trade and investment

This is a "Singapore issue" i. e. a working group set up by the 1996 Singapore Ministerial Conference has been studying it.

In the period up to the 2003 Ministerial Conference, the declaration instructs the working group to focus on clarifying the scope and definition of the issues, transparency, non-discrimination, ways of preparing negotiated commitments, development provisions, exceptions and balance-of-payments safeguards, consultation and dispute settlement. The negotiated commitments would be modelled on those made in services, which specify where commitments are being made—"positive lists"—rather than making broad commitments and listing exceptions.

The declaration also spells out a number of principles such as the need to balance the interests of countries where foreign investment originates and where it is invested, countries' right to regulate investment, development, public interest and individual countries' specific circumstances. It also emphasizes support and technical cooperation for developing and least-developed countries, and coordination with other international organizations such as the UN Conference on Trade and Development (UNCTAD).

Since the 1 August 2004 decision, this subject has been dropped from the Doha agenda.

Key dates: trade and investment

Continuing work in working group with defined agenda: to 5th Ministerial Conference, 2003 (in Mexico)

Negotiations: after 5th Ministerial Conference, 2003 (in Mexico) subject to "explicit consensus" on modalities with a deadline: by 1 January 2005, part of single undertaking. But no consensus; dropped from Doha agenda in the 1 August 2004 decision.

Interaction between trade and competition policy

This is another "Singapore issue", with a working group set up in 1996 to study the subject.

In the period up to the 2003 Ministerial Conference, the declaration instructs the working group to focus on clarifying:

- core principles including transparency, non-discrimination and procedural fairness, and provisions on "hardcore" cartels (i. e. cartels that are formally set up)

- ways of handling voluntary cooperation on competition policy among WTO member governments

- support for progressive reinforcement of competition institutions in developing countries through capacity building

The declaration says the work must take full account of developmental needs. It includes technical cooperation and capacity building, on such topics as policy analysis and development, so that developing countries are better placed to evaluate the implications of closer multilateral cooperation for various developmental objectives. Cooperation with other organizations such as the UN Conference on Trade and Development (UNCTAD) is also included.

Since the 1 August 2004 decision, this subject has been dropped from the Doha agenda.

Key dates: trade and competition policy

Continuing work in working group with defined agenda: to 5th Ministerial Conference, 2003 (in Mexico)

Negotiations: after 5th Ministerial Conference, 2003 (in Mexico) subject to "explicit consensus" on modalities with a deadline: by 1 January 2005, part of single undertaking. But no consensus; dropped from Doha agenda in the 1 August 2004 decision.

Transparency in government procurement

A third "Singapore issue" that was handled by a working group set up by the Singapore Ministerial Conference in 1996.

The Doha Declaration says that the "negotiations shall be limited to the transparency aspects and therefore will not restrict the scope for countries to give preferences to domestic supplies and suppliers"—it is separate from the plurilateral Government Procurement Agreement.

The declaration also stresses development concerns, technical assistance and capacity building.

Since the 1 August 2004 decision, this subject has been dropped from the Doha agenda.

Key dates: government procurement (transparency)

Continuing work in working group with defined agenda: to 5th Ministerial Conference, 2003 (in Mexico)

Negotiations: after 5th Ministerial Conference, 2003 (in Mexico) subject to "explicit consensus" on modalities with deadline: by 1 January 2005, part of single undertaking. But no consensus; dropped from Doha agenda in the 1 August 2004 Decision.

Trade facilitation

A fourth "Singapore issue" kicked off by the 1996 Ministerial Conference.

The declaration recognizes the case for "further expediting the movement, release and clearance of goods, including goods in transit, and the need for enhanced technical assistance and capacity building in this area".

In the period until the Fifth Ministerial Conference in 2003, the WTO Goods Council, which had been working on this subject since 1997, "shall review and as appropriate, clarify and improve relevant aspects of Articles 5 (Freedom of Transit), 8 (Fees and Formalities Connected with Importation and Exportation) and 10 (Publication and Administration of Trade Regulations) of the General Agreement on Tariffs and Trade (GATT 1994) and identify the trade facilitation needs and priorities of Members, in particular developing and least-developed countries".

Those issues were cited in the 1 August 2004 decision that broke the Cancún deadlock. Members agreed to start negotiations on trade facilitation, but not the three other Singapore issues.

Key dates: trade facilitation

Continuing work in Goods Council with defined agenda: to 5th Ministerial Conference, 2003 (in Mexico)

Negotiations: after 5th Ministerial Conference, 2003 (in Mexico) subject to "explicit consensus" on modalities, agreed in 1 August 2004 Decision.

Deadline: originally by 1 January 2005, now unofficially the end of 2006, part of single undertaking

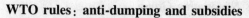

WTO rules: anti-dumping and subsidies

The ministers agreed to negotiations on the Anti-Dumping (GATT Article 6) and Subsidies agreements. The aim is to clarify and improve disciplines while preserving the basic, concepts, principles of these agreements, and taking into account the needs of developing and least-developed participants.

In overlapping negotiating phases, participants first indicated which provisions of these two agreements they think should be the subject of clarification and improvement in the next phase of negotiations. The ministers mention specifically fisheries subsidies as one sector important to developing countries and where participants should aim to clarify and improve WTO disciplines.

Negotiations take place in the Rules Negotiating Group.

Key dates: anti-dumping, subsidies

Start: January 2002

Stock taking: 5th Ministerial Conference, 2003 (in Mexico)

Deadline: originally by 1 January 2005, now unofficially the end of 2006, part of single undertaking

WTO rules: regional trade agreements

WTO rules say regional trade agreements have to meet certain conditions. But interpreting the wording of these rules has proved controversial, and has been a central element in the work of the Regional Trade Agreements Committee. As a result, since 1995 the committee has failed to complete its assessments of whether individual trade agreements conform with WTO provisions.

This is now an important challenge, particularly when nearly all member governments are parties to regional agreements, are negotiating them, or are considering negotiating them. In the Doha Declaration, members agreed to negotiate a solution, giving due regard to the role that these agreements can play in fostering development.

The declaration mandates negotiations aimed at "clarifying and improving disciplines and procedures under the existing WTO provisions applying to regional trade agreements. The negotiations shall take into account the developmental aspects of regional trade agreements. "

These negotiations fell into the general timetable established for virtually all negotiations under the Doha Declaration. The original deadline of 1 January 2005 was missed and the current unofficial aim is to finish the talks by the end of 2006. The 2003 Fifth Ministerial Conference in Mexico was intended to take stock of progress, provide any necessary political guidance, and take decisions as necessary.

Negotiations take place in the Rules Negotiating Group.

Key dates: regional trade

Start: January 2002

Stock taking: 5th Ministerial Conference, 2003 (in Mexico)

Deadline: originally by 1 January 2005, now unofficially the end of 2006, part of single undertaking

Dispute Settlement Understanding

The 1994 Marrakesh Ministerial Conference mandated WTO member governments to conduct a review of the Dispute Settlement Understanding (DSU, the WTO agreement on dispute settlement) within four years of the entry into force of the WTO Agreement (i. e. by 1 January 1999).

The Dispute Settlement Body (DSB) started the review in late 1997, and held a series of informal discussions on the basis of proposals and issues that members identified. Many, if not all, members clearly felt that improvements should be made to the understanding. However, the DSB could not reach a consensus on the results of the review.

The Doha Declaration mandates negotiations and states (in par 47) that these will not be part of the single undertaking—i. e. that they will not be tied to the overall success or failure of the other negotiations mandated by the declaration. Originally set to conclude by May 2003, the negotiations are continuing without a deadline.

Negotiations take place in "special sessions" of the Dispute Settlement Body.

Key dates: disputes understanding

Start: January 2002

Deadline: originally by May 2003, currently no deadline, separate from single undertaking

Trade and environment

New negotiations

Multilateral environmental agreements. Ministers agreed to launch negotiations on the relationship between existing WTO rules and specific trade obligations set out in multilateral environmental agreements. The negotiations will address how WTO rules are to apply to WTO members that are parties to environmental agreements, in particular to clarify the relationship between trade measures taken under the environmental agreements and WTO rules.

So far no measure affecting trade taken under an environmental agreement has been challenged in the GATT-WTO system.

Information exchange. Ministers agreed to negotiate procedures for regular information exchange between secretariats of multilateral environmental agreements and the WTO. Currently, the Trade and Environment Committee holds an information session with different secretariats of the multilateral environmental agreements once or twice a year to discuss the trade-related provisions in these environmental agreements and also their dispute settlement mechanisms. The new information exchange procedures may expand the scope of existing cooperation.

Observer status. Overall, the situation concerning the granting of observer status in the WTO to other international governmental organizations is currently blocked for political reasons. The negotiations aim to develop criteria for observership in WTO.

Trade barriers on environmental goods and services. Ministers also agreed to negotiations on the reduction or elimination of tariff and non-tariff barriers to environmental goods and services. Examples of environmental goods and services are catalytic converters, air filters or consultancy services on wastewater management.

Fisheries subsidies. Ministers agreed to clarify and improve WTO rules that apply to fisheries subsidies. The issue of fisheries subsidies has been studied in the Trade and Environment Committee for several years. Some studies demonstrate these subsidies can be environmentally damaging if they lead to too many fishermen chasing too few fish.

Negotiations on these issues, including concepts of what are the relevant environmental goods and services, take place in "special sessions" of the Trade and Environment Committee. Negotiations on market access for environmental goods and services take place in the Market Access Negotiating Group and Services Council "special sessions".

Ministers instructed the Trade and Environment Committee, in pursuing work on all items on its agenda, to pay particular attention to the following areas:

The effect of environmental measures on market access, especially for developing countries.

"Win-win-win" situations: when eliminating or reducing trade restrictions and distortions would benefit trade, the environment and development.

Intellectual property. Paragraph 19 of the Ministerial Declaration mandates the TRIPS Council to continue clarifying the relationship between the TRIPS Agreement and the Biological Diversity Convention. Ministers also ask the Trade and Environment Committee to continue to look at the relevant provisions of the TRIPS agreement.

Environmental labelling requirements. The Trade and Environment Committee is to look at the impact of eco-labelling on trade and examine whether existing WTO rules

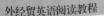
stand in the way of eco-labelling policies. Parallel discussions are to take place in the Technical Barriers to Trade (TBT) Committee.

For all these issues: when working on these (market access, "win-win-win" situations, intellectual property and environmental labelling), the Trade and Environment Committee should identify WTO rules that would need to be clarified.

General: ministers recognize the importance of technical assistance and capacity building programmes for developing countries in the trade and environment area. They also encourage members to share expertise and experience on national environmental reviews.

Key dates: environment

Committee reports to ministers: 5th and 6th Ministerial Conferences, 2003 and 2005 (in Mexico and Hong Kong, China)

Negotiations stock taking: 5th Ministerial Conference, 2003 (in Mexico)

Negotiations deadline: originally by 1 January 2005, now unofficially the end of 2006, part of single undertaking

Electronic commerce

The Doha Declaration endorses the work already done on electronic commerce and instructs the General Council to consider the most appropriate institutional arrangements for handling the work programme, and to report on further progress to the Fifth Ministerial Conference.

The declaration on electronic commerce from the Second Ministerial Conference in Geneva, 1998, said that WTO members will continue their practice of not imposing customs duties on electronic transmissions. The Doha Declaration states that members will continue this practice until the Fifth Ministerial Conference.

Key date: electronic commerce

Report on further progress: 5th Ministerial Conference, 2003 (in Mexico)

Small economies

Small economies face specific challenges in their participation in world trade, for example lack of economy of scale or limited natural resources.

The Doha Declaration mandates the General Council to examine these problems and to make recommendations to the next Ministerial Conference as to what trade-related measures could improve the integration of small economies.

Key date: small economies

Recommendations: 5th and 6th Ministerial Conferences, 2003 and 2005 (in Mexico and Hong Kong, China)

Trade, debt and finance

Many developing countries face serious external debt problems and have been through financial crises. WTO ministers decided in Doha to establish a Working Group on Trade, Debt and Finance to look at how trade-related measures can contribute to find a durable solution to these problems. This working group will report to the General Council which will in turn report to the next Ministerial Conference.

Key date: debt and finance

General Council report: 5th and 6th Ministerial Conferences, 2003 and 2005 (in Mexico and Hong Kong, China)

Trade and technology transfer

A number of provisions in the WTO agreements mention the need for a transfer of technology to take place between developed and developing countries.

However, it is not clear how such a transfer takes place in practice and if specific measures might be taken within the WTO to encourage such flows of technology.

WTO ministers decided in Doha to establish a working group to examine the issue. The working group will report to the General Council which itself will report to the next Ministerial Conference.

Key date: technology transfer

General Council report: 5th and 6th Ministerial Conferences, 2003 and 2005 (in Mexico and Hong Kong, China)

Technical cooperation and capacity building

Through various paragraphs of the Doha Declaration, WTO member governments have made new commitments on technical cooperation and capacity building.

For example, the section on the relationship between trade and investment includes a call (par 21) for enhanced support for technical assistance and capacity building in this area.

Within the specific heading "technical cooperation and capacity building", paragraph 41 lists all the references to commitments on technical cooperation within the Doha Declaration: paragraphs 16 (market access for non-agricultural products), 21 (trade and investment), 24 (trade and competition policy), 26 (transparency in government procurement), 27 (trade facilitation), 33 (environment), 38 – 40 (technical cooperation and capacity building), 42 and 43 (least-developed countries). (Paragraph 2 in the preamble is also cited.)

Under this heading (i. e. pars 38 – 41), WTO member governments reaffirm all technical cooperation and capacity building commitments made throughout the declaration and add general commitments:

The Secretariat, in coordination with other relevant agencies, is to encourage WTO developing country members to consider trade as a main element for reducing poverty and to include trade measures in their development strategies.

The agenda set out in the Doha Declaration gives priority to small, vulnerable, and transition economies, as well as to members and observers that do not have permanent delegations in Geneva.

Technical assistance must be delivered by the WTO and other relevant international organizations within a coherent policy framework.

The Director-General reported to the General Council in December 2002 and to the Fifth Ministerial Conference on the implementation and adequacy of these new commitments.

Following the declaration's instructions to develop a plan ensuring long-term funding for WTO technical assistance, the General Council adopted on 20 December 2001 (one month after the Doha conference) a new budget that increased technical assistance funding by 80% and established a Doha Development Agenda Global Trust Fund. The fund now has an annual budget of 24 million Swiss francs.

Key dates: technical cooperation

Technical assistance funding raised 80% ; Development Agenda Global Trust Fund set up: December 2001

Director-General reports to General Council: December 2002

Director-General reports to ministers: 5th and 6th Ministerial Conferences, 2003 and 2005 (in Mexico and Hong Kong, China)

Least-developed countries

Many developed countries have now significantly decreased or actually scrapped tariffs on imports from least-developed countries (LDCs).

In the Doha declaration, WTO member governments commit themselves to the objective of duty-free, quota-free market access for LDCs' products and to consider additional measures to improve market access for these exports.

Members also agree to try to ensure that least-developed countries can negotiate WTO membership faster and more easily.

Some technical assistance is targeted specifically for least-developed countries. The Doha Declaration urges WTO member donors to significantly increase their contributions.

In addition, the Sub-Committee for LDCs (a subsidiary body of the WTO Committee on Trade and Development) designed a work programme un February 2002, as instructed by the Doha Declaration, taking into account the parts of the declaration related to trade that was issued at the UN LDC Conference.

Key date: least-developed countries

Reports to: General Council: July 2002, 5th and 6th Ministerial Conferences, 2003 and 2005 (in Mexico and Hong Kong, China)

Special and differential treatment

The WTO agreements contain special provisions which give developing countries special rights. These special provisions include, for example, longer time periods for implementing agreements and commitments or measures to increase trading opportunities for developing countries.

In the Doha Declaration, member governments agree that all special and differential treatment provisions should be reviewed with a view to strengthening them and making them more precise.

More specifically, the declaration (together with the Decision on Implementation Related Issues and Concerns) mandates the Trade and Development Committee to identify which of those special and differential treatment provisions are mandatory, and to consider the implications of making mandatory those which are currently non-binding.

The Decision on Implementation—Related Issues and Concerns instructed the committee to make its recommendations for the General Council before July 2002. But because members needed more time, this was postponed to the end of July 2005.

Key date: special and differential treatment

Recommendations to General Council: July 2002, July 2005

Cancún 2003

The Doha agenda set a number of tasks to be completed before or at the Fifth Ministerial Conference in Cancún, Mexico, 10—14 September 2003. On the eve of the conference, on 30 August, agreement was reached on the TRIPS and public health issue. However, a number of the deadlines were missed, including "modalities" for agriculture and the non-agricultural market access negotiations, reform of the Dispute Settlement Understanding, and recommendations on special and differential treatment. Nor were members near to agreement on the multilateral geographical indications register for wines and spirits, due to be completed in Cancún.

Although Cancún saw delegations move closer to consensus on a number of key issues, members remained deeply divided over a number of issues, including the " Singapore " issues—launching negotiations on investment, competition policy, transparency in government procurement, and trade facilitation—and agriculture.

The conference ended without consensus. Ten months later, the deadlock was broken in Geneva when the General Council agreed on the "July package" in the early hours of 1 August 2004, which kicked off negotiations in trade facilitation but not the three other Singapore issues. The delay meant the 1 January 2005 deadline for finishing the talks could not be met. Unofficially, members aimed to complete the next phase of the negotiations at the Hong Kong Ministerial Conference, 13—18 December 2005, including full "modalities" in agriculture and market access for non-agricultural products, and to finish the talks by the end of the following year. (*Source*:*http*://*www. wto. org*)

Notes

[1] subsidiary 附属机构
[2] sour 使失望，使变酸
[3] discord 不调和，不和
[4] deadlock 僵局，停顿
[5] Singapore issues 新加坡议题
[6] General Council 总理事会
[7] Doha Declaration《多哈宣言》
[8] controversy 争论，争吵
[9] stringent 严厉的；银根紧的
[10] eligibility 合格，合格性
[11] negligible 可以忽略的，无用的
[12] fraud 欺骗，欺诈
[13] interim 中期；暂时的
[14] subsidize 补助，资助，补贴
[15] countervail 补偿，抵消
[16] encompass 围绕，包括
[17] prejudge 预先判断
[18] slash 删减
[19] annex 附件
[20] escalation 扩大，增加
[21] reticence 无言，沉默，勉强
[22] patentability 取得专利的可能性

［23］folklore 民俗学，民间风俗，民间传说

［24］explicit 详述的，清楚的，直言的

［25］hardcore 核心部分，中坚分子

［26］plurilateral 多边的

［27］Cancún 坎昆（墨西哥城市）

［28］catalytic 催化的

［29］convention 大会，协定，惯例，约定

［30］scrap 扔弃，敲碎，拆毁

Exercises

I. Match the following words in Column A and Column B

Column A	Column B
1. eligibility	a. 沉默，勉强
2. fraud	b. 争论，争吵
3. annex	c. 合格，合格性
4. escalation	d. 附属机构
5. reticence	e. 附件
6. subsidiary	f. 新加坡议题
7. discord	g. 取得专利的可能性
8. deadlock	h. 不调和，不和
9. Doha Declaration	i. 欺骗，欺诈
10. controversy	j. 多哈宣言
11. patentability	k. 民间风俗，民间传说
12. folklore	l. 僵局，停顿
13. hardcore	m. 核心部分
14. convention	n. 扩大，增加
15. Singapore issues	o. 协定，约定
16. General Council	p. 总理事会

II. Translate the following sentences into Chinese

1. The WTO Director-General is to ensure that WTO technical assistance gives priority to helping developing countries implement existing WTO obligations, and to increase their capacity to participate more effectively in future negotiations.

2. The declaration reconfirms the long-term objective already agreed in the present WTO Agreement: to establish a fair and market-oriented trading system through a programme of fundamental reform.

3. Accordingly, the services negotiations started officially in early 2000 under the Council for Trade in Services. In March 2001, the Services Council fulfilled a key element in the negotiating mandate by establishing the negotiating guidelines and procedures.

4. The declaration also extends the deadline for least-developed countries to apply

provisions on pharmaceutical patents until 1 January 2016.

5. WTO rules say regional trade agreements have to meet certain conditions. But interpreting the wording of these rules has proved controversial, and has been a central element in the work of the Regional Trade Agreements Committee.

6. Multilateral environmental agreements. Ministers agreed to launch negotiations on the relationship between existing WTO rules and specific trade obligations set out in multilateral environmental agreements.

7. The issue of fisheries subsidies has been studied in the Trade and Environment Committee for several years. Some studies demonstrate these subsidies can be environmentally damaging if they lead to too many fishermen chasing too few fish.

8. When eliminating or reducing trade restrictions and distortions would benefit trade, the environment and development.

9. Small economies face specific challenges in their participation in world trade, for example lack of economy of scale or limited natural resources.

10. The WTO agreements contain special provisions which give developing countries special rights. These special provisions include, for example, longer time periods for implementing agreements and commitments or measures to increase trading opportunities for developing countries.

III. Cloze

The TRIPS Agreement provides a higher level _____ protection to geographical indications _____ wines and spirits. This means they should be protected even if there is no risk _____ misleading consumers or unfair competition. A number of countries want to negotiate extending this higher level to other products. Others oppose the move, and the debate _____ the TRIPS Council has included the question of whether the relevant provisions of the TRIPS Agreement provide a mandate _____ extending coverage _____ wines and spirits.

The Doha Declaration notes that the TRIPS Council will handle this _____ the declaration's paragraph 12 (which deals with implementation issues). Paragraph 12 offers two tracks: "(a) where we provide a specific negotiating mandate _____ this Declaration, the relevant implementation issues shall be addressed under that mandate; (b) the other outstanding implementation issues shall be addressed as a matter of priority _____ the relevant WTO bodies, which shall report _____ the Trade Negotiations Committee [TNC], established under paragraph 46 below, by the end of 2002 for appropriate action."

Ⅳ. Underline the important sentences in the text, which give you useful information

Ⅴ. Retell or write down what you learn from the text in English or in Chinese

Unit Fourteen

The Seventeenth APEC Ministerial Meeting Joint Statement

THE SEVENTEENTH APEC MINISTERIAL MEETING
Busan, Republic of Korea
15-16 November 2005
JOINT STATEMENT

APEC Ministers from Australia, Brunei Darussalam, Canada, Chile, the People's Republic of China, Hong Kong, China, Indonesia, Japan, the Republic of Korea, Malaysia, Mexico, New Zealand, Papua New Guinea, Peru, the Philippines, Russia, Singapore, Chinese Taipei, Thailand, the United States of America, and Viet Nam, representing economies which collectively account for forty-six percent of world trade, fifty-seven percent of the global GDP and forty-five percent of the global population, gathered in Busan, Korea, on 15—16 November 2005, in order to participate in the Seventeenth Asia-Pacific Economic Cooperation (APEC) Ministerial Meeting. The APEC Secretariat was also present. The Association of Southeast Asian Nations (ASEAN) Secretariat, the Pacific Economic Cooperation Council (PECC) and the Pacific Islands Forum (PIF) attended as official observers. The meeting was chaired by H. E. Ban Ki-moon, Minister of Foreign Affairs and Trade and H. E. Hyun Chong Kim, Minister for Trade of the Republic of Korea.

Ministers focused discussions around the APEC 2005 theme: "Towards One Community: Meet the Challenge, Make the Change." They reaffirmed their commitment to achieving trade and investment liberalisation and facilitation in the APEC region by 2010 and 2020, and resolved to continually push it forward in this regard.

Ministers reviewed the key achievements of APEC 2005, which was hosted by the Republic of Korea, and agreed upon initiatives to be undertaken during the APEC 2006 year, which will be hosted by Viet Nam.

Ministers agreed to the following:

Strengthening the Multilateral Trading System

1. APEC's Contribution to the World Trade Organisation (WTO) Doha Development Agenda (DDA) negotiations

Ministers reaffirmed the utmost importance APEC economies attached to the successful conclusion of the DDA negotiations by the end of 2006 with an ambitious and overall balanced outcome.

Ministers agreed that the 6th WTO Ministerial Conference in Hong Kong, China would be a critical step in achieving this goal and that significant progress must be made in the Ministerial in resolving considerable divergences, and a clear roadmap for completing the Round in 2006 must be established.

In this regard, Ministers recommended the Leaders to adopt a stand-alone statement on the DDA negotiations that provided strong political leadership and commitment necessary to produce a sound platform for successfully concluding the negotiations in Hong Kong, China, and urged all other WTO Members to show flexibilities needed to move forward the negotiations by and beyond the Hong Kong Ministerial.

2. WTO Capacity Building

Ministers reaffirmed the importance of trade-related capacity building as a tool to enable developing economies to accede to the WTO, fully participate in the WTO negotiations, enjoy the full benefits of the WTO membership, and maximise the potential of trade as a tool for social and economic development.

Ministers welcomed the first policy-oriented WTO Capacity Building Workshop on Best Practices in Trade Facilitation Capacity Building held in Jeju in May, and urged Officials to continue work in this area based on the workshop's recommendations. Ministers welcomed the outcomes of the APEC/WTO Trade Facilitation Roundtable 2005 held in Geneva in February, which provided a unique opportunity to share APEC's expertise in trade facilitation with WTO members. They also welcomed the Seminar on the Information Technology (IT)/Electronics Industry held in Gyeongju in September as an effective measure for capacity building and raising awareness of future trade expansion of IT/electronic products.

Ministers instructed Officials to continue to implement capacity building activities across the full range of areas included in the WTO DDA negotiations, and to continue to evaluate APEC's past capacity building activities, drawing on the expertise of APEC members as well as international organisations, and to report their progress at the Ministers Responsible for Trade (MRT) meeting next year. They called for further APEC attention to the issues of multi-stakeholder and intra-governmental consultations, recognising that these were crucial tools for APEC members to identify their interests and build consensus before and during trade negotiations.

3. Accession of APEC members to the WTO

Ministers welcomed the progress that has been made in the WTO accession negotiations for the Russian Federation and Viet Nam, and looked forward to the rapid conclusion of these negotiations for their early accession.

4. APEC Geneva Caucus

Ministers commended the work undertaken by the APEC Geneva Caucus to advance the DDA negotiations, especially in the area of tariff elimination of IT products and of trade facilitation, and instructed it to continue its work with a view of sharing APEC's experience with WTO Members, contributing to the successful outcome of the 6th WTO Ministerial Conference and promoting an ambitious and balanced conclusion of the DDA negotiations. They highly welcomed the visit by members of the APEC Business Advisory Council (ABAC) to Geneva in June in an effort to provide business input into the DDA negotiations.

Mid-term Stocktake of the Bogor Goals

Ministers endorsed the report, A Mid-term Stocktake of Progress Towards the Bogor Goals: Busan Roadmap to the Bogor Goals. They commended the report for demonstrating APEC's good progress towards the Bogor Goals and for developing a roadmap to achieve the Bogor Goals and to meet the expectations of the business community in facilitating business activities. Ministers agreed to recommend that Leaders endorse the report.

Ministers recognised that APEC economies had achieved significant liberalisation and facilitation of trade and investment since 1994. They also noted that the rewards from these policy choices had been substantial and had contributed to sustained economic growth and significant welfare improvements in the region.

Ministers remained fully committed to achieving the Bogor Goals of free and open trade and investment in the Asia-Pacific by 2010 for developed members and 2020 for developing members as stipulated in the Bogor Declaration. Ministers emphasised that the

Bogor Goals, the core organising principle of APEC, aimed at promoting sustainable growth and prosperity in the region.

Recognising that the environment for trade was constantly evolving, Ministers expressed the need for APEC to adapt its focus accordingly and to continue to deliver concrete and business relevant outcomes in the years ahead to realise the Bogor Goals. They agreed that, while the APEC agenda should be revitalised to keep pace with the new international trade environment, APEC must ensure the achievement of the Bogor Goals.

In order to accelerate progress towards the Bogor Goals, Ministers particularly emphasised the Busan Roadmap to the Bogor Goals, which outlines key priorities and frameworks, such as support for the multilateral trading system, strengthening collective and individual actions, promotion of high-quality regional trade agreements and free trade agreements (RTAs/FTAs), the Busan Business Agenda, a strategic approach to capacity building and the pathfinder approach, ensuring APEC to better respond to the new business environment and continuing to drive free and open trade and investment in the region through work on intellectual property rights (IPR), trade facilitation, anti-corruption, investment, and secure trade.

Ministers reaffirmed their deep commitment to the multilateral trading system and their support for the WTO. They agreed that APEC economies would continue to make contributions towards the successful outcome of the WTO DDA negotiations and that the APEC Geneva Caucus must redouble its collective efforts to advance the negotiations in all areas of the DDA. They agreed that, once the results of the DDA negotiations were known, APEC members would need to consider what further liberalisation steps would be needed to help reach the Bogor Goals.

Ministers agreed that Individual Action Plans (IAPs) and Collective Action Plans (CAPs) were the major vehicles in achieving the Bogor Goals. They agreed to strengthen the IAP Peer Review processes and make them more transparent and accessible to business. Ministers consequently agreed that the next round of the IAP peer reviews would be conducted from 2007—2009 under the strengthened review framework.

They agreed that high-quality RTAs/FTAs maximised the contribution of these agreements to APEC-wide progress towards the Bogor Goals. Ministers agreed that APEC would develop by 2008 comprehensive model measures on as many commonly accepted RTA/FTA chapters as possible by building on its work in developing model measures for trade facilitation, taking into account the diversity of APEC economies. They agreed that this would be a valuable contribution to maintaining consistency and coherence across RTAs/FTAs in the region.

Ministers agreed that APEC must develop a comprehensive business facilitation program along with strategies, taking into account the diversity of member economies with respect to economic development and domestic policy objectives that also addressed behind-the-border administrative burdens and impediments to trade and investment.

They also underscored the need for APEC to continue to put emphasis on economic and technical cooperation (ECOTECH) to ensure that the Bogor Goals were not only reached, but that their potential benefits were distributed as broadly as possible within the Asia-Pacific community.

Ministers encouraged the implementation of the decisions and commitments taken in the APEC context, both individually and collectively, while preserving APEC's core principles of voluntarism, comprehensiveness, and consensus-based decision-making.

Trade and Investment Liberalisation and Facilitation (TILF).

Ministers endorsed the 2005 Committee on Trade and Investment (CTI) Annual Report to Ministers on APEC's Trade and Investment Liberalisation and Facilitation activities, including the revised/enhanced CAPs, and commended the progress made by the CTI in implementing the CAPs. They welcomed the achievements, in particular, in the following areas:

1. Advancing Trade and Investment Liberalisation and Facilitation

Individual and Collective Action Plans:

Ministers reaffirmed the importance they attached to the Individual Action Plans (IAPs) as one of the principle vehicles for reaching the Bogor Goals. Ministers endorsed the 2005 IAPs and welcomed the measures undertaken by individual economies to liberalise and facilitate trade. Ministers also welcomed the report of the newly included issues in the IAPs: RTAs/FTAs and Implementation of General and Area-Specific Transparency, all of which would contribute to greater transparency in the activities undertaken by member economies.

Ministers welcomed the successful completion of the IAP Peer Reviews of all twenty-one member economies as our Leaders had instructed in 2001, which confirmed that all member economies were making good progress towards achieving the Bogor Goals. Ministers also welcomed the continuation of the IAP Peer Review Process for the next three years in a strengthened manner, including a greater focus on what APEC members were doing individually and collectively to implement specific APEC commitments and priorities. Ministers endorsed the revised IAP Peer Review Guidelines and the timetable to carry out the next round of reviews, noting that this would provide greater opportunities for business to raise its views.

Ministers welcomed the progress made in the CAPs and instructed Officials to continue to review and update them in order to substantially contribute to APEC's commitment to free and open trade and investment in the Asia-Pacific region by 2010— 2020.

Ministers endorsed the APEC-OECD Integrated Checklist on Regulatory Reform (Checklist), which is a voluntary tool that member economies may use to assess their respective regulatory reform efforts. They instructed Officials to continue to explore ways of working with the OECD to disseminate the Checklist as well as to assist economies in utilising this tool.

Ministers noted the progress in improving the reporting mechanism of Strengthening Economic Legal Infrastructure (SELI) and a work plan to develop a new SELI IAP template in 2006.

Investment:

Ministers noted the importance of investment flows to and from the APEC region and reaffirmed the importance of investment liberalisation and facilitation in the progress towards the Bogor Goals. The APEC Investment Opportunities Conference 2005 to be held in Busan in November would provide a useful overview of diverse investment climates in the APEC members, offering a forum for member economies to exchange information on individual investment frameworks. Ministers welcomed Viet Nam's proposal to hold an APEC Seminar on Experiences in Attracting Investment from Trans-National Corporations (TNCs).

Ministers noted the important contribution made by the APEC Non-Binding Investment Principles (NBIP), which were concluded in 1994 to achieve more liberal investment regimes in the APEC region. Ministers welcomed the efforts to strengthen interaction with ABAC and reaffirmed the need to improve the investment environment for business in the region and instructed Officials to further intensify their efforts to achieve investment liberalisation and facilitation.

Ministers welcomed the outcomes of the APEC Seminar held in Tokyo in September, focusing on the recent developments of the investment elements in RTAs/ FTAs and bilateral investment treaties (BITs). Ministers stressed the need to strengthen work in the investment area, including assistance to APEC economies in identifying the impact of investment liberalisation and a further study on the interaction and relationship between various agreements on investment.

Ministers noted the APEC-OECD seminar on policy framework for investment held in November, which identified many areas where APEC and the OECD could strengthen cooperation on investment for development.

Customs Procedures:

Ministers commended the work done to reflect the growing needs of trade facilitation and security through simplification and harmonisation of customs procedures in the region and in that context welcomed two new CAP items, i. e. the Time Release Survey, which is a useful tool to find and improve bottlenecks in customs related procedures, thereby facilitating trade.

Ministers welcomed the release of an "APEC Customs and Trade Facilitation Handbook", which would give Asia-Pacific businesses better access to information on customs laws and regulations in APEC member economies. The handbook offers an invaluable resource for business people to avoid costs incurred by a lack of knowledge of procedures and regulations.

Business Mobility:

Ministers noted the importance of business mobility in trade facilitation. They welcomed the entry of Viet Nam as the 17th member of the APEC Business Travel Card (ABTC) Scheme and commended efforts within APEC to facilitate business mobility while making travel more secure.

Standards and Conformance:

Recognising that the alignment of domestic standards with international standards contributed to trade facilitation in the region, Ministers welcomed the results of a comprehensive review that showed a very high level of achievement of the alignment work in the agreed upon priority areas. Ministers instructed Officials to launch new voluntary alignment works on the International Electro-technical Commission (IEC) standards for electrical equipment, especially for those that were covered under the IEC System for Conformity Testing to Standards for Safety of Electrical Equipment (IECEE) Certification Bodies (CB) Scheme to be completed by 2010.

Ministers also welcomed the publication of the first CTI Sub-Committee on Standards and Conformance (SCSC) blueprint, which summarised the activities undertaken in the areas of Standards and Conformance in APEC, noting that it would enhance the knowledge of the business community on standards and conformance related work.

Private Sector Development:

Ministers acknowledged that issues like trade facilitation, transparency and business regulations and administrative procedures had noteworthy effects on the development of the private sector, especially SMEs. They welcomed the initiative to develop a Private Sector Development agenda to improve the business environment in the region and to continue to support the development of SMEs in terms of raising their competitiveness in the marketplace. They noted that such efforts would build on existing areas of APEC work such as trade facilitation, transparency and regulatory reform, promote the sharing of best practices and support the outcomes of the 12th APEC SME Ministerial Meeting and focus on capacity building.

2. Trade Facilitation Action Plan (TFAP)

Ministers welcomed the progress made by economies towards meeting the target established under the 2001 TFAP of a five percent reduction in trade facilitation costs by 2006. They agreed to another five percent reduction by 2010.

Ministers commended the progress made by the member economies in implementing the APEC TFAP and welcomed the reports by the economies on actions and measures taken in the areas of movement of goods, standards and conformance, business mobility and e-commerce.

Ministers welcomed the preparatory work underway for the final review in 2006 and endorsed the TFAP Roadmap to 2006 that proposed a work program to ensure that APEC accomplished the goal of the aforementioned five percent reduction in transaction costs across the region by 2006. They also instructed Officials to develop a work plan that would take the TFAP beyond 2006.

Ministers instructed Officials to carry out further concrete actions in identified priority areas, such as improving customs procedures, enhancing the alignment of domestic standards with international standards, facilitating business mobility and fostering a paperless trading environment, with a view of producing tangible benefits for the business community and stressed the need to promote capacity building in the aforementioned four areas to enable all economies to fully implement the TFAP.

Ministers welcomed the fruitful outcomes of the APEC Symposium on Assessment and Benchmark of Paperless Trading held in China in September. Ministers urged all member economies to strengthen cooperation in this area with a view of reinforcing mutual cooperation and pushing forward the achievement of APEC's paperless trading goals.

They welcomed the initiative by Australia and Viet Nam for a targeted process of 2006 and endorsed the development of a comprehensive business facilitation program, which builds on the gains made by the TFAP and the Santiago Initiative for Expanding Trade in APEC and also draws in the APEC Finance Ministers' Process and ABAC to develop effective strategies and modalities.

Ministers welcomed outreach efforts by the CTI and the APEC Secretariat to showcase APEC's achievements and future plans in the area of trade facilitation, including the publication of a business outreach brochure.

3. RTAs / FTAs

Ministers emphasised the importance they attached to APEC's work on RTAs/ FTAs. APEC members view high-quality and comprehensive RTAs/FTAs as one of the principal avenues for reaching the Bogor Goals. Ministers noted that there was a window of opportunity for APEC to help ensure that the spread of RTAs/FTAs in the region was consistent with the Bogor Goals. Ministers instructed Officials to continue their work on developing policies towards RTAs/FTAs.

They agreed that APEC should continue to play a constructive role in this area by exchanging information and experiences on APEC member economies' RTAs/FTAs as well as by taking concrete measures to enhance transparency in IAPs and to strengthen targeted capacity building. In this regard, they welcomed efforts by the parties to the Trans-Pacific Strategic Economic Partnership to brief other APEC members on the recently concluded agreement.

Ministers agreed that the RTAs/FTAs Best Practices document agreed upon last year helped to promote a common understanding of and greater convergence and coherence among RTAs/FTAs. Ministers also agreed to continue efforts to use the Best Practices document on a voluntary basis as a meaningful reference in RTAs/FTAs negotiations.

Ministers took note of the successful 3rd Trade Policy Dialogue on RTAs/FTAs held in Jeju in May and welcomed the work program, initiated at the Dialogue, on developing model measures for RTAs/FTAs chapters. In this regard, they welcomed the Model Measures for Trade Facilitation in RTAs/FTAs and expressed their conviction that these non-binding model measures, which APEC members were encouraged to follow, would serve as a reference for APEC member economies achieving high-quality free trade agreements, making a genuine contribution to the liberalisation and expansion of trade in the Asia-Pacific region.

Ministers supported capacity building assistance to help member economies, especially developing economies, to enhance negotiations skills for RTAs/FTAs and for addressing the concerns of domestic industries. They welcomed expanding initiatives in this area, including the Workshop on Preferential Rules of Origin in Seoul, and looked forward to the forthcoming workshop on investment and market access issues in Malaysia, the advanced workshops on negotiating FTAs in Indonesia, and the APEC Workshop on Best Practices in Trade Policy for RTAs/FTAs: Practical Lessons and Experiences for Developing Economies to be held in Viet Nam in 2006.

4. Strengthened Intellectual Property Protection and Enforcement

Ministers recognised that the protection and enforcement of Intellectual Property Rights (IPR) is essential to building a knowledge-based economy and are key factors for boosting economic development, promoting investment, spurring innovation, developing creative industries and driving economic growth.

Ministers fully supported the APEC Anti-Counterfeiting and Piracy Initiative adopted at the June 2005 meeting of APEC Ministers Responsible for Trade. Ministers endorsed the APEC Model Guidelines to Reduce Trade in Counterfeit and Pirated Goods, to Protect Against Unauthorised Copies, and to Prevent the Sale of Counterfeit Goods over the Internet, as called for in the APEC Anti-Counterfeiting and Piracy Initiative. Ministers agreed that the model guidelines and templates were a timely policy response to the emerging challenges of online piracy and trade in counterfeit and pirated goods and are valuable tools to help economies strengthen their IPR protection and enforcement regimes, as well as to raise public awareness about the importance of this issue. Given the importance of strong IPR regimes in the region, Ministers instructed economies to take further steps that build on the APEC Anti-Counterfeiting and Piracy Initiative in the coming year, in consultation with the private sector so as to reduce trade in counterfeit and pirated goods, curtail online piracy, and increase cooperation and capacity building in this area.

Ministers called on economies to complete the exchange of information on their IPR websites, IPR enforcement officials and steps they had taken to apply the APEC Effective Practices for Regulations Related to Optical Disc Production before SOMII2006, and to take steps to further this work.

Ministers welcomed members' progress in advancing the CAPs on IPR including the establishment of eleven IPR Service Centres and encouraged members to make further progress.

Ministers noted the success of the APEC High-level Symposium on IPR held in Xiamen in September, which marked an important step to strengthen cooperation on IPR protection among members and to enhance the dialogue between the public and private sectors.

5. Pathfinder Initiatives

Recognising that pathfinder initiatives were valuable tools for furthering trade and investment liberalisation and facilitation, Ministers stressed the importance of ensuring progress and retaining momentum in such initiatives. They encouraged Officials to hold further discussions on the implementation of current initiatives as well as to continue their efforts to identify additional areas in APEC that could serve as potential candidates for the pathfinder approach in accordance with the Guidelines on Pathfinders adopted last year, and encouraged further discussions on their implementation.

Trade and Digital Economy:

Ministers welcomed the progress made in implementing the Pathfinder on Trade and Digital Economy, in particular, the completion of the survey of member economies' Best Practices for Combating Optical Disk Piracy and the discussions on possible technology choice principles. They welcomed the successful workshop on technology choice held in February to discuss issues/policies aimed at maximising users' and suppliers' choices of innovative products and services. Ministers recognised the outcome of the dialogue on technology choice in February 2005, which focused on the relationship between the promotion of innovation and the development of knowledge-based economies and technology neutral policies and regulations; open, international, and voluntary standards; and non-discriminatory, transparent, technology neutral, and merit-based government procurement policies. Ministers agreed to continue discussion on these concepts in 2006, with a view to developing a set of technology choice principles for inclusion in the Leaders' Pathfinder Statement to implement APEC Policies on Trade and the Digital Economy.

APEC Sectoral Food Mutual Recognition Agreement (MRA) Pathfinder Initiative:

Ministers welcomed the fruitful outcome of the first APEC Sectoral Food MRA Pathfinder Initiative Meeting hosted by Thailand in June and endorsed Thailand's proposal to host a Seminar on the Development of Sectoral Food MRAs in June 2006. Member economies' active participation in this event is encouraged as it would help this pathfinder initiative make progress and facilitate trade in food products, which is important to the region and APEC's overall goals.

6. Food Cooperation

Ministers welcomed the progress made by economies towards strengthening food safety cooperation across APEC and noted the outcomes of the Food Safety Cooperation Seminar held in Gyeongju, co-sponsored by China, Australia, Thailand and Viet Nam. Ministers were encouraged by the ongoing work towards achieving a stocktake of the activities of relevant international and regional organisations aimed at promoting food safety, and they welcomed the establishment of an Ad Hoc Steering Group on food safety cooperation under the CTI SCSC. In completing its mandate, the Ad Hoc Group was expected to take input from and work in close collaboration with the Agricultural Technical Cooperation Working Group (ATCWG).

APEC Food System (AFS):

Ministers also welcomed the joint and cross-cutting actions being implemented by all APEC member economies and APEC fora, such as the ATCWG, to implement the APEC Food System. They encouraged further work to develop agriculture in the APEC region, including further work to develop rural infrastructure, to promote trade in food products and to disseminate technological advances in food production and processing.

Anti-Corruption and Transparency Standards:

Ministers recognised that APEC's goal of economic prosperity could not be achieved unless corruption, both in the domestic economies and in international business transactions, was effectively addressed and those individuals guilty of corruption were denied a safe haven.

Ministers agreed that corruption undermined economic performance, weakened democratic institutions and the rule of law, disrupted social order, destroyed public trust and provided an environment for organised crime, terrorism and other threats to human security to flourish. As it is one of the largest barriers to APEC's road to free trade, to increase economic development and to greater prosperity, Ministers reaffirmed that they would continue to look for avenues to effectively address this important issue within APEC as well as in other fora.

Ministers welcomed the outcomes of the APEC Anti-Corruption and Transparency Symposium (ACT Symposium) and urged greater action to combat corruption and to improve transparency. They applauded Korea for hosting the ACT Symposium and commended the APEC Anti-Corruption and Transparency (ACT) Task Force for beginning its important work. Ministers stressed the importance of capacity building programs and encouraged member economies to develop and submit capacity building projects in support of APEC works in transparency as well as in anti-corruption.

Ministers encouraged all APEC member economies to take all appropriate steps towards effective ratification and implementation, where appropriate, of the United Nations Convention Against Corruption (UNCAC). Ministers encouraged relevant APEC member economies to make the UNCAC a major priority. They urged all member economies to submit brief annual progress reports to the ACT Task Force on their APEC anti-corruption commitments, including a more concrete roadmap for accelerating the implementation and tracking progress. Ministers also encouraged the ACT Task Force to continue closer coordination with the APEC CTI and all other relevant APEC sub-fora.

Ministers welcomed the anti-corruption pledge that would be made by CEOs at this year's APEC CEO Summit and encouraged continued collaboration between the APEC ACT Task Force and ABAC. Ministers welcomed the private sector's call for a synergistic collaboration with the ACT Task Force to improve corporate governance and seek to strengthen this important public-private partnership. Ministers pledged to intensify regional cooperation to deny a safe haven to officials and individuals guilty of corruption, and encouraged greater cooperation in the areas of mutual legal assistance, where appropriate, extradition, asset recovery, and forfeiture of the proceeds of corruption. Accordingly, Ministers supported greater cooperation and information exchange among member economies as well as the sharing of expertise and experiences and supported capacity building on the denial of a safe haven, the UNCAC implementation, anti-bribery best practices, anti-corruption and SMEs, and other relevant areas including those as recommended in the ACT Course of Action (COA).

Ministers agreed to continue APEC's collective efforts to promote good governance, integrity, and transparency, as they were indispensable to APEC members' aspirations for a more secure and prosperous community in the Asia-Pacific region and beyond.

Ministers reiterated the importance of fulfilling the APEC Transparency Standards and the area-specific Transparency Standards. They welcomed the first comprehensive submission of IAP reports on the implementation of Transparency Standards, as formulated at APEC Los Cabos and Bangkok Leaders' Meeting in the Leaders' Statement to Implement Transparency Standards.

Human Security

Ministers shared the pain of bereaved families in the areas stricken by terrorist attacks and natural disasters, and expressed their deep condolences. They stressed the need to achieve the objectives of human security and trade and investment liberalisation and facilitation and highlighted the activities being undertaken in the areas of counter-terrorism, non-proliferation, infectious diseases, emergency preparedness and energy security.

1. Counter Terrorism and Secure Trade

Ministers reiterated that terrorism was a serious threat to the security, stability and growth of the APEC region. They continued to review the progress on APEC's commitments to dismantle transnational terrorist groups, to eliminate the danger posed by the proliferation of weapons of mass destruction, their delivery systems and related items, as well as to confront other direct threats to the security of our region in the future. Ministers encouraged APEC economies to continue to develop new initiatives in these areas, and to implement existing commitments to eliminate the danger of terrorism and secure trade unilaterally, bilaterally, multilaterally and in APEC, building on the comparative strengths of APEC.

They applauded the improved counter-terrorism coordination measures adopted by APEC within its own fora as well as other international counter-terrorism action groups. Ministers highlighted the benefits to human security of the APEC Counter Terrorism Action Plans (CTAP) in identifying capacity and gaps in regional security frameworks. Ministers looked forward to sharing the results of the APEC CTAP Cross-Analysis with relevant donor bodies. Ministers reiterated their resolve to securing trade in the APEC region. They welcomed the outcomes of the 3rd Secure Trade in the APEC Region (STAR Ⅲ) Conference in Incheon in February, and looked forward to the 4th STAR Conference (STAR IV) in Viet Nam. They stressed the need for enhancing public-private partnerships to strengthen cooperation in combating terrorism and stressed the importance of building business confidence by working closely with private sectors and publicising information on measures taken to secure trade. In this connection, Ministers welcomed Singapore's initiative to host a symposium on Total Supply Chain Security in 2006.

Ministers recognised the need to further facilitate secure trade, to reduce public health hazards and to reduce the threat of economic disruption through incidents related to radioactive materials, and applauded the agreement of relevant APEC economies to aim at implementing the International Atomic Energy Agency Code of Conduct on the Safety and Security of Radioactive Sources as well as the Guidance on the Import and Export of Radioactive Sources by the end of 2006. Ministers underscored the efforts to mitigate the threat of Man-Portable Air Defense Systems (MANPADS) to civil aviation and welcomed the agreement by all APEC economies to undertake a MANPADS Vulnerability Assessment at international airports by the end of 2006. Mitigating the threat of MANPADS attacks and enhancing the security of civil aviation in APEC would ensure the continued flow of people and services for business and tourism.

Ministers commended the significant progress made by the CTI Informal Experts' Group on Business Mobility to secure people in transit, including the development of improved standards for border control and enhanced immigration services.

Ministers thanked Australia and the United States for the report on the start of the pilot Regional Movement Alert List (RMAL), which is an important step in fighting terrorism in the region. They welcomed the expansion of the pilot RMAL to New Zealand in the near future. Ministers noted the supporting progress in developing a Multilateral Legal Framework for those economies choosing to join RMAL and in examining legal issues associated with accessing lost and stolen passport data and instructed Officials to progress this work in 2006. Ministers instructed officials to advance an APEC initiative on capacity building for machine readable travel documents and biometrics technology to enhance regional security. They also called for further cooperation to ensure that all APEC member economies issue machine-readable travel documents, if possible, with biometric information by the end of 2008. Ministers thanked Korea for raising the awareness on international conduct standards for Immigration Liaison Officers (ILO) and best practices of Regional Immigration Liaison Officer Cooperation.

Ministers confirmed their agreement to voluntarily begin providing information on lost and stolen travel documents to the existing database of the International Criminal and Police Organisation (ICPO) on a best endeavours basis by the end of 2006.

Ministers instructed Officials to advance an APEC initiative on capacity building for machine readable travel documents and biometrics technology to enhance regional security, and they encouraged the development of capacity building initiatives for developing economies to achieve this goal.

Ministers reiterated their common understanding that APEC needed to continue building capacities and stressed that appropriate capacity building activities and best practices should be identified and made available to developing economies for the implementation of security measures. They commended the additional APEC work this year to help enhance security and welcomed, in particular, the following capacity building and implementation actions undertaken by APEC economies this year:

Steps to advance compliance with the International Maritime Organisation's

International Ship and Port Facility Security (ISPS) Code through cooperative capacity building efforts and by encouraging follow-up visits to Viet Nam, Indonesia, the Philippines, Malaysia, Thailand, Peru and Papua New Guinea to enhance the work already completed;

· Continued work in APEC to develop effective export control systems, such as Japan's export control survey on APEC Key Elements for Effective Export Control Systems and the efforts this year by individual economies to offer voluntary capacity-building on export controls;

· Commencement of the projects to strengthen the anti-money laundering regime in Indonesia, Thailand and the Philippines through the Asian Development Bank's Regional Trade and Financial Security Initiative, as well as the pending launch of four additional projects to combat terrorist financing and to strengthen maritime and civil aviation security;

· Delivery of a workshop on Airport Vulnerabilities and Counter Measures to APEC economies, as well as interested regional partners;

· Delivery of MANPADS Component Pocket Guides by the United States to all APEC economies to assist the detection and prevention of MANPADS smuggling;

· Progress on the STAR goal of 100 percent baggage screening for passengers, expected to be reached by the end of 2005; and

· Progress in implementing, concluding, or aiming to conclude an Additional Protocol with the International Atomic Energy Agency, reflecting APEC's determination not to allow illicit nuclear activities in our region through the collective commitment to expanded transparency on nuclear-related activities. They welcomed the recent signing of the IAEA Additional Protocols by Singapore and Thailand as well as the Board approval of the Protocol with Malaysia, and encouraged relevant APEC economies to conclude such agreements on a priority basis. Assistance of other APEC economies to relevant non-signatory economies in this field is welcomed.

In implementing counter-terrorism commitments, Ministers noted the importance of minimising costs associated with cross-border business transactions. With this in mind, as APEC continues its progress on trade facilitation, economies will work to apply improved technology and procedures, and offer capacity-building to this end. Ministers affirmed their commitment to ensure that any measures taken to combat terrorism comply with all relevant obligations under international law, in particular international human rights, refugee law and humanitarian law. Ministers welcomed the outcomes of the APEC Human Security Seminar co-hosted by Japan and Thailand in Tokyo in October.

Ministers welcomed the work on the APEC Framework for the Security and Facilitation of Global trade, which is based on the World Customs Organisation (WCO) Framework of Standards to Secure and Facilitate Global Trade and to create an environment for the secure and efficient movement of goods, services and people across the borders. They noted that the APEC Framework would lead to the implementation of international standards for securing and facilitating the global supply chain within the APEC region.

2. Health Security

Avian and Pandemic Influenza:

Ministers noted with concern the threat that the highly pathogenic avian influenza posed to the APEC region as well as to the world. In this regard, Ministers are committed to accelerating APEC's ongoing work on infectious disease threats such as avian influenza and HIV/AIDS. They agreed it was critical to ensure that APEC was prepared for and had the capacity to effectively respond to infectious diseases at the individual, regional and international levels, in cooperation with specialised international organisations, in particular the World Health Organisation (WHO), the Food and Agricultural Organisation, and the World Organisation for Animal Health (OIE).

Ministers noted with particular satisfaction the outcomes of the APEC Meeting on Avian Influenza Preparedness held in Brisbane in October and November, and they endorsed the report and recommended it to Leaders. They further called for support to strengthen their regional and international surveillance and response systems. Ministers welcomed Singapore's offer of the use of the Regional Emerging Diseases Intervention (REDI) Centre to assist APEC's efforts in enhancing rapid regional pandemic response. Ministers welcomed Viet Nam's proposal to host an APEC Ministerial Meeting Responsible for Avian Influenza in 2006 to consolidate APEC work, taking into account Brisbane's recommendations and ongoing regional and international efforts.

Ministers endorsed the initiative on Preparing for and Mitigating an Influenza Pandemic, with the aim of strengthened collective action and individual commitment on a multi-sectoral basis to prepare for and respond to an influenza pandemic. Ministers welcomed the proposed extension of the scope of the APEC LSIF disease biomarker project to include infectious diseases, such as avian influenza, and noted that the associated cohort study would facilitate monitoring of these diseases if conducted across multiple economies. Ministers also endorsed the recommendations of the cross-sectoral APEC Symposium on Response to Outbreak of Avian Influenza and Preparedness for a

Human Health Emergency held in San Francisco in July, which sought to minimise the threats to animal and human health, including the threat of transmission from animal to human, as well as the economic consequences of avian and other pandemic influenza.

Ministers welcomed the efforts of the Health Task Force (HTF) and Task Force on Emergency Preparedness (TFEP) projects initiated by member economies in enhancing preparedness for pandemic influenza. Ministers instructed all APEC fora to continue to work cooperatively with the TFEP and the HTF to achieve this goal.

They underscored the importance of timely and accurate reporting and capacity building efforts to enable adequate, systematic and well-coordinated prevention. In this connection, Ministers looked forward to active participation in the APEC Symposium on Emerging Infectious Diseases to be held in China in April 2006.

HIV/AIDS:

Ministers commended the HTF's efforts to address the growing threat of HIV/AIDS in the APEC region, as directed by Leaders last year, and called for further work in this area. They welcomed the outcome of the APEC Workshop on HIV/AIDS Management in the Workplace in Bangkok and the APEC Workshop on HIV/AIDS and Migrant-Mobile Workers to be held in Manila in December. They welcomed these two initiatives as demonstrating ways in which APEC could add value and work with various working groups and fora in APEC and relevant international organisations, such as the Joint United Nations Programme on HIV/AIDS (UNAIDS) and WHO, as appropriate, in the fight against HIV/AIDS. They noted that, as the private sector was the largest employer in the region, it had the greatest potential to contribute to the well-being of the people living with HIV/AIDS by providing them with the opportunity to live with dignity as a productive working member of society. In this regard, Ministers recognised the importance of the activities of the Global Fund and called for its further contribution. Ministers welcomed the upcoming international AIDS Conference in Toronto in August 2006 and encouraged the effective engagement of APEC economies in the conference.

Ministers stressed the need to enhance prevention, treatment, and care capacity in developing economies, including the provision of anti-retroviral (ARV) in developing economies.

3. Emergency Preparedness

Ministers recalled that APEC Leaders stated when they met in Vancouver in late 1997 that they "recognised that unexpected disasters which affect one of us can affect all of us, and that we can benefit from sharing expertise and collaborating on emergency preparedness and response. " Ministers noted that the Leaders' statement had proved particularly true when the APEC region was hit by a series of devastating natural disasters rarely seen before in human history: the earthquake and seismic tidal waves that struck the regions bordering the Indian Ocean last December; earthquakes in Indonesia; Hurricane Katrina and Rita in the United States; Hurricane Wilma in Mexico; and a series of typhoons in China. These natural disasters reminded Ministers that APEC had exerted collective efforts to fight against and respond to natural disasters in the past and that APEC should build on the past and continue to play its value-added role in strengthening emergency preparedness and disaster recovery measures, to complement activities in other fora, such as those under the Hyogo Framework for Action adopted by the UN World Conference on Disaster Reduction in January.

As a response to the earthquake and seismic tidal waves in December 2004 and to enhance preparedness for future disasters of all kinds, Ministers endorsed the APEC Strategy on Response to and Preparedness for Emergency and Natural Disasters and welcomed the establishment of the APEC TFEP to coordinate work in APEC, identify gaps in member economies and explore ways to enhance APEC's preparedness for disasters and emergencies of all kinds. They looked forward to the launching of the APEC Website on Emergency Preparedness.

Ministers noted the outcomes of the TFEP stocktake and commended the work in relation to emergency preparedness done or to be done by various APEC fora. They acknowledged the Task Force's report on the progress to date and commended the work that had been conducted under its auspices.

Ministers called upon Officials to explore new initiatives and to continue the development of appropriate measures to enhance disaster preparedness and response in the Asia-Pacific region and instructed all APEC fora to work in a coordinated way, trying to get all APEC economies better prepared for future natural disasters: from natural disaster early warning systems, to the best practices for emergency management, and to rapid social and economic recovery from the damages caused by natural disasters.

Ministers welcomed the development of the APEC Small and Medium Enterprises (SMEs) Disaster and Emergency Preparedness Checklist and emphasised the importance of preparedness and mutual cooperation between member economies in reducing the costs arising from disasters.

Ministers welcomed the Transportation Working Group (TPTWG) Seminar on Post Tsunami Reconstruction and Functions of Ports Safety held at the 26th TPTWG meeting in Vladivostok. They recognised the importance of information and communication technology（ICT）in response to natural disasters and acknowledged the need to deploy the communication infrastructure in each economy to disseminate warning messages and gather information for initial reaction. They also welcomed the Seminar on Tourism Crisis Management organised by Korea in October in Hanoi, which laid out a plan to reduce the damage by the devastating crisis to the tourism industry.

Ministers welcomed the APEC-EqTAP Seminar on Earthquake and Tsunami Disaster Reduction co-hosted by Japan and Indonesia held in Jakarta in September, which contributed to both disaster management capacity building and the enhancement of preparedness for natural disasters in APEC member economies, as an indispensable step towards attaining sustainable development in the region.

Ministers underscored the importance of the All Hazards Workshop hosted by the United States in June that brought together high-level decision-makers from around the region and experts to examine the requirements and capabilities of establishing end to end early warning systems essential to saving lives and protecting property. They noted that this effort strengthened regional and within-economy cooperation and preparedness to provide better warning capabilities in the immediate future. Ministers looked forward to an all hazards forecast and warning compendium, a product of the workshop to be disseminated in 2006 to continue the effort.

4. Energy Security

Ministers noted with concern that sustained high oil prices caused by factors such as increased demand, low spare production capacity, insufficient refining capacity, speculative trading and heightened concerns on the longer-term adequacy of oil supply, might have adverse impacts on the economies of APEC, and emphasised that access to adequate, reliable, affordable and cleaner energy was fundamental to the region's economic, social and environmental well-being.

Ministers agreed that effective responses to high and increasingly volatile oil prices required a broad range of supply and demand-side measures to increase oil production, enhance the security of oil supply, improve the efficient operation of the global oil market and promote energy diversification, efficiency and conservation. Ministers also noted that the economies of APEC faced considerable challenges in bringing energy supply and demand into balance while reducing the environmental impact from energy production and consumption and agreed that, to address this, it was essential to promote efficiency and conservation, expand cross-border trade, attract investment and accelerate technology development.

In recognising the need to urgently respond to these challenges, Ministers noted that Energy Ministers met in October to consider individual and collective responses, such as holding a dialogue with the Organisation of Petroleum Exporting Countries (OPEC) and discussing findings from recent APEC studies on the impact of high oil prices on trade and the downstream oil market. Ministers welcomed outcomes from this meeting, and instructed the Energy Working Group (EWG) to continue their broad-based approach by implementing measures developed under the APEC Energy Security Initiative (ESI), the CAIRNS Initiative as well as the APEC Action Plan to Enhance Energy Security.

Ministers also encouraged the EWG to undertake further actions, including engaging more closely with other international energy fora; implementing initiatives on LNG public education and communication, and financing high performance buildings and communities; establishing a biofuels task force, building the capacity of the economies of APEC to collect and analyse energy data; identifying best practices, benchmarks and indicators to assess energy efficiency improvements; and supporting the establishment of the APEC Gas Forum. In undertaking these actions, Ministers instructed the EWG to work closely with business and also financial and research communities.

Ministers highlighted the important role of renewable energy among APEC economies, especially developing economies. They welcomed the APEC Workshop on the Development of Renewable Energy held in China in September.

Ministers joined APEC Energy Ministers in recognising the need to accelerate energy technology development and instructed the EWG to increase its cooperative activities to support the development and uptake of technologies for new and renewable energy, clean fossil energy including clean coal, carbon capture and storage, hydrogen and fuel cells and methane hydrates. Ministers also recognised the growing importance of nuclear energy in the APEC energy mix, and encouraged interested APEC economies to join the ad hoc group on nuclear energy and to progress activities identified in the nuclear framework endorsed at EWG27 to support nuclear power while ensuring optimal safety, security, seismic protection, health and waste handling, including trans-border effects.

Ministers emphasised the need to develop increased energy resources in ways that addressed poverty eradication, economic growth, and pollution reduction, and the need to address climate change objectives. In this context, they welcomed the UN Climate Change Conference in Montreal later this month.

Economic and Technical Cooperation (ECOTECH)

Ministers reaffirmed the importance of ECOTECH in contributing to sustainable growth and achieving common prosperity, and its significant role in ensuring the achievement of the Bogor Goals. Ministers commended the progress made this year in advancing the ECOTECH agenda and in reinforcing the complementarity of TILF and ECOTECH and called for efforts to further advance ECOTECH. They stressed that the benefits of globalisation and liberalisation should be shared by all, through APEC's better-focused and more targeted economic and technical cooperation activities, particularly capacity building. Ministers also recognised the need for APEC to interact with bilateral, regional, and international organisations and financial institutions with a view to fostering cooperation, broadening support and leveraging financial resources to boost ECOTECH activities.

Ministers commended the achievement of the SOM Committee on Economic and Technical Cooperation (ESC) in making progress to promote ECOTECH activities in APEC and endorsed the 2005 Senior Officials' Report on Economic and Technical Cooperation and the recommendations therein. They welcomed the Officials' decision to strengthen the coordination of ECOTECH activities by establishing the Steering Committee on ECOTECH (SCE).

Ministers noted the conclusion of the second Policy Dialogue between APEC and International Financial Institutions (IFIs) and the Organisation for Economic Cooperation and Development (OECD) held in Gyeongju in September, which was convened to find synergy in promoting capacity building for Micro, Small, and Medium Enterprises (MSMEs) and trade facilitation for developing member economies in APEC. They noted the way forward as recommended by the meeting to enhance collaboration with International Financial Institutions (IFIs) and relevant international organisations and acknowledged that the Financial Ministers' Process should be closely consulted in any future dialogues. Ministers also welcomed the collaboration between the APEC Secretariat and the World Bank's Global Development Learning Network (GDLN). They looked forward to concrete programs supported by IFIs and other relevant international organisations.

Ministers recognised that a complete quality assurance process, from the initial project proposal to the implementation and evaluation stage, was key to enhancing the successful implementation of ECOTECH activities, and had the potential to attract external resources from IFIs as well as the private sector. Ministers welcomed the addition of the Monitoring and Evaluation Framework, as contained in the 2005 Senior Officials Report on Economic and Technical Cooperation, as an important tool to significantly improve the quality of APEC's ECOTECH projects.

Ministers welcomed the establishment of the APEC Support Fund (ASF) as an important means to supplement resources available for APEC's capacity building work and welcomed Australia's contribution of three (3) million Australian dollars towards the establishment of the fund. Ministers urged member economies to consider bestowing contributions to either the ASF or the TILF accounts as a means to broaden APEC's funding base.

Ministers welcomed the outcomes of the APEC Workshop on Invasive Alien Species held in Beijing in September and co-sponsored by China and the United States, and endorsed the APEC Strategy on Invasive Alien Species. Ministers commended on the progress regarding the establishment of the Asia-Pacific Finance and Development Centre (AFDC) in Shanghai and recognised it as an important step forward for promoting financial stability and development, financial system reform and capacity building in the region.

Ministers welcomed the work undertaken this year on the issue of sustainable development. They endorsed the recommendations of the Workshop on the Role of Voluntary Initiatives in Sustainable Production, Trade, and Consumption Chains held in Santiago, which is to be coordinated by the SCE. Ministers looked forward to the outcomes of the upcoming High-level Meeting on Sustainable Development to be held in July next year in Santiago.

Human Resources Development

Ministers recognised human resources development as an important foundation for the economic and social development of the APEC region. Ministers noted the important role of the Human Resources Development Working Group (HRDWG) in building the capacity of economies, through policy dialogues and exchanges in areas such as education. Ministers also commended the work on developing a Strategic Action Plan for English and other Languages in the APEC Region, while noting that the scope of a comprehensive strategy extended beyond the mandate of the HRDWG as such.

Ministers recognised the important role that the Labour and Social Protection Network (LSPN) could play in promoting training and employment policies, enhanced productivity, improved workplace practices and strong and flexible labour markets through the development of useful labour market information and policies.

Ministers welcomed the successful conclusion of the APEC Symposium on Strengthening Social Safety Nets under Rapid Socio-economic Changes held in Seoul in August. Ministers noted the symposium's finding that globalisation and liberalisation needed a complementary social agenda to ensure that change was brought about smoothly, minimising negative social consequences and maximising its benefits to all. Ministers welcomed the intention of the Social Safety Nets Capacity Building Network (SSN-CBN) to develop a future work programme in 2006. Ministers also encouraged Viet Nam and Australia to host meetings of the SSN-CBN in 2006 and 2007, respectively.

Reaffirming the great importance of promoting education and training, Ministers welcomed the achievements made by the APEC Future Education Consortium and the APEC Education Foundation in accomplishing a learning community and a stable supporting system for educational development in the APEC region. Ministers also welcomed the APEC e-Learning Training Program as a systematic and sustainable initiative to expand digital opportunities for education policymakers, school administrators and teachers in the region.

Ministers noted the significant work being carried out by Human Resources Development—Capacity Building Network (HRD—CBN) in preparing business leaders and managers for globalisation, focusing on such themes as entrepreneur development, risk management, international rules and standards, and trans-boundary environmental issues. Ministers also welcomed the close collaboration between APEC and ABAC in implementing the project, Capacity Building for Recycling Based Economy (RBE) in APEC.

Industrial Science and Technology:

Ministers envisioned APEC as providing a platform where member economies could promote common prosperity through enhanced cooperation in industrial science and technology.

Ministers welcomed the establishment of the APEC Climate Centre (APCC) and underscored the need to set up an institutionalised communication channel for more effective exchanges of information on regional climate prediction and innovative techniques to mitigate adverse effects caused by extreme weather and climate events in the APEC region. They also welcomed the establishment of the electronic International Molecular Biology Laboratory (eIMBL) to facilitate a more effective network in the biotechnology sector.

Ministers recognised the importance of the Emerging Technologies in APEC Workshop scheduled for December 2005 in Bangkok, which would provide an opportunity for member economy experts to discuss and share information on successful approaches to understanding emerging technologies, including information technology, biotechnology, and nanotechnology; and the challenges faced by domestic and organisational innovation systems in nurturing investment, capacity, development, and commercialisation of such technologies.

Ministers welcomed the outcome of the APEC Biotechnology Conference held in Chinese Taipei, which identified factors needed for the growth of the biotech industry in the APEC region.

SMEs and MEs

Ministers recognised that innovation was the main driving force that created dynamic SMEs and MEs, and sustained growth in the current globalised marketplace. Ministers also recognised that SMEs in developing as well as developed economies had the potential to play a vital role in advancing innovation, given their flexibility and ability to respond more quickly to current conditions. Ministers emphasised the importance of APEC cooperation in developing appropriate economic and policy environments for APEC SMEs to reach their full innovative potential.

Ministers welcomed the Daegu Initiative on SME Innovation Action Plan adopted at the 12th APEC Ministerial Meeting on SMEs, which provided the Innovation Action Plans for member economies to review and improve their economic and policy environments for SME innovation, both individually and collectively. They welcomed the APEC SME Innovation Centre in Korea that would link SMEs with supporting organisations of member economies. They also recognised the importance of the APEC process in developing and supporting the emergence and sustainable growth of SMEs in the Asia-Pacific region.

Ministers were encouraged by the progress made to advance the goals of the APEC SME Coordination Framework, and applauded the efforts undertaken by the SME Working Group (SMEWG) in this regard. Ministers encouraged the SMEWG to continue its outreach to other APEC fora and to consider highlighting other SME-related activities at the next SME Ministerial Meeting.

Ministers stressed the need for additional APEC activities to promote international trade for SMEs and MEs that had high export potential but lacked a formal channel to export their products and services and committed to continue working to reduce and remove existing impediments for SMEs and MEs to enter international markets. They agreed on the need to continue building on entrepreneurship as well as on the need for further emphasis on microfinance.

Ministers placed particular importance on capacity building, mostly while addressing the social dimension of globalisation with regards to the poverty alleviation dimension of MSMEs.

Ministers welcomed the continued participation of the Women Leaders' Network (WLN) in the Micro Enterprises Sub Group, the SMEWG and the SME Ministerial Meetings, and reaffirmed the importance of the WLN and its efforts to work with APEC on the advancement of gender issues and the promotion of women as an engine for economic growth and job creation throughout the region.

Transportation

Ministers affirmed the importance of the transportation sector in trade and economic development. Ministers affirmed that measures to secure transportation services should not be operated in a way that reduced trade in the sector.

Ministers affirmed the current policy emphasis of the TPTWG, including the eight options to liberalise air services and nine shipping policy principles to encourage free and competitive access to international liner shipping markets, maritime auxiliary and intermodal services as well as use of technology to enhance efficiency in the transport sector, capacity building, harmonisation of vehicle standards and measures to enhance the security of aviation and maritime services in the region.

Sharing Prosperity of the Knowledge-Based Economy (KBE)

In today's global economy that is increasingly interconnected by technology, Ministers recognised the importance of expanding and improving the digital capabilities and skills of all APEC member economies. Ministers were confident that this would greatly enhance the ability of economies to participate in and contribute to the global economy, thus facilitating trade and investment. Ministers noted the liberalisation process of the telecommunications sector in the APEC region and commended the ongoing work of Telecommunications and Information Working Group (TEL) in advancing this objective.

Ministers welcomed the Best Practices on Implementing the WTO Telecommunications Reference Paper mentioned in the 2005 Lima Declaration by Telecommunications and Information Ministers (TELMIN), which can serve as a guide for economies to implement the principles contained in the WTO Telecommunications Reference Paper.

Ministers welcomed TEL's continuous work on updating Progress Towards Adopting and Implementing the WTO Reference Paper on Basic Telecommunications.

Ministers also recognised the importance of developing regimes that would enhance the ICT regulatory investment and user environments in each economy and welcomed the

Effective Compliance and Enforcement Principles adopted by TELMIN. Ministers noted that these documents were important capacity building tools for APEC members towards supporting the WTO Doha Round and achieving the Bogor Goals.

Ministers also noted the progress that had been made by APEC economies in implementing the APEC Mutual Recognition Arrangement on Conformity Assessment, which has facilitated the free flow of telecommunications equipment within the region.

Ministers reaffirmed that the Asia-Pacific Information Infrastructure (APII) was an essential basis for ensuring competitiveness of the region and instructed Officials with TEL to intensify their efforts to achieve an Asia-Pacific Information Society (APIS).

Ministers commended the achievement of more than doubling Internet access in the APEC region since 2000, noted the TEL report Achieving the Brunei Goals Moving Forward and welcomed the Key Principles for Broadband Development in the APEC Region that were adopted at the 6th APEC Telecommunications and Information Industry Ministerial Meeting (TELMIN), which set a new objective of universal broadband access. They recognised the tremendous economic and social benefits that access to and increased use of the Internet and broadband could provide, such as increased productivity and commerce, access to education, health and medical services, as well as information dissemination in cases of pandemics and disasters. Therefore, Ministers encouraged APEC economies to follow these principles and to develop and implement domestic policies and regulatory frameworks that maximised broadband deployment, access and usage, including people with disabilities and special needs; facilitation of continued telecom market competition and liberalisation; and confidence building in the use of broadband networks and services.

Ministers reaffirmed the understanding shared among TELMIN that in ensuring marketplace choice and competition, promoting security, encouraging innovation, affirming transparent, technology-neutral and balanced policies, and realising open standard-based interoperability, both open source software and commercial software played an important role.

Ministers recognised the importance of the second phase of the World Summit on the Information Society (WSIS) to be held in Tunisia in November, commended the work undertaken by TEL regarding APEC's input to the WSIS II, and welcomed the report of From APII to APIS: A Contribution to the World Summit on the Information Society to be delivered to the WSIS II meeting.

Ministers continued to encourage efforts aimed at enhancing the digital capabilities of all APEC economies. For this reason, Ministers noted the significant progress made by the APEC Digital Opportunity Centre (ADOC) aimed at turning the digital divide into digital opportunities. Ministers acknowledged the need for continuing APEC's work in this increasingly important area, and looked forward to future progress that enabled all APEC economies to better participate in the Digital Economy.

Ministers recognised that fulfilling the e-APEC Strategy depended on the integrity and security of the e-commerce environment and commended the work TEL had undertaken in this area.

Ministers welcomed the APEC Strategy to Ensure a Trusted, Secure and Sustainable Online Environment developed by TEL; encouraged APEC member economies to take action in the areas identified; and instructed TEL and other appropriate APEC fora to consider means to facilitate implementation of this strategy. Ministers further welcomed TEL's outreach to other relevant international fora, in particular, the successful APEC-OECD workshop on e-Security and Spyware that resulted in a commitment to intensify cooperation and information sharing between the OECD and APEC, including joint research and analysis.

Recognising the importance of uninterrupted information flow, Ministers endorsed the International Implementation Guidance Section of the APEC Privacy Framework and commended the Electronic Commerce Steering Group (ECSG) for its completion and publication of the APEC Privacy Framework, taking note of the two successful technical assistance seminars on domestic and international implementation of the Framework.

Macroeconomic Issues

Ministers supported the Finance Ministers' statement that all economies had a shared responsibility to take advantage of relatively strong global economic performance to address key risks and vulnerabilities in their respective economies. This would help ensure the orderly adjustment of global imbalances and to help achieve more sustainable external positions and stronger medium-term growth.

Ministers endorsed the Economic Committee's (EC) reports for 2005: 2005 APEC Economic Outlook; KBE/New Economy project titled Patterns and Prospects on Technological Progress in the APEC Region; and TILF project titled Follow-up Study on the Impact of APEC Investment Liberalisation and Facilitation.

Ministers commended the EC's continued efforts in maintaining its analytical functions while becoming more policy and action-oriented in its mandate to coordinate and contribute to the structural reform agenda in consultation with the relevant APEC fora and the Finance Ministers' Process.

Structural Reform

Ministers acknowledged that structural reform was a key "behind the border" issue facing APEC economies and an essential vehicle to realise the benefits of trade and investment liberalisation and facilitation.

Ministers, therefore, welcomed the new role of the EC of coordinating structural reform activities across APEC and encouraged the development of capacity building initiatives to narrow gaps identified in the APEC Structural Reform Action Plan.

Ministers welcomed the success of the APEC-OECD Structural Reform Capacity-Building Symposium, which facilitated the sharing of experiences by APEC and the OECD. Ministers welcomed the key findings of the symposium with regard to the contribution that regulatory reform, a key part of structural reform, could make to more open and competitive markets in the APEC region and encouraged the EC to undertake additional work in this area.

Ministers welcomed the APEC Work Plan on LAISR towards 2010 (LAISR 2010) established by the EC, which set out a roadmap to address structural reform issues across APEC over the next five years consistent with the LAISR declaration. Ministers looked forward to further developing this "whole of APEC" approach to structural reform in 2006, which would include establishing closer links and better coordination with other relevant APEC fora, including the CTI SELI and the CTICPDG, and the Finance Ministers' Process. Ministers encouraged these groups to collaborate closely with the EC on structural reform issues.

Interaction with the Business Community

1. Dialogue with the APEC Business Advisory Council (ABAC)

Ministers recognised the role of ABAC in providing advice on concrete initiatives to improve the business environment in the Asia-Pacific region. They committed themselves and instructed Officials to take such advice into account, where appropriate. Ministers also appreciated ABAC's contribution to the Mid-term Stocktake of APEC's Progress Towards the Bogor Goals. Ministers emphasised the need to continue to strengthen the working relationship between the government and the business sector and affirmed the continuation of a partnership between ABAC representatives and Officials through closer communication so that APEC could share the views of the business community in a timely manner.

2. Industry Dialogues

Cooperation with the industries and other stakeholders in APEC through industry dialogues has developed as a highly effective mechanism for the implementation of key APEC trade facilitation objectives. Ministers welcomed the work of the industry dialogues to improve understanding between the public and private sector and to bolster APEC's contribution to the DDA, including trade facilitation, tariff and non-tariff barriers and transparency.

Automotive Dialogue：

Ministers noted the Auto Dialogue's efforts to respond to their call for support of the DDA and encouraged the group to expand on its work. Ministers noted the group's growing attention to IPR issues and encouraged the group to more clearly identify issues of concern to the automotive industry, and to coordinate with the Intellectual Property Rights Experts' Group (IPEG), when appropriate. Ministers endorsed the Auto Dialogue's ECOTECH activities, which focused on aiding ASEAN parts suppliers as well as a project to implement customs best practices at the Manila Port in the Philippines.

Chemical Dialogue：

Ministers continued to be concerned over the potential impact of product-related environmental regulations, including the proposed EU Registration, Evaluation and Authorisation of Chemicals (REACH) legislation and the Restriction of Hazardous Substances (RoHS) on international trade, and the burden they could impose on businesses. Ministers called for continued consultations bilaterally and in appropriate international fora to ensure that these initiatives resulted in the protection of human health and the environment without placing unnecessary restrictions on the facilitation of trade. Ministers welcomed the chemical dialogue's report to the MRT on the role of APEC in the implementation of the Globally Harmonised System of Classification and Labelling (GHS). They encouraged APEC member economies to continue to implement the GHS and welcomed the planned APEC Seminar on GHS Implementation and Technical Assistance in Thailand next year.

Life Science Innovation Forum (LSIF)：

Ministers noted that there was a growing imperative for enhanced cooperation to develop an environment that fostered innovation in the region to promote the development of a bio-medical life sciences economy and to meet emerging health and economic challenges, including infectious and chronic diseases and the trend in ageing demographics. Ministers welcomed the successful conclusion of the 3rd APEC Life

Sciences Innovation Forum (LSIF) in Gyeongju in September. Ministers noted the progress and encouraged continued efforts in implementing the APEC Strategic Plan for Promoting Life Sciences Innovation endorsed by Leaders in Santiago in 2004. They endorsed the recommendations of the LSIF to implement projects in priority areas, including research, access to capital, harmonisation with international standards, and health services.

Non-Ferrous Metals Dialogue (NFMD):

Ministers welcomed the 1st Non-Ferrous Metals Dialogue (NFMD) and looked forward to its contribution to a better understanding on the issues related to facilitating the non-ferrous metals trade. Ministers also welcomed the work plan agreed upon at the 1st NFMD containing the following elements: formation of a network of non-ferrous metals industries, development of questionnaires for industries to identify the most important areas of cooperation, and development of a matrix of non-ferrous metals industries business recommendations. Ministers noted, particularly, that collaboration with the Chemicals Dialogue and the CTI SCSC this year set a good example of creating synergy in APEC.

High Level Policy Dialogue on Agricultural Biotechnology (HLPDAB):

Ministers acknowledged the importance of realising the benefits of agricultural biotechnology through increased agricultural productivity, improved food security and the protection of environmental resources. Ministers welcomed the outcomes of the 4th APEC High Level Policy Dialogue on Agricultural Biotechnology held in the margins of SOMI in Seoul in March. Ministers noted the Dialogue's recommendations that many factors, including cost implications and the value of a transparent, science-based approach to agricultural biotechnology, were relevant to a discussion on the implementation of international treaty obligations, including the Cartagena Protocol on Biosafety. Ministers also acknowledged the value of encouraging intra-governmental dialogue as member economies considered the development and implementation of biotechnology policies, including the implementation of the Cartagena Protocol on Biosafety.

Ministers supported the 5th High Level Policy Dialogue on Agricultural Biotechnology, which will be held in Viet Nam in 2006.

Ministers also encouraged APEC economies to participate in the upcoming Conference on Biosafety Policy Options, which will take place in January 2006 in Manila, and to facilitate discussions at the 5th High Level Policy Dialogue. The conference will focus on exploring policy options for Biosafety regulations in the APEC region.

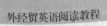

Cross Cultural Communication

Ministers welcomed the 2005 report of the APEC Focal Point Network on Cross-Cultural Communication (CFPN) and endorsed its recommendations. Ministers commended the work of the CFPN in identifying areas to foster mutual understanding among member economies.

Ministers instructed Officials to make an effort to undertake CFPN's recommendations to enhance intercultural understanding and the visibility of APEC. These included: strengthening information sharing through the APEC website; APEC Cultural Cooperation Events; an APEC Young Artists Gala; and an Annual Coordinator's Report to Senior Officials on CFPN Activities.

Ministers welcomed the successful hosting of the APEC Film Week: A Special Screening for APEC Films held in Busan in October. Ministers recognised that it contributed to enhancing mutual understanding among APEC member economies and paved the way for further development of APEC's cultural cooperation activities.

Ministers noted that cultural exchange and cooperation would allow APEC to advance closer towards APEC's vision of an Asia-Pacific community. They encouraged members to continue to work for promoting cross-cultural communication within APEC.

Gender Integration

Ministers welcomed the report of the Gender Focal Points' Network (GFPN) and commended the efforts of the GFPN to integrate gender issues into APEC processes and activities.

Ministers reaffirmed the important contributions of women in APEC economies and acknowledged that women's participation in trade and investment as workers, entrepreneurs, and investors, particularly through women-owned and -managed MSMEs, was a key factor to sustained regional economic growth.

Ministers recognised that critical to achieving and reinforcing APEC's goals on gender integration, further initiatives to promote and facilitate the increased participation of women in decision-making was needed. Ministers welcomed the proposal of the GFPN to deliver periodic gender information sessions and gender analysis training to Officials to improve their understanding of the differential impact of trade liberalisation and facilitation on men and women and to increase the effectiveness of the design, implementation, monitoring, and evaluation and communication of policies and projects so as to include gender considerations through gender-responsive policies and projects.

Ministers noted the need to improve the implementation of the Framework for the Integration of Women in APEC and called upon fora and economies to take measurable steps to apply and advance the Framework. Ministers also encouraged APEC fora and economies to appoint a Gender Focal Point who could participate in the GFPN meetings. Ministers welcomed the Initiative for APEC Women's Participation in the Digital Economy 2005 Training for Women's IT Capacity Building in APEC economies. They also noted the progress in follow-up activities to the APEC project Supporting Potential Women Exporters by the CTI to identify and implement trade facilitation and transparency measures that met the needs of women exporters and small business and called for the adaptation of research results in local languages and wide dissemination in APEC member economies. Ministers endorsed two GFPN project proposals—Integrating Gender Expertise Across Fora and Gender Analysis Training—to further promote and intensify gender integration in APEC.

Youth

Ministers welcomed the success of the APEC 2005 Youth Plaza held in Korea in August under the theme APEC Youth in the Cyber World. They also welcomed the Seoul Declaration towards a Healthy e-World and recognised the need to expand digital opportunities to APEC Youth. Ministers welcomed the APEC Youth Technology Innovation Collaboration (TIC 100) Conference that was held in September. Ministers encouraged and supported Viet Nam's proposal to organise APEC Youth Camp 2006.

Non-Member Participation

Ministers endorsed the newly Revised Consolidated Guidelines on Non-Member Participation in APEC Activities, which will replace the 2002 Guidelines when it expires at the end of the year. Ministers welcomed the newly revised Guidelines as an effective way to strengthen the cooperation between APEC and ABAC by facilitating ABAC's participation in APEC activities.

APEC Reform

Ministers endorsed the report on APEC Reform and Financial Sustainability that focuses on three areas: APEC financial reform, higher efficiency through better coordination and continuous reform. They commended the 2005 APEC reform achievements as they contributed to keeping APEC relevant and effective in the rapidly-changing international environment with the adoption of measures that secured financial sustainability, developed a more effective work structure and pursued continuous reform.

Ministers noted the shared understanding among Officials to increase members' annual contributions in 2007 and 2008 in accordance with each member's financial

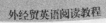

procedures as a way to ensure APEC financial sustainability. They also welcomed the decision of improving the project assessment procedure through appropriate division of labour between the Budget and Management Committee (BMC) and the APEC Secretariat.

Ministers welcomed the decision of Officials to transform the SOM Committee on ECOTECH (ESC) into the SOM Steering Committee on ECOTECH (SCE). They acknowledged that an enhanced mandate to undertake the coordination function and to rank project proposals of Working Groups by the reconstituted SCE would contribute to strengthening coordination of ECOTECH activities. They also welcomed the decision for better coordination among the sub-fora, Working Groups and Task Forces through such measures as reviewing their terms of reference and quorum.

Ministers instructed Officials to keep the APEC reform agenda a priority item in the future and to make APEC more effective and reliable.

Ministers urged member economies to consider bestowing contributions to either the ASF or the TILF account as a means to broaden APEC's funding base.

Sectoral Ministerial Meetings

1. Energy and Mining Ministerial Meetings

Ministers welcomed and supported the outcomes of the 7th Energy Ministers' Meeting held in Gyeongju in October, as aforementioned in the Energy Security section. Ministers also welcomed the success of the 2nd Meeting of Ministers Responsible for Mining held in Gyeongju in October and confirmed their commitment to the economic, environmental, and social dimensions of sustainable development, and recognised the importance of the mining and metals industry as a platform for reaching greater development in many APEC economies.

2. APEC Ocean-Related Ministerial Meeting

Ministers welcomed the outcomes of the 2nd APEC Ocean-Related Ministerial Meeting held in Bali in September. Ministers commended the Bali Plan of Action (BPA), which contained practical commitments to progress the 2002 Seoul Oceans Declaration by taking substantial and concrete steps to balance sustainable management of marine resources and the marine environment with economic growth. Ministers instructed all relevant APEC fora to take due note of the BPA in order to ensure coherence and consistency among the broad range of APEC activities that were supportive of it.

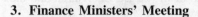

3. Finance Ministers' Meeting

Ministers welcomed and supported the outcomes of the 12th APEC Finance Ministers' Meeting (FMM), which had noted that all member economies needed to put in place the appropriate policies and strategies to address the importance and urgency of the challenges that came with ageing populations in the APEC region, and emphasised the importance of open, well-supervised and systemically sound financial services sectors in promoting free and stable capital flows in the region. Ministers also welcomed domestic reform and international cooperation espoused in the Finance Ministers' Jeju Declaration, aimed at addressing the common concerns of member economies regarding the issue of population ageing.

Ministers also welcomed the FMM's deliberations on the financial services negotiations in the Doha Development Round, combating terrorist financing, promoting FDI, and the need for further improvements in remittance services and their oversight to facilitate more efficient transmission of this increasingly important international financial flow.

4. SME Ministerial Meeting

Ministers welcomed the aforementioned outcomes of the 12th APEC Ministerial Meeting on SMEs held in Daegu in September, in particular the adoption of the Daegu Initiative on SME Innovation Action Plan and the APEC SME Innovation Centre.

5. Ministerial Meeting on the Telecommunications and Information Industry

Ministers welcomed the aforementioned outcomes of the 6th Ministerial Meeting on the Telecommunications and Information Industry (TELMIN 6) held in Lima in June, in particular the adoption of the Lima Declaration and the Program of Action for TEL.

APEC Secretariat

Ministers noted with satisfaction the Report of the Executive Director of the APEC Secretariat and commended the APEC Secretariat for its efforts throughout the year in support of the host economy and the APEC process at large.

Ministers welcomed the successful conclusion of negotiations on the Supplemental Agreement to the Agreement between the Government of Singapore and the Secretariat of the Asia-Pacific Economic Cooperation Organisation relating to the Privileges and Immunities of the APEC Secretariat and noted that the Supplemental Agreement would

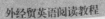
provide greater clarity to the maintenance responsibilities of the APEC Secretariat and the Government of Singapore.

Ministers took the opportunity to express their appreciation to the Government of Singapore for the hospitality it had extended to the APEC Secretariat since its inception in 1993.

ACMS and AIMP

Ministers welcomed the development by the APEC Secretariat of the APEC Collaboration and Meeting System (ACMS) and an APEC Information Management Portal (AIMP).

Guidebook on APEC Procedures and Practices:

Ministers welcomed the Guidebook on APEC Procedures and Practices prepared by the APEC Secretariat as a key reference document for hosts in preparing future APEC meetings.

Official Observers

Ministers welcomed APEC's interaction with its Official Observers, the ASEAN Secretariat, Pacific Economic Cooperation Council (PECC) and the Pacific Islands Forum (PIF), and noted their recommendations for APEC such as contained in the PECC Seoul Declaration adopted this year.

Future Meetings:

Ministers noted the preparations for APEC 2006 by Viet Nam. They noted that future APEC Ministerial Meetings would be held in Australia in 2007, Peru in 2008, Singapore in 2009 and Japan in 2010.

Approval of SOM Report

Ministers approved the SOM report, including the decision points therein, in particular, the proposed APEC budget and the assessment of members' contributions for 2006. (*Source*: *http://www. apec. org*)

Notes

[1] Busan 釜山(韩国)

[2] theme 主题，话题，题目

[3] divergence 分歧

[4] Jeju 济州(韩国)

[5] Gyeongju 庆州市(韩国)

[6] caucus 领导人会议，核心会议

[7] Ministerial Conference 部长级会议

[8] stocktake 盘点

[9] reward 报酬，酬谢，赏金

[10] Bogor Declaration《茂物宣言》

[11] Bogor Goals 茂物目标

[12] anti-corruption 反腐败

[13] impediment 妨碍，障碍物

[14] disseminate 传播，宣传

[15] template 样板，模板

[16] diverse 不同的，变化多的

[17] bottleneck 瓶颈

[18] alignment 校正，对齐，对准

[19] noteworthy 值得注目的，显著的

[20] conviction 信服，坚信

[21] knowledge-based economy 知识经济

[22] spurring 鼓励，刺激，激励

[23] curtail 缩减，剥夺

[24] pathfinder initiatives 探路者机制

[25] Ad Hoc Steering Group 特别指导小组

[26] mandate 指令，要求

[27] corruption 腐败，贪污

[28] disrupted 使分裂，使瓦解

[29] address 对付

[30] ratification 批准，承认，认可

[31] implementation 实行，履行，实施

[32] synergistic 协同的，协作的

[33] corporate governance 公司治理

[34] extradition 引渡逃犯

[35] forfeiture 没收，没收物，罚金

[36] bribery 行贿，受贿

[37] reiterate 重申

[38] bereave 使孤寂，使丧失

[39] condolence 哀悼，吊唁

[40] hazard 危害

[41] disruption 崩溃，瓦解

[42] biometrics 生物统计学

[43] liaison 联络

[44] anti-money laundering 反洗钱

[45] smuggling 走私

[46] protocol 草案，备忘录

[47] illicit 违法的，被禁止的

[48] pandemic 大流行的，大流行病

[49] avian influenza 禽流感

[50] preparedness 准备状态，战备状态

[51] surveillance 监视，监督

[52] prevention 预防

[53] devastating 毁灭性的

[54] seismic 地震的

[55] auspices 赞助，保护

[56] deploy 展开，配置

[57] Doha Development Agenda（DDA）多哈发展议程

[58] counterfeit and pirated goods 赝品和盗版产品

[59] intellectual property rights（IPR）知识产权

[60] minimise 使减到最少/最小，使降到最低限度

[61] Individual Action Plans（IAPs）个别行动计划

[62] Collective Action Plans（CAPs）集体行动计划

[63] Committee on Trade and Investment（CTI）贸易与投资委员会

[64] regional trade agreements and free trade agreements（RTAs/FTAs）区域贸易协议
与自由贸易协议

[65] Trade and Investment Liberalisation and Facilitation（TILF）贸易与投资的自由化
与便利化

Exercises

I . Match the following words in Column A and Column B

Column A	Column B
1. DDA	a. 茂物目标
2. divergence	b. 批准，承认，认可
3. caucus	c. 引渡逃犯
4. stocktake	d. 多哈发展议程
5. Bogor Goals	e. 盘点
6. anti-corruption	f. 集体行动计划
7. impediment	g. 行贿，受贿
8. alignment	h. 走私
9. knowledge-based economy	i. 草案，备忘录
10. pathfinder initiatives	j. 反腐败
11. Ad Hoc Steering Group	k. 区域贸易协议与自由贸易协议
12. ratification	l. 崩溃，瓦解
13. implementation	m. 探路者机制
14. corporate governance	n. 个别行动计划
15. extradition	o. 妨碍,障碍物
16. bribery	p. 禽流感
17. disruption	q. 校正,对齐,对准
18. anti-money laundering	r. 实行，履行，实施
19. smuggling	s. 监视，监督
20. protocol	t. 知识经济
21. avian influenza	u. 特别指导小组
22. surveillance	v. 赞助,保护
23. auspices	w. 分歧
24. counterfeit and pirated goods	x. 反洗钱
25. IPR	y. 贸易与投资的自由化与便利化
26. IAPs	z. 领导人会议，核心会议
27. CAPs	aa. 贸易与投资委员会
28. CTI	bb. 赝品和盗版产品
29. RTAs/FTAs	cc. 公司治理
30. TILF	dd. 知识产权

Ⅱ. Translate the following sentences into Chinese

1. Ministers reaffirmed the importance of trade-related capacity building as a tool to enable developing economies to accede to the WTO, fully participate in the WTO negotiations, enjoy the full benefits of the WTO membership, and maximise the potential of trade as a tool for social and economic development.

2. Ministers welcomed the progress that has been made in the WTO accession negotiations for the Russian Federation and Viet Nam, and looked forward to the rapid conclusion of these negotiations for their early accession.

3. Ministers remained fully committed to achieving the Bogor Goals of free and open trade and investment in the Asia-Pacific by 2010 for developed members and 2020 for developing members as stipulated in the Bogor Declaration. Ministers emphasised that the Bogor Goals, the core organising principle of APEC, aimed at promoting sustainable growth and prosperity in the region.

4. Recognising that the alignment of domestic standards with international standards contributed to trade facilitation in the region, Ministers welcomed the results of a comprehensive review that showed a very high level of achievement of the alignment work in the agreed upon priority areas.

5. Ministers welcomed the fruitful outcomes of the APEC Symposium on Assessment and Benchmark of Paperless Trading held in China in September. Ministers urged all member economies to strengthen cooperation in this area with a view of reinforcing mutual cooperation and pushing forward the achievement of APEC's paperless trading goals.

6. Ministers recognised that the protection and enforcement of Intellectual Property Rights (IPR) is essential to building a knowledge-based economy and are key factors for boosting economic development, promoting investment, spurring innovation, developing creative industries and driving economic growth.

7. Ministers recognised that APEC's goal of economic prosperity could not be achieved unless corruption, both in the domestic economies and in international business transactions, was effectively addressed and those individuals guilty of corruption were denied a safe haven.

8. Recognising that pathfinder initiatives were valuable tools for furthering trade and investment liberalisation and facilitation, Ministers stressed the importance of ensuring progress and retaining momentum in such initiatives.

9. Ministers reiterated their common understanding that APEC needed to continue building capacities and stressed that appropriate capacity building activities and

best practices should be identified and made available to developing economies
for the implementation of security measures.

10. Ministers reiterated that terrorism was a serious threat to the security, stability
and growth of the APEC region. They continued to review the progress on
APEC's commitments to dismantle transnational terrorist groups, to eliminate
the danger posed by the proliferation of weapons of mass destruction, their
delivery systems and related items, as well as to confront other direct threats to
the security of our region in the future.

III. Cloze

Ministers reaffirmed the importance they attached to the Individual Action Plans
(IAPs) as one of the principle vehicles _____ reaching the Bogor Goals. Ministers
endorsed the 2005 IAPs and welcomed the measures undertaken _____ individual
economies to liberalise and facilitate trade. Ministers also welcomed the report _____
the newly included issues in the IAPs: RTAs/FTAs and Implementation of General and
Area—Specific Transparency, all of which would contribute _____ greater transparency
_____ the activities undertaken _____ member economies.

Ministers welcomed the successful completion of the IAP Peer Reviews of all
twenty-one (21) member economies _____ our Leaders had instructed in 2001, which
confirmed that all member economies were making good progress _____ achieving the
Bogor Goals. Ministers also welcomed the continuation of the IAP Peer Review Process
_____ the next three (3) years in a strengthened manner, including a greater focus on
what APEC members were doing individually and collectively _____ implement specific
APEC commitments and priorities. Ministers endorsed the revised IAP Peer Review
Guidelines and the timetable to carry _____ the next round _____ reviews, noting that
this would provide greater opportunities for business to raise its views.

IV. Underline the important sentences in the text, which give you useful information

V. Retell or write down what you learn from the text in English or in Chinese

附录

KEYS

Unit One   10 Common Misunderstandings about the WTO

I.

a-5	b-1	c-8	d-11	e-2
f-6	g-15	h-20	i-3	j-9
k-7	l-14	m-10	n-17	o-19
p-4	q-12	r-18	s-13	t-16

III. Cloze

In addition, the system and its rules can help countries allocate scarce resources more efficiently and less wastefully. For example, negotiations have led to reductions in industrial and agricultural subsidies, which in turn reduce wasteful over-production.

A WTO ruling on a dispute about shrimp imports and the protection of sea turtles has reinforced these principles. WTO members can, should and do take measures to protect endangered species and to protect the environment in other ways, the report says. Another ruling upheld a ban on asbestos products on the grounds that WTO agreements give priority to health and safety over trade.

What's important in the WTO's rules is that measures taken to protect the environment must not be unfair. For example, they must not discriminate. You cannot be lenient with your own producers and at the same time be strict with foreign goods and services. Nor can you discriminate between different trading partners. This point was also reinforced in the recent dispute ruling on shrimps and turtles, and an earlier one on gasoline.

Also important is the fact that it's not the WTO's job to set the international rules for environmental protection. That's the task of the environmental agencies and conventions.

Unit Two　10 Benefits of the WTO Trading System

Ⅰ.

a-5	b-18	c-13	d-22	e-12
f-23	g-6	h-9	i-20	j-16
k-10	l-24	m-7	n-19	o-1
p-8	q-2	r-11	s-25	t-3
u-17	v-14	w-4	x-21	y-15

Ⅲ. Cloze

The short-sighted protectionist view is that defending particular sectors against imports is beneficial. But that view ignores how other countries are going to respond. The longer term reality is that one protectionist step by one country can easily lead to retaliation from other countries, a loss of confidence in freer trade, and a slide into serious economic trouble for all-including the sectors that were originally protected. Everyone loses.

Confidence is the key to avoiding that kind of no-win scenario. When governments are confident that others will not raise their trade barriers, they will not be tempted to do the same. They will also be in a much better frame of mind to cooperate with each other.

The WTO trading system plays a vital role in creating and reinforcing that confidence. Particularly important are negotiations that lead to agreement by consensus, and a focus on abiding by the rules.

Unit Three   European Union

I .

a-4	b-16	c-13	d-21	e-5
f-8	g-9	h-1	i-2	j-18
k-12	l-20	m-10	n-15	o-6
p-3	q-17	r-11	s-7	t-14
u-19	v-22			

III. Cloze

The European Commission has already (in July 2004) published its proposals for a new-look and more integrated regional policy for the period 2007-2013 after present programmes run out. Procedures will be simplified and funding concentrated on the most needy regions of the 25 member states. For the new period, the Commission proposes a regional policy budget of 336 billion, still the equivalent of one third of the total EU budget.

The idea is to divide the spending into three categories. Of the total amount, 79% would go on reducing the gap between poor and richer regions while 17% would be spent on increasing the competitiveness of poor regions and creating local jobs there. The remaining 4% would focus on cross-border cooperation between frontier regions.

Unit Four   EU-China: Closer Partners, Growing Responsibilities

I.

a-6	b-9	c-21	d-22	e-10
f-11	g-7	h-12	i-8	j-13
k-1	l-4	m-25	n-5	o-15
p-2	q-14	r-3	s-16	t-18,
u-27	v-30	w-19	x-28	y-29
z-20	A-23	B-17	C- 24	D-26

III. Cloze

Build a stronger relationship. A key objective of the negotiations for a new Partnership and Cooperation Agreement, which will also update the 1985 Trade and Cooperation Agreement, will be better access to the Chinese market for European exporters and investors, going beyond WTO commitments, better protection of intellectual property and mutual recognition of geographical indications. China is already a major beneficiary of the international trading system and should assume a responsibility commensurate with those benefits, making a substantial contribution to reviving and completing the WTO Doha round.

Many of these steps are not only in EU's interest. They are strongly in China's interest and an integral part of China's progress towards balanced and sustainable growth and development and global leadership and responsibility. The accompanying trade policy paper sets out a comprehensive approach to EU-China trade and investment relations for the medium term.

Unit Five   International Chamber of Commerce

I.

a-4	b-21	c-5	d-10	e-24
f-22	g-6	h-25	i-2	j-13
k-16	l-26	m-17	n-14	o-20
p-9	q-11	r-1	s-3	t-8
u-12	v-15	w-19	x-7	y-18
z-23				

III. Cloze

ICC members belong to an organization representing businesses <u>from</u> all sectors all over the world. ICC is the only world business organization. It promotes business enterprise and investment <u>as</u> the most effective way of raising living standards and creating wealth. ICC works <u>for</u> the liberalization of trade and investment <u>within</u> the multilateral trading system.

Being a member of ICC enables you to take part in the work of ICC's commissions and special working groups, composed of a total of more than 500 business experts who regularly meet to scrutinize proposed international and government initiatives affecting their subject areas. Members of ICC learn what really matters for their companies at an early stage and win time to make the right decisions.

Through ICC's many working bodies, members shape ICC's policy and elaborate its rules. ICC gives priority <u>to</u> the issues that most urgently concern its members. It is the members who set ICC's agenda.

ICC members are <u>at</u> the forefront of business self-regulation. ICC is world leader in setting voluntary rules, standards and codes for the conduct of international trade that are accepted by all business sectors and observed <u>in</u> thousands of transactions every day.

Unit Six   Trade and Development Report

I.

a-3	b-8	c-13	d-4	e-7
f-19	g-2	h-14	i-1	j-5
k-11	l-18	m-16	n-9	o-10
p-12	q-6	r-15	s-17	t-20

III. Cloze

At the international level, recent increases in the prices of some primary commodities and improvements in the terms of trade of a number of developing countries may not have changed the long-term trend in real commodity prices or altered the problem of their volatility. Wide fluctuations in primary commodity prices are not in the interest of either producers or consumers. This has also been recognized by the IMF's International Monetary and Financial Committee, which, at its April 2005 meeting, inter alia, underscored "the importance of stability in oil markets for global prosperity" and encouraged "closer dialogue between oil exporters and importers". Although primary commodities other than oil may be less important for the developed countries, they are nevertheless equally, if not more important for those developing countries that depend on exports of such commodities. And since in many of the latter countries extreme poverty is a pressing problem, the issue of commodity price stability is of crucial importance not only for the achievement of the MDGs but also for global prosperity in general. Consequently, in the spirit of a global partnership for development, the international community might consider reviewing mechanisms at the global or regional level that could serve to reduce the instability of prices of a wider range of commodities, not just oil, to mitigate its impact on the national incomes of exporting countries.

Unit Seven　　US-China Joint Commission on Commerce and Trade

I.

a-4	b-7	c-11	d-14	e-15
f-2	g-12	h-1	i-3	j-10
k-5	l-9	m-13	n-16	o-6
p-8				

III. Cloze

The CLWG also sponsors the US-China Legal Exchange, a series of joint legal seminars that foster mutual understanding of the legal regimes governing trade and investment in both countries. The seminars offer US audiences the opportunity to learn about the legal reforms taking place in China and provide Chinese participants the chance to learn about US practices. Under this program, the United States and China send delegations of legal experts to speak on topics of current interest. Both private sector and government attorneys have been featured at the seminars, which are open to government officials and academicians as well as the local business and legal communities. In December 2002, Vice Minister of Foreign Trade Long Yongtu led a delegation of Chinese legal experts to the United States to talk about the legal changes necessary for China to implement its WTO accession commitments. General Counsel Kassinger reciprocated, leading the most recent Legal Exchange delegation to China in November 2003 to discuss both recent developments in corporate governance practices in the United States as well as to discuss a variety of trade remedy measures used to safeguard fair trade between the United States and its trading partners, including China.

Unit Eight   Association of Southeast Asian Nations

I.

a-4	b-6	c-14	d-17	e-3
f-10	g-1	h-5	i-11	j-9
k-13	l-7	m-16	n-18	o-8
p-12	q-2	r-15		

III. Cloze

ASEAN's strategy shall consist of the integration of ASEAN and enhancing ASEAN's economic competitiveness.

In moving towards the ASEAN Economic Community, ASEAN has agreed on the following:

　* institute new mechanisms and measures to strengthen the implementation of its existing economic initiatives including the ASEAN Free Trade Area (AFTA), ASEAN Framework Agreement on Services (AFAS) and ASEAN Investment Area (AIA);

　* accelerate regional integration in the following priority sectors by 2010: air travel, agro-based products, automotives, e-commerce, electronics, fisheries, healthcare, rubber-based products, textiles and apparels, tourism, and wood-based products.

　* facilitate movement of business persons, skilled labour and talents; and

　* strengthen the institutional mechanisms of ASEAN, including the improvement of the existing ASEAN Dispute Settlement Mechanism to ensure expeditious and legally-binding resolution of any economic disputes.

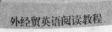

Unit Nine　Declaration of the Beijing Summit of the Forum on China-Africa Co-operation

I .

a-10	b-7	c-3	d-5	e-2
f-6	g-9	h-8	i-1	j-4

III . Cloze

We hereby solemnly proclaim the establishment <u>of</u> a new type of strategic partnership <u>between</u> China and Africa featuring political equality and mutual trust, economic win-win co-operation and cultural exchanges. <u>For</u> this purpose, we will:

■ Deepen and broaden mutually beneficial co-operation and give top priority <u>to</u> co-operation <u>in</u> agriculture, infrastructure, industry, fishing, IT, public health and personnel training <u>to</u> draw <u>on</u> each other's strengths.

■ Increase exchange of views <u>on</u> governance and development to learn <u>from</u> each other.

■ Enhance the Forum <u>on</u> China-Africa Co-operation.

Unit Ten   Declaration on Fifth Anniversary of Shanghai Cooperation Organisation

I.

a-3	b-14	c-13	d-6	e-7
f-11	g-15	h-25	i-10	j-5
k-8	l-1	m-2	n-17	o-19
p-4	q-22	r-26	s-9	t-20
u-18	v-21	w-2	x-12	y-16
z-24				

III. Cloze

To expand economic cooperation among them, SCO member states need to coordinate their efforts in implementing the Programme of Multilateral Trade and Economic Cooperation among SCO Member States by carrying out major priority projects of regional economic cooperation. They need to work together to promote trade and investment facilitation and gradually realise the free flow of commodities, capital, services and technologies.

The SCO welcomes participation by relevant partners in specific projects in priority areas like energy, transportation, information and communications and agriculture. The SCO will endeavour to actively participate in international campaigns against communicable diseases and contribute to environmental protection and rational use of natural resources.

To strengthen and expand the social foundation for friendship and mutual understanding among SCO member states is an important way to ensure the SCO's resilience and vitality. To this end, SCO member states need to institutionalise bilateral and multilateral cooperation in culture, arts, education, sports, tourism and media. With the unique and rich cultural heritage of its member states, the SCO can surely serve as a model in promoting dialogue among civilisations and building a harmonious world.

Unit Eleven   Deepening Economic Interdependency between China and Japan and Challenges for the Future

I.

a-4	b-10	c-1	d-9	e-3
f-2	g-16	h-11	i-13	j-6
k-12	l-5	m-7	n-14	o-8
p-15				

III. Cloze

The fair was comprised of three parts: an exhibition, a symposium and industrial tour for missions visiting the country. The exhibition was a success, with nearly 600 exhibitors from China, Japan and Korea; the total number of attendees and visitors to the fair (Industrial Fair) exceeded 15,000. CCPIT, KOTRA and JETRO have agreed to hold a similar event in Korea next June and one in Japan in 2008.

JETRO, together with relevant organizations and associations, also holds the Japan-China Economic Conference every autumn in Osaka, bringing together key Chinese entrepreneurs and Japanese firms interested in doing business in China's fast-growing economy. Some 330 representatives from over 200 Japanese firms and 170 representatives from 120 Chinese firms took part in last year's conference.

A business-matching event is held concurrently with the event, which, in past years, has led to quite a number of successful business deals. I cordially invite Chinese firms and interested parties to take part in this year's conference, which will take place November 16th and 17th.

Unit Twelve　Investor's Guidebook to Russia

I.

a-4	b-19	c-22	d-6	e-10
f-25	g-21	h-11	i-1	j-20
k-3	l-12	m-2	n-26	o-14
p-9	q-16	r-7	s-24	t-13
u-8	v-15	w-17	x-5	y-18
z-23				

III. Cloze

According to WTO data, Russia's share in world exports does not exceed 1. 5%, and in imports, it does not exceed 0. 7%, whereas Russia's participation in the global services trade is purely symbolic. Nonetheless, over the years of economic reforms, exports have become the largest sector of the economy, accounting for over one-fourth of GDP (in the former Sovet Union this figure did not exceed 10%). Twenty to 80% of the national production of basic commodities and semi-finished goods are bound for the world markets. It should be noted that qualitative indicators of exports do not resolve the task of raising competitiveness of the Russian-made products at the world markets so long as the structure of the Russian exports has an obvious energy and commodities leaning. The structure of exports is evident of the lopsided development of the Russian economy with high-tech industries still lagging behind.

The share of machinery and equipment in Russian exports was a mere 5. 6% in 2005. The imports are dominated by consumer goods (primarily foodstuffs and raw materials for their production and household appliances), accounting for about one half of the total Russian imports.

Unit Thirteen   The Doha Agenda

Ⅰ.

a-5	b-10	c-1	d-6	e-3
f-15	g-11	h-7	i-2	j-9
k-12	l-8	m-13	n-4	o-14
p-16				

Ⅲ. Cloze

The TRIPS Agreement provides a higher level <u>of</u> protection to geographical indications <u>for</u> wines and spirits. This means they should be protected even if there is no risk <u>of</u> misleading consumers or unfair competition. A number of countries want to negotiate extending this higher level to other products. Others oppose the move, and the debate <u>in</u> the TRIPS Council has included the question of whether the relevant provisions of the TRIPS Agreement provide a mandate <u>for</u> extending coverage <u>beyond</u> wines and spirits.

The Doha Declaration notes that the TRIPS Council will handle this <u>under</u> the declaration's paragraph 12 (which deals with implementation issues). Paragraph 12 offers two tracks: "(a) where we provide a specific negotiating mandate <u>in</u> this Declaration, the relevant implementation issues shall be addressed under that mandate; (b) the other outstanding implementation issues shall be addressed as a matter of priority <u>by</u> the relevant WTO bodies, which shall report <u>to</u> the Trade Negotiations Committee [TNC], established under paragraph 46 below, by the end of 2002 for appropriate action. "

Unit Fourteen The Seventeenth APEC Ministerial
Meeting Joint Statement

I.

a-5	b-12	c-15	d-1	e-4
f-27	g-16	h-19	i-20	j-6
k-29	l-17	m-10	n-26	o-7
p-21	q-8	r-13	s-22	t-9
u-11	v-23	w-2	x-18	y-30
z-3	aa-28	bb-24	cc-14	dd-25

III. Cloze

Ministers reaffirmed the importance they attached to the Individual Action Plans (IAPs) as one of the principle vehicles for reaching the Bogor Goals. Ministers endorsed the 2005 IAPs and welcomed the measures undertaken by individual economies to liberalise and facilitate trade. Ministers also welcomed the report of the newly included issues in the IAPs: RTAs/FTAs and Implementation of General and Area-Specific Transparency, all of which would contribute to greater transparency in the activities undertaken by member economies.

Ministers welcomed the successful completion of the IAP Peer Reviews of all twenty-one member economies as our Leaders had instructed in 2001, which confirmed that all member economies were making good progress towards achieving the Bogor Goals. Ministers also welcomed the continuation of the IAP Peer Review Process for the next three years in a strengthened manner, including a greater focus on what APEC members were doing individually and collectively to implement specific APEC commitments and priorities. Ministers endorsed the revised IAP Peer Review Guidelines and the timetable to carry out the next round of reviews, noting that this would provide greater opportunities for business to raise its views.